TheRoadHome

Christina Berry

Black Rose Writing | Texas

ISBN: 978-1-68433-742-2
PUBLISHED BY BLACK ROSE WRITING
www.blackrosewriting.com

Printed in the United States of America
Suggested Retail Price (SRP) $19.95

The Road Home is printed in Georgia Pro

*As a planet-friendly publisher, Black Rose Writing does its best to eliminate
unnecessary waste to reduce paper usage and energy costs, while never
compromising the reading experience. As a result, the final word count vs. page count
may not meet common expectations.

For Mom, Karen, Mattie & Callie, Nancy & Lucy, Catherine, Nanyehi,
and so many others.

You are the women who gave me life and inspiration to be a strong,
resilient, and creative ᏣᎳᎩ woman.

ᎦᎸ

TheRoadHome

1—Wednesday July 13, 2005 12:45AM

"Bottoms up," Ryan says, lifting his shot. Dillon and I follow his lead and drink the round. I'm not sure who our whiskey benefactor is tonight. Not that it really matters—there's always someone buying drinks for the bands.

Gigging musicians don't make a lot of actual cash money in Austin, but if booze were currency, we'd all be fucking rich. This is our third round of free whiskey tonight, a pretty good haul for a Tuesday night show.

I glance at the time. It's tomorrow already, and I have two guitar lessons to teach. I need to make it an early night. And if I want to make it home safely, that will have to be my last drink. With the whiskey working its way into my bloodstream, I turn to Tom and ask for water.

"Jake, what'd you think of the set?" Ryan asks.

I look at the guy and almost have to squint at the sight of him. He's a Ken doll, rocking the sun-kissed surfer look. Shining from a lather of stage sweat, the dude practically glows. For a bass player, Ryan is very pretty. I'd argue he's the hottest guy in the band. He'd probably counter I hold the title, though we've never discussed it.

I shrug. "Seemed off."

"Off?" Dillon asks from the other side of Ryan, but with the music blaring from the stage, I see the question on his lips more than hear it.

Our drummer, Dillion—a dead ringer for Animal, the Muppet (if Animal were tattooed from head to toe)—is definitely *not* the prettiest member of Nebulous, and that's a badge he wears with pride. "Off how?"

"Not you two." Ryan and Dillon were great, as always. We've been playing together for five years for a reason, but tonight, I sucked. I missed a key change on one of our oldest songs, and my vocals felt shaky throughout the set. I shout to be heard when I clarify, "Me. *I* was off."

They nod. They'd noticed it too but weren't going to be the first to address it during this postmortem of our set.

I announce, "I'd like to work on some new material."

Ryan raises a brow. "It's about damn time. We haven't written anything new in almost a year."

Has it been that long? Surely not. Then again, I have had other shit on my mind lately. I guess watching the marriage of your two best friends fall apart can be a little distracting.

Ryan's girlfriend—the Barbie to his Ken—returns from the lady's room. Ryan's focus shifts entirely to her as she fits against him and kisses his chin. He's hopelessly devoted to her, has been for years. It's sweet. It should be inspiring, the embodiment of relationship goals, but a relationship has never been one of my goals.

In no mood to witness the contented lovebirds chirp and peck at each other, I look away, glancing around to the stage lit up with red and yellow lights, where some outfit out of Baltimore is wrapping up their tour of the Southwest. At their feet, the dark sea of people undulates to the rhythm of the music. When the band hits a high-energy part, a pit opens up, all punching arms and kicking feet. It's a good crowd for a Tuesday.

I tilt my head back to drink my water and nearly spit half of it out when Ryan elbows me in the gut and stage-whispers, "Incoming, dude."

As signals go, it's not subtle, but it's effective. I instantly know what he means: Rebecca approaches.

In all her beautiful, blonde, and curvy glory, she settles into a sexy lean against the bar at my left. She's gorgeous, and she knows it. And as much as I hate to admit it, she holds power over me. We're polar opposites, so of course there's some sort of magnetic pull, an undeniable attraction to this woman—this body, those lips, that wicked little tongue.

There was a time when I thought I could love her, but for the life of me, I can't remember why. We'd given it a try, only to learn we couldn't tolerate each other for more than about a week. Sadly, it took us almost three months to come to that stunning revelation.

Rebecca had been angry when I broke up with her. She'd thrown a fit in my apartment, broken a couple albums in my collection. I hated her for a while. Then one night, I ran into her at a show and fucked her in the bathroom. I thought it was a final goodbye, a farewell fuck.

So why have I fucked her half a dozen times since then?

Something in my posture must shift. I don't feel the change myself, but I see it in Rebecca's eyes: the moment when she knows I'm under her spell.

The guys must recognize the change as well, they groan with irritation. They've never liked Rebecca, not that they've ever said a word about it; we're not that kind of friends.

Unless you've been playing music together since grade school, bandmates inhabit a weird nonspace on the friendship spectrum, somewhere around coworker and neighbor (except we've all seen each other naked at least once during our various tours). Despite the nudity aspect, we generally stay out of each other's business. We see everything but say nothing—it's one of the unspoken rules of band life: hear no evil, see no evil, speak no evil—even when one of us is dating a succubus and could really use an intervention.

Ignoring the rest of the band, as usual, Rebecca focuses her clear blue gaze on me, and licks her lips when she says, "You were good tonight."

Liar. I ignore the compliment as I lean against the bar, gesturing for Tom to bring me more water.

"Water? Really?" Rebecca scoffs. "Don't you want a shot? I'm buying."

"I have to drive home."

Rebecca leans toward me, presumably to hear me better. This close, I catch a whiff of her perfume. It burns my nostrils. I never liked the stuff, yet the familiar scent triggers some sort of sense-memory stimulant, sending a rush of blood from my brain straight to my cock.

"Then maybe we should have shots at your place." Never one to beat around the bush, her frankness is one of the things that first attracted me to Rebecca. Looking back, though, I'm at a loss to remember the other things.

Well, the sex. Definitely the sex. The sex was great. *The sex is still great.* But aside from that dubious desire to fill the space between her legs, there's nothing else for us.

Hands shaking, I twist the cap off my second bottle of water and guzzle a good portion of the contents, trying to reclaim my faculties. With a refreshed gasp, I wipe my mouth on my arm and frown at Rebecca. "I've got an early day tomorrow."

If she's disappointed by my rejection, she doesn't show it. With a shrug, she gives me a "your loss" expression and turns her attention to Tom behind the bar, who can't take his eyes off her breasts. She orders a whiskey shot, and Tom pours two, drinking with her. *Hey man, good luck to you.*

"See you at practice," I say to Ryan and Dillon, both riveted by the drama playing out before them. I grab my guitar and head out the back door to the alley where I've parked my truck. It takes me a few minutes to lug my amp out, lift it into the bed, and strap it down. Then I slide my guitar in beside it and climb into the cab.

With a crank of the ignition, I toggle the headlights on and startle as they illuminate the figure standing about twenty feet in front of my bumper. *Rebecca.* She stands perfectly still, a goddess statue bathed in light. Though I'm sure she can't see me from the blinding beams in her eyes, she stares right at me, practically right through me.

I stare back for a good long minute, weighing my options, then I do exactly what I know I should not. I slide across the bench seat, unlock the passenger door, and swing it open, wide and inviting.

A corner of her mouth quirks up in a grin as she saunters toward the truck. I squeeze my fists on the steering wheel while I wait for her to fasten her seat belt, then accelerate toward the end of the alley to Red River Street.

The part of my brain still working nags me with questions like: Why are you taking her home with you, you moron? Why do you continue to have sex with this woman, even when you know there's no future in it?

On Seventh Street, I glance over my shoulder to change lanes and notice the bag of cocaine she's pulled out of her purse. "What the fuck are you doing?"

"What does it look like I'm doing?" She smirks at me as she fishes a fingernail into the powder and brings it to her nose.

"Are you fucking kidding me? You're snorting fucking cocaine in my fucking truck as we drive past the fucking police station?"

Rebecca answers my question with a hearty snort, sucking a bump into her other nostril.

"Rebecca, put that shit away right goddamn now before you land us both in jail!"

"Relax," she mumbles as she pinches her nose and sniffs again. Then, cheerily oblivious, she holds her stash toward me, offering.

"Rebecca, I'm not asking, I'm telling. Put it away, or I'm dumping you by the side of the road, and you can walk your ass home."

With an exasperated huff, Rebecca closes up the baggie of drugs and stows it in her purse. I drive the rest of the way home like I've got a stick up my ass—maintaining perfect lane position, signaling a good half block before turning corners, no racing through yellows or rolling through stops.

I hold my breath until I pull into a spot near the mailboxes at my apartment complex. Rebecca silently lets herself out of the truck and sways those hips as she makes her way to my unit, likely expecting me to follow like a dog. She's forgotten I have a load to carry.

In a supremely passive-aggressive move, I make Rebecca wait for me to make the two trips up and down the stairs with my guitar and amp before I unlock the door to let her inside my apartment. When I finally slide my key home, she's wilted by the heat and perturbed by the wait. I'm perversely pleased and a little creeped out with myself for it.

Not waiting for me anymore, Rebecca makes her way to the kitchen, finding my whiskey stash in the place it's always been and the shot glasses on the shelf below. She pours two generous shots and sets them on the bar that separates the kitchen from the main room.

In no rush, I lug my gear to the corner, where I've set up a weight bench and keep the books I save for the road. I stare at her as I toss the contents of my pockets onto the coffee table, tug off my shirt and boots, then pull my hair out of its braids and finger comb it into loose waves.

Rebecca hikes herself up onto my kitchen counter, crossing her legs in a way that makes it abundantly clear there's nothing under her dress. When I don't respond, she huffs with boredom and pulls a cigarette from her purse, lighting up with my favorite lighter. With a long, slow exhale, she blows a stream of smoke through perfectly puckered lips.

It's that mouth that does the trick. Slowly, I cross the room to join her. Silently taking one of the two shots, I drink it down before she can come up with something to toast to. She drinks her shot, then pours two more. We drink again.

I don't know why I'm letting her get me drunk. Maybe I'm just not in the mood to be sober. Maybe I'm tired of the running commentary in my brain urging me to stop this nonsense. Maybe I just want a little mindless fun, a brain haze while I get my cock sucked and fucked.

I reach for the cigarette in Rebecca's hand, take a deep drag, then toss it into the sink. Without a word, I take her hand and tug her off the counter, leading her toward the bedroom.

• • •

"So beautiful," Rebecca sighs. She's still straddling me, my cock spent and wilting inside her. She smooths her fingertips across my forehead, down the line of my nose, across the planes of my cheeks, and finally traces the edge of my jaw. "And so cruel."

"What?"

"Beautifully cruel." She sighs again, sounding far more melancholy than I've ever heard her before.

"You think I'm cruel?"

"Your eyes are cruel; deep and dark and hard. No one sees it but me." She rubs her thumbs across the ridges of my cheekbones, just beneath my eyes. She's scaring me. This talk is too intimate, and I don't trust her when she's this close. Her thumbs pause in their caress, and my discomfort ratchets up to a bone-deep fear. Afraid that Rebecca might poke my eyes out with her thumbnails.

With a sad sigh she asks, "Why did we break up?"

I push up to sit. The movement effectively dumps Rebecca off my chest and onto the tangle of sheets at my side. I move to my feet and walk to the kitchen, tossing the used condom in the trash as I make my way toward the fridge. I grab a beer, consider getting one for Rebecca, hesitate, then pull a second beer from the fridge before heading back to the bedroom. She's digging through her purse for that little baggie of coke again.

"When did you start doing that shit?" I ask as I hand her a beer.

She smirks. "When I was fifteen."

I blink, stunned. She's been a cokehead this whole time? How did I not notice? "Well, there's a good reason why we broke up. I obviously wasn't paying any attention to you."

Rebecca nods thoughtfully, then snorts a bump of coke and washes it down with a slug of beer. "But we were good together—"

"We were awful together. All we ever did was fuck or fight." I lean against the wall to drink my beer, in no rush to get back into bed with her.

She snorts another bump, then sets it aside and turns onto her hands and knees, crawling toward me across the bed.

Her expression is mischievous, promising so much. My cock twitches at the sight of her sweetheart ass and the way her breasts sway heavy between her arms.

"See?" Rebecca bites her bottom lip. "Little Jake misses me."

I roll my eyes as I chug my beer, then set the empty on the dresser and walk to the edge of the bed, my cock right at her eye level. "Little Jake is an idiot cyclops with a gluttony problem. And can we stop calling my dick *little*?"

Without another word, Rebecca slides Little Jake—worst dick name ever—into her mouth. She opens her throat, hollows out her cheeks, and sucks me so deep that I, too, forget why we ended things.

2—Wednesday July 13, 2005 9:42AM

"Ari's been hit by a car."

What? I bolt upright in bed and nearly drop the phone. "What?"

"She's okay." Greg pauses, lets out a ragged breath. "I mean, she's going to be okay—she has to be okay. I don't know... They won't tell me anything, but...she has to be okay."

My brain struggles to process what Greg is saying, and it doesn't help that my mind keeps flashing back to that terrible night all those years ago, echoing the sound of my grandmother's trembling voice on the phone. *Usdi Yona, there's been an accident.*

Panic hits me like a swift kick to the chest. I look around the dim bedroom of my shitty apartment, desperately seeking some sign that this is a terrible nightmare, and if I could just wake up—

I find my proof-of-nightmare in the bed beside me: Rebecca, naked and sprawled across the tangle of sheets. *What in the hell is she doing here?* I stare at her, taking in the sight of her smeared makeup and her blonde hair, tufted and tangled from sex and sleep. Flashbacks of the night before flicker through my mind like a pornographic slide show.

This is definitely a nightmare. I look back at the phone clutched in my hand, held at arm's length like a snake about to strike. On the other end, Greg mumbles, "Someone should call Alex, but I don't have his number."

Alex. Shit. This is real, not a nightmare. My hands start to tremble. I squeeze them into tight fists. The phone groans with complaint as I pull it back to my ear and ask, "Where is she?"

"The hospital downtown." Greg's voice teeters over each syllable.

"What happened?" I stand on wobbly legs, aimlessly circling as I look for a pair of clean jeans. I grab the first pair I can find, cinching the phone between my ear and shoulder as I yank them on. Not bothering with my boots, I slip my feet into a pair of ratty flip-flops and grab the closest T-shirt, tugging it over my head as I head out to the living room.

Keys. Cigarettes. Lighter...lighter...where's my fucking lighter—?

"What's going on?" Rebecca asks from the hallway, still completely naked.

"I gotta go. Let yourself out." I give up on finding the lighter and turn for the door.

"But..." Rebecca cocks her hip and arches her back, a tempting pose. "I thought we could—"

"Greg, talk to me, brother. What happened?" I direct into the phone and force my trembling hand to turn the doorknob. Finally outside, the humid morning air drowns my lungs as I jog down the stairs and across the grassy expanse of common grounds toward the lot where I left my truck.

There's no answer from Greg, just a labored, shaky breath, his silence hanging as heavy as the damp air. I steady my hands to open the truck door, then sit inside for a moment, staring blankly out of the windshield.

"Greg, what happened?" I raise my voice, trying to snap him out of his fugue state.

"I was going to work..." He takes a deep breath, then starts talking again. "Ari was walking to the café on the corner to write. I pulled out of the driveway and turned my head back toward the intersection. That's when I saw the guy run the stop sign..." Greg's voice drifts off into nothing, just those shaky breaths again.

"He hit her?"

Greg lets out an audible shudder and repeats himself. "Someone should call Alex, but I don't know his number." Then he adds, "And Ari's phone was...crushed."

Crushed? That word sends a cold-as-ice panic through me, sinking with a dizzy dread as the terrible imagery plays out in my imagination. I crank the ignition and haul ass out of the parking lot to head south toward the hospital. Brake lights ahead, and I nearly rear-end the car in front of me. I shake my mind out of its tailspin. I need to focus. This is not a conversation to be had over the phone while driving, not if I want to arrive alive.

"Listen, brother, I'm ten minutes away."

"Okay."

"I'll talk to you then."

"Okay."

"Hang in there."

"Okay."

I hang up and drive, focusing on the lanes of the road, the gauges on the dash, the bumpers of the cars in front of me. But the traffic isn't enough to distract me from my horrific imagination. I picture the absolute worst scenario: Ari's smile fading just as she hits the windshield. Then my mind imagines something far worse: her smile disappearing just as she goes under the wheels. I picture her bleeding and broken in the road...*crushed.*

A pathetic whimpering sound fills the cab of the truck, and it's coming from me. I sound like I'm the one who's been hit by a car, broken and bleeding and mewling in agony.

At the hospital, I circle the parking lot like a buzzard until I find a spot. I barely pause to lock the door before running across the asphalt toward the sliding glass doors of the emergency room.

Stepping into the waiting area is like stepping back in time. I've taken great pains to avoid places like this for most of my life, and for a very good reason: the smell. Hospitals have a unique scent, which I despise. And as those wide doors slide open with a gasp, the miasma overwhelms me.

Death and disinfectant, that's what I smell. To be fair, I'm probably just imagining the stench of death. No one else is reeling from the horrifying odor.

I hate this pathetic weakness quivering inside me. I need to be strong. I take a deep breath of the awful air and focus on the task at hand: walking. My flip-flops make a cheery little *thunk, thunk, thunk* sound as I cross to the nurses' station, but I course correct when I spot Greg leaning against the far wall.

The guy looks like death warmed over. His hair stands on end in places, like he's been pulling at it. His light eyes are bloodshot with dark circles underneath them, and his already pale skin is practically translucent. Whatever tie he'd been wearing is gone now and so is the top button of his shirt. But worse than all that is the blood. A patch of dark red stains the front of his white Oxford shirt, and the cuffs of his sleeves are practically dripping red. His hands are stained too.

Ari's blood. Fuck.

My knees give out. I support myself on the wall beside Greg, though there are empty chairs all around us.

Greg is surprised to see me. He blinks his bloodshot eyes and emerges from his fog, sounding stoned when he says, "All they'll tell me is she's in surgery."

I nod, trying to appear calm.

"I called her parents. Talked to her mom. They're going to fly down." Greg's face pinches in pain, and he starts to tug his hair again. "She started crying..." He doesn't finish his sentence. He doesn't have to. I've been here before. I know firsthand the terror Steve and Kathryn Goody are experiencing right now.

Usdi Yona, there's been an accident.

My mind bouncing between past and present, I come unmoored, suddenly adrift. I need to grab onto something. I stare at the ivy plant in its pot on the table in front of me, and I want to clutch it in both hands. I want hurl it at the wall and watch it shatter into pieces. I want to destroy the table where the plant now sits, too, and chairs to either side, smashing them with my feet, stomping them to nothing. I could lay waste to this whole place.

"—don't know how to reach Alex."

Greg's voice snaps me from my fit of impotent rage. I blink at him, a little surprised he's so eager to get in touch with Alex. Not that I have anything against Alex, but he's Ari's new boyfriend. Considering Greg is Ari's husband, it's a bit odd. Then again, lately, all the shit between my friends has been a bit odd.

It's been eight months since Ari and Greg mutually agreed to open their marriage and give each other "space." I'd made it clear from the beginning the idea was colossally stupid. But did they listen? No. Now, eight months later, Ari's in love with Alex, Greg is fucking his secretary, and Ari and Greg are on the cusp of a divorce.

Greg pushes a hand through his hair, "I'm sure she'd want him to be here."

And that's reason number eight million six-hundred thousand and twelve why I love this guy like a brother; he's not a selfish shithead. He truly loves Ari and wants what's best for her. And right now, what's best is to surround her with her people—*all* her people.

"I don't have Alex's number."

Greg furrows his brow, trying to concentrate. "What about that friend of hers with the colorful hair? What's her name? Carol?"

"Sheryl." Also known as Sher Nobyl, a wickedly cute little roller derby dynamo, and Ari's new best friend. "I don't have her number either, except...actually, I might be able to get their numbers." I fish my phone out of my pocket. "Give me a minute. I'll see what I can do."

I bolt for the exit. Outside, I breathe deep of the sweltering summer air as the glass doors shush shut behind me. The fresh air works wonders on my head, even so, I need a cigarette. I shove one of my smokes between my lips, relaxing a bit with the familiar feel of it. Oral fixation to the rescue. But, searching my pockets, I don't have a lighter.

I scan the sidewalk, looking for the obligatory "smoking area." It's on the left. Just a single trashcan with an ashtray mounted on top, set beneath an awning to protect smokers from the sun and rain. Thankfully, there's a woman lighting up her own cigarette. She's in scrubs, a nurse's badge on a lanyard around her neck. Her messy ponytail and weary posture suggest she's been on shift for a while.

I approach, slow and steady, the unlit smoke hanging from the corner of my mouth. She glances my way, does a double take, then smiles. I get that a lot. One of the advantages of being the only six-foot-three, full-blooded Cherokee Indian in Austin, Texas is I stand out in a crowd. When I join her beneath the awning, it only takes a sidelong glance and the beseeching raise of my eyebrow for the woman to lean in and light my fire.

I give her a friendly thanks, then take a couple of long drags as I scroll through the contacts on my phone. It doesn't take long to find who I'm looking for. She's in the "A" section under "Arson Nic." Nicole Rollins.

The fiery-hot yet cold-as-ice derby chick booked my band to play the half-time show at the roller derby championship bout last season, and I still have her number. From my first interaction with the woman, I found her to be utterly fascinating and incredibly intimidating, an enigma.

Everyone in town calls her a "crazy bitch," probably because of the brutality she brings to the skate track. As a derby skater, she's infamous: strong, fierce, fast, and violent—likely the best skater in the premiere derby league she helped to create. But it's this league-creator side of her that I've had the pleasure of knowing. In working with her to book my band, I found her to be neither crazy nor a bitch. Intense, yes, but also smart, professional, courteous...and really fucking hot.

My strange attraction to her, in and of itself, is part of the enigma. Nicole Rollins is not my type. She's the opposite of my type. I like the simplicity of soft edges, easy access, and gentle goodbyes; one look at Nicole, and I'd known she was none of those things. Still, I found her athletic beauty distracting, her big green eyes bewitching, her raspy come-hither voice sexy as hell, and the sway of her hips mesmerizing. A definite snake charmer, that woman. But off limits, because when I first met Nicole a year ago, she'd had a boyfriend—Alex Balfour. Alex, who dumped Nicole for Ari a few months later.

My, how things have changed.

In light of all the drama, I doubt Nicole will appreciate my call now. I stare at her number for a moment, take another long, soothing drag off my cigarette, then dial.

"Hello." The voice on the other end of the line is vaguely feminine, but it sounds like she's just gargled with a cup of gravel.

"Nicole?" *Duh, jackass. Of course it's Nicole. You just called her.*

"Yeah." She sounds annoyed and about to hang up.

"Hey, listen, it's, uh, Jake Sixkiller from Nebulous. You booked my band back in—"

"You're Ariana's friend, right?" she cuts me off.

I take a deep inhale of my coffin nail...*annnnnd exhale.* "Yeah."

"What do you want?"

"I need...listen, this is going to sound shitty, and I'm sorry, but I need Alex's phone number, and Sheryl's number too."

There's a long pause. You could park a tank in the middle of that pause. Then she laughs. But it's not a good laugh. It's hollow, utterly lacking in humor. "If you want Alex's number, why don't you ask Ariana? You know, the little bitch he dumped me for."

Yep. I figured this would be like pulling teeth. "Okay, first of all, don't call Ari a bitch. Second of all—"

"Fuck you, Jake Sixkiller from Nebulous. Don't call me—"

"Listen, Ari's been in an accident. Please just be a decent human being, for fuck's sake. At least give me Sheryl's number."

"Why should I?"

"Because I want to believe you're not the colossal cunt everyone says you are. Prove me right." I cringe, prepared to hear her hang up. Instead there's another long pause: a big, wide, deep, ugly pause.

"Whatever." That's all she says before that dreaded click, and she's gone.

"Fuck!" I shout at the phone, then wince and shrug in apology to the nurse with the messy ponytail. *Internal voice, Jake, use your fucking internal voice: "Motherfucking, cocksucking, asslicking fuckity fuck fuck!"*

I pace and smoke, trying to think of who else would have the numbers I need. Ryan, bass-playing boy wonder, knows everyone in Austin. Also, I'm pretty sure Steven Lowe is desperately in love with Sheryl. I could call him to get her number, and maybe Sheryl has Alex's—

My phone chimes to announce an incoming text. I flip it open to a text message from Nicole. No words, just two phone numbers. *Well, hot damn! I owe that woman a beer.*

I text her a quick, **TY! You're a peach**, then hit the first number and listen to it ring.

"Hello?" It's Sheryl. I don't know Sheryl very well, but in my interactions with her, she'd always struck me as a bit flighty. How will she react to this news?

"Hey, Sheryl, this is Jake Sixkiller, Ari's friend."

"Hiya, Jake."

"Listen, I have some, uh, Ari is in the hospital. She—"

"What?"

"She was hit by a car. She's in surgery now. I'm here with Greg, calling Alex next. I just wanted you to know. You're one of her closest—"

"Which hospital?" The tone of her voice is completely changed, any hint of humor gone. Hearing her concern raises her up a few pegs in my estimation.

"It's the hospital downtown."

"I'm on my way." There's a rustling sound on her end, and then she's gone.

I finish my cigarette as I return to Nicole's text and hit the second number. That first call, that was the easy one. I nervously tap my foot as I wait through the rings. One...two...three... I'm preparing myself for voicemail when Alex answers, all business. "Balfour."

"Alex, it's Jake."

"Hey man, what's up?"

Fuuuuck. "Listen, it's Ari...she's in the hospital."

"What? What happened? Is she okay?" The guy's tone is something awful, pain with a side of panic.

"She's been hit by a car. I don't know a lot of details, just that she's in surgery—"

There's a jangly, metallic sound on his end, the pace fast and frantic—no doubt his toolbelt bouncing against his hips as he bolts for the door at his job site. "Where?"

I explain, and Alex hangs up. I stand there for a moment, listening to the dead air left in Alex's wake, and watch Greg through the sliding glass doors of the emergency room. He's listing to one side, like a capsizing ship.

. . .

"Where is she? Is she okay?"

Greg and I both look up at the sound of Alex's voice. Expecting information, he jogs across the waiting room and comes to a full stop in front of me. When I don't have anything to tell him, he turns his pleading gaze to Greg.

It occurs to me this is the first time Ari's soon-to-be ex-husband is meeting her new love. I'm struck by how different they appear. Alex is tall and muscular, a brawny workingman look. Ari tells me he's in construction, but he's too good-looking for actual construction work. He's like the porno version of a construction worker.

Greg, on the other hand, in his expensive shoes and haircut, carries himself with a classic-Hollywood elegance. Though the refinement of his style is dramatically offset by the stains of Ari's blood on his shirt. He's like the horror movie version of a businessman.

There's a moment when they make eye contact and come to some sort of accord, a peace between the two men who love Ari most in the world (aside from me and her dad, of course). I'm glad to see it. Despite all the recent drama, this awful situation unites them toward a common goal: Ari's well-being.

Alex stares at the blood covering Greg's hands, and with a deep, shaky breath, he asks, "What happened?"

Greg's fog lifts, and when he speaks, it is with a clear voice and calm cadence. "She was crossing the street, and a car ran the stop sign, a blue Honda Civic. The driver saw her at the last minute and swerved to miss her. I think that saved her. Instead of hitting her straight on, he clipped her. She went up onto the hood, then rolled off to the side."

Greg's face pinches like he's picturing that moment again, then he clears his throat and continues. "The driver stopped. He called 911 while I tried to take care of Ari. She'd fractured her left leg. That much was obvious. Also, she had a big cut on her arm, which was where most of the blood came from. I, uh, made a tourniquet with my tie..." He pauses and looks down at his hands, flexing his fingers into tight fists. Fissures and cracks form in the crimson coating of Ari's dried blood.

What little color Alex had in his face drains out. He wobbles on his feet before collapsing backward into one of the chairs beside the ivy plant I'd been eyeing before. Bending over like he might puke, he remains there, frozen and staring at the tile floor, practically catatonic.

Greg and I exchange a glance then park our asses too. And this is how we remain. It seems like hours, days, weeks pass while we wait there, sitting together, but alone; each trapped in our own head, all imagining the same horror.

• • •

"What happened? Is she okay? When can we see her?"

Greg, Alex, and I look up at the sound of Sheryl's voice. She stands a few feet away, her hands braced on her hips, a frown creasing her pretty little pixie face. As small as she is, she looks even smaller now. It's the boots, or lack thereof. She's wearing a pair of basic sneakers, which don't give her the height boost her patent leather platform boots normally do.

More than just shorter, she looks entirely different today. Instead of her usual leather, latex, and spandex, she's wearing green scrubs patterned with little tacos. She's not wearing any makeup, either, and her shock of hot pink hair is tied in a messy knot on top of her head.

It occurs to me I've never seen Sheryl out of costume, which is basically what her style is: costumes and masks. Today, though, the mask is off, and it's the real Sheryl who stands before us.

"We don't know anything yet. She's still in surgery," I say.

Sheryl harrumphs as she drops into the seat beside Alex. Looking at him like a big sister helping out her little bro, she laces her fingers through his and squeezes his hand. "How are you holding up, big guy?"

Alex glances at Greg and me, then grimaces when he says, "She's strong. She'll be okay. I have to believe that."

Sheryl looks across the aisle at Greg's bloody hands and clothes. "What happened?"

Greg explains again. Sheryl asked several pointed questions, making it clear she has some medical training. Greg can't answer them, making it clear he does not.

I sit quietly, trying to ignore them. I sing songs in my head—Cherokee versions of old gospel songs from my childhood, stupid pop songs from the radio, Slayer—anything I can think of, so I don't have to listen to Greg outline the litany of horrors again.

I tune out all the sounds, focusing instead on the sights, mainly the sight of us all together for the first time. We make quite the motley crew—Greg in his bloody shirt, Alex in his construction safety gear, Sheryl in her veterinarian garb, and me...well, shit, my shirt's on inside out and backward. I yank it off, flip it right side out, and slip it back on. Iron Maiden, and it's relatively clean.

All eyes have turned to me—including messy ponytail nurse at the front desk—as if my impromptu striptease is the most interesting thing in the room. I shrug and smirk—*show's over, folks*—then, turning my attention back to Greg, Alex, and Sheryl, I grimace at what I see.

There is a clear divide between us. On one side of the aisle sit Greg and I, the old guard—her once and former lover and friend. And across from us, Alex and Sheryl, the new guard—her now and future lover and friend. Once upon a time, I'd thought I was irreplaceable in Ari's life. Now, staring my replacement in the face, I'm less certain.

It's been almost thirteen years now that I've known Ari, and I still remember every detail of the day she walked into my life. I'd just smoked a fat joint in the stockroom of the bookstore—where someone had the bad idea to give me the title and responsibility of assistant manager—when Ari strutted right up to me and asked for a job.

She looked like a vampire: all gothed out with jet-black hair, porcelain skin, a lace and velvet dress, and thick, heavy combat boots. She was trying so hard to look mean. It was adorable. I laughed in her face, but only because I was *really* high and thought she was joking. When she asked me again, I hired her on the spot.

I'd fallen instantly in love with her on that day. I was too old for her, of course, twenty to her seventeen, but I loved her in all the other ways a man can love the people in his life.

Greg was slightly less scrupled about the age gap, and he effectively put the kibosh on my affection for Ari ever turning romantic. Regardless, the moment Ari walked into my world, my world got better.

Sitting here now, with Ari in surgery for God-knows-what injuries, looking across the aisle at her new life, her new best friend and her new love, the prospect that I could lose her looms over my head like a dark cloud.

I frown. I don't want to be on this side of the aisle. I don't want to be part of Ari's past. I want to be in her past, present, and future. I consider changing seats, getting up and crossing the aisle to sit beside Sheryl.

But what about Greg? I can't leave him behind. But I can't shoehorn him into Ari's new life, can I? Would Ari want that? Would Greg want that? I glance over at Greg, who's eyeing Alex—as if he's come to the same conclusion I have.

· · ·

"You're her husband?"

Greg nods vacantly at the doctor, whose light blue scrubs are spotless, pristine. I take comfort he's not covered in blood like Greg is, then fret again: *do doctors go through a wardrobe change between the operating room and the waiting room?*

"And you are?" The doctor glances at me over the patient chart in his hands.

"Her brother." Well, it's sort of true, in a her-parents-love-me-like-a-son kind of way.

Doc turns to Alex next, and it's all eyes on him as he fidgets. *Oh, won't this be awkward.* How many patients have a husband and a boyfriend? Then again, this is Austin.

"He's her other brother," Greg blurts out, surprising everyone. The doctor glances between me and Alex, no doubt curious about the contrast in our complexions.

I improvise. "I'm adopted. So what's up, Doc?"

We all give the doctor a hurry-up-and-speak look as Sheryl flutters in with an armful of donuts and a round of coffees. We unload her haul as Greg again takes care of the introductions with the doctor. "Sheryl is her sister."

The doctor looks weary but doesn't delve into the truthfulness of our family ties. He just looks at the chart in his hands. "As I was saying..." He then starts to rattle off a whole lot of blah-blah-blah. I hold my breath, waiting for him to get to the part where he says, "Oh and by the way, miracle of miracles, Ari doesn't have a scratch on her, darndest thing. Also, she's hungry for blueberry pancakes and asking for you, Jake."

That part never comes.

Instead, I hear things like "set fracture of tibia...three bruised ribs...observation for signs of concussion."

A tremendous pressure starts to build in my chest. I press my palm to my heart and wince. Sheryl notices and wraps an arm around my waist. I'm surprised by her support. She doesn't know me from Adam, yet she's letting me lean on her like a crutch. She quietly assures me, "She's okay, Jake. Our girl's going to be okay. Are you going to be okay?"

Numbly, I nod.

"When can we see her?" Alex asks, his voice steady even as his hands shake at his sides.

"She's through recovery and in an ICU room, so you can visit her now," the doctor says, then instructs us on how to find her room. He adds, "When she wakes, she'll be disoriented. It could be good to see a familiar face, but I don't want all of you crowding into her room at once."

When he finally finishes talking, we turn as one, the old guard and the new walking in perfect sync, a surreal lockstep as we haul ass upstairs to see her.

On level three, it's a hurried scan of room numbers until we finally find her. The door is open, and at the first sight of her, I'm equal parts sick to my stomach and elated beyond measure.

First thought: *Jesus, she looks like roadkill.*

Second thought: *Thank Christ she's not actual roadkill.*

Ari's face is a patchwork of scrapes and angry bruises. Her arms and hands are just as shredded, with one arm covered in thick bandages and the other a pincushion for the IV. Her left leg is wrapped in a giant cast, with her little toes sticking out the end, the trim nails painted bright purple.

Seeing her like this is a total mindfuck. My brain misfires, and my eyes deceive me. In a flash, I'm in another time, another place, a different hospital room. Instead of Ari lying before me, battered and bruised, I see my mom's comatose body supine and still, surrounded by an array of beeping and blinking machines.

I stagger backward, nearly knocked on my ass as I blink and rub my eyes, confused and pained by what I see, both in the here and now and in the past. While I stumble, Greg goes stock-still, as if frozen to the floor, and Sheryl winces and wobbles.

Alex, though, doesn't hesitate, not even for a millisecond. With an assertive gait, he rushes through the door and kneels at her bedside faster than a vampire drawn to a juicy vein. He clasps one of her hands and whispers words into her ear. I want to look away, feeling like an intruder in their private moment.

As quietly as we can, Greg, Sheryl and I ignore the doctor's orders and all crowd into Ari's room. There aren't enough chairs, just two for the four of us. What's the protocol here? Who gets to sit—old guard or new? We all shuffle awkwardly from foot to foot until Sheryl speaks, her voice cracking the silence like a whip. "I'm going to find a couple more chairs."

She disappears, and it's just me and Greg, doing the awkward shuffle as we try not to focus on Alex as he tenderly touches Ari's hair. There's a bang behind me and I turn as Sheryl wrestles a chair through the doorway. The thing is twice her size and weighs more than she does. Greg is quick to help, maneuvering the thing into the room while Sheryl disappears to find another one. When she brings that one in, I help and we each sit—Alex at Ari's side, holding her hand, while Sheryl, Greg, and I dot the corners of the room.

I don't know how long it is we wait; it feels like eons. The beeps and blips of Ari's machines remind me too much of the past. I lean forward and dump my head in my hands, covering my ears so I don't have to hear those sounds, so I don't have to hear anything, until—

"Hey," Alex says, and I perk up. "She's waking up."

We all rocket to our feet and circle her bed, anxious for any twitch of movement, any sign of life. There's a flutter of her eyelashes, a twitch of her fingers. Then she opens those big brown eyes, and it's like watching the sun rise—there will be another day.

Ari looks around the room, confused. She winces from the glare of the bright lights, and I hurry to shut them off, so the only illumination comes in through the window at her side.

"Hey there, Little Hare," Alex's voice purrs. "Do you know where you are? Do you remember what happened?"

She blinks away some of her confusion and tries to nod, flinching as if the movement hurts. Alex flinches, too, like her pain hurts him. Ari sees the torment on his face, and whispers in a raspy voice, "I'm okay."

Alex slumps with relief, looking practically boneless without all the tension and panic to hold him upright. On a gust of breath, he sighs, "Thank God."

Alex kisses her temple, because the rest of her face is a maze of bruises no man could navigate. Her eyelids flutter, and she grins a little as he whispers secrets into her ear. When he pulls away, Ari pinching the fabric of his dayglo safety vest. "What are you wearing? You look like a traffic cone."

"I hope you like it. Cuz if you keep playing in traffic, I'm going to insist you wear one of these every time you leave the house."

"I should go," Greg whispers to me and takes a step toward the door.

"Greg, wait," Ari calls out.

Greg stops in his tracks as she beckons him forward. "Do you need anything? I can bring you something from the house, just name it—"

"Thank you." Ari's eyes tear up.

Shit. How close did we come to losing her today?

She reaches out and squeezes Greg's hand, her voice watery when she repeats, "Thank you."

"I...uh..." Greg's eyes water, and he looks down at the floor. He shakes his head, then sets his jaw in a rigid line when he looks back up at her and clears his throat. "I'm just glad you're all right."

When Ari smiles, Greg does too, but it's still weird to see them like this. For years, they were inseparable, a unit; all of us—we were the Three Musketeers. Now everything is so awkward.

On the other side of her bed, Alex offers his hand to Greg. The two men have sat together for hours now, waiting for news about Ari, waiting for her to wake. And never during that time did they actually do the whole meet-and-greet thing. Now, with Ari's fate known, they shake hands for the first time.

"Hey, guys, don't bogart the babe," Sheryl hollers as she clomps forward and makes her way to Ari. It's just the right amount of levity to calm everyone's twitchy nerves. Dialing back her usual bone-crushing action, Sheryl gives Ari a hug that is downright gentle. It looks weird.

"Sherrie!" Ari grins at her friend, then asks the room, "Geez, was there an article in the newspaper? How'd you all know I was here?"

"Jake," Alex and Sheryl answer in unison.

Actually, Nicole helped me get in touch with everyone, but I don't mention that, because, yeah, *awkward.*

"Hey, Jake." Ari levels her gaze at me. She gives me that heart-stopping smile of hers. Despite all the black and blue, her face is as sweet as an angel's.

"Hey, Two Shoes." I come to the side of her bed.

"I tried something new today."

"Heard about that."

"I don't recommend it."

"Heard that too." I smirk. "And here I thought your days of experimentation were over."

She giggles, and the sound soothes my jangled nerves.

I swoop in for a hug, trying not to hurt her as I gingerly drape my arms around her. In return, Ari squeezes the ever-loving shit out of me, then grumbles that I've hurt her. Her grousing is music to my ears.

"My baby," the strained and reed-thin voice comes from behind me. Ari's parents stand in the doorway, looking haggard and stricken by the sight of Ari in that hospital bed. They got here fast. I check the time on my phone, surprised that the day has slipped by while we sat and waited.

At the sight of her parents, Ari's mask of bravery slips, and with a whimper, she crashes. "Mom," Ari whispers tearfully.

In a flash, Ari's mom is at her bedside, hugging her only child. At the other side of her bed, Alex hustles out of the way to make room for Ari's dad, and the big man wraps his arms around his wife and daughter.

"I need to get out of here." Greg mumbles at my side.

"Yeah, man, I'll come with you." I murmur back. A bit louder, so everyone can hear me, I say, "We'll give you guys some privacy. Call if you need anything."

"Greg," Kathryn calls to him as he moves toward the exit. He freezes as his mother-in-law approaches with warm eyes, clearly surprised when she wraps him in a loving embrace. "Thank you for calling us, sweetheart, and thank you for...being there...and..." she steps back, taking in the vision of his bloody attire, and blanches but quickly recovers. She grasps both of his hands, which he'd had the good sense to wash clean of blood a few hours ago. "Just, thank you," she finishes.

Greg forces a flat smile, but says nothing.

Next, Kathryn turns her attention to me. "Jake, honey, are you okay? You look a little pale?"

"It's been a long day, Mrs. Goody, but things are looking up."

She wraps me in a hug, and as her warmth envelopes me, I feel at peace for the briefest moment. Steve follows his wife over and offers us each a solid handshake before he and Kathryn return their attention to their daughter and the new people in her life. *Time to go.*

I look to my left, but Greg is already gone. I have to jog to catch up with him in the hall as he marches toward the exit of the hospital, "Hey man, wait up."

Greg stops and waits for me.

"So." I take a deep breath of the summer air when we're finally outside and turn to Greg, squinting in the sun. "Want to go out tonight and get completely shitfaced?"

"God yes."

3—Thursday July 14, 2005 12:14AM

"Two more shots of Jack." I order from Manic—a retired sideshow circus performer who adores Ari and has been eyeing Greg with curiosity since we came in. I'd forgotten this bar is Alex and Ari's regular spot when I suggested it for drinks.

Since our parting at the hospital, Greg's showered and changed out of his bloody clothes. But he still looks like a wreck. And he's too wrapped up in his own misery to notice he's being watched. I nudge him with an elbow. "You were saying?"

"Fuck you. I wasn't saying anything," Greg grumbles as Manic delivers our drinks. Greg picks up his whiskey shot and stares into it like it's a crystal ball. To the din of bar chatter and The Scorpions rocking us like a hurricane, we do our shots without a toast. Only then does Greg start talking. "Man, shit sucks."

I settle into my seat for the long haul. Greg has this way of not sharing a damn thing about himself until the whiskey starts to flow and then it's an all-out emotional-upchuck. Cue the word vomit: "We were fine, you know. I mean, maybe a little stale, but isn't that what marriage is supposed to be like? You settle into a comfortable—"

"Numbness?"

"I wasn't numb. I loved her. I still love her. *Fucking hell,* I still love her. But she wanted to open things up, and honestly, the idea excited me, and then the whole thing with Kate...That was a mistake."

Welcome to the Greg and Ari Show. I've been in the live studio audience for almost thirteen years. Lately, it's been a fucking soap opera. "What's the story there? Are you and the secretary no longer a *thing*? Because I thought you were in love with her."

"She's my assistant, not my secretary, asshole." Greg huffs and takes a swig of his beer. "I thought I was in love with her too. Turns out, I had it all wrong...what love is."

"What is love?" I ask with a chuckle.

Greg frowns at me. "If you start singing that Haddaway song, I will break your nose."

The thought had occurred to me, but I abstain and take a sip of beer, remaining silent, waiting for Greg to share whatever insights he has to offer.

"I used to think love was about the good times. I thought it was just about being happy with someone, or at least being content with them."

"It's not about being happy?"

"Well, of course everyone wants to be happy, but the good times...that's the easy part. The real shit, the true test of mettle, that comes out during the bad times. That's when love really matters. And I...I screwed it up. I took things for granted. I took *her* for granted." Greg presses his palms to his bottle of beer and holds the thing out like he's reading the label. "And when things got bad, I didn't even notice. I figured, if I'm content, then she must be, too. I didn't put any work into it. I didn't think I had to."

I roll my eyes at him, "For a smart guy, you're kind of an idiot. What did you think all those marriage vows about sickness and health and richer and poorer are about? Marriage is supposed to be about the good *and* the bad times, or did no one ever explain that to you?"

"Yeah, but that's my point." Greg's eyes twinkle, and he shifts on his seat to face me, ready for a debate, ready to let the analytical part of his brain take over from the emotional part for the first time today. "We've got plenty of money, and we've both been healthy. We never had those obvious sources of stress to contend with. Most couples fight about, what? Money, sex, kids...well, the money and sex have always been good, and no kids so—"

"If the sex was so good, why was she in such a hurry to fuck other dudes?" I don't know why I say it. It's a needlessly cruel observation, and one I'm sure Greg has spent many nights wondering about himself. Still, it's frustrating that Greg was so blind to what was really happening in his own marriage. When his wife had asked to open the marriage, he'd jumped at the chance rather than taking a moment to wonder *why* she was asking. He'd just assumed all was well at home, never noticing that his wife was withering away in the house he'd bought her, a fucking Rapunzel wanting to let down her hair.

Greg scowls at me again. "If it were just about sex...It wasn't about the sex."

"And Kate...how does she fit into this?"

He groans and finishes his beer, then orders another and a round of shots. "Kate...Kate *was* about the sex. I conflated my curiosity of the newness, my sexual attraction to her, and my genuine admiration of her into some big emotional...thing, then confused that *thing*, whatever it was, with love. And I'm not sure what Kate felt toward me, but it wasn't love."

"You've put a lot of thought into this."

"I've had a lot of time to think lately." Greg grimaces and takes a drink of his fresh beer. He pauses in deep thought for a moment before adding, "This morning, when Ari was hit...All I could think was, 'I'm going to lose her. I'm going to lose her.' And then, at the hospital...seeing her with Alex, it all became clear. I've already lost her. I mean...Shit, that came out wrong. I'm not equating her leaving me with her dying. I just meant—"

"I know what you meant, brother."

With a relieved exhale, he muses, "I had the love of my life, and I didn't even realize how lucky that made me. And now look at me...getting drunk and pining over everything I've lost."

Welcome to my life, Greg. I drown that pathetic bout of self-pity with another chug of beer, then grab one of the shots. Greg takes the other, and with false cheer in my tone, I go with an old toast, one we made up back in college. "To the two hottest guys in the bar."

Greg remembers it, too, and graces me with a nostalgic smile as he raises his glass to clink mine. "To them, whoever they are." We both chug our drinks. With a low groan, Greg rubs his hand over his face and asks, "Enough about me. What about you? Anything new?"

"I fucked Rebecca again last night," I admit with a heavy sigh.

Greg chokes on his beer. Laughing and coughing and pounding his chest, he jokes, "Well, aren't we a fine pair?"

Can't argue with him there. I glance across the bar to a blonde and redhead who've been giving us their come-hither looks for about fifteen minutes now. The redhead is cute in the face, and the blonde has a massive set of tits that jiggle when she laughs. I turn to Greg. "Speaking of a fine pair, there's a fine pair of ladies making eyes at us, ten o'clock. Shall we fuck them?"

"Yes. Let's..." Greg toasts the air and then downs the rest of his beer. "Or...no, wait. I need to go home, curl into the fetal position on the bathroom floor, and weep until I pass out."

"Sounds like a party. Wear a condom."

Greg smirks at me as he ambles to his feet, tosses a couple of twenties on the bar for Manic, and leaves without another word. In his absence, the heavy weight of my foul mood only sinks lower. Without Greg here to cry in my ear about losing Ari, I'm left to my own thoughts, and lo and behold, they stray to Ari as well.

We could have lost her today.

The weight of that reality settles on my shoulders like Atlas's burden. What would I do without her? I close my eyes, and in an instant, my traitorous mind morphs my thoughts back to those memories of before, images of the woman I *did* lose. I see my mom lying in her hospital bed, the left side of her face covered in thick bandages, a tube shoved down her throat to push air in and suck it back out of her lungs. Her body broken beyond repair—

I blink and rub my eyes, wanting to wipe my memories away, then look over at the blonde and redhead. How much work would it take to get them into a threesome? The way they're looking at me, not much. So why does the thought of it exhaust me?

Too tired to fuck? That's a new one.

I stare at the bottom of my glass and contemplate leaving, but where would I go? Back to my apartment, to stare at the bottom of a different glass…or bottle? Alone? But I'm alone here too. Always alone. I glance across the bar at the blonde and redhead again, recognizing the opportunity for what it is. I don't have to be alone; not for tonight, anyway.

I gulp down what's left of my beer, leave some money on the bar for Manic, stand on stiff legs, and weave my way through the crowd. As I near, the two women adjust their postures and paste inviting grins on their plump lips. I consider the prospect of burying my sorrows in them. But at the last minute, I continue past their corner of the bar and go outside to find a cab.

• • •

There are no cabs. I walk around the block, but there's nothing. Well, not *nothing*; there are plenty of people—all crowded onto the cobbled sidewalk, already inebriated, eager to get a head start on their weekend drinking—but there aren't any cabs.

I contemplate returning to the bar, to the warm bosoms of the redhead and the blonde. A threesome could be fun tonight, a good way to take my mind off of, well, everything. I close my eyes and let myself imagine it for a moment, then think better of it and open my cell to call the cab dispatch office. I nearly yelp with surprise when the phone chirps in my hand, announcing the arrival of a text. It's from Nicole.

You owe me one.

Grinning, I type a reply: **I owe you two. I'll buy you a couple beers next time I see you.**

"Make it a couple whiskey shots, and you're on."

I jump at the sound of that gravelly femme-fatale voice coming from behind me. I turn and there's Nicole standing a few feet away. *Well, fuck me sideways 'till Tuesday; this is a surprise.*

A combination of fear and awe arise within me as she saunters in my direction. Goddamn, the woman is hot. I thought it the first time I laid eyes on her, and I've thought it every time I've seen her since. She exudes sensuality. Every gesture and movement she makes lingers, a slow seduction. And I can't drag my eyes away from the hem of her short skirt as it rides the tops of those tight thighs as she moves. *Shit. Did I just lick my lips?*

She's not even your type, I try to remind myself...again. Yeah, but she's so damn pretty. No, scratch that—with her pouty plum lips, big green eyes, lean, lithe body, and legs for fucking days—she's nothing less than gorgeous. Just the sight of her gets my heart racing. It doesn't hurt she's wearing a latex dress. *Who wears a rubber dress in July? Sweet baby Jesus, the thing is practically painted on.* I go a little lightheaded as all my blood rushes south.

"Well, hello there," I say, then want to kick myself. *Well, hello there? Really?* I try to play it cool, but I have no clue how to play this at all—which is new. This shit usually comes so easy for me. I'm a grade A Casanova, a fucking legend at the game of seduction. If there were a certification course in The Chase, I'd be the goddamn instructor. So how is it that in a matter of seconds, this woman has thoroughly scrambled my brain and turned me into a bumbling idiot?

Nicole's smile turns wicked, and she bats those long eyelashes at me, laying the groundwork for my undoing. *Jesus Christ, the woman is terrifying.* She's a clear and present danger, a maneater, a praying mantis, a black widow. And me, I'm the poor bastard unwittingly tangled in her web, about to have my head bitten off.

"About those drinks. Can I get a rain check?" I try to save myself from impending doom. "I was just about to catch a cab and head home."

"I can give you a ride." *Oh good lord, the double entendre.*

I tilt my head, watching her with suspicion as I ask, "Why would you want to do that?"

"Maybe I don't want to drink alone." She cocks a hip and that skirt inches farther north. "Do you have anything to drink at your place?"

I nod dumbly, speechless.

"Well, then..."

I shake some sense into my head. "Actually, I can stick around here for a couple more." I gesture toward the bar I've just left. Nicole follows me inside, where I find us two stools at the bar. Across the way, the blonde and redhead aren't smiling at me anymore. I turn my focus to

Manic who approaches with a knowing smirk as he comes to take our order.

"Two shots of Jack—"

"Jack? No." Nicole turns to Manic. "Make those Jameson."

I raise an eyebrow. Nicole crosses those long legs, then says only, "Trust me."

Trust? That's a tall order. When Manic brings the two shots over, Nicole slides one in front of me. I eye the drink with suspicion and not because it's Irish rather than Tennessean whiskey, but because it's trouble. This little fucker will be to blame for all the bad decisions I make for the rest of the night. *Wasn't me. Oh no, not my fault. Blame the drink.*

Nicole lifts her shot as she asks, "What should we drink to?"

I have no idea.

"How about to trying new things," she says as she clinks her drink against mine. Speechless, I follow her lead, then nearly choke on my own drink as I watch her throat move when she swallows.

Nicole sets aside her glass and turns her whole body to face me, her crossed legs the only thing between me and the bottom hem of that rubber dress. *Shit, I'm staring at her crotch.*

I look up with a jerk of my head. Nicole smirks; she's caught me. For a good long minute, neither of us speak; neither of us do a thing. We just stare at each other. Then, slowly, she tilts her head and lifts her hand like she's going to touch my face. Instead, she reaches for a lock of my hair. I flinch with surprise as her delicate fingers twirl and play with the ends.

During the summer, I almost always wear my hair in braids, but after the day I've had, I couldn't be bothered. In a brief trip home for a shower and change, I only had the energy for a comb through before I tugged my clothes on and came to the bar. It's dry now and shines in the warm lights.

"You have nice hair," she says.

I blink. I swallow. I clear my throat as if to say something, but I'm speechless. What do you say to that? Thanks?

"It's so black, it's almost blue."

I tilt my head, and the movement sends more of my hair falling around my shoulder to brush against her hand. She strokes her fingers through the strands and the sensation makes me lightheaded. Distracted by her touch, I nearly yelp when she places her other hand flat on the top of my bar stool, right between my legs. I shrink away to avoid the fingers-brushing-against-my-dick form of physical contact. I'm already mostly hard, and I'd rather she didn't know it.

Nicole's expression is mischievous as she leans into my space. Her breasts brush against my chest and her mouth hovers at my ear for a long moment. All I can sense is where she's touching me and the feeling of her hot breath against my cheek. Then, with that phone sex voice of hers, she purrs, "It's funny you called me a peach in your text. I've been told I taste like one." *Fuck. Me.*

With that, I'm fully hard and salivating like Pavlov's dogs. I nearly bust out in a choking cough but manage to keep it together, maintaining my outer cool even as my inner lech wants to dive to his knees and learn the truth of that statement firsthand.

With the deadly grace and patient prowl of a panther, Nicole straightens up, pulls her hand off my chair, and slides her ass back onto her stool.

Heart racing, cock hard as fucking steel, I watch her every move, practically panting. Hot *damn, she's seducing me. I'm being seduced.* This rarely happens. I'm usually the seducer, not the seducee. Gotta say, the view from this side of the fence doesn't suck.

Getting off on the idea that this goddess wants me enough to chase me, I get some of my swagger back. I give her my version of a wicked grin and ask, "Does that offer for a ride still stand?"

• • •

I burrow my hands under that tight rubber skirt and clasp my palms to Nicole's bare ass as I pick her up. She wraps her legs around my waist and moans when I slam her back against my fridge. I can't wait another minute to be inside her, and I yank her strip of a thong aside to push my way in. *Incredible. She feels incredible.*

I drive deep into her, making her moan. I love the sound of it. I want to hear it again. I fuck her harder, faster, anything to get a reaction.

Even though I've got her suspended against my fridge, she still manages to take charge. Hugging her arms around my neck, she grabs fistfuls of my hair and yanks. My head falls back, and I hiss at the pain. It hurts so damn good. When she bites me on the neck, I howl and almost come.

I stumble, and we nearly hit the deck, but I recover and turn, flattening her back on the kitchen table. I pull her arms off my neck so I can stand up straight with her laid out like a feast before me. I grab at the top of her dress and tug it down until her tits pop out. I fill my mouth with one and my hand with the other as I proceed to fuck the everloving shit out of her. She arches up and screams when she comes, and the sound of her ecstasy is a gift I savor.

Then she pulls away, and in an instant, she's turned the tables again. She pushes me backward until my ass hits the chair by the wall. Before I can recover or complain, she springs onto me and seats herself back on my cock, her knees planted on the chair on either side of my lap. I groan when she grips the chair behind me and rides me like a bucking bronco. *My God, she's a fun fuck.*

I look up at her and she's staring down at me, watching me while she fucks me. When we make eye contact, she holds my stare, and I wouldn't dream of looking away even if I could.

In that moment, it's like I connect with her, fully fucking connect, and it's like nothing I've ever experienced. I see her, hear her, feel her, taste and smell her, but I want more. I want to know her. The thought terrifies me, and I nearly lose my erection. But then she smiles, and it's so beautiful. I come right then and there, and watch in awe as she rides my orgasm to her own. *Damn that was good. No. Better than good, that was—*

Nicole's expression flips from bliss to blasé, like a switch turned off. And I feel a chill on my lap when she moves off me. Standing in the middle of my kitchen, she pulls her thong and dress back into place. Crap, we're both still fully clothed, my pants wrapped around my ankles like an idiot. I raise my ass up to tug my jeans back on, tossing the condom in the trash bin before I button the fly.

I'm usually so much more suave, taking my time, enjoying all the sights, sounds, and flavors before I move in for the kill. But not this time. The instant I had Nicole in my apartment, she beelined for the kitchen, looking for a beer. I practically tackled her as I fell to my knees and pressed my face between her legs, desperate for a taste. *A peach, indeed.*

But now—*shit,* things are awkward, and not in the usual "Thanks for the tumble, maybe I'll call you" sort of way. More in the "Where do we go from here?" sort of way.

It's too quiet. I feel the need to speak, to say something clever. But what do you say after you've just nailed the ex-girlfriend of your best friend's new boyfriend? And, insult to injury, it's some of the best sex you've ever had in your life?

I reach into my back pocket and yank out my smokes. As I light up, I offer one to Nicole. She shakes her head and crosses the room to my fridge, yanking out two long necks. She slides into the chair across from me and pops the caps off using the edge of the table. *Hot.*

"So." Nicole takes a sip of her beer as she pushes the other one across to me. "What was the emergency today? What sort of *accident* did Ariana have?"

She wants to talk about Ari? *Now?* "Uh…"

Nicole watches me closely as she takes a long sip of her beer, then licks her lips.

"She was hit by a car," I mumble, mesmerized by that mouth.

"Oh shit." Nicole actually looks genuinely concerned for Ari, and that makes me like her—which is funny, considering I just fucked her. "Is she okay?"

"She's banged up pretty bad, but she's tough. She'll be okay." I shrug, if only to mask how much the day's events have affected me. "Thanks again for the phone numbers."

Nicole stares at me for a moment, then stands. "Well, listen, this has been fun, but I gotta go."

Uh…okay. I feel oddly bereft as I walk her to the door. I think I want her to stay. I kind of want to sit with her, maybe smoke and drink with her—or, I don't know, fuck her again or just watch some TV. I frown. *What the hell is wrong with me?*

At the door, I search my head for something witty to say, but nothing comes to mind. We stand for an awkward moment before I lamely offer, "Drive safe."

Nicole turns to leave. I surprise us both when I clasp her hand and pull her back around to face me. Then I kiss her.

In the first instant our lips meet, I realize it's our first kiss. And, man, I am such an ass for completely skipping that step earlier during all the sex.

In the second instant, as her velvet-soft lips move against mine, I realize I really like kissing her. She tastes so damn sweet, and those lips are pure heaven. I cinch my arms around her waist and pull her against me as the kiss grows more intense. Her hot breath punches into my mouth as I slide my tongue into hers, taking her with long, languid strokes.

Holy. Christ! Kissing shouldn't feel this good. Kissing has never felt this good. This feels too...right. It's almost—*fuck me*—it's almost romantic. Abruptly, we snap apart, blinking and breathless.

"I have to..." She backs away, her shaky hand going to her lips.

"Yeah."

She turns and leaves. I never once take my eyes off her, and I'm disappointed she never once turns back to look at me. She just saunters off, those killer hips swaying with each step she takes to leave me.

I have to physically clutch onto the doorframe to stop myself from jogging after her, finding her at her car, bending her over the hood, and sliding home again.

Home? I shake my head to dislodge the thought. *What the hell is wrong with me?*

. . .

I wake with a jolt, my head throbbing and my body sore, and curse as the memories of last night come to me. *Fucking hell, you fucking fuck!*

What was I thinking when I nailed Nicole? If there were ever a woman who's off limits, it's her. How am I supposed to befriend Alex and stay close with Ari if I have this hanging over my head?

As Ari distances herself from Greg, I suffer a paranoid fear she'll leave me too. Simple solution: befriend Alex. Because, if it's not going to be Greg, Ari, and me, then it's going to be Alex, Ari, and me. I will be part of the equation. Period. But did I just screw everything up when I fucked the wrong woman?

With a groan, I hop in the shower and wash once, twice, three times, trying to scrub away any trace of Nicole. Forty-five minutes later, loaded with an armful of Stargazer lilies—Ari's favorite—I trudge up the third-floor corridor of the hospital, aimed for her room.

As I approach, I see the doctor looking in at her, a peculiar expression on his face. My heart starts to race, and I quicken my pace, asking as I approach, "Everything okay?"

The doctor smirks at me, then looks back into Ari's room. Inside, Alex has crawled into Ari's bed and the two are cuddled up close, fast asleep.

They don't look entirely comfortable. Alex has contorted himself into an awkward pretzel around Ari's leg cast and her IV pincushion arm. Still, they look utterly content, their sleeping faces relaxed in an enviable peace. Her head rests on his arm like it's the perfect pillow, and she hugs his other arm across her middle like it's the best blanket.

"Her brother, eh?" the doctor asks with a smirk.

Oh right. I give the doctor a sheepish grin when I admit, "Uh, no, he's not her brother. Ari's relationships are complicated, but they're not *that* complicated."

The doctor just shakes his head as he walks away. I turn my attention back to Ari and Alex. The sight levels me with a bittersweet combination of emotions—from joy and relief to loneliness and envy.

Envy? I shake the thought from my head and step into the room. The bouquet's cellophane wrapper crinkles, and the obnoxiously loud noise echoes within the confines of the quiet space.

I cringe, not wanting to wake them, but before I can retreat, Ari and Alex both blink their eyes open at me. Alex stretches and Ari sits up as best she can, sniffing the air. "Something smells good."

Shit! I should have taken a longer shower. I should have soaked in a vat of scrubbing bubbles. It's like Nicole has marked me with her scent, and every time I move, I catch little whiffs of her on me, dripping from my fingers and chin, seeping through my pores—a dead giveaway to my nefarious nocturnal activities.

Ari reaches out to take the bouquet from me and gives the flowers a long sniff. *Idiot, she was talking about the flowers.*

"So, the doctor thinks there's some incest happening in here," I lamely joke, because nothing spells "ice breaker" like incest jokes.

"What?" Ari squawks.

Alex chuckles. "Kind of figured telling the doctor I was her brother would come back to bite us in the ass."

"What?" Ari repeats as Alex and I laugh.

"So, when can we spring you from this joint, Two Shoes?"

Ari announces, "Right now. Let's go."

Alex scolds her. "Nice try, Little Hare." To me, he explains, "Doc says she should be cleared to leave by this afternoon."

Ari lets out a mighty huff, pouting like a precocious child, and whines about boredom. Alex whispers something to her. Under the bedsheet, he must be tickling her, because she starts to giggle and squirm. *Okaaaay. Awkward.*

"How's my little girl?" Kathryn Goody chirps loudly as she and Steve step into the room, blanching when they see Alex in bed with their daughter.

Adding to the awkwardness, Alex responds like he's been caught stealing. Yanking his hands out from under the blanket, he looks like they have him at gunpoint when he sputters, "I didn't...we weren't...I mean...shit...er...crap." He takes a moment to find his words, then surprises us all when he announces, "Sir, ma'am, to be clear, I have every intention of marrying your daughter, just as soon as she'll have me."

You could hear a pin drop, it's so quiet in here. Everyone holds their breath for a good long minute, stunned by what Alex has just said. And no one is more stunned than Ari. She looks at him with what can only be described as wonderment. He smiles and winks at her, and if a wink could say a thousand words, that one does.

I don't belong here. I've never felt more out of place than I do in that moment. I'm an interloper in Ari's life now. While Ari's busy falling in love with this new man and the new life he can promise, I'm still fucking up and fucking around. I see Ari's future moving ahead while I stand still. I see my place in her heart shrink to nothing, a star sucked into a black hole.

I need to get out of here, clear my head. Interrupting the moment, I croak out some lame line about needing to go to work, and then I leave. I don't need to go to work, but that's a lie I can live with. Instead, I swing by my apartment to pick up my guitar and amp, then head straight for the band's practice space.

The room is dark and dank, small and windowless with walls painted matte black and covered by hundreds of show flyers and Hustler centerfolds. The only illumination comes from two strands of Christmas lights stapled to the walls, but the dimness is good for deemphasizing the detritus that piles up when three guys share a space for five years and no one bothers to bring a vacuum. The floor is littered with bits of busted guitar and bass strings, shards of broken drumsticks, forgotten guitar picks, wadded up pieces of duct tape, and a half-empty bottle of blue Gatorade that's been repurposed as an ash tray.

I plug in, plop my ass onto a whiny old metal chair, light a cigarette, and prepare to play something...anything...

Nothing comes. My fingers don't work right, and my head has forgotten all the lyrics. I groan in frustration and rocket to my feet, setting my guitar aside and pacing the floor. Finally, I stop at Ryan's corner, dig through his stash—probably the real reason I came here, if I'm being honest—and roll myself a joint.

I lay down on the floor and stare up at the ceiling as I light up. *It's fucking pathetic.* My best friend was lying in a hospital, being semi-proposed to, and I ran out on her like a grade A asshole—just to come lie here on the dirty floor and smoke a joint, alone.

Always fucking alone. That goes without saying.

No, that's not true. With Greg and Ari, I was never alone. I was part of their unit: a third wheel, sure, but together, we were a magnificent fucking tricycle. It never once occurred to me that it could change, that I could lose what I had with them.

But of course it would change; of course I would lose it. Everything is fleeting, temporary. Life is just a hiccup, a blink in time. And those of us currently living life—we're not special, just lucky. We're nothing more than bags of bones wrapped in flesh, obsessing about our insignificant struggles and successes until we, too, shuffle off this mortal coil to make room for the next generation of victims to life's greatest illusion—an illusion that we have any control, that what we do matters. It's all a crapshoot, a coin toss. Live or die—go over the car or under it, get on the doomed plane or miss the flight, hit a tree at sixty-two miles per hour or follow the bend in the road to safety.

We all weave our little tales of a greater purpose, a larger meaning, creating a tapestry out of the loose threads of life, never wanting to acknowledge how easily that fabric can be cut or torn, and—

Damn, this is some good weed. I laugh and God laughs with me.

• • •

"I mean, she said, 'while I recover,' but I think she intends to stay there." Greg takes another hit from the joint before passing it back to me. *Note to self: I owe Ryan twenty bucks.*

I take my own hit. I still haven't told him about Alex's preproposal. How would that make the guy feel? He's already taken a kick square in the nuts today when Ari called him to tell him that she'll be picking up some things tomorrow and then staying with Alex indefinitely.

"What do you think? Will she...come back?"

Feeling the need to be a smartass, I sing about it being against the odds she'll return to him.

"Did you seriously just sing Phil Collins at me?" Greg shakes his head and tries to stifle his smile.

"Who do you think I am? Of course I sang Phil Collins at you." I take a swig of beer before I level with him. "Look, man, you gotta face facts. She's moving out. I mean, sure, right now it's about her healing. And with her crutches, it just makes sense for her to stay—"

"With him." Greg groans. "And once she's there..."

"Hey, you know what? You should move in with me."

Greg takes a big hit, holds it, then coughs when he laughs. "Sorry, dude, but I don't like you like that."

"Whatever." I flip one of my braids over my shoulder like I'm flirting. "Everyone likes me like that."

"You keep telling yourself that, buddy." Greg smirks.

With a laugh and a long pull from my beer, I offer again, "Seriously, though, I've got that spare room. You're welcome to—"

"I know." Greg grimaces. "Thanks, brother."

There's a long silence between us. We finish the joint, and I light a cigarette. As I stare out at Greg's yard, I remember helping him and Ari put the flower bed in all those years ago. The purple sage and prickly pear are huge now. I remember that prickly pear sticking the everloving shit out of me because I was too manly and stupid to wear gloves while planting a goddamn cactus. Which reminds me...

"Man, I screwed up last night." I exhale my words on a gust of smoke, saying it so quickly I don't have time to stop myself.

Greg looks over at me and gives me room to elaborate.

"I fucked Nicole Rollins."

"Arson Nic? You had sex with Arson Nic?" Greg cracks up laughing. I mean, the guy actually holds his side like he's going to bust a gut from laughing so hard.

"Fuck you, asshole." I groan and take another drag off my smoke.

"Dude." Greg is practically hyperventilating as he wipes away a tear. "Why would you have sex with Alex's ex-girlfriend? What are you, an idiot? And more importantly, are you going to tell Ari?"

"Fuck no." I take another long drag and finish my beer. "Actually, I probably will. I can't keep shit from her; she's part bloodhound."

"So?" He waggles his brow.

"So what?"

"Was it good?"

Now I laugh and shake my head before finally admitting, "Yeah, it was...good." *Probably the best sex of my life, at least top five.*

"Gonna hit that again?"

"No," I say it unequivocally, as if there is no doubt in my mind.

4—Saturday July 16, 2005

"Well, hello there, Jake Sixkiller from Nebulous." That femme-fatale voice sends a zap of electricity straight through me. I spin around and look down into the crowd, searching for her. She's at the edge of the stage, staring up at me, her lips slightly parted with so much promise. *Nicole.*

She's even more beautiful than I remember. In her skintight, leopard-print dress, she looks like a jungle cat—lithe, gorgeous, and deadly. I practically purr at the sight. I try to play it cool, even as my pulse races and my palms get clammy with sweat. "Well, hello to you too."

Nicole gives me that sexy little grin of hers but doesn't say anything more. And that's a shame, because I really want to hear her voice again.

Trying to play it cool, I yank my T-shirt out of my back pocket and use it to wipe the sweat from my face and chest, drawing her eyes to my pecs. It occurs to me that after performing in front of a few hundred people, I'm wearing less clothing than I was the night I fucked her.

I set my guitar case at the side of the stage and jump down into the crowd. I get a couple one-armed hugs from former fucks, a few chest-press hugs from future fucks, and several hearty back pats from some of the dudes in the crowd. I hardly pay attention as I swagger toward Nicole, my sights set, missile locked.

"You're very talented," Nicole says.

She smiles and I'm knocked stupid by the sight, desperate to see it again. I try to think of something clever to say, but she's short-circuited my brain. So I just say, "Thanks."

Then things get awkward. I'm too close to her, and have to keep from rubbing my bare chest against her leopard-printed breasts each time someone pushes through the crowd behind me. God, I need a drink. I gesture toward the bar. "Can I buy you a drink? I still owe you one."

"I think it's time I bought *you* a drink," Nicole counters, then leads the way to the bar. As I follow, my eyes lock onto the sexy sway of her hips and the way her tight dress cups her amazing ass.

What the hell are you doing, Jake? My brain begs the question, even as every other part of me whistles and sings "la-la-la-la-la-la-la," pretending not to hear logic. Deep down, though, I know better than to court this dangerous liaison. I *should* have given Nicole a one-armed hug like I've given every other former fuck in this room.

But *should* is not in my vocabulary tonight. Despite my better judgment, I'd rather do what I *want* to do. And right now, all I want to do is get her under me, clawing and coming and screaming my name.

Greg is at the bar, smirking at me. *Terrific.*

"Hey," Greg greets me then turns to Nicole, ratcheting up the charm with his Cary Grant grin as he offers his hand to shake. "I don't believe we've formally met. I'm Greg Hendricks."

"Nicole Rollins." She shakes his hand, and gestures to the wall of alcohol behind Tom, the bartender who stands ready to take our orders. "I'm buying shots. Would you like one, Greg?"

"No, thank you." Greg says. When she turns away to place her order, he raises an eyebrow in silent judgment. If eyebrows could talk, Greg's would say: "Are you crazy? Just two days ago, you said never again."

My brows hit my hairline in silent rebuttal: "What? It's just a drink. Doesn't mean a goddamn thing."

Greg rolls his eyes at me. When Nicole turns back around, shots in hand, Greg fakes a yawn and says, "Listen, I'm going to head home.

Early start tomorrow. You kids have fun." With a cocky smirk, he leaves me to my doom.

Nicole offers me one of the two Jameson shots. We down our drinks without a toast and then face more silence.

Once upon a time, I had game. *Where the hell did my game go? Cleveland?* I'm about to say fuck it all and ask her if she wants to get some food with me, or coffee. We could do coffee...or, you know, some alone time.

But I don't get as far as opening my mouth when Nicole opens hers and cuts through the quiet like a knife. "So listen, about the other night..."

Oh boy. That's never a good start to any conversation.

"I don't know what I was thinking. I shouldn't have...I think, maybe in a way, I was using you."

Uh... I frown, but she's not looking at my face. She's looking at my bare chest. I suddenly feel too naked, too vulnerable. I slip my T-shirt back on and cross my arms over the black cotton.

Nicole still won't look me in the eyes, even as she continues talking. "I think I used you for revenge sex, and I'm sorry."

"Revenge against who?" Oh, who am I kidding; I know the answer to that. It's so obvious, a blind man could see it.

"Ariana," she confirms, and her voice sounds meek and thin, no longer the seductive femme fatale. "I just..." Now, finally, she looks up at me. I see something in her eyes, a sadness I've never noticed before. Then, in a blink, it's gone, and her entire demeanor changes. Her defenses slide into place before she shoots me a hard look, this time maintaining eye contact. "Ariana stole Alex from me, and...well, I'm a tremendous bitch, or colossal cunt, as you so aptly put it, and I wanted to hurt her like she hurt me, and you're close to her, so I used you." She furrows her brow, then adds, "I just wanted to apologize. You seem like a nice guy."

Stunned. Reeling. Pissed. Hurt. It's the hurt that surprises me most. Her words register as actual pain in the center of my chest, and with each word out of her mouth, that pain ratchets up another notch.

The next emotion to zing through my head is disbelief. There is no way Nicole can convince me I mean nothing more to her than a prop in her petty little revenge drama. Not after that kiss. The sex, sure; it's easy to fake emotions during sex, but she'll never convince me she didn't experience that kiss on the same level I did. Maybe I was alone for the rest of it, but not then.

I've barely reconciled my disbelief when I'm flooded with the red rage of pure, stupid fury. Did she seriously just call me a *nice guy*?

Fuck this shit. No more Mr. Nice Guy. Nicole has hurt me, so I'll hurt her back. I open my mouth, and the absolute worst thing I can think to say comes right out. "Sorry to burst your bubble, *sweetheart*, but I'm afraid you gave your gash to the wrong guy. If it's revenge you were looking for, you should have spread your legs for Greg, not me. I'm just the friend. He's the husband. I'm Tonto. He's the Lone Ranger. But hey, thanks for the easy lay. Always nice to get a nut off without having to actually try."

Nicole flinches.

I convince myself I don't care. I turn and walk away. In a matter of minutes, I've packed my guitar and amp into the bed of my truck, and I'm about to get into the cab when the backdoor of the bar opens and closes. I turn to look back, stupidly hoping it's Nic—

It's Rebecca. *Terrific.*

"Hey," Rebecca says as she saunters toward me. "I was hoping we could talk. After the other night—"

"Look, Rebecca, this is not a good time, and that was a mistake."

"What was a mistake?" Her voice takes on a teasing tone, the sort of tone people use when they talk to dogs or children. It's the tone she always takes with me whenever I said something she doesn't want to hear.

"The other night." I pinch the bridge of my nose to fight the onset of a headache. "I was drunk. I...it was a mistake. It won't happen again."

"What won't happen again?" She's still using that Rover-come-over tone. And as she speaks, she moves closer to me, so close I can't breathe without sucking in a lungful of the burning stench of her perfume.

"You and me..." I don't want to use words like "us" and "we" with Rebecca, so I go with a neutral pronoun. "*It* didn't work the last time, and it won't work—"

"*It* worked pretty well the other night." With that, she winks and plasters herself against me as she grasps for *it*, adeptly attempting to manipulate my cock through the layers of denim and boxer-brief cotton.

I try to jerk away from her, but I'm stopped by the rigid metal of my pickup truck. I plaster myself against the machine, blindly grasping for the door handle, desperate to escape. But my hands lack the coordination to manipulate the door handle, just as Rebecca is unable to manipulate my handle.

"Little Jake" remains unmoved in my pants. Rebecca furrows her brow in confusion. I'm confused too. In the months we've circled each other in this on-again-off-again dance of ours, I've felt a lot of conflicting emotions when it came to Rebecca—indifference was never one of them.

Rebecca bites her bottom lip in stubborn resolve, determination in the face of adversity, and tries to kiss me. I shake my head and turn away, toward the head of the alley. And what do you know, we have an audience. Her face is in shadow, but her telltale leopard-print dress gives her away. *Nicole.*

With her arms crossed over her chest and her hip cocked to one side, Nicole watches Rebecca sink to her knees. *Shit. I don't want this to happen.* I want to stop Rebecca, but when I open my mouth, nothing comes out. I look back toward Nicole, hoping for...what, help? A visual aide?

I hear rather than feel Rebecca unzip my jeans, but I definitely feel it when she slides my cock into her mouth. Not numb anymore, I'm instantly hard as Rebecca sucks me deep. I groan, some combination of pleasure and frustration, and let it happen.

Bracing myself against the truck, I glance back to our audience. Nicole is still there, still watching. I can sense the disapproval rolling off her in waves. It's a turn-on. Is it her presence, rather than Rebecca's hard work, that's got me stiff as steel?

At the moment, I don't care. I keep my attention focused on Nicole, watching her with longing as she watches me with disdain. But all too soon, she shifts from one foot to the other, then turns and walks away, disappearing out of the alley entrance to return to Red River Street and the flow of Friday night foot traffic.

I feel her absence acutely, which makes me angry. *Good riddance and revenge fuck you, too, Nicole.* I cringe at the ugly thought and look down at Rebecca's blonde head, bobbing as she works her magic.

Shit. I'm doing the same thing to her Nicole did to me, aren't I? I'm using Rebecca's mouth for revenge and nothing more. Guilt courses through me, and I groan as I pull myself free of Rebecca's lips with a juicy pop. She looks up at me with surprise as I tuck myself back into my pants and zip up.

"Sorry." Am I apologizing for *not* using her mouth like she's some whore in an alley? I look around at where we are and groan, then feel the need to nobly add, "I can't do this to you."

As I speak, I try to work the raw edge out of my voice so I sound kind to her. Though I don't feel anything remotely resembling kind right now. I feel raw, empty—a user who's been used. And how shitty is it that even as I try to make things right with Rebecca, my mind is laser-focused on the hurt left by another woman?

"Do what to me?" Rebecca wipes her mouth with the back of her hand as I help her get back to her feet.

"This. It's not right."

Rebecca huffs in exasperation. "*This* what? What are you talking about, Jake?"

"This," I practically yell as I gesture between us. "You and me. It's not going to happen, and..." I huff, too, frustrated with my inability to just say what I mean. But I hate talking about this kind of shit. Which is probably why I avoid "relationships," and a large part of why my "relationship" with Rebecca has lasted as long as it has.

But as I stare at her now, I see the vulnerable, hurt person she's always worked so hard to hide from me. What have I done? I've let this thing, whatever it is, go on for far too long. I've been stringing this woman along for months. It was...what...six months ago that I thought I'd finally severed the cord connecting us. I'd been inspired to end things after Greg had revealed the news of the open-marriage plan with Ari. I'd meant to make a clean break, and yet here we are.

Maybe Ari's near-death has delivered me to this place of clarity, but as I stand here now, staring at this woman—a woman who once told me she loved me then pretended she was joking when I didn't say it back to her—I see things differently than ever before. My weakness has hurt her. My vacillations have to stop. I owe it to Rebecca and to myself to end this mess once and for all.

"It's over." I say the words with steel in my voice, and so there's no room for misunderstanding, I add, "We're over."

She smirks. "You've said that before."

"Yeah, I know, and I'm sorry for that. This time, I mean it."

She puts on her flirty mask, and when she speaks, it's with that baby-talk, puppy-love voice again as she reaches down to stroke me in my jeans. "Sure you do."

I bat her hand away and speak through gritted teeth. "Stop it."

With a pout, she says, "Jake, I'm getting tired of these games. You act like you don't want me one minute, then you're all over me the next."

I close my eyes in shame, remembering bits and pieces of the other night. *All over her* is putting it mildly. "I...Yeah, I'm sorry, Rebecca, truly. I treat you like shit, and you let me. It's not good for either of us. It has to end. You need—"

She slaps me soundly across the face. My vision spots, my cheek stings, and my ear rings. I stare at her, struck dumb. She's slapped me before, but never when she was this sober and never with this much anger in her eyes. When she speaks, the words hiss out. "Don't you tell me what you think I need. You don't get to do that."

There's an awkward pause, during which I just stare at her, this stranger standing before me. She hardly resembles the woman I once knew.

Almost instantly, her face changes back. With a little shake of her head, she slips her mask back into place, and with a bat of her lashes, she reaches up to stroke the cheek she's just hit, to soothe the pain she's just caused.

I shake my head, and she lowers her hand back down to her side. She waits for me to do something, to say something. Maybe she expects me to soothe the pain I've just caused her.

I don't. I won't.

Silently, I turn my back on her. Probably not a smart thing to do, but I'm not thinking all that clearly right now. I find the latch to my truck door, open it up, and climb inside. "Goodbye, Rebecca," I say before I close the door. Then I leave.

I take Red River south to the band practice space to drop off my guitar and amp, then climb back into my truck and stare out the windshield. I don't want to go home. I don't want to go anywhere, so I just drive. I circle and weave through the city. I navigate my truck up and down busy blocks lit by bright neon signs labeling bars and billiards, restaurants and shops. I dodge drunk pedestrians, aggressive pedicabbers, horse-drawn carriages, and double parkers before I finally leave the bright lights of downtown.

I head north, but not toward my place. Instead, I go to Greg and Ari's place. Correction: Greg's place. I park in the driveway and stare out the windshield for a moment before mustering the energy to reach for the door latch.

My phone rings, and I fumble it out of my pocket to look at the screen. It's Rebecca. I send her to voicemail and unlock my door. My fingers are on the door handle, about to open up, when my phone rings...again. It's Rebecca...again.

"Are you kidding me?" I ask the empty seat beside me, then send her to voicemail...again.

I open the truck door with a little too much anger. The door panel swings too wide, too fast. It comes right back at me like a boomerang, closing me inside the cab of the truck just as my phone starts to ring a third time.

"What do you want from me?" I answer, not trying to hide the irritation in my voice.

"Jake?" Not Rebecca. The voice is lower, breathier, phone-sexier.

Could it be...? I look at the Caller ID. Holy shit! "Nicole?"

"Yeah."

"Uh..." It's like she's slapped me too. My brain must be bruised because I can't think of what to say, so I go with the blunt and obvious. "Why are you calling me?"

She exhales, and even that sounds sexy. "To apologize."

x

"Why?"

"Listen, Jake...I need to talk to you."

"Huh?"

"Where are you? Are you with that chick from the alley?"

I burst into a fit of laughter. *Christ, when did my life get so absurd?* "No, I'm not with her."

"Then where are you?"

"Why do you keep asking me that? Why do you care where I am?"

"Because I'm at your apartment, and you're not here."

"Oh, please tell me you're joking. Look, Nicole, I don't know what kind of game you're playing, but I'm tired—"

"I need to set you straight on something."

"What?" Curt, humorless, impatient.

"When I seduced you last night, that was about revenge—"

"You've said all of this already—"

"But later," she hurries to interrupt my annoyed rant. "It was different. Later on...it...changed for me."

I close my eyes and let out the breath I've been holding.

"I don't expect you to—"

"When did it change?" My words come out almost like a growl.

Silence. I get nothing but painfully empty silence from her. I want to hang up, but instead, I wait. I sit in the stifling heat of the truck cab for what could be hours, staring out the windshield at the yard. The blades of grass reflect the moon's glow, shining silver like a bed of nails.

When my patience runs out, I demand, "*When.*"

In a tiny voice, little more than a whisper, she finally admits it, "When we kissed."

I knew it! I fucking knew it! That kiss. That fucking kiss.

I've kissed a lot of women. Yet, never did I feel even a hint of the spark I felt with Nicole. Nicole's kiss unhinged me.

And now, Nicole has admitted to her own undoing. My chest puffs up with satisfaction. I'm not alone in this. Nicole might have started this to royally fuck with my head and Alex's head and Ari's head, but I've managed to fuck with her head too.

That night, I'd stupidly given her power over me, a power which she'd brutally abused tonight with her cruel admission. But now, as I imagine her sitting alone on my porch stoop, desperate to see me, desperate for more of me, she's given me all the power. Now I'm the one in control. I'm the one who can hurt her, deny her—respond to her cruelty with my own.

But I don't want to. I don't want to deny her or treat her cruelly. I want to kiss her and touch her and taste her and take her, any way and every way I can. *Which is a problem.*

No matter what I want, or how badly I want it, this woman is completely, totally, and irrevocably off-limits to me. One trip down that rabbit hole was one too many. It'd be moderately excusable to have one night of bad judgment. That's a story I'm pretty confident I could spin to Ari and Alex. But two nights? Not so much. I need to back off from this. I need to think with my head, not my—

"Jake, please." That word. That magical word coming from Nicole, spoken in her phone-sexy voice, does strange things to my nervous system.

I close my eyes and groan. "Wait there. I'm on my way."

•   •   •

Nicole straightens from her seat on the top tread of my stairs, and I take her mouth before she can utter a single word. The sensation is the same as that first kiss—fire, pure and scorching. I groan into her mouth, and she moans in response. *Fuck. Me.*

I'm completely captivated by this woman's mouth. Which is noteworthy, because I've never been much of a fan of kissing. There are so many other things I'd rather do with my mouth. But with Nicole, everything is backward, upside-down, and inside-out. She's got me all twisted up, and I think I like it.

I pull away to suck in some oxygen, and Nicole surprises me when she cups her hand over my crotch and tightens her grip. "That whore in the alley, was that your way of getting back at me?"

I'm a little surprised that I'm really fucking hard right now, despite—or perhaps because of—her punishing grip. But, eager to regain control, I grab Nicole's wrist and twist her arm until it's pinned at an awkward angle behind her back. She writhes in my grasp, rubbing her tight little body against me. Good God, is she turned-on by this? I tug her arm a little tighter behind her back, and she purrs like a contented cat. *Fuckin' A!*

Wanting another reaction from her, I shift so she feels my hardness and whisper in her ear, "Sounds like you're jealous it wasn't you on your knees in that alley."

Anger flairs in her eyes. She's so sexy when she's mad. *I'm taking such perverse pleasure in this power play. What the hell is wrong with me?*

In a moment of clarity, I release her arm from my hold and step back. "Enough with the games. I want to fuck you. Do you want to be fucked?"

Nicole comes to me now, her lips close to mine, and whispers, "Yes."

I take her mouth with a brutal kiss while I fish the keys out of my pocket and get us inside the apartment. This time, I direct her straight to the bedroom and toss her onto the bed. I dive down to her hips, shove her skirt up to her waist, and press her thighs apart with bruising force. With one hard yank, I rip her lace thong to shreds, and in the next instant, I have my mouth on her.

She's dripping wet. She's getting off on the rough stuff, and so am I, which is news to me. I've been known to spank a pert ass now and then, maybe tug a ponytail on occasion, but I've never been straight-up rough before. Gotta say, this shit is hot. Everything about Nicole is so damn hot. And she tastes so damn sweet—peaches and cream, indeed. I devour her, feasting, gorging, until she comes on my tongue.

When I crawl back up her body, I realize she's still fully clothed. Enough with this quickie shit; I'm getting her naked. I find the zipper on her dress and tug it off. Okay, so I could be more gentle about it, but I'm still kind of mad. She pulls my shirt over my head as I awkwardly kick my jeans off and dig a condom out of my pocket. Within a matter of seconds, I'm buried deep inside her.

"How does your revenge feel now?" I growl into her ear.

She moans and twists her hips up to meet my punishing rhythm.

"Tell me," I demand.

"Fuck me harder," she says as she digs her nails into my back. "Oh God, yes."

I silence her with a rough kiss. She adds her own violence to the mix, her teeth tugging my lip like she wants to draw blood. Hovering out of reach of her sharp kisses, I take full control of her body, pinning her wrists over her head. She bucks up to meet me, trying to twist free of my control, always challenging me. I tighten my grip and quicken my pace until she comes with a scream.

Nicole gazes up at me, her eyes glazed in postorgasmic bliss. I release her wrists, and she pushes me off her. I land on my back, and she climbing on top. Now she's in command, a jockey riding her racehorse.

God, this view. My eyes follow the smooth line of her stomach to the curves of her breasts, moving along with her rhythm, to the long line of her neck and the delicate features of her face, softened with the afterglow of her latest orgasm.

I reach up and clasp my hand on the back of her neck, pulling her down to me, and lock eyes with her as I use my other hand to stay her hips. She looks confused—until I begin my own pace. Unlike the gallop of before, I take her slow this time, moving in deep, long strokes.

I watch her, all those sweet glints of ecstasy in her eyes building to her next orgasm. And when it hits, she keeps her eyes open, watching me as I watch her. *Christ, eye contact is hot.*

I come with her this time and see stars. When it's all over, there's only the sound of our jagged breathing and my racing heart booming in my ears like the ticking of a clock...a doomsday clock.

Shit. I did it again. I took another taste of this mighty fine peach, my forbidden fruit. The woman is a habit, a bad one that I desperately need to quit. But *fuuuuuck*, she's better than any drug I've ever tried. And right now, my perfect drug is draped across me like a warm blanket.

What do I do now? Should I touch her, kiss her, talk to her, ask her to leave? Nicole is the first to move. She slides up onto an elbow and stares down at me. With gentle fingers, she strokes my cheek, the same spot where Rebecca hit me. "I'm sorry, Jake."

"I like the way you apologize."

She kisses me sweetly and it's like heaven. I wrap my arms around her and kiss her too. I twist us onto our sides and fish my thigh between her legs, locking every part of us together as we make out.

We're doing it all backward again, getting the main course of fucking out of the way so we can savor this dessert. But what a sweet dessert it is.

After all the sex and hours of making out, my energy flags. I tuck Nicole against me, playing big spoon to her little. I've never been much of a cuddler. I'm a hugger, true, and a toucher, yes, but I'm not a cuddler. *Or am I?* I press my face into the crook of Nicole's neck and take a deep breath, inhaling the scent of her hair and her skin as I drift off to sleep.

5—Sunday July 17, 2005

He's a giant, my Uncle Eli. His arms squeeze around my chest like a vise as he pulls me away from my brother, making it hard to breathe, to scream. The tattoo on his forearm is the only thing I can see. Its black lines blur with the tears in my eyes until it looks just like the frantic up-and-down tics and squiggles of Mom's heart rate monitor.

I don't remember him being so big, but when he straightens to his full height with me pinned against his chest, my feet leave the floor. I kick, aiming for anything I can injure—his shins, his knees, his balls. I don't care what I hit. I just need to hurt him so he'll set me free. I claw at his hands. I try to hit his face, gouge his eyes, but with my arms pinned at my sides, he's out of my reach.

"Calm yourself, Usdi Yona," he says, and I can smell beer on his breath. His words and that rank stench only enrage me more. I fight harder, but it does no good. Nothing I do has an impact. After all, he's a giant, and I'm just a fourteen-year-old kid.

If only I were stronger and bigger, more of a man. Maybe then I could break free of his control and scramble back across the floor to my brother. Maybe if I were bigger, I could protect him like a big brother should. Maybe I could do what the doctors and nurses can't. Maybe I could save him.

I scream through my tears, shouting the same word over and over, like I've forgotten all but his name. "Tommy!"

. . .

I wake with a start, disoriented for a moment as I sit up and blink my eyes open. I quickly recognize the tangled sheets and beige carpet of my bedroom. I look to where *she* should be—empty...empty arms, empty bed, and from the sound of silence that greets my startled awakening, the apartment is empty too. At some point in the night, my perfect drug wore off, or more accurately, my perfect drug wandered off. And in the harsh light of day, I feel...Well, what exactly is this that I'm feeling? A hangover? Withdrawal?

I should be glad Nicole is gone. Makes everything easier. Thing is, though, I'm pretty sure I wanted her to stay. I kind of wanted to see her dark pixie hair clumped and tangled with bedhead. I wanted to watch those gorgeous green eyes flutter open and see her smile illuminated by the morning sun.

What kind of lame-ass poetry shit is that? Besides cheesy, it's absurd. Nicole is hardly a sunshine and dew drops kind of woman. Nicole is an after-dark sort of woman, and come to think of it, I'm fairly certain I've never seen her in the daylight. *Maybe she's a vampire. Oh, she's* definitely *a vampire.*

Ambling out of bed, I head for the kitchen to start the day with coffee and a cigarette. I stop dead in my tracks at what I find on the kitchen table. Laid out neat and tidy is a lacy black thong, torn not-so-neatly in half. *Did I do that?*

Beside it, a note: You owe me a new thong. You can bring it tonight.

Tonight? I move the note aside and there beneath it, printed on blue cardstock paper, is a single ticket to tonight's flat track roller derby bout.

Holy. Shit. Nicole has invited me to see her skate. More than that, though, she's given me her complimentary ticket. As a performer, I know the significance of that. There's a huge difference between telling a chick "Come see me play sometime," versus putting her on the guest list to a show. This ticket is Nicole's guest list.

I'm honored. I howl up at the ceiling in triumph. I stare at the thing like it's golden and grants me access to Willy Wonka's lair. Tonight, I have a date with Nicole...at her behest. She invited me. *She* invited *me*! Doors at six-thirty. First whistle at seven. And me with no show, no band practice, there's nothing else I have to do. *Hell yeah!*

My phone rings; it's Ari calling. "Hey, little sis, how's it hangin'?"

"I'm sore and lonely."

" 'Sore and Lonely' has got to be the saddest country and western song ever written, Two Shoes." I start to make yodeling sounds with made-up lyrics about being sore and lonely.

Ari laughs, then grumbles about how much it hurts to laugh, and now she's calling me a jerk for hurting her. I chuckle. There are few things in this world as cute as Ari when she's miserable.

"Are you busy today," she asks.

I glance at the blue ticket in my hands, my golden ticket. "Why? What's up?"

"Alex has to work overtime, so I'm all alone, and I forgot to bring a book with me when I came over here." With a sad sigh, she asks, "Want to hang out?"

Of course I'll hang out with Ari. There's no question. She's my best friend. And there's no way in hell I could, in good conscience, leave her "sore and lonely" while I go out carousing with her nemesis. I close my eyes and swallow the frustrated groan trying to claw its way up my throat. "Sure thing."

"Yay!" she hollers. "Will you bring over *The Lost Boys* and *Near Dark*? I'm in the mood for a movie marathon."

"The Blood for Blood Marathon? Is it that time of the month already?" I'm confused. Our vampire movie marathons are usually reserved for when Ari's got cramps, and if I'm not mistaken, that's not for another two weeks. And how screwed up is it I've memorized my best friend's menstrual cycle? I shake my head, a little freaked out.

"Well, since I almost got killed by a car and lost a lot of blood in the process, I figured we could make a special allowance."

"Good point." I try to sound jovial, even as I wince at the thought of Ari hurt and bleeding on that road, her blood trickling down the hill and dripping into a storm drain. I have to shut my eyes and shake my head to get the images out. I force humor into my voice when I say, "Of course, you're owed a special allowance for taking out that Honda. I'll bring *The Hunger* and *Fright Night* too."

"My hero," Ari sighs.

"How you doing on food? Want me to pick something up on the way?"

Ari moans, "Yes, please," in response, and gives me Alex's address. I grab a pen and use the back of Nicole's note to jot down the details. *Awkward.*

"See you soon?" Ari asks sweetly.

"You got it, little sis. Candy striper Sixkiller reporting for duty."

"Now I'm picturing you in a candy striper outfit." Ari lets out a boisterous laugh. "Ouch, my ribs hurt. Stop being funny, ya jerk."

I chuckle and get her off the phone.

And...silence. Without Ari's cute little giggles in my ear, the apartment is too quiet, too still. I look around at my space, the space I've occupied for almost three years. The off-white walls are dreary and scuffed in places, with no photos, no posters, no art. The cheap plastic mini blinds are standard issue, ill-fitting and slightly askew. In the living room, the furniture is old and worn, bought secondhand years ago. In the dining area, I've temporarily shortened the chain on the chandelier with zip ties to make room for my weight bench and a set of dumbbells.

It's all temporary, transient—for years, I've lived here like I'm ready to leave at any moment. As if the next time I go on tour, I might not come back. And how did I not notice that before? The only mark I've made on my space is the brownish discoloration of the walls from years of accumulated cigarette smoke.

I look at my pack of cigarettes there on the counter, waiting for my morning ritual. I pick them up, turn them over in my hand, then chuck them across the room into the garbage. Nothing but net. They land with a satisfying splat. I wait for the nicotine draw to kick in, for the addiction panic to seize me—but there's nothing, only a strange sense of calm.

Next, I pick up the bright blue ticket left for me by Nicole. I turn it over in my hands and clutch it tight until the edges start to wrinkle and bend. I walk over to the garbage can and drop it in too. With a deep breath in and out, I walk away without a backward glance—

Two steps. That's as far as I get before I turn and dive for the trashcan. I rummage through the coffee grinds, cold pasta, stale cigarette butts, and cracked eggshells until I find it—that blue ticket, my golden ticket. I wipe it clean and take it with me as I head for the shower.

• • •

"How are you feeling?" I ask as Echo & the Bunnymen launch into their cover of "People Are Strange" and we get our first glimpse of Santa Carla, Murder Capital of the World (because of all the damn vampires).

"Peachy keen," Ari chirps with faux cheer.

I flinch at her mention of peaches—that forbidden fruit will never taste the same—and squirm a bit in my seat, the blue derby ticket burning a hole in my back pocket. I pop the top of a foam food container and pass it to her.

"You brought me pancakes?" Ari tears up.

"Of course I brought you pancakes."

Ari gives me a big smile. The bruises on her face and arms have turned into that sickly combination of purple and yellow, which means they're getting better, even though they look worse.

"How's the leg?" I ask around a mouthful of food.

"Itchy." Ari grumbles from her perch on the couch as she takes a bite. "But Alex pulled down one of the mini blind wand thingies for me to use as a scratch stick. Without this beauty," she holds up the stick like it's a magic wand, swishing it through the air a couple times, "I become a super whiny little bitch."

I chuckle from my seat on the floor. "Is Alex just now meeting the super whiny side of you? Poor guy has no clue what he's gotten himself into."

Ari sticks out her tongue in mock offense. "How's life for you, Jake-i-poo? You're quiet." She eyes me with suspicion, and I want to cower under her keen gaze. She's always had the uncanny ability to flay me with a single glance and see right inside. Usually, it's not a problem.

There's rarely much going on inside my head that's not reflected on the surface. Today, though, is different.

"Life is...life. You know? It is what it is."

"That's either very deep or utter bullshit. I'm leaning toward utter bullshit. What's going on, big bro?"

I shrug and keep my eyes focused on the movie when I say, "Nothing you need to worry your pretty little head about."

"Fine, don't tell me. Want to hear more about my problems?"

"Absolutely." I exhale with great relief.

"I can't take a shower with this thing on. I have to take baths and keep my leg out of the water. Normally, I love baths, but now Alex has to help me in and out like an invalid, and I hate it." She gives me an exaggerated pout.

"Something tells me Alex is not complaining about having to give you baths. In fact, I'll bet right now the guy is thinking, 'Man, I can't wait to get home and get my girl naked and wet and scrub behind her—'"

Ari throws a wadded-up napkin at me and groans. "Shut it, dirty boy." She rolls her eyes, "Anyway, the point is, I suck at being laid up like this. Last night, I started crying because I couldn't bend over to pick a napkin up off the floor. I've gone batshit crazy with hormones or cabin fever or something. Poor Alex probably regrets letting me move in."

"Probably," I agree, and Ari swats me with her scratch wand. "So what's the story with that? Are you moving in here permanently? Greg thinks you're coming back after you heal up."

Ari blinks, and that's all the answer I need. It's permanent, and of course it is. She's in love with Alex; why wouldn't she want to move in with him. Paperwork aside, Greg is already an ex in her mind. He's her past, and Alex is her future. And why does that thought terrify me?

I cough, then cough again. I need to take a moment, and I need to take a piss. I climb to my feet, avoiding Ari's gaze as I ask, "Bathroom down the hall?"

Ari nods as she chews a big bite of food. She gestures like she's trying to get my attention, and mumbles with her mouth full, "The door on the right." But it's too late. I've opened the door on the left, and—

Holy. Shit. Inside is an entire room filled with torture devices of the erotic variety. I stand there dumbfounded, and try to take it all in. There is everything from a cherry red spanking bench and sex sling with purple stirrups to a St. Andrew's cross in the corner and thick-gauge chains hanging from the ceiling like something out of an Alice Cooper video.

"Goddamnit, Jake, I said the door on the right?" Ari is on her feet and at my side, teetering on her one good leg.

Completely stunned, all that comes out is, "Holy fucking shit, Ari." She groans.

"Holy fucking shit, Ari!" Clearly my brain has hit a skip in the record, but seriously, "*Holy. Fucking. Shit. Ari!*"

"Jake," Ari huffs and tries to close the door, but I won't let go of the knob. "Oh, come on, close the damn door, you nosey ass."

I let go when she smacks at my hand and shimmies past me to close the room off. She wobbles and I snap out of my stupor to help, acting as a crutch to get her back to the living room and comfortable on the couch. I can't sit—I'm too wired—so I pace in front of the television.

Ari huffs. "The bathroom is the first door on the *right*."

"Fuck that. I have questions."

She raises an eyebrow, waiting.

I point toward the hall, and my mouth opens and closes as I search for words, finally settling on, "Is this...I mean...dude. Are you into that sort of thing?"

Ari starts to chew her bottom lip, which is one of her tells, a dead giveaway.

"Holy shit, Ari. You are!"

"Yeah," she huffs. "I am. So what?"

I stare at her, dumbfounded. Thirteen years! Thirteen years I've known this woman, and never once did I suspect she might be a freak in the sheets. But looking at her now, my eyes are open. And I'm in awe. *She's just full of surprises, isn't she?*

Not sure what to say or ask, I finally settle on "Alex got any booze in this place?"

Ari points to a huge hole in the wall that leads into the kitchen. "There's tequila and whiskey in the cabinet to the right of the fridge and glasses to the left of it."

I follow the directions to the letter this time, not ready for any more surprises today. I grab the whiskey—Alex, like Nicole, drinks Jameson, apparently—and two glasses, then join Ari on the couch.

She lifts her legs so I can sit beside her, then she drapes her legs over my lap. It's a relief. This is how we've always sat when we watched movies together, but this is the first time we've sat this way since Alex entered the picture. Maybe stumbling across that hidden room has eased some of the unspoken tension between us—one less secret.

I ease into the seat and help her get comfortable, elevating the broken leg on a pillow on my knee. I pour a finger of whiskey into each glass and hand her one. We toast and take our sips. As the burn slides down my throat, I relax.

"So, little Goody Two Shoes is into the kinky shit, eh?"

Ari groans and covers her bright red face. It's hard to reconcile this Ari, cute and blushing, with the new image I have of her.

I finish the whiskey in my glass and pour us each another. I turn my attention to the movie, watching Michael eye Star while that greased-up beefcake plays the saxophone. But in my head, I'm treated to a whole litany of images I'd rather not see—Ari strapped to that St. Andrew's cross while Alex whips her or bent over the spank bench for a paddling.

I close my eyes to those thoughts, but they're just replaced by different images, and this time, the starlet is Nicole. Her response to my rough treatment last night makes a lot more sense when I imagine the kinky sort of shit she did with Alex. For two years, she slept with a guy with a sex sling, and not one...but three variations of the cat o' nine tail whip—

"Hey." Ari punches my arm, pulling me from my thoughts. "Do you think less of me now?"

"What? No, of course not. Ari, shit, no."

She furrows her brow, skeptical.

I turn as much as I can without jostling her legs on my lap and say with sincerity, "Ari, I am absolutely not judging you. I do not think less of you. If you've found something that makes you happy, then fuckin' A, that's awesome."

A hint of a smile crosses her lips.

I clear my throat and ask the big question before I have time to chicken out. "But...he's good to you, right? He doesn't hurt you...without your consent, right?"

Ari laughs like what I've asked is utterly absurd. When she speaks, her tone is unequivocal. "Alex would never hurt me. Not. Ever," she continues, her voice strong and unwavering when she adds, "He's very good to me, Jake. The kinky stuff...it's fun and challenging and—"

"I fucked Nicole." The words tumble out of my mouth like a herd of bison chased over the edge of a cliff.

Ari blinks, confused by the interruption.

"I fucked Nicole," I repeat, still a skipping record, but hung up on a new groove this time. "Twice. I fucked Nicole twice, so, there, I said it."

Ari purses her lips together. I flinch, not sure what it means when Ari does that with her mouth. Then she bursts into laughter, moans in pain, then laughs again, then grimaces.

"Jesus, woman, stop it. You might break something new."

"I can't"—she groans—"help it. *Ouch.* It's just, *shit,* your face. You look so serious. It's, *ow,* hilarious." She tries to stop laughing, only to burst into another wave of the giggles.

I laugh, too, and it feels good. Finally, I ask, "You're not mad?"

"Why would I be mad?"

"Because...she's...your nemesis."

That gets another eruption of stuttering laughter and groans of pain. "My *nemesis*? You make us sound like supervillains."

I smirk at her. "I just mean...She's Alex's ex."

"So?"

"It doesn't bother you?"

"No. Should it?"

Well, don't I feel like a dumbass.

"Jake, for a big city, this town is really small. Honestly, as much as you get around, you've probably had sex with several of Alex's exes."

"Hey!" I feign offense, but she's got a point.

"So, what's she like? The stories I hear make her seem a bit...larger than life."

"She's cool."

"Oh my God." Ari covers her mouth with her hand in that way women do when they're being overly dramatic. "The way you just said 'she's cool' was so...Jake, you like her."

"Well, duh, that's rule number one when you stick your dick in someone."

"Oh please," she scoffs. "A: you know as well as I do, that's not even true. And B: you *like her* like her."

"Oh, for fuck's sake. What is this, junior high?"

"You *like* her. You *like* her. You *like* her." She does an awkward little shimmy dance and points her fingers at me in exaggerated swoops and circles.

I roll my eyes. "God you're annoying. Where does Alex keep the ball gags?"

Ari laughs. "Ow, don't make me laugh, jerk."

"Serves you right, little sis. Now sit still and watch the movie."

She smirks, but turns back toward the television. I do, too, but nearly jump out of my skin when she hollers, "It's Bout Night! What are you doing here? You should go watch Nicole skate."

But what kind of friend would I be if I just left her here, sore and lonely?

Like she can read my mind, Ari says in a firm tone, "Jake, go."

I check the time on my phone. "I can finish *The Lost Boys*." Settling a little more comfortably into the couch, I rub Ari's feet as we watch the rest of the movie, occasionally refreshing our drinks and regularly quoting along with the dialogue, particularly the Frog brothers.

• • •

"Arson Nic does not look happy as they send her to the Texecutioner's Chair for that elbow block to Doctor Mid-Nite's nose. Good news is, the nose ain't broke, folks, so we're going to give away some raffle prizes while our cleaning crew wipes up the blood."

Indeed, Nicole does not look happy as she is reprimanded by the ref. But damn, she really nailed the woman, and the fight that ensued was pretty hardcore. Now the two skaters scowl at each other, with Doctor Mid-Nite holding ice to the bridge of her nose as blood dries on the dark skin of her chin and stains the front of her top. *Holy shit. Nicole is a bit terrifying. So why am I really turned-on right now?*

Nicole finally complies and goes to sit in the Texecutioner's Chair, which is decked out to look like an electric chair. She crosses her arms over her chest, and I'm reminded of the pose she struck at the end of the alley, when she watched Rebecca and me.

I shift a little to get a better look at her. She's gorgeous, with the face of an angel and a body formed by the devil himself. She looks long and lean in that little plaid schoolgirl skirt, fishnet tights, and knee pads. *Good God, those knee pads are sexy.* Up top, she's got a little white shirt unbuttoned and tied in a knot just below her breasts, which are displayed stunningly in a black satin pushup bra.

Man, what I wouldn't give for fifteen minutes alone with her in that outfit. Actually, I'd probably only need ten, but let's make it twenty. I groan and adjust my pants. *And, wow, note to self: be less of a creeper.* I cross my arms over my chest, trying to act natural.

Nicole still hasn't spotted me. Does she think I've blown her off? Does she care? Probably not, she's far too involved in the bout to notice anything else.

Anyway, I'm not sure I want Nicole to know I'm here. I mean, what the hell would I say to her if I were to run into her?

Thanks for the comp ticket.

Thanks for all the phenomenal sex and the comp ticket.

Sure hope you never hit me like you just hit that blocker.

No, thanks, let's avoid all that. I keep to the edges of the giant building, one of those massive, Texas-sized metal Quonset huts. The place is an old roller rink dating back to the seventies, complete with arcade and concessions toward the front, with the skating rink filling up the back. Overhead, an assortment of lights shine in a rainbow of colors, blinking and shifting to the tempo of some song barely audible over the rumble of the crowd. At the very center of the rink is a spinning disco ball shaped like a giant roller skate.

Down below, the derby organizers have built a four-turn oval track using red rope lights fastened to the floor with package tape. Ringing the track are scores of fans sitting and standing everywhere. Some fans sit on the floor, so close to the track edge their knees overlap the tape. Behind them, several rows of chairs are set up in concentric rings and are filled with people wearing their favorite team colors.

Each team has a corner where their fans tend to congregate. The fans of Sheryl and Nicole's team gather at turn three, the one closest to me, and a particularly spirited set of supporters holler for Nicole's attention. She's either ignoring them or can't hear them above the din. *Were I to stand at turn three hollering for her attention, would she ignore me too?*

Nicole has to sit out a round in the penalty chair, but as soon as the refs let her back in, she's on the line and raring to go. She's like a cat about to pounce, crouched low on the toe stops of her skates, a star on her helmet, her eyes fixed on the track ahead, waiting for the ref to blow the second whistle.

The star on her helmet indicates she's a jammer—her team's sole point-earner for the jam. She's a bit unique for the position, far taller than most of the others, but she's fast, so fucking fast, and mean, so fucking mean. Her team is in the lead, and it's mostly due to Nicole and Sheryl—their other jammer—who is much smaller and skates like a ghost, able to slip through tiny holes and gaps in the pack, often undetected and usually untouched. Nicole, on the other hand, *makes* holes and gaps.

When the ref blows the second whistle, Nicole moves as fast as lightning, her body low and her long legs pumping hard to get the early lead. When she loops around the track and reaches the back of the pack, one of her teammates gives her a helpful push. She careens straight into a wall of opponents, knocking them over like bowling pins and breaking through the front to secure her position as lead jammer. Before her opponent can even reach the back of the pack, Nicole is already on her heels and laps her as well as the entire pack...again. When she's broken through the wall of blockers, she shoves her hands onto her hips, which, as lead jammer, signals an end to the jam. The ref blows a long whistle, and the skaters all scatter to their respective benches while Nicole keeps skating, circling slowly, bent over at the waist, her palms on her knees as she catches her breath. And God, what a vision that is.

What am I doing here, stalking in the corner, sporting a hard-on at the sight of a woman I can't shake from my mind? I shouldn't be here. I should leave.

I chug my beer and glance at the exit to my left. Pretty sure it's a fire door and opening it will result in a blaring alarm. *Bad idea. Really bad idea.* Still, I inch closer, contemplating it.

When the guy wearing the paisley polyester leisure suit and purple velvet cowboy hat booms out the start of intermission, I scope out my escape options and make a dash for the front door. Outside the air is hot, damp, and electric with the threat of a storm. I cut through a row of cars, making my way to the side parking lot.

"Jake."

I stop cold and close my eyes. The sound of my name in that femme-fatale voice scrapes down my spine like fingernails. I turn and see Nicole a few feet away, hot and sweaty and sinfully sexy in that tiny little Catholic schoolgirl outfit. In the dim light of the parking lot, I can only make out the angles of her expression, not the specifics, but memory fills in the gaps and my breath goes ragged.

"Where are you going?" she asks.

"I... uh..."

She lets go of the door she'd propped open with her hip and skates toward me, her red plastic wheels clattering over the uneven pavement. When she reaches me, she stops just shy of her breasts smashing into my chest. If only she weren't such a good skater; I wouldn't have minded that crash landing. I swallow hard as she stares up at me. In her skates, she's almost as tall as me, but she still has to angle her face up to look me in the eyes. And now, with her jaw tilted up at a stubborn angle, I get a good look at her...so pretty. All the air rushes out of my lungs.

"Did you bring me a new thong?"

I grin as I reach into my back pocket and yank out a virgin-white lace thong. It's one of six I bought in a whole assortment of colors at the lingerie store on my way here. There was a buy-five-get-one-free sale, and I'm planning ahead, considering I intend to rip my way through several more.

Nicole reaches for it, and I snap my arm back, hiding it behind my back. She smirks.

I give her my best smile, the thousand-watt panty-melter—big dimples and bright white teeth—and take a step closer, bridging the gap between us. Quietly, I ask, "If I give you this, will you give me something in return?"

"What do you want?"

Everything. "Will you come to my place tonight?"

Nicole leans up, balancing on the toe stops of her skates. Her lips hover just inches from mine, then she moves her mouth close to my ear and delivers my undoing when she whispers one single, perfect word. "Yes."

"Will you give me the chance to rip this thong off of you too?"

No hesitation. "Yes."

Damn, she's hot when she's agreeable. It takes every muscle in my body to hold back from laying her out on the hood of the Prius parked behind her. Every nerve in me is itching to do inappropriate things to her, things that would get us arrested for indecency and some other stuff too. I swallow hard as I deliver my next demand. "Will you keep this outfit on?"

Nicole bats her lashes. "My my, does Jake Sixkiller have a schoolgirl fetish?"

"I didn't until tonight." I give her a long, deliberate once-over, tilting my head to the side to get a real good look at her, then add, "You'll want to keep your knee pads on too."

Her laugh vibrates straight down into my cock, and *then* she licks her lips. I go lightheaded and wobble a bit on shaky legs.

"Any other wishes I can grant you before you give me my new thong?" she asks.

I clasp her hand in mine, giving her the thong as I reach up with my free hand and touch her cheek. "Let me cook you breakfast in the morning."

Nicole recoils, taking a full step away from me. In an instant, the sex kitten who'd only a moment ago been purring against my chest transforms to someone I hardly know—the hard-edged, tough girl who's just spent the last quarter busting noses and kicking asses. *My Nicole is gone.*

She looks over her shoulder, speaking with a rigid tone when she says, "Intermission is almost over. I need to get back."

I watch, stunned, as she turns and skates across the parking lot toward the entrance, then disappears inside without a backward glance. *What the hell just happened?*

I remain unmoved, trying to figure it out. An amber cone of light beams down from the streetlamp overhead to illuminate my confusion, the distant rumble of thunder punctuating the silence like the gods themselves are laughing at my humiliation. The Texas heat bakes me where I stand. Frankly, at this moment, I wouldn't mind if I melted into a puddle on the pavement. To be nothing but an oily stain on the concrete—now that's the good life.

"Wow."

I close my eyes at the sound of Sheryl's voice. *Terrific. Because that's exactly what my moment of epic rejection needed, an audience.*

"I didn't know you two were—"

"Obviously we're not *anything*. Or did you miss that last part?" I glare at Sheryl, not because she's done anything wrong, but because she's the closest target for my bitterness.

"Jake…" Her tone is so gentle, like a mom's comforting words when you've scraped your knee, and that pisses me off even more.

"Sheryl, just back off, *please*."

There's a long silence, during which I start to feel like an asshole for taking my shit out on Sheryl. I drop my head and pinch the bridge of my nose as I hear her skates start to roll. *Note to self: apologize to Sheryl—umph!*

I don't see it coming. Sheryl rolls into me with the force of a compact car and wraps me in a hug I'll be feeling for days. How does such a tiny little thing contain so much power? She squeezes me so tightly I run out of air and can't refill my lungs within the vise of her iron grip. I stand there like an idiot, arms at my side, more confused than ever. *What is happening right now?*

When she releases me, she pats me on the shoulder. "Better?"

"What was that for?"

"Sometimes we all just need someone to be nice to us. I figured this was your time."

Well, shit. She's such a sweetheart—

Before I can finish that thought, she grabs my hand and yanks. She revs her little engine with a couple of runs on her toe stops, and then it's full speed ahead as she skates toward the entrance to the rink, dragging me along with her. I have to hustle to keep up or risk a face full of gravel.

"What the hell? Where are you taking me?"

"Intermission is almost over. We need to get back inside."

Oh hell, no. I plant my feet like an anchor in the seabed, and Sheryl is forced to spin around or end up flat on her ass. She recovers from the momentum shift like a pro and skates around in a graceful circle, then lifts my arm to skate under it, like we're dancing. I don't move a muscle. "I'm not going back inside. I'm leaving."

"Don't be stupid. Of course you're coming back inside."

"No, I'm not."

"Jacob Motherfucking Sixkiller—"

"My middle name is Mitchell, actually, but you're close—"

"Let's go, big guy. Time to pull up your big girl panties, and come back inside."

"My big girl panties?" I laugh. My momentary distraction is a fateful mistake. Sheryl uses it to gain leverage over my dead weight. Skating forward, she knocks me off balance, so I have no choice but to follow her when she pulls me toward the door.

Before I know what's hit me, I'm back in the frigid environs of the massive HVAC-cooled arena, with Sheryl tugging me like an excited puppy on a leash. She doesn't stop when we've made it inside the door, though. Oh no. The tiny little thing keeps her hooks in me until she's dragged me all the way around the track to the far corner. Without any warning, Sher spins on a dime, and I have to stop short or risk a graceless face plant into the penalty chair. She shoves my shoulders, knocking me off-balance. I go down, and my ass lands in an empty chair in the reserved VIP area.

"There. Now shut up and enjoy the show." With that, Sher kisses me on the forehead, turns to skate away, and flips up her little skirt to flash me a look at her underwear. The words "Kiss My Grits!" are scrawled in red-sequined letters across her ass.

I can't help but laugh. Sheryl has managed to seat me as far away from the exit and as close to the action as possible. Not only is there no hope for an easy escape, but now there is no way Nicole will miss me sitting here. Especially considering I'm sitting right next to the penalty chair, and Nicole has a knack for getting penalized.

Terrific! Ter-fucking-riffic! I curse Sher as I try to get comfortable in the rigid plastic chair. A moment later, Sheryl comes steaming up to me with a tall boy of Lone Star beer wrapped in a bright pink koozie. She hands me the beer, winks, and skates away. With a sip of my free beer, I relax a bit.

When Nicole takes to the track, she glances at me a couple times though she tries to ignore me. Me on the other hand, I baldly stare at her. After all, if I'm going to be stuck here, I might as well enjoy the view. And frankly, Sheryl is right. If I want to win the heart of a tough girl like Nicole, then I can't run away every time she presents a challenge.

Who said anything about winning her heart?

I groan at the thought of it and stretch in my chair, a little sore from Sheryl's vise-grip hug. I shift my shoulders and twist my abdomen, trying to work out the kinks in my back and neck. It's on my third half-assed twist toward the right that I notice the redhead. She's sitting on the floor at turn two, looking curvalicious and retro, with Victory rolls in her hair and a tight little polka-dot top.

She winks at me, and I look away, turning my attention back to the action. But Nicole has noticed the flirting too. She eyes the pretty temptress with a scowl. "Oh shit" is the only thought I can muster before all hell breaks loose. With the moves of an angry cat, Nicole pops one of her opponents right in the shoulder, and the burly blocker sinks like a stone into the floor seats at turn two, right into the buxom redhead's lap. The skater rolls to the side to avoid hurting anyone in the crowd, but the redhead's beer cannot be saved. It flies out of her hand, end over end, spilling everywhere.

There's a procedure for this sort of thing at Austin roller derby bouts—a ritual of shame which accompanies any spillage of beer. While the cleanup crew wipes the beer off the track, the announcer does everything in his power to humiliate the beer spiller. It's tradition.

"Shame! Shame! Shame!" a chorus rings out as the entire room chants.

"Say it with me, everyone," the announcer shouts gleefully. "What do you do when a skater is coming your way? What do you do with your beer? You..."

"Lift!" shouts the crowd. Everyone holding a Lone Star—the "National Beer of Texas," and the only beer served at these bouts—lifts and then takes a drink of their beer. *God bless Texas*. I chuckle to myself as I take a sip of my own beer.

Sorry, redhead, apparently you winked at the wrong guy. And what the fuck is that about? Nicole rejects me one minute, then gets violently jealous the next? *Not cool*.

As the commotion settles down, and the wet spot is wiped dry, the refs do exactly what they should do—they put Nicole in the Texecutioner's Chair. Right. Next. To. Me. *Sweet!*

She studiously ignores me as she sits down, her head situated just beneath the old porch light fashioned to look like an electric chair helmet. I'm having none of this ignoring me bullshit, though. I've got Nicole exactly where I want her, a captive audience. She can't run away now. In the background, whistles and cheers provide the perfect camouflage for our conversation as the next jam starts.

I lean close to her but not so close the crowd will notice. "Did you do that on purpose?"

"Do *what*?"

"Take out the redhead?"

"Who?"

I angle my chin toward turn two.

Nicole doesn't answer, so I go on. "I'm starting to sense a pattern with you." I fold my fingers under my chin, assuming a thoughtful pose. "It's the jealousy that turns you on. You don't give me the time of day until someone else does. Then you get all hot and bothered and spread your legs for my attention. It's cute, really."

"What are you talking about?"

"First, it was your petty revenge-fuck bullshit which got you on my kitchen table. Then watching another woman suck me off in the alley had you camped out on my doorstep. And now...that poor little beer-spiller over there gets a blocker to the lap because...why? Because she flirted with me?"

"Oh my God, get over yourself."

"No, no, I think I'm onto something with this. Jealousy is the key, isn't it? It's your aphrodisiac." I hold my Thinking Man pose like I'm Sigmund fucking Freud. "This is very interesting, because *this,* I can work with. Though in the future, I'd prefer you take your aggression out on me, not them. No need to beer-shame the flirty little redhead when you can just revenge-suck my dick in the men's room."

Nicole looks like she wants to claw my eyes out. And it's a good thing we're having this little heart-to-heart in front of hundreds of people—otherwise, she might just do it.

"Fuck you, Jake. Go revenge-suck your own dick!"

Sadly, Nicole picks the exact wrong time to shout those words at me. There's a lull in the action as the jam ends, and it's time for her to leave the penalty chair and return to the game. Her words echo through the arena like a shot. Parents gasp as they react too late to cover their kids' ears, and the announcer makes an amusing "oh" face as he blinks with surprise. Nicole clears her throat and slowly stands, then skates back onto the track. Seated on the benches across the way, Sheryl tries to stifle a smile as she winks at me.

Yeah, how you like them big girl panties?

• • •

I'm ignored for the rest of the bout. Not only does Nicole avoid all eye contact, she's also extremely careful not to foul anyone so egregiously that she'd land her ass back in the penalty chair next to me.

She's shut me down right and proper, and it's not a big surprise. Really, I deserve it. This is her world, and I've come in and shit all over it. I feel very bad about it, actually. I deserve to be shut down.

The only solace I take is the assurance that my bullshit doesn't fuck with her head in the slightest. There is nary a wobble in her roll as she goes on to lead her team to a resounding victory.

Good. As much as I enjoy ruffling her feathers, I don't want to fuck with the shit that matters to her. Good for her for not letting me.

When the bout is over, the crowd goes wild. Nicole, sweaty and gorgeous, is waylaid by a documentary film crew putting together a story about the origins of this all-women-owned, first-of-its-kind derby league.

I watch for a moment, in awe of her achievements. Then I plot my escape. After the awkward confrontation at halftime, I'm ready to go home alone. I spot my opportunity and slip around the back of the announcer's booth unseen. This time, I don't dawdle in the parking lot. I jog to my truck, crank the engine, and take off for home before anyone can stop me.

The thing is, despite my little performance art piece with Nicole during the second half, I'm still a bit stung by her reaction in the parking lot. The look on her face when I suggested she spend the night hurt.

I crank the volume on the stereo to drown out my thoughts. The college station is halfway through metal hour, and the DJ is playing Metallica's "Ride the Lightning." I bang my fist on the steering wheel as I sing along with the song. Outside, rain pelts the windshield, and steam rises from the hot pavement. Thunder booms and rumbles, and lightning pulses and flickers to the beat of the song. It's cathartic, better than therapy.

By the time I hit my place, I'm feeling like my old self again. I strip out of my shirt and boots, turn on some porn, and flop onto the couch to jerk off.

I wake with a jolt, cock still in my hand. The doorbell buzzes again, and I glance at the clock. It's almost eleven. The bell rings a third time, then a fourth. *Who rings a bell four times this late on a Sunday night? Okay, fine. If it gets to ten rings, I'll answer the door.*

I wait.

There's five.

Why is six afraid of seven? Because seven ate nine. Drum roll...

Silence. *What. The. Fuck? Really? You'll ring my bell nine times, but not ten? Oh, for fuck's sake.*

I climb to my feet, take the four steps to the front door, and swing it wide open. Nicole is there, dripping wet from the rainstorm that rages behind her. She's slouched against the wall like it's the only thing strong enough to hold her up.

Without a moment's hesitation, I charge straight for her and kiss her so hard, the back of her head nearly hits the brick. She moans, and I take that as my cue to clasp my hands on her ass and lift her up, carry her into my apartment, and kick the door shut behind us.

Once inside, I drop her onto the couch and go to the kitchen for a couple beers. Upon my return, Nicole frowns at me. A sexy moan comes from the TV, and I glance over. The porn is still playing, and right now some guy is jabbing his tongue into some chick's asshole.

That's right, baby, class act right here. I shrug at her as I plop down on the couch. Reaching for the remote, I mute the volume but let the pictures roll.

"You kept the kneepads on. Nice touch." I gesture at her incredibly hot roller girl ensemble.

She looks down at her outfit, then lifts her beer to her kiss-swollen lips for a long sip.

"So tell me, Nicole, are you planning to spend the night?"

She furrows her brow as if confused.

"That was a condition, remember?"

"You can't be serious. You actually want to cook me breakfast?"

"I'm as serious as rectal cancer, darlin'."

She tries to suppress a smile. "That's pretty serious."

"You bet your sweet ass it is."

"What if I say no?"

"Well, then I'd say you know where the door is."

She laughs like I'm joking, but I just take a long sip of my beer and stare at her, steady and emotionless, trying to gauge her mood. I'm pushing her buttons, no doubt, but I have no idea how far is too far.

"Okay." She sets her beer on the coffee table, then proceeds to leave. *Wait. What?*

"You're leaving. Are you serious?"

"Serious as rectal cancer." She steps back out into the rain.

Oh, fuck all that noise. I rocket to my feet and dive for the door. She's barely gotten ten feet before I wrap my arms around her waist and pull her backward into my apartment.

"Fine, I won't cook you breakfast. Whatever," I whine as I carry her into the bedroom and toss her onto the bed. "Just means more bacon for me."

She laughs, but I'm not joking. I'm tired and cranky and a little offended by her bizarre boundaries.

"Are you mad at me?" she asks in a coy tone and tilts her head to the side.

"Yes, I'm fucking mad at you," I say in truth, though I can't for the life of me figure out why.

"How can I make it up to you?" She slides off the bed onto those kneepads of hers and saddles up close to me. I forget my train of thought as she slides her hands up my thighs and parts my already-unzipped jeans. "I have a pretty good idea of what might put a smile back on your face."

And with that, she proceeds to give me the best blowjob of my life. I see stars and wobble so much my knees go out. I fall backward onto the bed as I come in her mouth, but she follows me where I land, swallowing every last drop.

It takes me longer than usual to recover, and while I desperately want to return the favor, I can't move. She senses that, and makes it easy for me. She shimmies out of her red bloomers, then crawls up and over my body, not stopping until she's straddling my head, a kneepad at each ear. I use what little strength I have to tear a hole in her fishnets so I can get at her. Then I grab onto her hips and pull her down until she's sitting on my face.

She comes twice riding my tongue, and by that point, I'm so turned-on, I can hardly see straight. I push her onto her back, grab a condom from the bedside table and mount her. With a moan, she takes me in and twists her legs around my waist as we fuck fast and hard. We both come, quick and easy.

I shift up onto my elbow and glance down at where I pull out of her, frowning at what I see. "Oh fuck!"

"What?"

"The condom broke."

She glances at my glistening dick, and reality dawns on her too. But her only reaction is a disinterested "Whoops."

I flop onto my back and cover my eyes with my arm. "Fuck."

"It's not a big deal. I can't get pregnant."

"It *is* a big deal. There's more than just pregnancy to think about." I roll onto my side and try to make eye contact with her, but she's staring at the ceiling. "Nicole, I get STD tested every other month. I'm clean. I swear to you, I'm safe."

"Well, that's good to hear, and you don't have to worry on my end. You're only the second guy I've had sex with in the last three years."

I'm stunned. The revelation she's only been with me and Alex in the last several years is a bit weird.

As my mind starts to settle back down from panic mode, something she said before begins to resonate. "You're on the pill, then?"

She frowns at me. "No. I'm not on the pill."

"Then how do you know—?"

"I just know, okay? I can't get pregnant, so you have nothing to worry about."

The tone of her voice sends a chill through me. While her words are harsh and angry, her tone is thin and sad, vulnerable.

I turn onto my side, running my fingers down her arm. I surprise myself when I say, "I'm sorry you can't get pregnant."

"What?" Nicole snaps her arm away from my touch. "Who says I want to get pregnant?"

"I didn't mean now. I just meant...You sound sad when you talk about it, like...maybe someday...shit. I'm sorry. It's none of my—"

"Yeah, you're right; it's none of your business." Nicole stands up and straightens her outfit. I hang my head in shame—yet again, I didn't even bother to get her fully naked. She's still in her kneepads. I'm such a prick.

"Nicole." I sit up and try to reach for her, but she steps away, then takes another step, increasing the distance between us. I stand and tug my jeans back up, then follow her, matching her step for step as she tries to broaden the gap and I try to close it. "Please talk to me."

"About what?"

"About you. Talk to me about you."

"Why?"

"Because," my voice rises, and I have to make a concerted effort not to sound pissed off when I say, "I want to know you."

"Why would you want to know me?"

Now I sound pissed off. "I don't know. I just fucking do."

She sets her jaw in that stubborn pose I'm starting to really like. "Fine. I'll tell you about me."

Yes.

"You want to know why I can't get pregnant?" She smirks. "I can't get pregnant because when I was fourteen, I went to a frat party in West Campus, and a guy I didn't know handed me a beer, and I was stupid enough to drink it. I woke up a few hours later on the frat house lawn, missing my underwear and my virginity, but I'd picked up a shiny new case of chlamydia."

It's as if every synapse in my head fires at once, my heart stops beating in my chest, and my lungs collapse in on themselves—total system failure. My knees go weak, and my weight shifts. I nearly hit the deck, so I tilt toward the wall, using the plaster as a crutch.

Nicole scrutinizes my reaction, waiting for me to say something, do something. But I don't know what to say; I don't know what to do. All I feel is rage, an overwhelming anger toward the bastard who hurt her, who took so much from her. But that's not helpful. I want to reach out and touch her, to wrap my arms around her and hold her close. I want to vow that no one will ever hurt her again, not if I have a say. But I can't touch her, not now—not when she's just revealed the pain and devastation another man has caused her.

Finally, all I can say, the only thing I have to offer is a pathetic, "I'm sorry."

It's not enough, not by a longshot. With a heavy sigh, she leans against the wall beside me and slides down until her butt hits the carpet. She drapes her arms over her knee pads and stares ahead of her at the blank wall. I slide down, too, until I'm beside her and staring at the same spot.

With a shrug, Nicole adds, "Anyway, point is, I'm all fucked up inside. So, you're safe."

That's the worst thing she could say. It guts me that she thinks I would be so dismissive about what's happened to her. I frown at her, and she stares back at me. I expect to see anger there, hurt, but all she's showing me is strength.

She's so strong; it takes my breath away. I want to thank her for trusting me. I reach up with a shaky hand and rest my palm on her cheek.

Nicole flinches, startled by the contact, and bats my touch away. "Don't do that. Don't be nice to me. I don't want that from you." After a moment, she asks, "Do you know what I like about you, Jake?"

No, but God I want to.

"You're an asshole."

Uh...

"You say the shittiest things to me, and I like that. Not because I'm a masochist, but because I can trust it. You don't say nice things to get what you want. You just say what's on your mind—good, bad, or ugly— and I trust that. I can trust you because you're an asshole and you're honest about it. So, if you start being nice to me..."

Shit. I clear my throat, and it takes me a couple tries to get the words out. "But what if I honestly want to be nice to you?"

She glances at me, then looks away toward the bed where I just fucked her with her clothes still on, her fucking kneepads still on. I cringe.

"Why?" she asks.

"Why what?"

"Why would you want to be nice to me?"

"I don't fucking know. I just do." I sound pissed off again. And I am kind of pissed off. Because she's asked a damn good question: Why *would* I want to be nice to her? This was just supposed to be a fun fuck or two...or three. It's not like I want to get involved beyond that. I mean, Nicole is cool and all, but I'm not looking for a relationship, and if this is what a relationship with Nicole is like, it's really hard work. *But she's worth it.*

Damn, is Ari right? Do I like Nicole? I mean, sure, I like her, but do I *like her* like her?

I stare at her long and hard, and she stares right back at me. She doesn't flinch or shy away from my scrutiny, and holy shit, there is nothing in this world more beautiful than this woman and her indomitable strength.

Oh hell. I think I do *like her* like her. And the most surprising part of that revelation is that it doesn't scare the crap out of me. She's straightforward and complicated, strong yet soft, bitter but sweet; she's ice cold and hot as hell, and I like every contradictory thing about her.

But I can't tell her any of this. So I button it up and tuck it away and just shrug and share with her some wisdom recently shared with me. "Sometimes we all just need someone to be nice to us. I figure this is your time."

She furrows her brow, watching me with cautious skepticism, then she cracks up laughing. "That's the corniest thing I've ever heard."

I really like the sound of her laughter.

She stands up, brushes the wrinkles out of her skirt, and steps over my legs on her way toward the door.

"Wait. Where are you going?"

"Home."

"But—"

"Jake—"

I stand and close the distance between us, then loop my arms around her waist and drop my head onto her shoulder. I'm clearly no good at buttoning and tucking when it comes to my emotions, because I lay it all out there when I whisper into her ear, "I don't want you to go."

Before she can argue, there is a tremendous crash of thunder outside. Wow, I hadn't even noticed it was still storming. I've been so wrapped up with Nicole, cocooned in our own little chrysalis, I'm oblivious to the world outside.

"At least stay until the storm passes. Don't make me worry about you out there. Please."

She exhales a harsh breath and agrees. I give her my megawatt smile and cinch my arms tighter around her waist, hugging her against me as I kiss my way up her neck.

"Nicole," I whisper, nibbling at her ear.

"Uh huh," she moans.

"Are you going to be mad at me if I'm accidentally nice to you tonight?"

"Uh huh," she moans louder as my nibbles turn to bites.

"Good," I growl. "You're so damn sexy when you're mad at me."

• • •

Clearly Zeus and Thor have got my back, because that heaven-sent thunderstorm lasts almost the entire night. To the dramatic flash and boom of the angry sky outside, I take my time getting to know Nicole, explore every damn inch of her with a real Lewis and Clark attention to detail.

I unclasp her kneepads and tug at her fishnets so I can have a little fun with her in just that tiny skirt and top. But eventually, those come off too, along with my jeans.

I lay her down in my bed to get her nice and comfortable as I worship her body with my hands, mouth, every part of me. As the storm drifts away, leaving only distant rumbling echoes and the quiet *drip, drip, drip* of raindrops falling from the eaves and the trees, I make love to her. She looks almost nervous as I move inside her, taking my time, letting our pleasure build at a slow simmer rather than the rolling boil we've come to know.

When she comes, her eyes grow large then flutter shut. She cries out and hugs me against her. The sounds she makes reverberate through my entire body, charging me headlong over that same cliff with her.

Sated, I cradle Nicole against my chest and cover us both with the bedsheets. I lazily run my fingers up and down her back and she rests her palm on my chest, right over my heart. She takes a long breath and sighs it out, and I love how relaxed her tight body feels wrapped up against mine. I feel relaxed too. I haven't known contentment like this, not in many years, and it feels good. But there's an anxiety that prickles within me too. I squeeze her a little tighter against me, trying not to cling, but I can't help how needy I feel. I've never been more afraid to wake up alone than I am right now.

6—Monday July 18, 2005

Roark steps back and looks over the heads of the linemen, scanning the field for a man open. I run hard, my lungs burning, my muscles screaming, as I try to lose my coverage. I glance around and see that none of the other eligible receivers have managed it, and Roark is on the run, avoiding a sack.

He makes eye contact with me, and I know it's coming. He throws. I push into my step, jump high, and make the catch. Securing the ball as my feet hit the ground, it's a mad dash toward the end zone. Only fifteen yards—

I don't see the hit coming. The free safety comes from my left and tackles me just as my feet hit the turf. He's a big guy, and he steamrolls me to the ground like fresh-laid pavement. I lose a shoe in the crush, but at least I don't fumble the ball. Not that it matters. The clock runs out. The game is lost.

The behemoth who took me out jumps to his feet and howls with satisfaction, and why shouldn't he? He won the game, while I lost it.

It takes me a little longer to get to my feet, retrieve my missing cleat, and brush the turf off my jersey and pants. I frown at the grass stains, knowing it will be hard for Mom to get them out.

With that thought, I glance over at the bleachers to see Mom waving at me. She gives me that there's-always-next-time grin, and it makes me feel better, though this is the last scrimmage of summer football camp, and my team—the white jerseys—have lost every game. At Mom's side, Dad and his twin brother Eli are hooting and whooping like I won. I ignore them, only smiling when I see my brother Tommy is already down on the field and sprinting toward me.

The kid looks like a miniature version of me, an exact copy of his big brother in every way, except that his twin braids are perfectly neat, where mine is surely mussed from my helmet and matted to my neck with sweat. When he reaches me, he's winded and puts his hands on his knees to catch his breath. He looks up at me like I'm the MVP, and he wants to put me on his shoulders and parade me around the gridiron with pride. "Jake! You kicked butt."

"Scoreboard doesn't agree, little man, but thanks." I give him a high five.

Greg approaches behind Tommy. He's taller than me but skinny. Normally, he's white as a ghost, but right now his cheeks are flushed pink from playing cornerback for the other team. He's my first (and only) white friend, and the only guy at this football camp who's been nice to me (the Indian kid). With a pat on the back he offers, "Tough break."

"Yeah."

"So," he continues, "some of the guys are going out for pizza. You should come, you know, if you want. My mom says you can stay the night at our house too."

I grin with excitement. I love staying over at the Hendricks house. They have MTV.

I glance back at my family as they come my way. Mom and Dad are arguing. Mom is walks with her back rigid and her arms folded tightly over her chest, her long hair falling over her face when she looks down at her feet. Dad struts beside her, looking more cowboy than Indian in his worn-out Stetson hat. He sports his usual smirk as he takes a drink from a brown-bagged can of beer. At his side, as always, dad's twin brother Eli looks like the Indian version of Dad's cowboy. They're both big, built strong and tall, but while Dad had to cut his hair for his factory job, Eli's jet-black braid snakes down his back. Eli's got a small blonde woman pressed up against him. I don't remember her from before. He must have met her here at my game.

"Yeah, that'd be cool. Let me tell my mom," I say to Greg.

"Mom's not going to like that," Tommy scolds me after Greg walks away. I shrug and pick him up. He kicks and squirms against me, complaining he's not a baby anymore and too old to be picked up. He's eight. He has a point. But at fourteen, I like reminding him who's the big brother. I put him down on his feet, but as he hops away, I loop my arm around his neck and rub my knuckles on his head until his hair is as mussed and frizzy as mine.

Mom reaches me before Dad and Eli, and she immediately hugs me. I grumble that I'm too old for hugs, and Mom steps back with a sad grin.

"You played good, Usdi Yona," she says. "I'm real proud of you."

"Thanks, Mom." I nearly roll my eyes, but I don't want to upset her before I ask, "Hey, Mom. Greg wants me to spend the night. That's okay, right?"

She frowns.

"Please?" I try not to sound too whiny as I beg.

Mom's frown deepens, but before she can speak, Uncle Eli is there and giving me a heavy clap on my shoulder with his massive hand— a hammer driving me into the ground like a nail. I flinch, and he chuckles. "Good game, kid."

"We lost," I grumble and kick my cleat at a divot in the turf, swinging my helmet in front of my knees. I hardly spare Eli a glance as I keep my focus on Mom, silently pleading with her.

"Yeah, well, maybe if you had more Indians on the team, you'd have won." Eli rubs his knuckles through my hair, forcing me to take my eyes off my mom to scowl at him.

"That's my son, the winner." Dad's there now, too, and when he says "winner" with a heavy exhale, I can smell the beer on his breath.

I wrinkle my nose. "I lost."

Dad shrugs and takes another drink.

"Jake, I was going to make pancakes with berries, your favorite," Mom says, trying to convince me to come home.

I don't have the heart to tell her Greg's mom's pancakes are better. She uses real milk, not condensed. "Mom, please."

"Please, what?" Dad looks between us, confused.

"Jake wants to spend the night with his friend again."

"That scrawny little white kid? Why?" Dad scrunches his face like something smells bad.

I ignore Dad and just stare at my mom, trying to plead with my eyes. Tommy watches the silent standoff, pouting out his bottom lip. He hates it when I leave him alone.

Dad shrugs. "Whatever. Come on, Callie. If the kid wants to spend his time with that white boy, let him."

I watch the light in Mom's eyes dim, and it fills me with guilt and regret. I think about taking it back. I think about hugging Mom, then following my family to the car to go home and sleep in my own bed—right next to Tommy's bed—and enjoy Mom's berry pancakes in the morning. But I don't take it back. I don't say anything at all.

Uncle Eli mumbles a brief goodbye and wanders toward his truck with his blonde friend in tow. Dad watches his brother go, then spanks Mom's butt and grabs her hand, tugging her to follow him back to our car. Reluctantly, she follows. Over her shoulder, Mom hollers, "Be good, Usdi Yona. Don't give them any trouble. We'll see you tomorrow."

"Bye, Jake," Tommy chirps up at me like a little bird.

"See ya, kiddo."

"I'm not a kid anymore." He pouts.

"Right." I roll my eyes. "See ya tomorrow, big man."

Tommy grins, and I can see the gap where his last baby tooth fell out a couple weeks ago. He turns and trots after Mom and Dad, and I stare at the sight of them walking away from me.

"I love you." I'm not sure why I say it. I never say stuff like that. It's silly and stupid, and I frown as soon as the words come out of my mouth.

All three of them pause in their stride and turn around to smile at me.

• • •

Another nightmare. I grumble and punch my pillow into the right shape as I lie down again, staring up at the ceiling, and remember the strange and wonderful night before, irritated by how empty the bed feels now.

. . .

"I fail to see the problem." Greg smirks at me from the passenger seat.

"How many times do I have to explain this?"

Humor in his tone, he scoffs, "Let me get this straight. You have this super-hot chick dropping by at all hours of the night to, and I quote, 'blow your fuckin' mind,' and then she leaves, and this is a problem for you?"

Well...yeah. "The problem is I *want* her to stay."

"You're not seriously going to kick her out of bed because she wants to do everything *but* sleep with you in it, are you? Because if so, then who are you, and what have you done with Jake?"

I frown at him.

Greg smirks. "My advice: stop crying and enjoy it while it lasts."

I roll my eyes, but Greg has a point. I should just chill out and let Nicole come and go as she pleases. What do I care if she likes to sleep in her own bed, just so long as she likes to fuck in mine?

As soon as that thought crosses my mind, I'm flooded with the memory of the look on Nicole's face when I made love to her last night. Jesus Christ, I actually *made love* to a woman last night. In all my years, I've always been a fucker, never a love-maker. In fact, I'm pretty sure I've never said the phrase *make love,* let alone consummated the act.

What is it about this woman? Why do I want to cuddle with her and protect her and make her smile and laugh and cry those weird tears of joy that chicks cry sometimes?

I groan.

Greg laughs. For a split second, he reminds me of the kid I grew up with. I think back to the hundreds of conversations we've shared over the course of our nearly twenty-year friendship. From talking about rounding the bases in the backseat of Greg's dad's car to dissolving a marriage and Greg's newly single status, we've always had each other's backs when it came to life shit.

I look at him now, a sharp dressed man in an Armani suit, a carry-on at his feet as I drive him to the airport, and I still see my best friend. Somewhere in that adult body is the awkward kid I used to play football and race dirt bikes with. Despite his expensive haircut, he's still the long-haired metalhead who helped me butcher our way through Black Sabbath's "Iron Man" at the high school talent show. We might be older now, wiser, more jaded, but he'll always be the bighearted best friend who shared his family with me when suddenly I found myself without one.

Which reminds me. "Do you remember those nightmares I used to get? I haven't had them in probably ten years...then two nights in a row."

"Why do you think they're back?"

"Probably seeing Ari in the hospital. Reminded me of my mom."

I don't need to say another word. He remembers that night too. That sort of thing will leave a permanent imprint on the mind of a fourteen-year-old kid.

"Anyway, it sucks, but when I'm with Nicole, it's like a weight gets lifted. You know? It's like...she soothes me—"

"Is that what the kids are calling it these days?"

"For fuck's sake." I groan. "Point is, when she's around, she...I don't know, she makes things better. And then she leaves, and the nightmares come."

"So, you think this hot piece of ass you've been nailing for a couple days is your living, breathing dream catcher?"

I smirk at him, irritated by his description of Nicole.

He's not finished talking, though, raising his finger to make a point as he says, "But consider this. Maybe she's the cause of your troubles, not the solution."

"What?"

"Think about it. The nightmares didn't start until Nicole came around. Right?" He stares out the windshield at some point in the distance as he talks. "What if she's one of those hags that sits on your chest and gives you night terrors? What if she's not your salvation at all, but actually your doom."

"What are you talking about?"

Greg glances at me, then turns his attention back to that far off place out the front window.

"Are you all right, brother?"

He feigns a casual tone. "Yeah, I'm fine."

I pull up to the curb at the airport drop-off area and shift the truck into park so I can stare at my friend, baffled by his bizarre mood swing. Greg hardly waits for me to come to a full stop before he's out the door. When he reaches into the footwell for his luggage, I ask, "Where are you flying this time?"

"New York."

"When are you back?"

"Few weeks," Greg answers absently, looking over his shoulder at the airport entrance.

"Okay. Well, take care of yourself. Call me," I say as he checks the time on his phone.

Greg looks at me now, staring me right in the eyes for a good long moment before he says, "Goodbye, Jake. I love you, brother," then closes the door on my reply.

. . .

From the airport, I go straight to the practice space. Stepping through the door, I'm overwhelmed by the stench. The place smells like sweaty gym socks, weed, and stale cigarettes. *Damn, stale cigarettes really stink. Is this what I've smelled like all these years?*

Ignoring it as best I can, I cross to my chair, prop my feet on my amp, and focus on tuning my guitar. When I'm finished, I lean back, balancing the chair on two legs, close my eyes, clear my head, and play.

I play old favorites I memorized as a kid and new favorites too. I play songs I've written over the years. And then I just play, putting chords together until something good comes out of it. I think up new riffs in my head and work them out with my fingers. Fingers on frets, pick plucking strings, I create. And it's the best feeling in the world. It's the closest thing I know to happiness. Even alone, here in this dark, dank room, I'm happy—

My phone buzzes in my pocket, and I startle. The chair I've been balancing on teeters backward, and I hit the deck, my guitar bouncing against my stomach with a bruising thump.

Groaning, I scramble to answer the call, not looking at the caller ID before I pick up. "Sixkiller."

"Jake, it's Caroline Evans. I wanted to confirm you're coming over for Jimmy's lesson today. Since you canceled on Maureen and Beth last Wednesday, I just—"

"Yes, ma'am." I check the time. *Shit, I'm late!* "I'm on my way." I hang up and scramble to my feet, shoving my guitar into its case and jogging for the exit.

Driving out to West Lake Hills is usually a fun part of my day. The winding roads and bumpy hills are a nice change of pace from downtown Austin's square grid, and the undulating slalom ride reminds me of the mountains and foothills back home. Today, though, I take the switchback roads at a clip, hustling to get to the Evans' house as soon as possible.

When I reach their street, I'm twenty minutes late. It irritates me; I'm never late. It's a point of pride. Long-haired, dark-skinned, heavy metal guys already get enough grief for the way we look, so I make it a rule to be punctual and reliable.

I park on the road and hop out, lugging my guitar with me as I jog up the long driveway. The house is huge, a massive Tuscan villa plopped right down in the middle of Texas. The grounds are well manicured, thanks to her lawn guys Manny and Juan, and overly green—despite the high heat and seasonal water restrictions. I wave at the guys as I run past them, as well as Carlos, the pool guy. They all wave back; comradery among "the help."

Mrs. Evans—a trophy wife turned divorcee and helicopter mom—opens the door before I've even knocked, a scowl marring her pretty face. For a stay-at-home mom on a Monday morning, her makeup is immaculate. She's got her hip cocked to the side, and her yoga-sculpted body looks stunning but stirs absolutely no interest in me.

I give her my most professional smile and apologize profusely for running late. She makes me wallow for a few moments but eventually lets me enter her home. Her son Jimmy is in his usual spot on the couch in the den, a little blonde shadow backlit by a window that overlooks the sparkling waters of their massive pool. He's strumming a vintage Les Paul.

Before I can stop myself, I'm doing the math in my head, adding up how much that guitar costs. I nearly scoff out loud at the thought that such a beauty is in the hands of an unskilled child. When I was a kid, I was learning to play on a cheap pawnshop guitar my dad busted his ass to afford—a guitar I still keep in my collection, despite its tinny sound.

"Jake, listen," Jimmy announces excitedly as I settle beside him on the calfskin couch and pull out my own guitar, a Gibson SG—which is almost as nice as his vintage Les Paul. He stretches his small fingers to span the guitar neck and strums the opening chords to a Kenny Chesney song he's asked to learn. The notes are a little flat, but he's improving.

"Awesome, my man, almost there." I encourage as I correct his finger position. He scrunches up his face as he concentrates, and when he finally gets it right, he smiles up at me. He's lost another baby tooth since my visit last week. In that moment, he looks so much like my little brother Tommy I have to look away.

It's absurd. The two kids couldn't be more different. Jimmy is as white as they come, blonde and blue-eyed, with freckles dotting his cheeks and the bridge of his nose. Whereas Tommy was FBI—full-blooded Indian—just like me. His dark eyes always smiling, his long hair always neatly braided—because Mom and I were always neatly braiding it for him—his goofy grin always a bit lopsided. I'd been teaching him guitar, too, that last summer.

I close my eyes, shake my head, and focus on helping Jimmy with his hand positions. Mrs. Evans comes in with a tray loaded with a pitcher of lemonade and cookies. I decline the offer, focusing on Jimmy, explaining the different methods you can use to hit the same notes.

"Jake, honey, would you prefer a beer?"

I scowl at her, irritated by her constant interruptions and a little surprised by her offer. "No thank you, ma'am."

"Oh Jake, please call me Caroline."

Caroline, my mom's name. I cringe. "No thank you, Caroline."

"How is he doing?" Caroline interrupts again.

"Great," I say; nothing more, nothing less. The time for my progress assessment comes *after* he's finished trying to make progress.

"Because we were thinking of having you come out more often, maybe three times a week, if you think it will help—"

My phone rings in my pocket, and I send up a little thank-you prayer for the interruption. Pulling it out, I frown at an international number I don't recognize and send it to voicemail. Before Mrs. Evans can start talking again, I launch into a new lesson with Jimmy.

An hour later, the lesson is over. Jimmy guzzles a glass of lemonade and stuffs a cookie into his mouth as I pack up my guitar and half listen to Mrs. Evans's chatter. All I can focus on are her idle hands. There is a checkbook in one and a pen in the other, and yet...

My phone buzzes in my pocket and I dig it out, answering without bothering to check Caller ID. "Sixkiller."

"Is this Jake Sixkiller of Nebulous?" The voice is unfamiliar and has an Irish accent.

"The one and only." I glance over at Mrs. Evans and mime the universal hand gesture for "write me the damn check, now, please." She finally puts pen to paper.

"Brilliant. I'm glad I found you. My name is Aidan Connor. I play in—"

"Mammoth." I say the name of the band like a teenage girl would say the name of her favorite Hollywood heartthrob. It's not my most metal moment. But *holy shit*, Aidan *fucking* Connor, guitar player and singer of *fucking* Mammoth, one of my favorite metal bands, is calling me on my *fucking* phone. I've seen Mammoth every time they've come through Austin, except for their most recent South by Southwest show, but only because my band was playing elsewhere at the same time. I have all four of their albums on vinyl, even the rare EP that was never released in the US. *Holy shit, why the hell is Aidan Connor calling me on my phone?*

"Yes, well, the reason for my ringing you is...I'm hoping you can help us."

"Yes," I say, because "Fuck yes, I'll do anything you ask," would sound too eager.

Aidan chuckles. "You don't even know what I'm asking ya."

"Answer's still yes." I glance at Mrs. Evans, who's holding my check. I take it and cover the phone with my hand to say, "Sorry, I have to take this. Same time next week?"

I don't wait for her response before I have my guitar case in hand, the phone back at my ear, and I'm headed out the door.

"You know our rhythm guitarist and second vocalist, Ian?"

Do I know Ian Murphy? What an absurd question. Who doesn't know Ian Murphy?

"His wife is pregnant and having a rough go at it, so he's flying home this week to be with her."

Ian Murphy has a wife? Ian Murphy is going to be a dad? I climb into my truck, crank the AC, and listen as Aidan continues. "Problem is, we still have three weeks left of our American tour. We need someone to fill in for Ian as we finish up our US dates. You came highly recommended."

Wait. What? Record scratch. "Me?"

Aidan asks, "Are you interested?"

"You want me to tour with you...as a member of Mammoth?" I think this bears clarification.

"Yes," Aidan answers patiently. "Are you interested?"

"I don't think 'fuck yes' is a strong enough answer."

Aidan laughs. "Great. Great. Are you available this afternoon? We have a rehearsal space rented in Austin. We thought maybe we could play a bit together, make sure it's a good fit. If it is, then we'll nail down the specifics regarding pay, schedule, and such."

I nod, then make sure to agree audibly in a reserved tone, while inside, I'm howling a victory war whoop.

Aidan gives me directions, and as soon as I'm off the phone with him, I hit the gas and drive back into town. Within twenty minutes, I've arrived, walking through the studio door, guitar in hand, heart in my stomach.

After the customary hellos, the guys head to their gear to get started. Dad-to-be Ian lets me plug into his amp, and we start out with the song "Inside." It's one of their two singles from the latest album. It's a great song, and I'm pretty sure I nail it—I can tell by the pleased expression on Aidan's face when we hit the climax of the song. Truth is, I can play every Mammoth song by heart. To say I'm a fan is an understatement.

About two hours into our practice session, they're all grinning as I hit one of Ian's tougher singing parts *and* nail the subsequent guitar solo.

I'm in. The rapport, the music—it all fits. I feel it. They feel it. And it feels fucking great.

Afterward, as we guzzle water and cool off, we plan for long practice sessions tomorrow and Wednesday, and then Aidan formally hires me. There's a ton of paperwork. I sign a contract with lots of fine print and details about my pay. I don't give a shit about any of it. I'd sign away my soul to the devil right now if they were to slip that page into the stack.

Aidan gives me a copy of the tour schedule as he says, "We'll make the official announcement at the show on Thursday. Invite anyone you want. Fill up the VIP section, if you like. I may have one or two additions to the guest list, but the rest is yours. This is your show."

"I already bought a ticket."

"You want a refund?"

I shake my head, overwhelmed by everything that's happened today, from the lowest low of waking from my worst nightmare alone to this, the highest high.

As we all say our farewells, I jog to my truck, climb inside, crank the air conditioning and call Nicole. Why she's the first person I call, I don't know. I try not to put too much thought into that. I mean, I should probably call Greg, my brother from another mother or Ari, my number one best girl, but—

"I can't talk long, I'm at work," Nicole says to me. Not, "Hello," not "Hi, how are you? I'm sorry I left you this morning with no goodbye, no note, no nothing."

I frown, but quickly recover. "Hey darlin', what are you doing on Thursday?"

"Why?"

"I've got a big show. Mammoth is playing, and—"

"I can't. I have skate practice."

"At eleven?" I scoff.

"That's past my bedtime."

"Ah come on. You can stay up one night. I'll make it worth your while. I'll put you on the VIP guest list, and—"

"Why?"

It's like facing a firing squad. "Why what?"

"Why do you want me to come?"

"Because I love it when you come." Yeah, I make sure the double entendre is crystal-fucking-clear.

She groans. "Why do you want me to come *to this show*?"

"Because...I'd like to see you."

"Why?"

"Why what?" I consider hanging up and calling back. Maybe I'll get a different version of Nicole on the second try.

She huffs, sounding tired. "What are we doing here, Jake?"

I blink, a bit stunned.

"Do you think we're dating? Because I'm not looking for a—"

I pinch the bridge of my nose, feeling a headache coming on. "Jesus, Nicole, lighten up, will ya? I thought I'd invite you to a show, but if you're going to bust my balls..." I pause. Take a deep breath. Stop myself from saying something I'll surely regret. Then finish with a curt "Thursday night, I'll text you the details. Maybe I'll see you, maybe I won't."

• • •

Alex's front door opens, and the man himself steps inside, pausing when he sees me. It's the Blood for Blood Marathon, Take Two. I'm under Ari's legs, rubbing her feet, and she's fast asleep as *Near Dark* runs on the television.

I flinch, half expecting the guy to come at me swinging—after all, I have my hands on his woman's feet—but he just grins at his peaceful sleeping beauty. Cool dude, this guy.

"Hey, man," he whispers as he drops his toolbelt and hard hat by the door. "What's up?"

"Vampire movie marathon."

"Sweet." Alex disappears down the hall. I hear the distant sound of a shower running, then Alex reemerges, clean and refreshed, and settles into the easy chair with a deep sigh. He leans close to Ari to gently push a strand of hair out of her face. She stirs a bit but doesn't wake.

"Shit, man, you want to sit here?" I indicate my position under Ari's legs.

"No, stay," Alex whispers. "I'm glad to see her sleeping so peacefully. She's been having nightmares since the accident."

"I'll bet." I know the feeling.

"So how are you doing?" Alex asks as he glances at the television.

"Pretty great, actually." I've been dying to tell someone the good news, but Ari fell asleep the moment I pressed play on the DVD, Greg's phone is going to voicemail, and...well, the conversation with Nicole didn't develop in the direction I hoped it would. "I'm going on tour as a fill-in for Ian Murphy of Mammoth for three weeks."

"Wow. That's awesome." Alex drops his jaw in awe, and I'm reminded that, yeah, it is pretty damn awesome.

"Yeah." I grin like an idiot. "My first show with them is Thursday. If y'all can come out, I'll put you on the VIP list."

"Hell yeah."

"I invited Nicole too. In case that's a problem..."

"Not a problem for me. Might be a problem for her." He smirks at me. "So the rumors are true then."

"There are rumors?"

With a shrug, Alex says, "Sher told us what went down at the last bout, and Ari confirmed you're dating Nicole."

"*Dating* is the wrong verb."

That gets a raised brow from Alex.

"Actually, there is no verb to describe whatever it is that's happening between us because nothing is happening between us. It's doubtful she'll even show up on Thursday."

Alex watches me as if trying to read between the lines of what I'm saying. And what the hell, I might as well open up to the guy. If he's a permanent fixture in Ari's life, then he's a permanent fixture in mine. Maybe a little share time is in order.

"Truth is, I like Nicole a lot, even though she confounds me and pisses me off, and every time I try to get close to her, she recoils like I'm a leper."

Alex nods knowingly.

"Is this weird, talking about her, considering y'all used to be together?"

"Not for me. It might bother her that we're talking about her, though." Alex considers for a moment before saying, "Listen, I'm not Nic's keeper, and I'm probably the last person she would want talking to you about this, but, honestly, I like you for her. I mean, I don't know you well yet, but Ari thinks the world of you, so you must be a good guy. Anyway, I have one piece of advice, if you're interested, and then that's all I'm going to say on the matter."

I agree, eager for any insight.

"Nic is a very private person, and she has her reasons. If you're looking to get close to her, I recommend respecting that. When she wants to share parts of her life with you, she will. But if you get pushy...just don't get pushy. Nothing good will come of it. And don't start something with her that you're not prepared to finish. She's been hurt a lot, most recently by me. I don't want to see her get hurt again. If you like her, great, go for it, but don't mess with her head just for the sex."

I blink, taken aback by his bluntness. Yet his words make me like him even more than I already did. Clearly, this is a man who takes care of his people, and obviously he thinks enough of Nicole to count her among that rank.

"Thanks" is all I can think to say, but it's so trite. I open my mouth to add something more, to express myself better, but the front door bangs open. Ari yelps and nearly falls off the couch, startled by the sound, and we all turn to see Sheryl standing in the doorway, swinging on a pair of crutches. "Get off your asses, people, it's Karaoke on Crutches night."

"It is?" Ari asks, clearly amused, despite the rude awakening.

"Duh." Sheryl gestures at her crutches.

"I don't have any crutches," I say.

"I do." Alex climbs to his feet and disappears down the hall. When he returns, he's carrying a set of aluminum crutches. He hands one to me and leans on the other.

I stare at the crutch, grateful to be included in whatever harebrained scheme this is. I help Ari move her legs off me and stand, then lean on my crutch as we head out, movie marathon forgotten.

Twenty minutes later, we're swinging into the bar, each of us leaning on a crutch or two. At the sight of us, Jared, the DJ, whistles into the microphone and asks, "Well, what do we have here?"

Sheryl hollers, "It's Karaoke on Crutches, bitches!"

Jared bellows over the speakers, "Shit, Ari, you sure know how to turn getting hit by a car into a party."

With that, I head straight for the DJ booth to put in a special request. And because Jared is a mooching fucker who owes me $50, he fast tracks us to the top of the play list.

"Okay, I have a special request for the Karaoke on Crutches contingency. Could everyone with crutches please make your way to the stage?"

Ari, Sheryl, and Alex look at me funny, and I shrug as we all head up there. When we're situated, I nod to Jared, and the song starts up. The expression on Ari's face when she recognizes it is priceless. Alex and Sheryl immediately join me as we serenade Ari with a hilariously off-key rendition of Bill Withers' "Lean on Me."

When the first tear traces down Ari's cheek, my own vision gets a little watery. I pull her into a hug and kiss the top of her head, then it's Sheryl's turn for a hug and kiss, and then into Alex's arms she goes. He smiles at me, singing as he hugs Ari to him and sways to the rhythm. And with that one contented look from Alex, I know my connection with Ari, my connection with them both, is much stronger than I had realized.

7—Thursday July 21, 2005

I push my way through the sea of people, my head on a swivel, constantly keeping an eye out for Nicole. I'd checked the small VIP overhang, but she wasn't there. So I've come down here to the large expanse of packed dirt that serves as standing room for general admission attendees, looking for her near the regular entrance. No sign of her here, either.

I try to quell my disappointment. I haven't seen or spoken to Nicole since that awkward phone call on Monday, so I'm not sure what I was expecting. Still, I'd hoped.

I need to move on. There are hundreds of gorgeous women here tonight; I need to stop fixating on the one who's missing. It's pathetic, and tonight is not the night to be pathetic.

Tonight's *my* night, and I've worked my ass off to be here. It's been a long few days of canceling guitar lessons with the kids of West Lake Hills for the next couple weeks, followed by countless hours practicing in the studio with Aidan, Glenn, and Sean. I've memorized every note and lyric to be sure I'm in sync with the rest of the band. The songs are practically tattooed across my brain. I'm ready. All the hard work of the past week will pay off tonight. And not just the past week—tonight is the payoff for the past twenty-two years.

I've been working toward this moment since I was ten and my dad bought me my first guitar at a secondhand store. I played that thing until my fingers bled and then calloused and I've been playing ever since. I dedicate tonight to every show that paid barely enough to cover the cost of gas to drive to the venue and back. To every time I had to play until two in the morning and then wake at six to schlep coffee or frame houses. To every penny of my own money I put into recording Nebulous's first demo and our first EP. To every time I thought about quitting, getting a "real" job and moving on...but didn't. All of it has brought me to where I am today, and it was all worth it.

"You not even gonna acknowledge me, rock star?" Dillon steps into my line of sight with an amused glint in his eyes.

I smile at my bandmate. I've been playing with Dillon and Ryan for years, and never considered them friends. But now, as I reminisce on all the shit we've slogged through together, I feel closer to him than ever before. "Sorry, dude, I was looking for somebody."

"And I'm a nobody? Is that how it's gonna be? Probably won't even remember us fugly fucks when you're snorting lines of coke off the ass cheeks of Playmates at Heff's mansion."

"Fuck you," I grumble. "You know I'm a breast man. I'll be snorting it off their tits, thank you very much."

Dillon slaps me on the shoulder. "Seriously though, I'm happy for you. They're lucky to have you."

His unexpected compliment chokes me up. "Thanks, D."

"Jaysus, Sixkiller, how can you stand this infernal heat?" Aidan moans as he approaches us and hands me a bottled water. He toasts with "Sláinte" then guzzles half his own. Around us, the crowd falls all over themselves to get a look at the pasty Irish celebrity in their midst. He hardly notices. He never does. In the half week I've spent with these guys, I've been impressed and a little surprised by how down-to-earth they are. It's as if they hit celebrity status when they weren't looking, and it still hasn't sunk in. Dillon stands beside Aidan in awe, wide-eyed and stunned.

"Aidan, this is Dillon, the drummer in Nebulous."

"Ah, brilliant. You guys are great," Aidan says and gives Dillon a firm handshake. "Hope you don't mind us borrowing him from ya."

Dillon, ever the comedian, quips, "This pain-in-the-ass pretty boy? He's all yours." He adds with an exaggerated eye roll, "And good luck getting laid when he's around. Hard to compete when Mr. Wind In His Hair is strutting around half-naked."

"You want to know how I stand the heat in Texas?" I gesture to my bare chest. "Less clothing." I don't mention that I perform shirtless in the winter too.

It's my only remaining ritual, to strip down to my jeans or leathers and carefully braid my hair before every show. But tonight, it's also practical. It's blazing hot out here. The crowded swath of packed dirt nestled between squatty old limestone walls should, in theory, be cooling off now that the sun has set, but there is no breeze blowing on this sweltering July night. Even shirtless, I'm slick with a layer of sweat. I glance toward the stage, a giant riser that fills the south side of the space, topped by a large awning striped with hundreds of lights illuminating everything with brilliant color. It's more lights than I've ever performed under. It's going to be scorching hot up there. The Irish blokes will surely melt.

And speaking of hot... Just over Dillon's shoulder, there by the main entrance, I see Nicole. Like a beacon in the dark, my gaze zeroes in on her the moment she comes into view. My brain fritzes out, all prior thoughts and conversations forever lost.

She's a goddess in a scarlet dress. And she stands out as the lone spot of color in a sea of black T-shirts. Already tall, her heels put her head and shoulders above most of the people around her. Her hair is gelled back to highlight the sharp lines of her face. Her green eyes are painted with a smoky gray to make them look even moodier and harder to read, and those luscious lips are a dangerous shade of crimson.

"The lady in red." Aidan waggles his brow. "She with you?"

"God, I hope so."

Dillon does a double take, but I don't care, my attention is riveted elsewhere. Nicole's eyes brighten when she sees me. She sways those hips on her way to meet me and the crowd between us parts like the Red Sea. Behind her, Sheryl's hot pink hair sweeps from side to side in sync with her bouncy steps. When she comes into view at Nicole's side, Aidan makes a sound like he's choking on his tongue, and Dillon whistles through his teeth. She's in a silver dress that looks like the wrapper off a stick of gum, and it's not much larger than one.

"Jaysus, Sheryl looks feckin' edible tonight," Aidan says under his breath.

I glance over at him. "You know Sheryl?"

Aidan ignores me, his focus on the approaching women. When they reach us, I attempt to make introductions, but Sheryl interrupts with a squeal as she pounces on Aidan.

"Hiya, cutie." Sheryl chokes him with a hug and punches him in the arm. "You don't call; you don't write...how's life treating you?"

"Quite well, and yourself?" Aidan rubs his arm, trying not to wince.

Nicole and Dillon and I watch in stunned disbelief, still not understanding how Sheryl knows Aidan. *Did they fuck—?*

"How's Ari?" Aidan asks her. "I've been meaning to give her a ring these last few days, but I've been busy with practice."

Wait. What? "You know Ari?" I ask Aidan. "How do you know Ari?"

Aidan furrows his brow, "*You* know Ari?"

"She's my best friend."

Aidan blinks, looking a bit confused. Sheryl laughs and I feel like I'm missing something.

"She's up in VIP with Alex," I inform Sheryl.

Sheryl clasps Aidan's hand in hers. "Come on, Aidan, I'll introduce you to Ari's new boyfriend."

Aidan mumbles as Sheryl drags him away, "Boyfriend? What happened to her husband?"

When they've gone, Dillon squirms awkwardly beside me, and I give him a reason to leave. "You're on the list for VIP with a plus one. Tell Ryan too, if you see him."

And then it's just Nicole and me. She glares at me like she's irritated.

"I'm glad you came," I say.

"Well, you put me on the list," she smirks. "Though apparently you put Alex and Ariana on the list too."

Fucking fantastic! The day that I'm no longer the monkey in the middle of this shit-throwing mess will be a good day. To lighten the mood, I go for the obvious diversion. "It's weird to hear you call her 'Ariana.' No one calls her that, except for Alex. Not even her mom."

"Whatever," Nicole huffs.

Sick of it all, I address the elephant in the room. "Why do you hate her so much?"

"You know why."

I cross my arms and flex my biceps for effect as I raise an eyebrow and smirk at her. Sure, I know why, but I want her to say the words. So I wait, stubbornly staring at her as I tap my foot impatiently.

I'd much rather be kissing her right now, but I don't. After our last phone conversation, I'm not sure if my kissing-permit is still valid or if it's been revoked. Also, she looks really pissed off.

Finally, she says, "She stole him from me."

"First of all, you can't steal a person. Alex was never your property. He has his own mind and his own heart, and he *chose* to be with Ari instead of you. Just like Ari *chose* to be with Alex instead of Greg. I get that it hurts for you and Greg, but that's life, sweetheart, so suck it up."

Nicole looks a bit stunned and stung. After a moment, she clears her throat and asks, "You said 'first of all,' so is there a second point you'd like to make?"

I soften my posture to appear less confrontational and ask the question that's been nagging me for days: "Are you still in love with Alex?"

She blinks once, twice, but she doesn't answer.

I can't read her expression, and that makes me nervous. And when I get nervous, my mouth tends to run away from me, like a dog without a leash. It does that now. "Because I don't think you are. In fact, I don't think you were ever in love with him. I think you enjoy being angry and take every opportunity you can to play the victim." *Fuck's sake! I need more than a leash; I need a goddamn muzzle...and to be neutered.*

If looks could kill. *Bang. Pow.* I'd be dead. Nicole narrows her eyes and flexes her fists. She looks like she'd be happy to help neuter me.

I should cower, but I'm feeling cocky tonight, and since I've already dug this hole, I might as well keep digging.

"Come here." I grab Nicole around the waist and pull her against me. I give her ample time to push me away. She doesn't. I'm pretty sure she thinks I'm going to kiss her. If I were smart, that's exactly what I'd do. But I'm not very smart, and this Ari/Alex thing is just going to keep hanging over us if I don't do something about it. So...

I pick her up in my arms, carrying her like a bride over the threshold. Nicole grumbles and complains, but she doesn't demand I put her down, so I don't. I don't stop until we're in the VIP area overlooking the stage. I pass Ryan and his girlfriend sharing a high table with Dillon and some cutie and join Aidan and Sheryl, who are standing across from Alex and Ari.

The happy couple are camped out at a tall table in the front corner with a great view of the stage. Ari sits in one chair, her plastered leg stretched across the other. Alex stands sentry at her side, making sure no errant drunks bump or jostle her. Ari looks a lot better and ridiculously cute in the denim miniskirt she's managed to shimmy over the massive cast on her leg and a Slayer T-shirt she's cut up and tied back together for some reason. The bruises on her face have mostly healed, and what discoloration remains, she's covered with makeup.

"Hey everyone," I say in a chipper tone as I set Nicole on her feet. "This is Nicole. She's pretty rad...when she wants to be."

Aidan says hello.

Alex blinks.

Ari's eyes go wide.

Sheryl chuckles.

Nicole grimaces at me.

I ignore them all and keep talking. "Ari, there's something you need to know. When you got hit by that car, your phone was destroyed, and I didn't have Alex's or Sheryl's numbers. Do you know who came through for me and gave me their digits, knowing full well they were for you? Nicole, that's who." I point at Nicole when I say it, in case there's any confusion.

Ari's expression turns to awe, and she looks like she might cry. With an awkward stumble she comes off her chair, teetering and wobbling without her crutches, and takes a hop toward Nicole. Nicole flinches like she wants to back away, but I form a solid wall behind her. I'm not going to let Nicole shrink away as Ari does what she does best— kill with kindness.

With a sweet smile that no one in their right mind could hate, Ari approaches Nicole and asks, "May I hug you?" Nicole blinks, and sort of nods, so Ari moves in for the kill, whispering, "Thank you."

The hug is one of the most awkward things I've ever witnessed. Ari teeters on her one good leg, while Nicole stands as stiff as a board, her eyes wide with panic. But when Nicole gives Ari a couple of weird little pats on the back, I can't help the dumb grin that slides across my lips.

When they eventually come apart, Ari looks Nicole straight in the eyes and says, "It meant the world to me that they were there when I woke up. I'm so grateful to you."

Nicole looks down at her feet, clearly uncomfortable with the attention and accolades. When she finally speaks, she has to clear her throat, and her words still sound stilted and awkward. "Really, you should thank Jake. If he hadn't pissed me off by calling me a colossal cunt, I probably would have just hung up on him."

Ari blinks, then bursts into laughter. Nicole slowly laughs too. And with that, the tension between us all seeps away. *Nice.*

"Hate to break up this touching moment, but..." Aidan looks at me and angles his thumb toward the stage.

I turn to my friends and take a deep breath. "Here goes nothing." *Lie. Here goes everything.* It's been years since I was nervous before a show. Tonight, though, I'm petrified.

Sheryl claps excitedly and bounces around a couple of times. Alex shakes my hand. Ari gives me a hug. "Break a leg, big guy."

I point at the massive cast on her leg. "Coming from you, that sounds like a threat." Ari giggles, and I kiss her cheek. "Big love, little sis."

Last but not least, I turn to Nicole, and before I can think twice about it, I pull her against me and kiss her. Correction: I kiss the ever-loving shit out of her. When we come up for air, Nicole stares at me wide-eyed and breathless, and her reaction does tingly things to my ego.

"I'm glad you came," I say with my lips against her ear.

She whispers, "I haven't come *yet.*"

"Trust me, darlin', that's on my list of things to do tonight. But first..." I wink as I turn to head down the stairs to the stage.

. . .

I love attention. Obviously. It's why I routinely strip half-naked and mount a stage under the glow of melting lights to sing my heart out to a room full of adoring fans. Writing music is what keeps me sane, sure, but performing is my passion. Performing is my life's blood. And tonight, that life's blood is pumping so hard my chest might explode.

I'm the last in line, following the other guys through the wings, humming with excitement, as giddy as a kid on Christmas morning. We make our way past rows of equipment, stepping over cords and weaving between sound monitors and lighting rigs, and I can hear the crowd out there, the dull murmur of a thousand conversations. There are over two thousand people out there, waiting to see us. I have to stifle a shiver.

It's not until we step out onto the stage, awash with yellow light, that the reality of this moment hits me. It's then, when the dull murmur becomes a roar, that I let myself truly believe it. *I'm here. I've made it.* I'm where I've always wanted to be. Sure, it's only a temporary gig, but I'm hardly splitting hairs over that right now. I damn near start to bawl, completely overwhelmed by the moment.

I head toward my setup on stage left, take a deep breath, then reach for my guitar and slip the strap over my head, letting the familiar weight fall to my waist. I dig a guitar pick from my pocket and do a quick tuning check. Even though I've been assured that the techs took care of sound check, I feel the need to verify. I'm not used to anyone but me tuning my guitar. A few strums, and it all sounds great. So I guess now there's nothing left to do but play.

With another deep breath, I turn to face the crowd for the first time and nearly start to cry again. It's a beautiful sight to behold, a sea of faces and devil horns as far as the eye can see. I'm overwhelmed, in awe, and in love with my life in this moment. All at once, I feel humbled and ten feet tall.

The sound from the crowd is incredible, an oceanic roar of adoration. Nebulous has a devoted following, sure, but we've only ever filled three-hundred-person capacity venues. Hearing the cacophony of adulation created by two thousand screaming fans is out of this world. This feeling is better than all the orgasms I've ever had, combined...except maybe those orgasms with Nicole.

Which reminds me...I look up to the VIP area, scanning for the faces I know. I see Dillon, Ryan, Ari, Alex, Sheryl...no Nicole. *What the fuck? Did she leave?* The disappointment threatens to ruin my amazing mood.

Whatever. I glance over to Aidan, waiting for his cue to start the first song, but he nods toward the foot of the stage. I look down, and there at the front of the crowd just inside the security barricade, where the photographers work, is a shock of brilliant red. How the hell did Nicole get into the photographer pit? She's staring up at me with her brow furrowed, her jaw hanging open—stunned. I would pay any amount of money for a photograph of the look on her face right now.

Slowly, Nicole's expression of surprise curls into a sparkling smile. The air rushes out of me in a gust, even as my chest puffs up with pride. Damn, this woman's got power over me, and I kind of like it.

I wink at her just as Aidan cues the first song, then turn all my focus to the music. I dive in feet first, concentrating on hitting every note and every stop. I rely on my long days of practice to fit right into the groove with the other guys. It comes easy, second nature.

Three songs into the set, Aidan calls for a break, and I guzzle half a bottle of water as Aidan talks to the audience. "Hello Austin! It's good to be back in this great city." The crowd goes wild. Aidan pauses graciously before continuing, "And speaking of your wonderful town, you might recognize one of your own up on stage with us tonight. We're pleased to have Austin's own Jake Sixkiller of Nebulous filling in for Ian as we finish our US tour."

I thought the crowd was loud before, but holy shit, they really flip out. It's more than I could have imagined. Down front, Nicole looks stunned again, and I can't tell if it's a happy stunned or sad stunned. Will she miss me while I'm gone? From VIP, though, there's no ambiguity. Dylan and Ryan howl like wolves while Ari and Sheryl go bonkers, with Alex looking worried as Ari bounces around on her hobbled leg.

Without further ado, we launch into the next song, one which is usually led by Ian, and now led by me. It's a challenging piece of music, demanding a rapid-fire guitar part as I scream my vocals in a syncopated rhythm. I nail it, and every song after it, laying waste to the music and throat-punching the lyrics.

When I growl out the last note of the last song, I glance over to see Aidan as he screams his final verse. The crowd boils over with energy, and the sound explodes through me. The guys are all smiling. It's been a phenomenal show. We nailed it, all of us, together.

I want to bottle this feeling. I'm fried, but I've never felt more alive. Every muscle in my body is seized up tight and screaming in agony. I'm drenched in sweat and as thirsty as a man stumbling through the desert. And it's absolute, pure bliss. Right now, I could leap tall buildings in a single bound and throw cars around. Nothing is out of my reach. Nothing is off limits to me.

As if on cue, I pass through the doors to the side stage and see my favorite color—red. I stomp over to Nicole, pull her against me, and kiss her like there's no tomorrow. I kiss her like she's the love of my life and there will never be another. I kiss her like I'm king of the fucking world and she's my queen.

When I pull away from her, she's breathless, her eyes glazed over like she's stoned. Before I can stop myself, I say, "Be mine."

Her eyes go wide with surprise, and I curse my stupid leash-free mouth.

"Tonight. Be mine tonight," I quickly amend.

She stares at me a beat too long, her expression unreadable. Slowly, a sexy smile creeps across those luscious lips.

. . .

"What was it like up there on stage in front of all those people?" she asks in a soft voice as her fingers trace down my chest. The movement tickles, and my muscles contract and flex in response. She does it again, enjoying the reaction she gets out of me.

And good lord, can this woman get a reaction out of me. After the show, we'd barely made it back to my place before I had her stripped naked and bent over the couch, then up against the front door; then finally, like the classy gentleman I am, I took her in my bed.

Now, here we lie, spent and content, her body entwined with mine, her hand exploring my chest as mine caresses her back. I consider my answer carefully, trying to think of the right way to describe the euphoria I felt on that stage tonight. All I can come up with is, "I tried heroin once. It was kind of like that."

Nicole perks up and leans on her elbows to look me in the eyes. "You did heroin?"

"I tried it once." I shrug. "I'll try anything, once."

"That's crazy. I've heard that once is all it takes to become addicted to that shit. People have OD'd on that first hit, you know?"

I chuckle and tickle her side.

"What's so funny?"

"Nothing, I just never expected the Nancy Reagan 'Just Say No to Drugs' speech from you of all people."

She frowns. "Me *of all people*—what the hell does that mean?"

Shit. "That came out wrong. I didn't mean..." I glance at her sheepishly. She's glaring at me, daggers in her eyes. *Fuck.* "I just meant, you have this reputation for being a bit wild and crazy. I didn't figure you for the staunch antidrug type...not that I'm prodrug...well, I mean, I think pot should be legal, but...shit, I'm babbling...about politics. All I meant was, it sounded funny coming from you, when it's something I'd normally hear from Little Miss Goody Two Shoes."

I glance at Nicole, who's trying to stifle a grin. "Little Miss Goody Two Shoes?"

"Ari," I clarify. "Her last name, before she married Greg, was Goody." Like that explains anything. I clarify further. "For years, she was this innocent little good girl, always wagging her finger at me for the stupid stunts I'd pull, so I called her Goody Two Shoes..." Images of Alex's playroom pop into my head as I add, "Though she's not much of a Goody Two Shoes these days, I guess."

When I finally shut my stupid mouth, there is a long, painful silence. *Shit.* What demon possessed me to bring up Ari while naked in bed with Nicole?

"I used to do a lot of drugs," Nicole says, saving me from myself. "Way too much cocaine. But I never tried heroin, never wanted to. I've always avoided opiates, benzos, and hallucinogens. I like to be aware, you know, awake."

Oh. Wow. Of course. After being roofied and raped, of course she would avoid a substance that could take her back to that vulnerable place. "Right. Makes sense. I imagine after having your conscious mind taken from you, you wouldn't want to...go there again."

She blinks at me, then rests her cheek on my chest. Annnnnd...more silence. I've managed to make it awkward again. I need to shut my mouth. Instead, I keep going. "For me, it was the opposite. Awareness was the last thing I wanted. When I used to get high, I was seeking...oblivion."

Nicole turns her head up and stares, her sharp gaze softened a bit around the edges. "Why would you seek oblivion?"

I'm not sure how to answer that. I could say any number of things, and they would be accurate enough without exposing the truth, but I don't. I give her the truth. "To escape the ghosts."

That gets her attention. "The ghosts?"

I immediately regret that I've opened this can of worms. I pull Nicole closer and nuzzle her neck, mumbling as I nibble at her throat. "Not literal ghosts; it's just an expression."

"An expression for what?" Nicole asks, not falling for my obvious distraction tactics.

I groan and keep nibbling and licking at her throat as I run my fingers down her belly to cup her sex in my palm. "Enough talking. We're wasting valuable time. I need to be inside you again...now, and later, and as often as possible before I leave tomorrow."

"Jake, look at me," Nicole insists. I stop what I'm doing to her body and lock eyes with her. "The other night, I told you something very personal about myself. And I'm still not sure why I did. So, the way I see it, you owe me."

There's something in her eyes in this moment that makes me want to open my heart and pour the contents at her feet. So I do. "When you were fourteen, you were raped." She frowns, but I press on. "When I was fourteen, I was orphaned."

She blinks at me, then shifts so she can watch me intently, ready to listen.

I take a deep breath, let it out. I stare into her eyes and tuck a wispy strand of her hair behind her ear. "My family was killed by a drunk driver." I clear my throat. "My father was the drunk driver."

Her brows lift in surprise, but she says nothing, waiting for me to tell her more; so I do.

"They were going home after watching me play football, this dumb scrimmage game for football camp. Not even an actual game. It was on the other side of the mountains, kind of a long drive, and no one had noticed how much my dad had been drinking during the game. On the way home, he missed a curve, hit a tree." Deep breath in and out. "Dad died on impact. The steering column crushed his chest. Mom wasn't wearing a seatbelt. A lot of people didn't back then. She was thrown from the car. She lingered for a few hours in the hospital, but never woke up. My little brother Tommy was in the backseat..."

A lump catches in my throat. Nicole leans in and kisses my shoulder and the emotion passes. I can talk again. I squeeze her tight against me as I start to tell her the whole thing, even the worst of it—a total confession.

"That summer, I begged my parents to let me go to football camp. We were pretty poor, and it wasn't cheap, but Mom scraped the money together and drove me across the mountains from North Carolina to Tennessee week after week, because it was the only thing that was likely to keep me out of trouble." I let out a hollow laugh, then continue, "And that's how I met Greg. You've met him, too, actually, Ari's soon-to-be ex-husband."

"The Lone Ranger," she smirks.

I grimace, wishing she'd forget all the shit I said to her that night. "He was my first white friend, if you can believe that."

Nicole's brows raise in surprise.

"You gotta understand, my family was traditional and my world at that age was very small. I grew up in the house my great granddaddy built in Sixkiller Hollow." I pronounce it "holler," the way everyone always did. "It was in a remote valley in the Qualla Boundary, the Cherokee reservation in North Carolina."

I'm stalling and have to stop myself from delving into a history lesson about the Eastern Band of Cherokee. *Not the right time.*

I start again. "I didn't know anyone outside of my community until Mom started taking me to football camp. Then I met Greg, and he was cool, and his family was nice to me. He'd invite me to spend the night sometimes, and I really liked staying at his place. It was a whole other world compared to what I knew. They had cable and an Atari, and, as shitty as it is, I wanted that to be *my* world. I *wished* it was my world."

I reach for Nicole's hand and kiss her palm before I set it on my chest. For some reason, I need her touch right now.

"That night, Greg invited me to sleep over at his house again. My mom tried to convince me to come home, but I was a stubborn little shit. I stayed at Greg's, and my family drove home without me. I got the call from my grandma a couple hours later." *Usdi Yona, there's been an accident.*

Nicole presses her fingers against my chest, warming me straight down to my heart.

"My brother, Tommy, was always copyin' me. He wanted to be just like his big brother, so on the drive home, he sat in my empty seat. I was always on the right side of the backseat, and he was always on the left. But that night, he sat on the right, behind Mom.

"He looked fine. He'd hit his head on the window, but otherwise, he was fine, so when Mrs. Hendricks drove me to the hospital and my grandma and Uncle Eli got there, they released him to us. And we went in to see Mom together, just Tommy and me. The grownups stayed out in the hallway, so we could spend time with her alone. It was awful. There were all these tubes going into her and machines beeping. It was hard to see her like that. My mom, she was so pretty, but that night she looked like a mummy, all wrapped up in bandages.

"Tommy said he felt funny, like he was gonna be sick. I just thought he was scared, you know, so I tried to be the big brother and hold his hand. But then he fell over, and I didn't know what to do. I tried to pull him back up, but he started to shake, and his eyes rolled back in his head and he..." *He pissed his pants.* I don't say that part out loud; it doesn't seem right. "Greg's mom said I screamed, that's how they knew to come in. I just remember my uncle grabbin' me and pullin' me away, and the doctors and nurses surroundin' my brother like buzzards on roadkill, and I just screamed and fought, tryin' to get back to him, to save him."

I can barely breathe. I take a moment to try to pull air into my lungs.

Nicole watches me for a long moment, concern in her eyes. When she speaks, she surprises the hell out of me. "It wasn't your fault."

What? I stare at her, stunned, then argue. "Of course it was my fault. I'm the reason they were even there. I'm the reason Tommy was in that seat. And, more than that, I wished it. Not just once, either. I wished over and over again that Greg's family was my family, that his life was my life." I shut my eyes when I admit, "I hated who I was. I hated that I was just a poor little Indian kid with an alcoholic dad. In those last few months, I remember that I hated my father for drinking, and I hated my uncle for encouraging him and my grandmother for making excuses for him, and I even hated my mom for putting up with him. I hated it all—our house, our poverty, my skin, my own flesh and blood—so I wished it all away. And then I got my wish."

I struggle to get my breathing under control again, waiting for what she might say next. But again, all she says is, "It wasn't your fault."

I huff. *Why does she keep saying that?*

"I used to blame myself too. I shouldn't have snuck out. I shouldn't have accepted that drink. I shouldn't have worn a skirt. I was asking for it—"

"No—" I want to argue, but she silences me with a finger over my mouth, then gently strokes my bottom lip.

"But one day, I realized the person who's to blame for everything that happened that night was the man who raped me. None of what *he* did was *my* fault. Just as none of what happened to your family was *your* fault. There's always, in the back of your head, that what-if-I'd-done-this-or-that-differently feeling. But it's too late for *what if*. All we have is *what is*. And Jake, *what is* the truth is that you did nothing wrong. What happened was awful, but it wasn't your fault."

I take a few deep breaths, trying to center myself and focus my mind, and when I focus, I focus on her. I am in awe of her. I raise my hand to her cheek, matching her tenderness with my own. "You amaze me. You're so strong, so much stronger than me."

She smiles, and it takes my breath away. Then she surprises me when she moves on top of me, her thighs straddling mine, her fingers stroking my cock. I groan. "Damn, woman, what will I do without you for the next sixteen days?"

Nicole smirks. "Please. We both know it won't even be twenty-four hours before you're balls-deep inside someone else. I suspect the bigger the tour bus, the better caliber of groupie."

I pull her hand off my dick—this is not a dick-in-hand sort of conversation—and tilt her chin to make eye contact. "You know there's no one else, right?"

"Tell that to the blonde on her knees in the alley."

I stare at her, a little stunned. "That was...that was me being an idiot because I was pissed at you. That night, you shredded me, Nicole. I was mad, and when I'm mad, I get stupid. But I didn't finish with her. As soon as you walked away, so did I. Since then, since that night with you, there's been no one else."

Now it's Nicole who looks stunned.

"Nicole, this thing between us, it's more than just sex. Or at least, it is for me. I don't know what it is for you, but for me...this means something to me. *You* mean something to me."

I cinch my arms tight around her waist, afraid that my words will send her running. She doesn't run. She doesn't move, doesn't even blink. It's like she's turned to stone, frozen in place. Finally, she quietly asks, "What do I mean to you?"

I don't know how to put it into words, but I try. "When I'm with you, I'm at peace."

Nicole looks like she wants to smile but won't allow it. I kiss her. It's a simple, sweet kiss, but with that kiss, I lay myself bare to her. Naked inside and out, I let myself be vulnerable. It's terrifying.

Then Nicole's lips move against mine, and it's the most incredible sensation I've ever experienced. It's a euphoria that's a hundred times better than performing, a million times better than any drug. *I'm hooked on this woman, and it's an addiction I don't want to kick.*

She wraps her fingers around my cock again. Then she shifts her hips over me and comes down, my length sliding into her hot, wet—

"*Fuck.*" I pull away from the kiss to protest. "I'm not wearing—"

"I know," she whispers against my lips as she seats herself fully onto me.

I watch in complete awe as she makes love to me. It's her response to everything I've just said, and it's a phenomenal reply.

When she reaches her climax, I come with her. And sated, we collapse together. With her atop my chest, I hug her tight and kiss her forehead. In that moment, I don't ever want to let her go. I would never leave this bed, skip the tour, miss meals, gladly lose all my jobs, if she would just stay like this: bared to me, connected with me.

• • •

"Jake." I don't remember falling asleep, but I wake gently to the sensation of Nicole petting my hair and whispering my name. I hesitate to open my eyes, enjoying her touch too much. *But...wait.*

I blink my eyes open to a room lit by the early morning sun. Nicole sits at the edge of my bed, fully dressed in last night's clothes.

"You spent the night," I croak, and the gravel of my morning voice masks some of the awe in my tone.

"But it's time for me to go now."

I glance at the clock. It's not even eight in the morning. I sit up, and the sheets pool at my waist as I slide closer to her.

She's so lovely in the daylight. I stare into her emerald eyes and run my fingers across her pale cheek and soft, pink lips. "You're not a vampire."

She laughs, and if I wasn't in love with her already, I certainly am now. *Wait...love?*

"Vampire?"

My hands are all over her now, one thumb tracing the line of her jaw while the other rubs along the ridge of her collarbone. Will I ever tire of touching her? Distractedly, I explain, "I was starting to wonder if that's why you'd never sleep over. Had to get back to your coffin, or you'd get ashed by the sun."

She laughs again, and I practically swoon. "I'm going to miss you while I'm gone. I haven't even left yet, and I already miss you."

"I can see that." She points at the bulge at my waist, popping a tent under the sheets. "But I think you'll find a way to take care of your loneliness without me."

"I'll be thinking of you every time I jerk off."

That cute little laugh again. "Charming."

"If it was charming you wanted, darlin', you've got the wrong guy." I hug my arms around her and flip her onto her back.

She sighs as I start to kiss and nibble her neck while I push her skirt up her thighs and pull her thong down. She opens the way for me, and when I enter her, she gasps, then admits, "Charming is overrated."

8–On the Road

Friday July 22, 2005—Houston

Prior to today, I've toured eight times in my life. The first was during college and was mostly an excuse for Greg, me, and the other guys in The Dark Hearts to consume as much drug, drink, and pussy as the East Coast had to offer. The other seven tours played on those same themes to varying degrees but with increasingly more emphasis placed on the music. And with each of those tours, I saw a marked improvement in transportation, lodging, and venues as we steadily built an audience and eventually signed to a small record label. But nothing compares with the experience of touring as a member of Mammoth.

Tours past, we'd have to cram all our gear into the back of a van and three-to-four smelly dudes into the front. On the last Nebulous tour, the label gave us enough money to rent a small trailer for our gear. We thought we were the kings of the road. Well, a trailer is attached to the back of the van again this time, but the van contains the three roadies hired to support the band. And the van is following behind our motherfucking bus.

Yep, that's right. I'm on a motherfucking bus with a driver and my own private bunk bed, and there's a lounge with a huge couch and television and kitchenette and a bathroom with a shower. How the hell am I supposed to go back to van living after this? *Note to self: start sending demos to larger record labels.*

I've spent the drive from Austin to Houston exploring the bus. I sat up front for a while, talking to Bruce, the driver who doubles as security for the band. He's a massive man who just returned from the war in Iraq, where he drove a damn tank. I feel very safe with Bruce at the wheel and at my back.

I spend some time unpacking the few belongings I brought—pants, shirts, socks, boxers, guitar strings and picks, earplugs, a few books, and my bathroom kit—into my private bunk, then wander back toward the lounge. Aidan is sprawled across one of the chairs, strumming his guitar, while Sean watches a movie on the television. I explore the kitchenette, which is loaded with Irish snack foods I've never heard of.

The small fridge is stuffed full of beer and soda, and when I swing the door open, Aidan pipes up, "Pass me a beer?"

I hand him one and give one to Sean too. I join them in their "Sláinte" toast and take a pull from my beer as I collapse into the chair across from Aidan.

"Everything to your liking?" Aidan asks as he tunes a string.

"This ride's fucking sweet."

"Took some adjusting for us too. Last time we were in the States, the lot of us stuffed ourselves in a van."

The guy remembers his roots. I appreciate that.

Aidan checks the time on his phone. "We should be there soon. Do you know how we might kill a couple hours in Houston?"

"NASA!" Sean hollers, and, in a strange version of an American accent, he adds, "Houston, we have a problem."

I cover my mouth to hide my laughter. Aidan laughs with me.

I look out the window at the suburban landscape streaming past us as we hit Houston's outer loop and shake my head. "No can do, guys. NASA is at least an hour's drive just to get there, and to see the rockets, you have to take this long-ass tour." I look across the aisle to Sean splayed on the couch, looking crestfallen. I feel like an asshole for shitting on his dreams of seeing Mission Control. I scramble for an alternative. "But I know a good titty bar not too far from here."

That does the trick. Sean grins from ear to ear, and Glenn peeks his head around the curtain of his bunk. "I vote yes to titties."

Aidan shrugs. I grab a cold water from the fridge and take it with me up to Bruce, giving him the refreshment as I direct him to the club. He radios our van to go ahead to the venue while we take a detour, then he drives us to, arguably, the best strip club in south Texas.

Inside, the Irish boys milk their accents for everything they're worth, putting a lot of bravado into their brogue. It's effective. We have our drinks served within a matter of minutes, and a whole bevy of dancers hover around our table.

"Chief Ladykiller, is that you?" I cringe at the use of that awful nickname, certain my mother, grandmother, and all my relations are turning over in their graves right now. Aidan raises a brow and mouths Chief Ladykiller at me. I scowl at him and shake my head, silently promising pain if he repeats it.

I turn to see Amber Lynn, gorgeous as ever, her curves—just as perfect as God and the surgeons have made them—squeezed into a dress that's not much more than a couple cocktail napkins knotted together to cover the parts of her body strictly regulated by the Texas Alcoholic Beverage Commission and Attorney General. She saunters toward us in a pair of stilettos and gracefully plops her perfect ass down onto my lap.

I give her my best smile, all dimples and teeth, and turn on the charm. "How ya doin', hot stuff?"

"Better now that you're here, sugar." Amber Lynn's syrupy Southern drawl is about as genuine as my bandmates' nineteenth-century Irish brogues. "You know I always enjoy it when my favorite road warrior pays me a visit."

Amber Lynn has been one of my favorite fucks for several years, a perennial detour any time I find myself in her city. Her hands roaming over me like a bad pickpocket, she's clearly got more of the same in mind for tonight. "What brings you to town, big guy?"

"On tour...with Mammoth," I gesture to the rest of the guys. "Allow me to introduce you to the band."

Before I can speak again, the guys jump in and speak for themselves, making certain she catches the lilt and cadence of their accents. Like the Pied Piper of Pussy, it's Aidan who attracts Amber Lynn's rapt attention. Within a matter of minutes, she has his hand in hers, leading him away to a private booth for a lap dance.

"Bloody hell. I think I'm in love," Sean mumbles as Amber Lynn walks away.

I straighten my T-shirt and jeans as I say a little prayer that Brandi isn't working today—

"Holy hell, is that you, Chief Ladykiller?" the voice comes from behind me. Again, I'm mounted. This time, the ass that lands in my lap belongs to Brandi, the genius who came up with my Chief Ladykiller moniker, an affront for which I still have yet to forgive her.

"Where have you been hiding, Chief?"

"You know how much I hate when you call me that. So why do you still do it?"

She pouts playfully like it's all a big joke. "You're just so sexy when you're mad. I can hardly help myself."

I scowl at her but change the subject. "Meet Sean and Glenn. They're from Ireland."

My God, I'd thought my Indian-warrior looks were a powerful chick-magnet, but I am truly humbled by the catnip that is the Irish accent. In a matter of seconds, the boys have Brandi sprawled across their laps, giggling as she asks them to say her name over and over again.

I appreciate the distraction, and use it to make my escape, leaving the table to lean against the bar near the back of the room. I look around me at the beautiful bodies and pretty faces and all I can think about is Nicole. I miss her smile, her scent, her taste. I want to be with her in my bed again, talking to her, listening to her, fucking her.

This tour is an amazing opportunity. It's a gift from the gods, no doubt. But it's come too soon. I wasn't ready to say goodbye to Nicole and leave for a stretch of sixteen long days and nights. They say absence makes the heart grow fonder, but don't you have to first be in a person's heart for that to work? *Am I in her heart? I have no clue.*

I mean, shit, it was only last night that I told Nicole she brings me peace. It was just last night that she made love to me and finally, blessedly, spent the night. It's all still so new, too new to take for granted. How will sixteen days of separation affect us?

I want to text her. All day I've wanted to text or call her, desperate to make contact. The sane part of my brain advises caution. *Don't be needy*, it says. *Don't cling, you fool. Play it cool. Wait at least a whole day, my man.*

I hate this shit. I'm no good at these bullshit games. I'm no good at waiting for what I want. *And you know what? Fuck all this noise. I'm texting her.*

I surreptitiously pull my phone out of my pocket, trying to avoid the attention of the bouncers. Quickly, I type out my message and send: **It hasn't even been a whole day, and already I miss your beautiful smile.**

"You know you're not supposed to be using that thing in here."
Busted.

I snap the phone closed and slide it into my pocket as Amber Lynn sidles up to me and leans against the bar at my left. She's posed like a model, aware of the best way to display her angles and curves.

She raises an eyebrow and gives me an appraising look. "Something is different about you, Jake. What is it?"

"I quit smoking."

Amber Lynn smirks at me, then looks back out at the room. "No, it's something else, something deeper."

I shrug, not looking to share my deep thoughts.

After a moment, she hazards a guess. "You got a girl messin' with your head?"

Well...

"Or is she messin' with your heart?"

Uh...

"Just tell me one thing. Is she prettier than me?"

"Impossible." I give her the million-dollar smile while I lie through my teeth.

My phone vibrates in my pocket, and I scramble to get at the thing, my suddenly too-big fingers clawing at my too-small pocket. I manage to yank it out and flip it open to a message from Nicole. She's sent me a photo, a selfie of her smiling wide, with the note: **Look what your text made me do.**

I grin at the photo like a moron and type the perfect response: **If I say I miss your tits, will you send me another photo?**

When I finish, I snap the phone shut and glance at Amber Lynn. She's been looking at my screen too. She smiles, and this time it's genuine. "She's very pretty."

I'm uncomfortable discussing Nicole with Amber Lynn. I don't have many ex-girlfriends in the strictest sense of the word—just Rebecca—but Amber Lynn and I have had some good times over the years. Talking to her about another woman seems rude. But if she's offended, she doesn't show it.

My phone vibrates again, and I grapple for it. Nicole has sent me another photo. The accompanying text is the same as before: **Look what your text made me do.** But this time, below it is a perfectly composed shot of her middle finger flipping me the bird.

I grin like an idiot.

Amber Lynn laughs as she looks at the image over my shoulder. "I like her."

So do I.

Sunday July 24, 2005—Day Off—New Orleans

Friday's show in Houston was even larger than Austin. As we walked out onto the stage, the crowd noise was so overwhelming, I nearly came in my pants. The Big Easy show last night was smaller and a little tamer, but no less fun, and having a day off in New Orleans is the perfect way to spend a Sunday. I play tour guide, helping my Irish friends fall in love with one of my favorite cities.

I take them out for beignets and coffee early. We grab muffulettas for lunch, munching as we listen to jazz in Jackson Square. Then the drinking starts. We hit Bourbon Street with a vengeance—karaoke, strippers, drag queens, and go-cups. Now, as the sun sets, we sit in the dark on a row of stools encircling a piano in the back of an old blacksmith shop, nursing a round of Hurricanes by candlelight and singing Irish drinking songs with the piano man.

My phone blinks and vibrates on top of the piano, and my first thought at seeing the caller ID is: *it's Nicole!* My second thought: *shit, I'm way too drunk to talk to her right now.* I answer the call anyway, taking a sip of my Hurricane to soothe my better judgment into submission.

"Hey there, Sugar Tits," I proclaim, louder than necessary.

She snorts, something between a laugh and a scoff. "Call me that again, and I'll feed you your spleen."

"Yes ma'am."

"How's the tour going?"

"Feckin' brilliant!" My attempt at an Irish accent gets a hardy laugh from Aidan at my side. "How's life on your end? What time is it there?" I ask her. "What time is it here?" I ask no one in particular.

Nicole doesn't answer any of my questions; instead, she asks her own. "How are the groupies treating you?"

"Oh, they're great. You were right. There is a correlation between bus size and the quality of the pussy." *Fuck, my mouth is off leash again.*

Aidan laughs at me and shouts to be heard over the piano music, "Hand me the bloody phone, you feckin eejit."

I'm just drunk enough to do as I'm told.

Into the phone, Aidan says, "'Ello, love, I'm here to report your man is a bleeding gobshite, but he's remained true." Aidan pauses for a moment, listening, then laughs. "Aye, that he is."

Aidan hands me the phone again with a smug smirk.

I wince as I put it to my ear, not sure if she'll be pissed, amused, or unmoved. "Yeah, I'm a bleeding gobshite...whatever that means. So how you doin', darlin'?"

Nicole laughs. "I don't think I've ever witnessed you drunk before."

"No. No, no, no, no. I don't do it often, but when on Bourbon Street, do as the Bourbon Street people do. That's what I always say."

Nicole laughs again, and it's like music, like the tinkling sound of rain hitting a metal roof.

Suddenly hit with a moment of clarity, I insist, "We need to go on a date."

"What?"

"We need to go on a date because I just realized all we ever do is have phenomenal sex. Not that I'm complaining at all. I love having sex with you, and I love that thing you do with your tongue when you—ouch!" I frown at Aidan, who's just hit me upside the head. He makes a hand gesture that either means "you're crazy" or "get to the point." I go with the latter. "Anyway, point is, we're always doing things backward, so we need to step backward and go on a date—with, like, flowers and food and a movie and some shit. I dunno. I don't do the date thing, but I've seen it in the movies, so I think I can wing it."

She cracks up. Not a good sign.

"So...whaddayasay? Want to do, you know, the date thing with me?"

I hold my breath and wait. Nicole eventually answers. "Sure, Jake, I'll do the date thing with you."

I hoot.

"Cool. So, how about when I get back...what day is that...Sunday, August 7. Will you go on a date with me on Sunday, August 7?"

"I can't."

"Can't?"

"I have a bout."

"A bout."

"What are you, an echo?"

"Echo. Echo. Echo."

"Are you even going to remember this conversation tomorrow?"

"Doubtful. I've had five hurricanes, and they are *amaaaaazing*. I love this city."

"Goodnight, Jake."

"Goodnight, Nicole. I think I love you."

Silence. Not a good sign. Finally, she breaks the silence with a cautious but amused "Okay, well, goodnight, drunk boy." And she hangs up.

Shit. "Did I just tell her I love her? I did, didn't I?" I look over at Aidan, his eyes wide with surprise as he cracks up laughing. "That was dumb."

Aidan laughs harder.

I groan. "Fuck off."

Monday July 25, 2005—Memphis, Tennessee

It's like that scene in *Spinal Tap* when a bunch of foreign rock stars try to harmonize an Elvis song while standing over his grave at Graceland. There's a crowd watching, enjoying the impromptu show. Normally, I'd be singing too. I do love attention, after all. But my head is killing me, and my thoughts are focused on Nicole. I want to call her. I *need* to call her. But if I do, will she even answer? *Fuck it. Let's find out.*

"Hey, drunk boy," she answers with a chipper voice.

I exhale the breath I was holding, relieved I didn't fuck everything up last night. "Oh no, that douchebag is still passed out on the bus. This is hangover boy speaking, but drunk boy asked me to tell you he's very sorry for anything stupid he might have said to you last night."

Nicole laughs. "How much do you remember about last night's conversation?"

"I remember asking you out on a date, but you turned me down." I gloss over the rest and hope she will too.

"Do you remember *why* I turned you down?"

"Actually, no." Fucking booze.

"I can't go out on Sunday because I have a bout."

"Oh." I pause. Waiting. Hoping for—

"You could come, if you want to—"

"Fuck yeah. I'll be there. Same time, same place?"

I can hear the smile in her voice as she gives me the details. She's comping me again, even after my drunken discourse last night.

"Talking to your lady in red?" Aidan nudges my shoulder then snatches the phone from me. He bats my grabby hands away as he speaks to her. "Nicole, love, we're at Graceland and feeling quite inspired by The King. We've got a little song for ya." Aidan winks at me, then busts out an impressive rendition of, "Can't Help Falling in Love."

Are you kidding me? I frown as Sean and Glenn join in. *Is this some Irish form of hazing, sing songs to the new guy's girl?* If it is, it's weird and strangely romantic, and by the second verse, I join in. Other tourists sing with us, the entire courtyard bursting into spontaneous song.

When we finish, Aidan hands the phone back to me, silently mouthing, "You're welcome."

"Wow," Nicole says when I get back on the line. "Did you guys just get all of Graceland to sing me a song?"

"Uh...yes?"

"That was pretty nice, Jacob Sixkiller. I thought I told you not to be nice."

I smirk, finally feeling like myself again when I say, "Well, in addition to being an asshole, I'm also contrarian and stubborn as fuck. The minute someone tells me not to do something, that's exactly what I'm going to do. So get ready, darlin', because I'm going to be so damn nice to you, you won't know what hit you. It'll be an F5 nice-nado...a Category 5 nice-icane. You're going to be blown away by my niceness."

Nicole laughs, unhindered and heartfelt, and the laughter rolls through me like an orgasm.

"I love your laugh." I sigh like a fucking fanboy, then want to kick myself.

"Yeah?" Nicole laughs again, and I wonder how many people know this softer side of her. It's an honor to be among that rank.

"Yeah."

"You know, Jake, I might have spoken too soon when I called you an asshole."

"Yeah?"

"Yeah."

Suddenly, the truth just tumbles out of my idiot mouth. "I miss you."

Silence.

I hold my breath as I think of all the horrible ways she could hurt me right now. I've given her all the power, and it terrifies me. I'm not accustomed to feeling vulnerable. With the exception of Greg and Ari, I've let no one in my adult life get close enough to hurt me. And that's how I like it. I'm a loner, a nomad roaming the desert, a minstrel with a traveling band. I have no roots to tether me, other than Greg and Ari. They've always tethered me to them. So, what happens now, as they split up, and my tether frays, about to snap.

Am I giving Nicole my tether? Because that would be epically stupid...even for me. Absolutely nothing in Nicole's words or deeds would suggest she wants to be my *anything*, let alone my fucking tether. At any moment, this fierce woman could reach into my chest, pull out my still-beating heart, and stomp it under the wheels of her skate—

"I miss you too."

"Yeah?"

"Yeah."

My chest feels like it might explode from the pounding of my heart.

"Jake?"

"Yeah."

"I need to get back to work."

"Oh...okay. Sorry," I stutter, then wonder out loud, "what is it you do, by the way? Your job, I mean?"

"I'm a librarian."

"You're joking."

She laughs. "No joke. I'm a librarian."

"Good lord! You are the embodiment of all my fantasies."

At that, she lets out a boisterous laugh. "Okay, hangover boy, safe travels."

She hangs up before I can say another word, but I don't know what I would've said anyway. My jaw is on the ground as a wave of erotic, library-centric images flood my imagination, mostly of Nicole in a pair of reading glasses and a pencil skirt, bent over to shelve books.

With my head still in the clouds, I turn to the guys. They're laughing at me.

"What?"

"Oh baby, you are the embodiment of all of my fantasies," Sean says to Glenn in a very girly, very exaggerated voice.

"Why not just cut off your bollocks to make her a wee little coin purse?" Glenn adds.

"Okay, okay," I grumble and pout. "Fuck all y'all straight to hell. And I'll have you know my bollocks would make a gigantic coin purse."

They laugh harder, but I don't care. The boys can have their fun. I'm on cloud nine, and no one can bring me down. My woman is a librarian by day, a derby skater by night, a hellcat in the sack, and she misses me. *She. Misses. Me.* No fantasy has ever been this good.

Wednesday July 27, 2005—Louisville, Kentucky

"Truth or Dare?" Nicole asks.

"Truth." I sit alone on a bench outside of a chicken restaurant somewhere in central Kentucky. It's hot as hell out here, but I hardly notice the beads of sweat that trickle down my spine. It's been six days since I joined the tour; six days I've been roaming the mid-South on a bus with a war veteran and three Irish blokes; six days with absolutely no privacy. So despite the heat and the rank smell wafting from the dumpsters near the side of the building, I savor this time alone on the phone with Nicole.

"I feel weird bringing this up, but I've been wondering...the other night when you talked about trying heroin...you said you were 'seeking oblivion.' Is that still true?"

Wow. Okay. She's not fucking around with this truth-or-dare game. With a pounding heart, I take a deep breath, let out the truth. "No. I haven't been that way in a long time. The night that happened was a bad night. It was the five-year anniversary of the accident. I'd managed the previous four anniversaries just fine. I mean, as fine as, well, you know...but that fifth year was the summer after my freshman year in college.

"I think part of my problem was the transition that comes with moving away from home to go to school, you know?" I pause, but Nicole is silent, so I keep going. "I hadn't realized how much I needed Greg's family and the normalcy of that dynamic until I moved out and was living in a dorm. Without Dan and Margie's help to keep me in line, I tended to overindulge. I was drunk or getting high all the time, fucking any chick who expressed interest in me...I was a mess, and I barely made it through that year. Probably only passed my classes because Greg helped me out a lot."

I'm getting sidetracked, talking too broadly. She asked a specific question about a specific event. Time to give her the specific answer. "That night, I was at a party, and this chick was flirting with me, so I went up to her room and we fucked, and then she offered me some H. I asked her what it was like, and she said, 'You get to float out of your skin,' and that sounded absolutely perfect to me, so I said yes. I'd never shot up before, so she did all the work. I just laid there, and in an instant, it hit, and, not gonna lie, it was *fucking* amazing. It was like I was being hugged by God himself.

"I didn't move for hours. I was bare-ass naked in some strange chick's room, and I didn't give a shit. Nothing mattered to me. That was the oblivion I'd been seeking, and it was bliss."

She exhales a long breath. I wait for her to say something, but she doesn't, so I continue.

"The next morning, though, I woke up in that room naked and alone...the girl was gone. I don't even think it was her room. I found my clothes, and I found the needle she'd used on me...on both of us. That's when I started to panic. What if she'd used a dirty needle? What if I'd just contracted AIDS or hepatitis? Everything just felt all wrong. My skin didn't fit right. But the worst part was that for the first time since the accident, I felt like they were watching me.

"You know when I said I was seeking oblivion to escape the ghosts? Funny thing is, it was actually the opposite. That was the night my ghosts found me, and they were so disappointed in me. I imagined my mother—the woman who'd given me life and sacrificed so much for me—and I could see the look of horror on her face as she watched her only living son shoot up heroin. I felt ashamed.

"That day, I went to the campus clinic and got tested for everything, and I started getting tested every other month after that, just to be sure. I stopped partying too. I still drank a few beers here and there, still smoked pot, and still hooked up with girls on occasion, but mostly I focused on school.

"Proudest moment of my life was the day I graduated college because I could feel my mom's eyes on me again, smiling this time."

"I think your mom would be proud of the man you've become," Nicole says with a quiet voice.

"I hope so." Tears burn the backs of my eyes as I'm overwhelmed with emotion. I glance at the restaurant window, relieved the guys are too focused on their bucket of chicken to care what I'm doing.

After a moment of quiet between us, Nicole offers, "I had a similar wake-up call."

I appreciate the change of subject. "Yeah?"

"Yeah. It was when I found out I couldn't have children. I didn't even realize I wanted them, but suddenly, I felt broken. Which is absurd. There are so many ways to contribute to society beyond just making babies, but I felt worthless as a woman."

I'm amazed by how open Nicole is when we talk over the phone. Would she be sharing these intimate thoughts if we were in the same room together? Maybe not, nevertheless, I wish I were there right now. I want to hold her. Instead, I hold my breath, waiting for her to continue.

"Maybe I was on a hunt for oblivion, too, because I started doing a lot of coke. This one night, I was drunk and coked up at a party in a hotel downtown. I went out on the balcony to get some air, and this guy kept crowding me and blocking my way back into the party. I was already having these weird fucked-up thoughts, and I got this crazy idea to jump off the balcony and then I just did it."

What. The. Fuck? "You jumped?" I'm practically hyperventilating at the image of what she's telling me.

"I jumped, right over the railing, and"—she laughs—"I landed in the pool."

I'm stunned silent. I can't believe she's laughing.

"Three floors down, and it hurt like hell; the worst belly flop of my life. I looked back up at the balcony and all these people from the party were looking down at me, completely shocked. It made me a legend in this city. They all think I'm batshit crazy, which is fine by me because nobody fucks with you when you're batshit crazy."

"You didn't mean to land in the pool, did you?" I ask, my voice cracking over each word. "You wanted to die."

There's nothing but silence on her end. A hollow, empty space where the sound of my own raspy breath amplifies and echoes back at me through the phone. Finally, with an exhausted sigh, she answers me. "I thought it would just be a few seconds of freefalling, and then lights out. I was so tired. And the idea of a freefall at the end sounded so easy."

"I'm sorry it came to that."

"I learned a lot in that instant. I think it's too bad when suicides are successful, because I always wonder if they had that same moment of clarity where they finally saw through all the bullshit and recognized how lucky they are just to be alive, and then...*splat*."

The sound effect she makes for "splat" makes me laugh. It's wrong to be laughing, but I can't help myself.

Nicole laughs, too, so I don't feel so bad. "Anyway, after that, I got my shit together. Got my degree, got my job, found derby... I remember when I heard that first whistle of that first bout, and I was so glad I'd landed in the water. I'm so lucky I survived my worst day, so I could have my best day."

"That's...really beautiful." I smile, but it falters as I ask what would have been too personal a question before today. "How do you know you can't have children?"

Nicole sighs long and heavy. Am I pushing her too far, asking too much?

But she answers. "When I was raped, I pretended like it didn't happen. Like if I never acknowledged it, then it couldn't hurt me. My parents were too busy to notice anything was different about me. And that made it easier to pretend everything was okay.

"Years later, when I was twenty, I was hit with severe abdominal pain. The pain got so bad my boyfriend at the time drove me to the hospital. That's when I found out I was pregnant, but it was ectopic, which means the fetus was attached in the wrong place. I also found out that the man who raped me gave me chlamydia, but it was asymptomatic—so all those years I was pretending everything was okay, it was silently destroying me inside."

She takes a long breath, and I do, too, feeling utterly heartbroken for her. Then she goes on. "That day, I lost my baby, and they had to remove one of my fallopian tubes as well. So now I have one barely functioning ovary and a uterus that looks like an Elm Street nightmare. It would take a miracle for me to have a successful pregnancy, and I don't believe in miracles."

Neither do I.

I slump forward, balancing my head on my hand as I stare at ants crossing the pavement between my feet. I want to say something to her right now, but it has to be the right thing, and I don't know what that is. Everything I could say just seems trite.

After too much silence, Nicole asks, "What are you thinking about?"

Everything. Nothing. Trying to decide if I should admit I'm probably falling in love with you. "You."

"What about me?"

"Your strength."

"I'm not that strong."

"Nonsense. I'm pretty sure you could pop my head like a grape with your thighs."

She laughs. We both stay quiet for a moment longer, each listening to the other breathe. I glance through the restaurant window; the guys are clearing the table. When they come outside one by one, the caboose, Glenn, lets out a loud belch.

"Guess that's your cue to get off the phone."

"Yeah. Can I call you tomorrow?" I don't know why I ask for permission. I've called her every night of the tour; why would tomorrow be any different? But I like the idea of asking her for things, and I like the sound of her saying yes.

"Yeah. Okay. Have a good show tonight. I'll talk to you tomorrow."

"I—" I almost say "I love you" to her...while sober. I blink a couple times in surprise. But it's too soon for that, and even if I were ready for that sort of talk, I wouldn't want that conversation to happen over the phone. When I finally say those words to the right woman, I will be looking her in the eyes. "Yeah, I'll talk to you tomorrow."

"Bye, Jake."

"Bye, Nicole." *I think I love you.*

Neither of us hang up. I listen to the sound of her breath as the guys climb the steps and disappear onto the bus. The longer the silence stretches between us, the more I want her to say something. Does she feel the same way I do? Is she as scared as I am to voice those feelings? When the last of the Irishmen turns and beckons me, I stand and start my walk toward the bus.

With a heavy sigh, I say, "Bye, Nicole."

"Bye, Jake."

Thursday July 30, 2005—Nashville, Tennessee

The venue is an old warehouse, enormously wide but with squatty low ceilings that give the place a claustrophobic vibe. It's packed to the gills with people, so that might be contributing to the cramped feeling. Also, the air conditioning must be broken. It's hot, practically flammable up on the stage.

Sweat drips into my eyes and flies from the tips of Aidan's hair as we sing the chorus to "Inside." We transition to the next verse with a key change and sync our guitars in a chugging rhythm as Glenn crashes his cymbals and Sean slaps a brutal beat on his bass.

This part of the song is hypnotic, a droning rhythm that mesmerizes. I close my eyes and sway along with the pulse of the music. And I'm not alone; everyone in the room is pulled into the same trance. This feeling right here, this communal euphoria, is what live music is all about.

We change tempo again, a fast, brutal guitar part as Dillon's machine-gun style double kick ratchets up the energy, and a pit opens up in the center of the floor. I watch the melee with a smile. Some people push backward, trying to get as far away from the flailing and churning bodies as they can. Others shove forward into the fray. There is a beauty to the brutality, a catharsis in the aggression. Metal saved me from my anger when I was an orphaned teenager with a chip on my shoulder. And I see more than a few young dudes down there who remind me of myself at their age, kicking and punching at the air, exercising their own ghosts.

When we finish the song, the audience shouts for more, but I can see from Aidan's face that there will be no encore tonight. He's bright red, and his light gray shirt is soaked dark with sweat. Back at the drums, Glenn has stripped out of his shirt, and Sean is panting like an overheated hound dog. These southern summer temps have been rough on the guys, but tonight's heat could be enough to send them to the hospital.

Despite Aidan's obvious exhaustion and possible heatstroke, he graciously thanks the crowd while the rest of us throw picks and sticks for the fans to catch. Then we race backstage to stand in front of the large swamp cooler that takes up one whole corner of the green room.

Bruce comes in with an armful of chilled water bottles. I want to kiss the man as I roll one across my forehead, then crack it open and drink all twenty ounces in a couple gulps. Aidan claims the first shower, and the rest of us use towels to dry off as we sprawl across the couches and chairs that litter the room. The walls back here are covered with graffiti where past bands have left their mark. Glenn picks up a marker from beside a tray of cookies on the table and adds Mammoth to the wall.

"Excuse me," squeaks a mousy voice from the door. I lift my head to peek over the back of the couch. It's a brunette in cat-eye glasses and a green dress. She doesn't look like a typical Mammoth fan; they usually just wear black. I collapse back onto the couch, half asleep, and leave it to Sean to do the talking.

"How'd you get in here, lass?"

"A big guy at the end of the hall let me through."

"That'd be Bruce. And why, pray tell, did he let you pass?" Sean asks.

"I'm looking for Jake Sixkiller."

My eyes rocket open, and I peek at her over the back of the couch again as I push myself upright to sit on the ratty sofa.

She smiles at me and trots across the room with her hand extended. "Hi! I'm Melissa Tanner with the Daily Beacon."

I shake the hand that's offered. "The Daily Beacon. That's the student paper, right?" I vaguely remember it from my days at the University of Tennessee.

"Yes. I was hoping to ask you a few questions."

"Why?"

Sean and Glenn chuckle. I narrow my eyes at them, but that only makes them laugh harder.

Melissa's smile wavers as she glances between me and the guys. "Because you're an alumnus," she answers. "I was hoping to interview you for an article."

"You drove all the way from Knoxville to interview me?" *That's a two-and-a-half-hour drive.*

Sean laughs again. "Give the bird a break, Jake. Answer her questions."

I try to smile for Melissa. It feels like it comes out wrong, a little lopsided, but I can't do any better. It's been a week of late nights and mediocre naps on the bus; it's taken a toll on my mental faculties. Not to mention, I stink. I can actually smell myself, and it's not pleasant. All I want right now is a shower, a snack, a little phone sex with Nicole, and some sleep. But this student journalist has driven a long way for this, so I relent.

"Okay," I hesitate. "What sort of questions do you have?"

Melissa settles onto the couch and starts. "The Music Department is extremely excited to have a graduate who's reached such an elevated level of success—"

"It's temporary."

"Sorry?"

"My elevated level of success? It's temporary. I'm just filling in." I glance over toward the far wall, where Sean and Glenn watch with strange expressions. Aidan has just come out of the bathroom in jeans, tugging a T-shirt over his head.

"Oh." Melissa does a double take when she sees Aidan half naked and clears her throat when she looks back to me. "Well, would you mind if I asked you a few questions anyway?"

"Okay."

Melissa shifts closer, too close. God, can't she smell me? I move away, pressing my back to the arm of the couch so I can face her as she messes with a small tape recorder and sets it on the cushion between us. She straightens her skirt, then consults her notes and asks, "You're an Eastern Band Cherokee who was born and raised in Cherokee, North Carolina, then attended high school and college in Knoxville before moving to Austin to jumpstart your musical career—"

"You've done your homework," I quip, already uncomfortable.

Melissa continues, "And now you're, uh, filling in with a band that's on the charts in the US and the UK—"

"Y'all are on the charts?" I turn to the guys, curious. I haven't paid a lot of attention to the news since we've hit the road. Aidan nods, Sean shrugs, and Glenn heads toward the shower.

Melissa clarifies for us all. "The single 'Inside' is at number three in the UK and number thirteen in the US on the Billboard rock chart."

"Cool." I'm impressed, but that has nothing to do with me, so I wait for her to continue. When she stares at me wide-eyed, I prod, "Is there a question in there?"

Her cheeks turn bright red with embarrassment, and she asks, "How did that all, you know, happen?"

I blink. That's a pretty broad question. We could be here all night. I choose to jump to the middle and keep things brief. "After college, I tried to start a few bands in Knoxville, but they never went anywhere. In Tennessee, if you want to play music you move here, to Nashville. I like Nashville, but the music scene isn't my style. For a while, I considered moving to LA, but when a friend got a job offer in Texas, I decided to tag along. When I arrived in Austin, I got a job the first week and joined a band the second. I played in four bands there before starting Nebulous five years ago. We're signed to a small label, but it's nothing like what these guys have going on."

I glance again at Aidan, who's listening to the interview as he snacks on a protein bar. "As for joining this outfit, Ian needed to return home for personal reasons, and the band happened to be near Austin, so they brought me in."

Melissa bites on the end of a pen. "Actually, I heard they vetted you pretty thoroughly."

"Where'd you hear that?"

"From the record label."

I frown at her, confused and too tired to care. "Okay."

Glenn returns from the shower, and now it's Sean's turn to clean up. I watch his retreat from the room with envy.

Melissa continues. "So, what inspired you to get into music?"

"My dad. He and his brother played music...before I was born. He always encouraged me to play and bought me my first guitar when I was ten."

My throat closes up, and I cough violently. Glenn tosses me a bottled water. I take a hearty drink, then cringe as I wait for Melissa's next question, somehow knowing—

"Speaking of your father, your family died when you were young. Can you—"

"You really have done your homework," I interrupt, looking for any distraction, anything to keep her from finishing that question. "No stone left unturned."

Melissa's keen gaze cuts right through me, peeling back the surface to see what's under my skin. I've underestimated her. She's a shark in these waters, not a guppy. "August 26, 1987—how much of an impact would you say the events of that night have had on your music?"

Flippantly, I pop off with a smart-ass answer. "I was a fourteen-year-old kid who lost his entire family, and now I scream into a microphone and play loud, aggressive music. What do you think?" I hear the attitude in my voice and reel it in to add, "It's had a profound impact on every part of my life, including music."

I glance over at the band. They're clearly listening, riveted, even if they are staring down at their feet.

Melissa's voice cuts through the quiet. "Can you tell me more about what happened that night?"

"Can we...not? I'd rather not discuss my personal life. If that's the focus of what you're writing, then I'd like to stop—"

"*It's* not the focus. *You're* the focus. But as you said, that night had a profound effect on you, so..."

I shake my head just as Sean comes out of the bathroom in fresh clothes, toweling off his hair. He looks around at the expressions in the room and asks, "Wha've I missed?"

I don't answer. No one does. Melissa and I sit in silence for a moment. Finally, she looks down at her notes and starts to flip through the pages like she's searching for her next question. The wait is excruciating. Please, God, nothing more about my dad and the car accident.

I clear my throat. "Listen, Melissa, I don't want to be rude, but I'm exhausted, and I'd like to hop in the shower. Do you have any more questions for me before I take off?"

She looks up at me with those big cat eyes and bites her lip in a flirty, cute expression. I'm unmoved. With a huff in her tone, she finally asks the question I've decided will be her last, and it's a softball. "Do you have any words of wisdom for current students of music at UT?"

Uh...am I the right person to be handing out advice? I glance at the guys, then back at Melissa. They're all staring at me as if I have something profound to say. *No pressure.* I think for a moment, then answer as best I can. "Don't give up. Don't quit. This life ain't easy, but nothing worth a damn ever is. So suck it up and do the work, because the payoff"—I look around the room, which isn't the best example of "making it," then glance over at the guys as I finish—"is worth it. To be able to play with incredible musicians, to express yourself through music and have an audience connect with that, that's worth all the bullshit that comes with it."

When I don't say anything further, Melissa reaches for her recorder. But before she turns it off, she asks, "Do you plan to visit your home while you're in the area?"

I blink at her, glance at the recorder in her hand, then look over at the guys and answer, "It's not on the schedule."

Melissa frowns at my answer. I feel bad for being so curt and impatient—I'm being a terrible interviewee—but her questions have opened old wounds and left me unsettled. She stops the recorder, pushes to her feet, and thanks the room for our time. Once she's gone, I leave, too, aiming for the shower.

The water feels good and cleansing, and I linger under the spray until it turns cold. When I'm clean, I pull on a pair of fresh jeans and comb through my hair before returning to the big room. Sean and Glenn are gone, and Aidan stands where I left him, staring at me.

"What's up, man?"

Aidan takes a deep breath. "I want to say...what that reporter said about the label vetting you. It's true. You know, who wants to be stuck on a bus for three weeks with some daft degenerate, so we checked—"

"And I'm not a daft degenerate?" I try to joke.

Aidan grins. "Point is, the stuff about your family...it came up."

"Okay."

Aidan stares at me for a moment, his expression tight, like he has much more to say, but he doesn't know where to begin. Finally, he offers, "If you want to talk about it..."

"No." I try to modulate my tone, not wanting to reveal how desperately I do *not* want to talk about it. "Thank you."

"And...if you want to visit your home...we can add it to the schedule."

I give him a curt nod.

After an awkward pause, Aidan moves toward the door. "Right. Well, so's you know, Bruce wants some sleep before we hit the road. The guys are in their bunks. I'm heading there myself now, so, if you want some privacy..."

"Yeah. If y'all don't mind, I'll hang out here for a while."

Aidan leaves and I'm glad to be alone. I'm on edge. There are very few people in my life who know about what happened to my family, and I like to keep it that way. Greg and Ari know the whole truth, of course, and now Nicole too. Rebecca knows the basics. But to find out all of Mammoth and their record label knows makes me uncomfortable. And now there's this reporter nosing around, looking for some sort of tragedy-to-triumph angle to an otherwise boring interview for a campus rag. The whole thing makes my skin crawl and my head hurt.

When Aidan's gone, I move to one of the couches and stretch out with my phone on my chest, considering whether or not to call Nicole.

It's late, later than I usually call. I don't want to wake her. But I desperately need to hear her voice.

Nicole answers on the first ring. With a sweet voice, she says, "I wasn't sure you were going to call."

"Sorry it's so late. It's been a long day."

"Oh? What happened?"

"You know, stuff and things. But I don't want to talk about me. I just want to hear about your day."

"My day? It was really boring, actually."

"Oh yeah? How so?"

"Well, I went to work, then I had skate practice, then I came home and reheated lasagna for dinner. Now I'm painting my toenails."

"What color?"

"Huh?"

"Your toenails."

"Black."

"Sexy." I close my eyes, picturing her feet with little balls of cotton stuffed between her black-tipped toes. "Speaking of sexy, tell me more about your day at work. Did you bend over a lot to reshelve books?"

"Perv."

"It's a legitimate question."

Nicole laughs and I settle into the cushions of the couch as I listen to her tell me all the ordinary details of her day. We talk for over an hour about nothing and everything, and it's one of the best phone conversations of my entire life.

Friday July 29, 2005—Chattanooga, Tennessee

"Where are you?" Ari asks.

I look out the window at the foothills of the Appalachian Mountains, whizzing by at seventy miles per hour. "Chattanooga."

"You planning to visit home while you're nearby?"

"No," I grumble.

"Whoa, Grandpa Grumpypants, who stepped on your lawn?"

"Greg," I huff. "Have you talked to him lately?"

There is a small, but telling, pause. *I'm such an idiot, of course she hasn't talked to him.* He's her ex. She has a new life now. "Not since I moved in with Alex. Why? What's going on?"

"He's in New York on business, and the last time I talked to him was when I drove him to the airport, almost two weeks ago. He was acting weird. I didn't think much about it at the time, but, I don't know, he's been depressed and...I'm worried. When I call his cell, it goes straight to voicemail now. I've left a dozen messages, and he hasn't called me back."

"That's weird."

"Yeah."

"Did Kate go with him?"

"I don't know. Probably. She's still his assistant, even if they're not..."

"They're not, what, together anymore?"

"No, Ari. He's alone." I flinch at the harshness of my tone. I'm talking to her like she's guilty of hurting Greg. It's not fair to her, but I can't control my frustration at the situation. "I haven't heard from him in eleven days. We haven't gone that long without talking since we were fourteen."

"Have you tried giving Margie and Dan a call? See if they've talked to him? Or his brother?"

"Not yet."

There's a pause, and I can picture Ari nibbling at her bottom lip as she thinks. "I'm sure he'll reach out to you soon. He loves you, Jake. He won't stay away for long."

I bite back everything I know I shouldn't say to Ari. I know it's not fair to blame her for Greg's pain.

But she's already blaming herself. With a sniffle she says, "Jake, I'm sorry he's hurting. If I could spare him that, I would."

Fuck. "Ari, please don't cry."

I look up; Aidan is watching me. I climb to my feet and head to the bathroom, the only true privacy afforded to us on the bus.

"And I'm sorry this is hurting you too." She clears her throat and her words come out scratchy and uneven when she tearfully adds, "I know you're angry at me. I know you wish none of this had happened.

I know you blame me, and, I mean, I blame myself too. I never meant for any of this to happen."

"I know, little sis, I know."

"It feels wrong. I feel bad I'm so happy with Alex, knowing that we've hurt all these people."

"Ari, shit, I'm sorry. It's not fair of me to bring all this up again and again. I'm happy you're happy; I truly am. I'm just in a shit mood, and I'm taking it out on you, and I'm sorry. Listen, just forget—"

Without a word, Ari hangs up on me.

"What the...?" I pull the receiver away from my ear and stare down at it, a bit stunned.

I consider calling her back, but instead, I call Nicole.

"Hey, you," she answers, sounding downright chipper.

The tension in my shoulders instantly loosens at the sound of her voice. "Hey to you, too."

"How's life on the road?"

"It's good." I sit on the edge of the sink and prop my feet up on the toilet seat, settling in for a nice, long chat.

"What's the matter, Jake? You seem off."

Damn, the woman already knows when I'm *off*.

"Everything okay?"

It feels weird to seek comfort from Nicole, but I do it anyway, "Have you ever thought you knew the direction of your life with absolute certainty, and then one day everything's changed around you and you don't know where you fit in anymore?"

She lets out a deep sigh. "This is about Ari and Greg, isn't it?"

Damn, she's good.

"Jake, I know they're important to you. But you need to stop trying to fit into their lives."

I frown, a little confused.

Like she's reading my mind, she clarifies: "You said it yourself that night you got the alley blowjob."

"Is *that* what we're calling that night?"

"Yes," Nicole answers before continuing. "When you were talking about Greg, you said, 'I'm Tonto, he's the Lone Ranger.' "

"Yeah, cuz I'm the Indian."

"No, you're the sidekick."

"Huh?"

"You've cast yourself as the sidekick in your own life story. And I get it; it makes sense. After you lost your family, you found yourself a new one with Greg's family and then with Greg and Ari, and you were so grateful to them for giving you a place, you made yourself subordinate to them. You've got to stop that. This is the Jake Sixkiller show, and you're the leading man, so start acting like it. Stop mooning over Ari and Greg and their precious feelings and let them moon over you and your precious feelings for a change."

First of all, ouch. Nicole's pep talks come with a bite. And second of all, holy shit, she's right.

"Huh," is all I can muster as her words of wisdom circle in my head and start to sink in.

There's a loud bang at the bathroom door, and I'm wrenched from my thoughts as Sean bellows, "Out of the jacks, lover boy. I 'ave to take a slash."

I grumble, but quickly exit and hurry to my bunk. Climbing in, I turn my back to the aisle and curl up as I keep the phone to my ear.

When I'm settled, Nicole says, "My advice to you is to get your shit together, figure out what you want in life, and go for it. If Greg and Ari are the friends you think they are, then they'll be by your side along the way."

"Huh." It's sound advice. "Anyone ever tell you you're wicked smart?"

"Oh my God, people never shut up about it."

My call-waiting chimes, and I look at the screen. It's Ari.

"Hey, Ari's calling me. Should I answer it?"

"Oh no, Tonto, my job here is done. I've reached my kick-in-the-pants-with-life-advice quota for the day."

"What?" I grumble. "Your quota is way too low."

"Oh yeah, well, how's this for a kick in the pants?" And with that, she hangs up on me.

Ari's call engages, and I let out an exasperated sigh. "Hey, little sis—"

"My calls went to voicemail too." The reason she hung up on me is clear now. "I called eight times. Greg never picked up. Jake, what if—"

"It's the middle of the day. He's probably in a meeting."

"But he hasn't talked to you in *eleven days*. What if he's..." Ari lets out a whimper, and I know she's beating herself up.

"Two Shoes, he's fine."

"You don't know that."

"Look, I'll call Margie and Dan, okay? I'll ask them to call him. If he doesn't answer a call from his own mother, *then* we should worry. But not before." I work nonchalance into my tone when I add, "It's probably nothing. Maybe he just needs some alone time. Please stop worrying, okay?"

"Okay," she says with a tearful sniff.

"You're going to worry anyway, aren't you?"

"Yeah."

"Knew I could count on you."

9—Sunday July 31, 2005

I'm too close. Like I've crossed into the Exclusion Zone surrounding a nuclear meltdown, the fallout from ground zero still colors the air. The past still falls from the sky in a shower of ash. It never stopped. I've just been ignoring it for a couple decades. But now, for whatever reason, the tinge in the sky, the scent in the air—it's all part of some nostalgic lure that's pulling me back home.

Home.

Sitting in this fast-food joint in the Buckhead neighborhood of Atlanta, I can look out the window and see the road that will take me home. My head throbs with tension. My skin feels too tight. I shake my head and drop my hands into my lap, clenching them into fists beneath the table, trying to stop fidgeting, even as my foot begins to tap against the floor.

"Hey guys, how would y'all feel about a home-cooked meal?" I speak the words before I can change my mind. No going back now.

They all perk up, setting down their mediocre coffees and bland breakfast sandwiches as they raise their eyebrows.

"Since we have the day off, I thought...you see...I grew up not too far from here, and...maybe we could pay a visit. Margie used to always fry chicken and bake a pie on Sundays. I don't know if she still does, but if I call ahead—"

"Do it," Sean demands. "Call ahead. Tell her to bake a pie—"

"Sean—" Aidan starts.

"Fuck's sake, Aidan, don't be a git." He picks up his breakfast sandwich and tosses it back down onto its wrapper. It lands with an unappetizing thud. "I'm sick of this shite. I want pie." Sean points at me. "And he gets to see his mum."

"She's not really my mom, but she's close," I clarify.

Glenn shrugs, and Aidan asks, "It won't be a bother?"

I laugh. *Fat chance.* Margie thrives when she has a house full of boys to feed. She'll be delighted. "Only thing is, the route we'd have to take to Charlotte goes through the mountains..."

Aidan leans over to the table across the aisle, where Bruce is reading my copy of *The Dark Tower*. The whole bus has been reading my books. More of that weird Irish hazing, I guess, or they forgot to pack their own. "Bruce, we're considering a detour, but the route would take us through the mountains—"

"Let's do it." That's the most I've heard from the guy in four days. "I'm bored with the interstate."

Aidan nods at me. "Crack on, then."

I call Greg's mom, and she answers in one ring. "Jake? Is everything okay?"

Yesterday, we'd chatted about Greg. He answered her call, and she described him as sounding "tired." He still hasn't answered my calls. But that's not what this call is about. I put a smile in my voice. "Hiya, Margie, everything's fine. I'm actually calling because, well, I'm in Atlanta."

"What?"

"I'm on tour with a band, and we have the day off. If it's not an imposition, we'd like to come—"

"An imposition? Listen to you." She lets out a hearty laugh. "Are you kidding me? What a rare treat. You come on home now and bring your friends. I'll make all your favorites for lunch."

My mouth waters at the thought. "No need for you to go to any trouble feeding us, Margie."

Sean scowls at me.

"Nonsense. You hush now and get on home."

When I hang up with Margie, Sean hollers, "Hallelujah," and tosses his breakfast sandwich into the trash.

"Uh, Sean, it's a three-hour drive, pal. You might want to go ahead and eat that."

. . .

Aidan reads on the couch in the lounge at the back of the bus. I hover awkwardly in the doorway, my fingers making and unmaking fists at my sides.

"You just going to stand there like a bleedin' tosser all mornin'?" Aidan asks, without looking my way.

I clear my throat, but the words don't come out.

Aidan finally glances over, and his expression shifts from irritation to concern. He sits up to face me, folding his book over his knee. "What's the matter?"

"There's something I need to ask you." I cross the room to sit across from him and lower my voice to say, "I know it's none of my business, but did you and Ari...?" *God, I don't actually want to know this.* "You know...?"

"That's what this is about?" Aidan asks and his lips quirk at the corners, like he's reminded of a fond memory.

I blink, a bit stunned. "Well, that's a yes."

Aidan frowns. "Yes. I was with her...briefly. Why?"

"Briefly?"

"Three days, but it was months ago, during South by Southwest. Why do you want to know?"

I blink again, a bit stunned. I cannot believe Ari didn't tell me. But that's a drama for a different day. For now... "These people we're going to go see, they're...Ari's husband's parents."

Aidan's brow practically hits the stratosphere.

"When my family died, Greg's family took me in, and that's who we're going to visit."

A blend of sympathy and awe is in his voice when he says, "I see." Leaning forward, he pinches the bridge of his nose like he's fighting a headache and in a hushed voice, explains, "About Ari...she said they had an arrangement—"

"Aidan, it's okay." *Does he think I'm upset?* "You're right. They did have an open arrangement. That's not why I brought this up. My point is Margie and Dan don't know all the details. They just know about the separation. And I didn't want anything awkward to come up in conversation. Figured it best to get everything said now, rather than later."

Aidan watches me cautiously.

I watch him, too, and after a moment ask, "Three days, huh?"

Aidan smiles wistfully but doesn't elaborate. He looks me straight in the eyes as he keeps her secret. And I've got nothing but respect for the guy for that.

· · ·

Knoxville looks different from the front seat of a tour bus. I feel strange, conspicuously out of place in this lofty position as I help Bruce navigate the winding suburban roads toward the Hendricks' house. When we arrive, it's an absurd scene to behold—a massive tour bus wedged between a Volvo and a Jeep at the end of a quiet cul-de-sac.

I step off the bus and stretch. Bruce and the guys follow behind me, taking in the expanses of freshly mowed lawns and the midsized colonial homes that dot them. Dan and Margie's house is virtually untouched by time. That consistency is comforting. Everything about this place is comforting and always has been.

From the front porch, Margie greets us with a big smile. My heart swells with affection for the woman who raised me like I was her own son. She wraps me in a hug, and I melt against her. Margie's hugs were a crutch that held me up more times than I care to count. When we pull away, I turn to Greg's dad, Dan, and shake his hand. He looks past me, staring in awe at the massive tour bus.

"Looks like you hit the big time, Jacob."

On that note, I proudly introduce everyone. Margie sweeps us into the house, which smells like chicken and cherry pie. Greg's Granny Millie is in her rocking chair by the window. Since her husband's death last year, she's been living with Margie and Dan, and it appears to be a comfortable arrangement for all. I rush over to hug her and introduce everyone. She graciously greets them, then allows me to escort her to the table.

Sure enough, Margie has prepared a true Southern feast. We sit around the giant oak table, and it's another familiar scene from my past. Margie was always the neighborhood mom. She's been known to host entire football teams and more than a few bands; everyone is welcome at Margie's table.

After a bit of small talk about the band and the guy's families back home in Dublin, Margie turns to me with a solemn expression and asks, "How is Ari recovering, Jake? Greg told us about the car accident."

"She's doing much better. Talked to her this morning, and it sounds like she'll be out of her cast in a couple weeks, so she's excited about that."

"Good, good. And...she's moved out of the house? Greg mentioned it, but..."

"Yes, ma'am, she's moved out."

With a heavy sigh, Margie asks, "This Alex, is he a good man? Does he treat her right?" Just when I thought she couldn't impress me more, she goes and does it.

"Yes, ma'am. He's very good to her. And, for what it's worth, she's very happy."

"Well, I'm glad to hear it."

Granny Millie smiles a bit. Even Dan is contented by that news. I glance across the table at Aidan, who's paying very close attention to his mashed potatoes as he shovels another forkful into his mouth. When Margie returns to her food and conversation lulls, I excuse myself and head up the long hall that leads toward the bathroom.

I peek into each room I pass. The rooms haven't changed much since I moved away. Greg's brother Matt's room is the only one that's any different. Once upon a time, the room had looked like the back office of a mechanic's shop—posters of cars and pinups of yesteryear covering every inch of wall space. Now, there is just a simple photo of

Granny Millie and Grandpa Chuck on the wall beside a small television and a cross nailed to the wall over the pink-afghan draped bed.

One door down, Greg's walls are plastered with photos of engineering marvels, with a massive poster of the Petronas Towers over his bed. In the corner stands the three-dimensional model of the Eiffel Tower he built out of toothpicks for the tenth-grade science fair.

Across the way is my old room. Just like Greg's, it's unchanged. My old twin bed is still covered in the blue quilt my mom made me when I was little. My bookshelf is still cluttered with math, science, and music books. Unlike Greg's old room, though, the walls of my space are bare, the tableau of my life in this house a blank slate—Tabula Rasa.

I sit down on the bed and the mattress springs groan under my weight. I stare at the plush carpet I used to feel underfoot each morning for four years, so soft between my toes.

"How are you doing, Jacob?" Margie asks from the door.

My head jerks up, and I force a smile. "Can't complain, ma'am."

"Well, that's nothing new. You never complain." She crosses the room to sit beside me, laces our fingers, and squeezes reassuringly. "I've been wondering how you're taking the separation. I know it's been hard on Greg, but I imagine it hasn't been easy on you, either."

"It is what it is." Not a real answer, but it's all I'm comfortable saying. I've been giving the subject a lot of thought lately, especially since my enlightening chat with Nicole a couple days ago, and the truth is, it's rough. Realizing my trusted circle of friends is only two people deep, and now witnessing those two people separate from each other has been hard. I'm exhausted. I shrug. "They'll figure it out...we'll figure it out."

"Oh, honey, I know you will. If anyone can, it's you. But I worry about you."

I'm not sure what she means by that. "I'll survive."

"Of that, I have no doubt. But life is about more than just survival. Jacob, honey, you have such a good heart. For as long as I've known you, you've always invested your energy into making sure the people around you are happy. But if you're investing all your energy into everyone else, what's left for you? You deserve happiness too."

I blink at Margie, surprised and a little amused by how similar her words are to Nicole's. I grin bashfully. "I'm workin' on it."

"Oh?" Margie raises an eyebrow, wanting details.

"There might be someone special."

"Might?"

"It's early still, but I like her...a lot. I think you'd like her, too, once you got to know her."

"Well, if she's the one who's put that smile on your face, I like her already."

I look at Margie, and it's the first time in a while I really see her. She's aged; more gray threads her hair, more wrinkles line her skin. But no matter how the years mark their passage, some things never change. The twinkle in her eyes and the calming smile on her lips—those are pure Margie and will never change. I will always see in her the woman who was there for me when I had no one else. I lean forward and wrap my arms around her.

"Oh," she gasps and hugs me back.

And I offer her the words I'll never be able to say enough. "Thank you, Margie, for everything you've done for me."

She sniffles, and I hug her closer. When we pull away, Margie wipes her eyes, and I do too. We sit together in silence for a while, holding hands on my old bed. After a moment, I clear my throat and commit to a decision I've been weighing since Atlanta. "I think I'm going to take the guys to Cherokee."

"Oh?" Those eyebrows rocket up again. Margie knows more than anyone what this means to me.

"I thought it could be interesting for them. Being from Ireland, they haven't seen an American Indian community before. You know?"

It's a cop-out, trying to play off the trip as though I'm a tour guide for the Europeans, but Margie doesn't comment.

• • •

"This is bloody brilliant!" Sean exclaims as he holds up a ceramic bald eagle with the American flag held aloft in its beak, an old musket gun clutched tightly in his talons.

"Welcome to Gatlinburg, gentlemen." I'd told them we were heading to the mecca of Southern Americana. Gatlinburg, Tennessee, does not disappoint.

"I never knew places like this existed in real life," says Aidan with awe as he stares at a display of black bear-themed tchotchkes and kitsch, including a toilet seat lid depicting a black bear at a waterfall, which he picks up for closer inspection.

"Never underestimate the absurdity of the American South," I say with a prideful grin.

Gatlinburg is fun for a few hours. We ride the Sky Lift up the side of Crockett Mountain for panoramic views of the quaint little town, then wander through a few of the shops, pretend to mine for gold at a roadside attraction, and stop for a beer at a country and western bar.

But now it's time to head farther east.

"Gentlemen, as you saw, that last town was a display of the absurdity of the American south. This next town is all about the American Indian," I say when we board the bus again.

Everyone's excited. They crowd up front with Bruce, watching out of the windshield as we make our way through the lush, green Smoky Mountains. It's nice to show them a bit of the beauty of this country, something other than the blur of highways and the indistinguishable clutter of fast-food joints, strip malls, and dirty rock venues.

I stand in the aisle behind them, staring at the old familiar scenery over their heads. Even after all these years, the mountains are unchanged; they are eternal. Once upon a time, I called this place home. These peaks were the backdrop for my entire world.

After my family died, I went west, like the Cherokee often do, but my Trail of Tears only took me as far as the west side of these mountains. And in that first year, I would often return. Margie would drive me on weekly trips to visit my grandmother in the nursing home. I would sit for hours with Granny Sixkiller, listening to her stories, letting her hold my hand and never wanting her to let me go. For eight months, she was the only family I had left. Then she died.

Sure, I still had Uncle Eli. But he'd shipped off to the navy the week after we buried my parents and Tommy, and when Grandma died, he'd sent flowers. It was at Grandma's funeral, as I sat alone mourning her, that I stopped counting Eli as part of my family. And it was at her funeral that I realized I no longer had a reason to return to my homeland, so I never did.

Why now, then, do I feel compelled to be here? What has changed? Just last month, I was climbing the hills east of Maryville with Ari and never once thought about the place on the other side of the mountains.

Is it because I walked down this memory lane with Nicole? Is it because that reporter dug up all the old graves? I never talk about what happened and try not to think about it much either. It's always there, though—buried deep, but an ever-present scar on my psyche.

Bruce steers through a sharp bend in the road, and there on the right are the markers: three discreet white crosses adorned with red ribbons that have faded over the years. They're overgrown with greenery now but easy to spot if you know where to look.

I clench my jaw tight, blink my eyes a few times, then return my gaze to the middle of the road, where it's safe. Emotions claw up my throat, but I don't let them out—not here, not now, not in front of the guys. I know having Bruce and the band here is a crutch and one I'd rather not admit to using, but it helps.

Once we're on the other side of the range and at the welcome center, we've arrived at my homeland: Cherokee, North Carolina, the Qualla Boundary, the reserved land of my Eastern Band of Cherokee kin. I take a deep breath, then explain the history as best I can to my Irish friends and Bruce.

"I read about the Trail of Tears once," Sean says. "What's that about?"

"That's the western Cherokee. They were forced to walk to Oklahoma. When you guys played Tulsa, you were close to the Cherokee Nation out there. My people, though...we hid here in the mountains. The government tried to hunt us down to send us west, too, but they couldn't find us. Eventually, they gave up and let us stay. My family has been here since before Columbus sailed the ocean blue in 1492."

I tell Bruce to turn left, and we go over the Oconoluftee River to where the town winds through the peaks. At first sight, the place seems almost unchanged. The log cabin and farmhouse-style buildings that skirt the river are the same as I remember, filled with many of the same souvenir shops, restaurants, and creameries. These days, though, colorful kiosks dot the parking lots, offering tube and kayak rentals, and the place is hopping with activity, tourists everywhere. I'd read that the new casino had boosted the town's economy, but it's something to see. The crowds collide with my memories of this place, making it all seem so different, unreal.

Feeling the urgent need to see something I remember in the way I remember it, I ask Bruce, "You think you can maneuver this bus up a windy valley road? There's a cool waterfall up that way."

Bruce puts his shoulder into turning the big wheel and navigates the small road as we wind through the valley beside the river. When we reach the falls, Bruce manages to create a parking spot out of thin air, and we all hop off the bus and follow the trail up the hill.

My tour group ogles the canopy of massive tree cover, the smells of nature, the peace and quiet. For me, the peace and quiet are filled with sounds and sights from a bygone time: carrying Tommy on my back up the hill, playing hide and seek in these woods with distant "cousins," Dad and Eli racing us boys up the steps while Mom and Grandma would hang back and take their time.

When we finally reach the base of the falls, it's mostly unchanged, and there is comfort in that. I stand in the spray of that roaring waterfall, feeling the thunderous beat of its current deep in my chest as its cool mist dampens my face.

Inside me, something eases, a weight lifts, a darkness lightens. Like a baptism, I am reborn. I once left this place a broken boy, but today I return as a strong man, a survivor, a warrior.

After a few moments spent in quiet awe of the site, we make our way back to the bus in silence, like the peace of the falls is something we can take with us. Back in town, we follow the winding road between mountain peaks, visit a few shops, and roll up our jeans to wade through the river to Island Park to feed Irish crisps to the ducks.

It's all so familiar and yet so foreign. Throughout our meandering tour, there are signs of growth and development in Cherokee, but nothing as foreign as the high-rise casino hotel which looms over everything but the mountains themselves. The massive monolith stands in stark contrast to my memory of this town and to the lush beauty of the nature that surrounds it. Inside, the noise and bright lights are a jolting juxtaposition to the peace we'd found at the falls.

Not even ten feet inside the door, I see a familiar face. An old family friend, Gayle Toineeta—Granny T to us kids—sits perched atop a stool, pushing buttons on a quarter slot machine. She glances over and a whole array of emotions pass over her face when she sees me—from surprise to confusion to recognition and excitement.

"As I live and breathe, Jacob Sixkiller, is that you?" Granny T hollers over the bells and whistles of the machines. She looks good for her age, considering she must be past seventy by now. There are a few more wrinkles, and her once jet-black hair is gray and cut into curls that halo her face.

"Yes, ma'am, it's me all right."

"Well, goodness gracious, let me get a look at you." She shimmies off her seat, setting her bucket of quarters there to save her spot, and comes at me. A full foot taller than I used to be, I bend to greet her, and she cups my face in her hands, assessing. "You sure came up handsome, didn't you? You're the spittin' image of your daddy."

Before I can react to her words, the woman releases my face and wraps her arms around my midsection, squeezing me with all her might. I let out an *oomph* as the air rushes out of my lungs, and I choke as I try to speak. "How you doin', Mrs. Toineeta? How is Jill?"

Granny T's granddaughter was the first girl I ever kissed—both of us thirteen at the time and hiding behind Granny T's garden shed. She'd found us and tanned my hide before sending me on my way back home.

"Jill? Well, she's married now with three little ones of her own, though not so little anymore. She's about to be a grandmother herself."

Jesus H Christ!

"And how are you, *Usdi Yona*?"

Usdi Yona. Little Bear. No one has called me that in years. I'd almost forgotten the nickname. I earned it for my tendency to fall asleep in class—like a hibernating bear, the teachers would say. "I'm well. I'm in Austin, Texas, now. Playing music. Actually, we're"—I gesture to the guys—"passing through town on tour."

"Oh." Granny T smiles widely. "A famous rock star now. Are you boys playing here at the casino? Goodness, I can't wait to tell Jill."

And by "Jill," she means the entire reservation. I blush, embarrassed, but Aidan plays on it, touting me up. "He's very talented, madam. You'd be rather impressed."

Granny T swoons a little, charmed by Aidan's accent, just like every other woman on this continent. I introduce the guys, who respectfully bow to her. Then Granny T turns to me and in Cherokee asks if I plan to visit my family.

I don't answer right away. In part because it takes me a moment to remember my native language, a language I haven't had the opportunity to hear or speak in close to twenty years, and because the answer is so awful. I've come all this way with no plans to visit their graves. Just coming to this town has been a big step. I can't be expected to overcome all my demons in one giant leap. Can I?

Even as I think it, I'm ashamed of my weakness. This is not the way of a warrior. A warrior would face his battles with steeled-spine courage. A warrior wouldn't need to take such little fucking baby steps.

Finally, in stilted, awkward Cherokee, I explain our bus can't fit on the road to the cemetery. *And hell yeah, listen to me, speaking my native language.* It feels good, right. I hope she asks me another question so I can answer it in Cherokee.

Granny T waves my words away like she's batting at flies, insisting she'll drive me.

Uh. I slip back into English. "Oh, no, ma'am. I couldn't ask you to do that."

She ignores my protests and turns to my bandmates. "Will you boys be able to entertain yourselves here for an hour or so?" She walks to her bucket of quarters and brings it back over, handing it to Aidan. He assures her he doesn't need her money, but she won't hear otherwise. "Play your luck," she insists *Utana Yona* and I have an errand to run."

I'm a bit stunned by the shift in my nickname—from Little Bear to Big Bear. Granny T winks at me, then takes my elbow and walks me out the doors, my Irish brethren left behind, holding a bag of coin.

· · ·

A Ford killed my family, and it's a Ford that takes me back to them. I fold myself into the passenger seat of Granny T's Taurus and glance over the center console at the baskets full of fake flowers piled into the backseat. "They're for Bingo," she says. As if that explains anything.

As we drive, Granny T updates me on all the goings-on in the Qualla Boundary. No need for a newspaper when they've got Granny T, town crier. No doubt, the news of my brief visit will make the rounds within the hour. By dinnertime, the Chief himself will know Little Bear Sixkiller passed through town and visited the graves of his family.

"Have you stopped by to see your uncle?"

"Eli?"

Granny T raises a brow at me. "Do you have any other uncles?"

"I thought he was in the navy in Guam or some shit."

She clucks her tongue at my use of foul language. "He retired ten years ago. Came back home, got a job at the plant, and married my youngest—Lisa."

"Oh." I haven't seen my uncle since the day we put my family in the ground. Except for his role in my nightmares, I haven't spared him much thought in almost two decades.

Thankfully, Granny T doesn't say any more on the matter. As we wind around a bend in the road, I catch a glimpse of the cemetery. My fists clench in my lap, and my breath hitches in my lungs.

We pass through the front gate of the graveyard, and Granny T takes the curved road around to the back. The population of the dead buried here has grown over the years, but back by my family, everything remains the same as I remember it. A small footbridge crosses a babbling brook and leads up a ridge to the Sixkiller plot.

Granny T turns the car around so she's parked facing the exit. She folds her hands in her lap and faces the windshield when she says, "Your father was a good man."

I scowl as anger flushes my face with heat. My hands fist tighter in my lap, and I open my mouth to argue, but she continues.

"He was far from perfect, but he loved your mom and you boys with all his heart." She glances at me, then back out the window again. "He'd be so proud of the man you've become, Jacob."

"Imagine the man Tommy could have become."

Granny T doesn't argue, because, how can she? She turns around and carefully plucks four flowers from the plethora of bouquets in the back seat. A carnation, a sunflower, a rose, and a lily. "The sunflower reminds me of your mom. It was her favorite flower."

I didn't know that. There's so much I didn't know about my mother.

"I'll be right here, *Utana Yona*. Take all the time you need."

I stare at the flowers she's carefully set in my hand, then look up at her and panic. I thought she'd come with me. I didn't realize I'd be crossing that little footbridge alone.

Sensing my weakness, Granny T takes my hand and says a quiet prayer. When she finishes, she nods at me. It's my cue to leave. I'm good at following cues. I exit the car, cross the footbridge, and take the narrow path up toward my family.

At the edge of the Sixkiller plot, I take one deep breath and another. I sway on shaky legs. The fabric petals of those fake flowers tremble from the tremors in my hands. My heart is in my stomach, and my head is filled with dread. Then I look up.

The sight of those four granite stones, all that's left of them, hits me like a punch to the gut. The air whooshes out of my lungs, and I shudder and gasp for a moment before I step forward—one step, two— then I walk the rest of the way.

My legs quit moving when I reach Granny Sixkiller's grave. It takes me a few blinks to clear my vision. I crouch and place the rose across the base of her stone.

"*Siyo, Elisi.*" *Hello, Grandmother.* It's all I can think to say. I remember all the good times I spent with her, before and after that awful night. I remember when she started to get sick. I remember watching her slowly fade away, how frail her fingers were when she'd hold my hand. I remember the sound of her voice as she'd tell me the old stories.

Her favorite was about the bears that would dance atop *Kuwahi*, the highest mountain in the Smokies. When they were sick, she'd say, they would go to Magic Lake to swim in the healing waters. After she died, when I'd watch the clouds swirl and bubble over those mountains, I'd imagine Granny there, swimming in the Magic Lake with the bears.

I wipe my arm across my face and groan, frustrated by the tears slipping down my cheeks. This was supposed to be the easy one. With Granny, I'd known she was going to die. She'd told me many times. She'd prepared me. I'd gotten to say goodbye to her. *I've always been so grateful for that.*

Still: "I miss you, Granny. I miss your stories and those butterscotch candies you always shared with me and your grape dumplings and your laugh." I'm flooded with memories of so many good times—helping her garden, listening to her stories as we'd hang clothes on the line to dry, sitting in the rockers on the porch drinking sun tea and watching the cat harass the dog. I laugh like she's here with me, and we're joking together like old times.

I take another deep breath and let it rattle out of my lungs, then push up to my full height. With my shoulders back and my spine straight, I turn and walk. I don't allow myself any time to think about where I'm heading. I just walk until I end up between Mom's and Tommy's graves. There, my legs buckle, folding under me like a lawn chair. I hit the ground, my knees landing hard on bits of the acorn shells. I stay that way, like I'm praying to God.

But it's not a prayer that comes out of me; it's a sob. It chokes me up, and I clear my throat a couple times, not ready to speak until I know I can trust my voice. I want to sound like the man I am, not the boy I was.

I lay the sunflower across Mom's stone and run my fingers over the engraved letters of her name, then trail my touch across the deep grooves that form her date of death. That night, I thought the worst thing that could happen was losing a football game. I had no idea how much more I had to lose.

"Hey, Momma, it's me, Jacob." *Idiot. She knows who you are.* I shake my head at myself but keep talking. "I'm sorry I haven't visited before now. I, well, I don't have a good excuse. But I hope you know how much I miss you, every day."

I clear my throat to continue. "I think you'd be proud of me. I got a degree in music and business, from the University of Tennessee." I smile to myself, proud to have realized her dream of sending her son to college. "I'm a musician. I'm on tour right now, playing in front of thousands of people." *Now I just sound like I'm bragging.* "I kept my hair long." *Okay, this is getting dumb.* "Sorry, I'm not very good at this." The breeze picks up and blows a loose strand of my hair into my eyes. I blink, then laugh and look up at the leaves on the trees and the dappled sunlight warming my face. Speaking to her like she's up there in the sky, I whisper to the wind, "I love you too, Momma."

With another deep breath and a few blinks of my teary eyes, I turn my head toward Tommy's stone. "Hey, big man, did you hear all that? Your brother's a rock star." I dig through my pockets, turning them inside out until I find a guitar pick, then set it on his stone, along with the carnation. "I miss you, kid."

I don't know what else to say, and every time I try to say anything, my throat closes up. So I think about all the things I've wanted to share with him over the years, but couldn't. I imagine all those things big brothers do for their little brothers: teaching him guitar, sneaking him into my shows when he was underage, serving him his first beer, giving him advice about girls. I imagine him growing up and starting a family of his own. *I'll bet he'd have been a good dad.* I imagine all those things he never got to try, all the love he never got to experience, all the life that went unlived.

And I cry. It's not a very manly thing to do but fuck it. I miss him. For as long as this little kid could walk, he'd been my shadow. He followed me everywhere. He copied every move I made. He adored and emulated me, and I hated it. I complained constantly about it. But now I miss it; I'd give anything to have my annoying little brother back. Like a phantom limb that's been hacked off, I still feel him there, my little shadow, my biggest fan.

My knees hurt. The solid ground covered with nuts and twigs presses against the fabric of my jeans and into the sensitive flesh below my kneecaps. I like the pain it causes. I need it. I focus on it, revel in it. It's fitting, the same ground which covers my family should leave its mark on me too.

I kiss my palm and press it to Tommy's stone, then struggle to stand again. I walk to the far side of Tommy's grave to visit my dad. This time, I stay on my feet. I stand above him, looking down at his stone. I twirl the fake lily in my fingers, hesitant to place it on his grave.

He doesn't deserve a flower. Giving him this lily would suggest that I forgive him, and he doesn't deserve my forgiveness.

All I have for my father today is all I've had for him since that terrible night: anger, blame, shame. I stare down at his grave and see the tomb of my brother's killer, my mother's murderer. It's deceptive, the sight of the three stones together. They all look the same—same color, same shape, same size, same end date—but they aren't the same, are they? Mom and Tommy died as victims, Dad, their victimizer. I can't forgive him for that.

But as I stand here, staring at the green grass that covers the six feet of soil separating me from what remains of my father, I see myself there. Every year as I've grown older, I've seen more of him in me. It's his face I see in the mirror every morning. It's his reflection that stares back from the surface of every shot of whiskey, at the bottom of every bottle. Like me, he loved music. He played the drums. He had plans, dreams, goals. Then along came a mistake named Jake, and Dad had to sell his drums to pay for a crib.

Last spring, when I turned thirty-two, I became older than my father ever was. That night, as I drank a shot of Jack Daniels, I thought of him, of his fate, and it hadn't made me angry. For the first time since the wreck, I felt sorry for him.

And that's what I feel again, now. I close my eyes and stop seeing that dreaded date of death. Instead, I see my dad's proud face when he bought me my first guitar with money he made working overtime shifts at the power plant. I see the man who cheered me on from the stands when I played wide receiver in peewee football. I remember the guy who tickled my mom until she squealed, then kissed her until she sighed.

When I remember him in those moments, I can see past the monster who killed my family; I can see my dad. I squat down next to my father's grave and lay the lily under his name, then do the one thing I never thought I could: I forgive him.

· · ·

On the road back to the casino, Granny T is kind enough to make small talk, filling the strained silence with inane details about a new restaurant in town and church choir gossip. But just as we're about to turn into the casino parking lot, she clears her throat and admits, "I talked to Lisa..."

Oh Jesus Christ, I know where this is going.

"She and Eli were excited to hear you're in town. She says she's cooking a big dinner, and you're more than welcome to come. You can bring your Scottish friends too."

I'd laugh if I weren't so pissed off. I should have known better than to trust the town crier to keep my visit on the down low. I glare over at Granny T, but she studiously ignores me, paying close attention to the road. She doesn't even glance at me when she adds, "It'd mean a lot to your uncle to see you. And your cousins too."

My cousins? I didn't even know I had cousins. Sure, there were always distant relations we called "cousins" for simplicity's sake, but Mom didn't have any siblings, and Dad's only brother had been an aimless Casanova when I knew him, always getting handsy with some blonde or another.

Why has it never occurred to me that I've grown up to be just like him? For as long as I can remember, I've been the big Indian with my hands all over some pretty little blonde.

When Granny T signals and turns into the casino parking lot, I spot Uncle Eli. He looks different, but the same. He was always big, but he's bigger now, with a gut that pushes out over his jeans and a pair of bright red suspenders that hold it all together. He's still got his long braid, though these days it's more gray than black. He's aged in the face, too, his dark eyes bracketed by wrinkles. He's talking to Bruce— the army guy and the navy guy trading war stories. Beside the van, Sean and Glenn kick a soccer ball with two little Indian boys who could easily be mistaken for Tommy and me twenty years ago.

Eli smiles broadly as we approach, and when he does, he looks like his old self, just like Dad. It fills me with sorrow that Dad never got to grow old like Eli.

"Well good goddamn, Gayle was right about you. You're no boy anymore. Look at you, *Utana Yona*, all grown up." Those are his first words to me since that night at the hospital, when his beer-battered breath warmed the side of my face as he repeated, "Calm yourself, *Usdi Yona*."

I let him hug me. It's one of those manly hugs that involves very little actual touching, mostly just a hearty pat on the back. When we step apart, I respond with the only thing that comes to mind. "Uncle Eli."

Unaffected by my awkwardness, Eli starts to speak animatedly, going loud enough that the guys stop their ball game and come over to join us. Aidan, too, comes over from a bench by the building, where he's been reading my copy of *On the Road*. "My wife's cooking up a feast. It's Indian taco night"—the two little boys jump up and down, hooting and hollering—"with the best damn frybread in Swain County."

"Them's fightin' words." I smile despite myself.

Granny T gets indignant when she defends her family honor. "No one fries it up better than a Toineeta, Jacob Sixkiller, and you well know that."

"What's frybread?" Sean asks, his eyes glimmering with excitement at the prospect of yet more home-cooked food.

I glance at the guys, who look ravenous despite having gorged themselves on Margie's lunch only a few hours ago. It would be a crime to deny them Indian tacos. "Well, I guess you're about to find out."

We all pile into my uncle's van. Bruce sits up front with Eli so they can continue their conversation. I sit in the back, hoping to be alone with my thoughts, but my two cousins climb into the seat beside me and eye me with curiosity.

"Who are you?" the bigger one asks, with the little one peeking at me around his brother.

"I'm your cousin, Jake. And you are?"

"I'm Hezekiah, but you can call me Kiah"—Dad's name—"and he's Thomas."

Eli glances at me in the rearview mirror, but I focus my attention on my cousins. "You were named after my dad. And you were named after my brother."

Little cousin Tommy gives me a wide grin, and just like his namesake, he's missing his two front teeth. *Shit.* I try to smile even as my eyes water. Clearing my throat, I ask, "How old are you guys?"

"I'm ten," Kiah answers for himself, then answers for his brother too, "and he's six. Is it true you're a rock star? Dad says you're a big deal and you make us proud, but I've never heard of you."

"Yeah, you're right, Kiah. I'm nothing special."

Uncle Eli turns onto the road to Sixkiller Hollow, and my breath steals out of my lungs. I didn't even know the house was still in the family. Technically, it had been Granny's house. She'd inherited it when Gramps died, and he'd inherited it from his father before him, but it had also been the house where I lived for the first fourteen years of my life.

I'm glad it's still in the family, but the thought of coming back to this place sends a shiver through me. I clench my fists in my lap and steady my breathing as we take another left onto the pitted dirt road. It's a bumpy route, and I steel my posture to keep from bouncing. At my side, my cousins giggle and bop around like it's their favorite roller-coaster ride.

From the outside, the house hasn't changed much. It's still painted a pretty shade of blue—like the sky in winter, Granny used to say. The yard is well tended, the garden thriving, with bright red and green tomatoes ripening on the vine. On the wide front porch, someone has hung several flowering plants, and there are a couple new rocking chairs next to the old ones.

I hear the hauntingly familiar yawn and slap of the screen door open and close as Lisa Toineeta, now Sixkiller, comes out to greet us all. She's still a looker—no surprise there, the Toineeta women were always gorgeous—small and curvy, with a mane of dark hair that flows down to her waist and a smile that covers most of her face. Her big eyes sparkle when she takes in the sight of her myriad dinner guests.

Ignoring everyone else, she cuts a line across the yard to me and gives me a warm hug. "Oh Jake, look at you. You're even more handsome than I imagined and so dang tall. Goodness, you're taller than Eli." She pulls away and shields her eyes from the setting sun as she looks me over. "Bet you're breakin' all the girl's hearts there in Texas."

"I'm semiretired from the heartbreaker game, actually."

"He's in love." Glenn gives a nice Irish lilt to the word *love*. I scowl at him.

"Is that so?" Lisa elbows me in the gut when she adds, "Lucky girl. Nothin' beats a Sixkiller in the sack."

I cough with surprise, and Eli raises a brow at his wife.

Lisa winks at her husband, then turns to speak to the lot of us. "You boys hungry?"

"Yes, ma'am," comes the chorus.

Inside, the house smells like ground chuck and frybread, and the scent guides most of the group directly toward the dining room. I linger to look around.

The house has changed so much. I hardly recognize it, and that makes this easier somehow. It's brighter now that the dark wood paneling has been removed, the walls painted a crisp white. Instead of the heavy, beige curtains, sheer white drapes let in the waning light of the evening sky. The big boxy TV is replaced with a more contemporary unit, and beneath it is a PlayStation, its controller cords tangled on the floor like the tentacles of an octopus. Two boy-sized sleeping bags stretch out across the wood floors, which were once covered with avocado green carpet.

Dozens of family photos dot the wall behind a black leather sofa, five generations of Sixkillers peering out from the assortment of frames. Three matching photos in identical cherrywood frames are centered in the middle of the family gallery.

All three pictures feature two young boys arm in arm out beside the old hickory tree behind the house. The photo on the left is the oldest; it's Eli and my dad when they were probably about twelve, each with a fishing pole and holding up a trout they'd caught in the river behind the house. The photo on the right is the most recent, my cousins Kiah and Tommy giggling as they eat ice cream together. It's the middle photo, though, that catches the breath in my lungs. It's me and my brother, my arm draped over Tommy's shoulders as we laugh at a joke long forgotten.

Overwhelmed with emotion, I turn away. Eli watches me from the doorway to the dining room. He says nothing, his expression sad like he feels it too, then goes into the other room. I wait a beat, taking another moment for myself before I follow him in to dinner.

The one thing that appears to be unchanged about the house is Granny's old dining table. I stare down at the familiar oak surface and recognize most of the dings and scratches in the honey-colored wood. I remember all the times I traced the pock marks with my little fingers while pouting at my mom, refusing to eat my peas. I trace a finger over one of those scars now, feeling the smooth edges of the old wood with my thickly calloused fingers.

At the head of the table, where my dad used to sit, Eli leads us in prayer. He does it in Cherokee first, then English for the guests. When Eli finishes, he passes around plates stacked high with fluffy deep-fried dough bread, as well as bowls of ground beef, beans, cheese, sour cream, shredded lettuce, and diced tomatoes—all the usual fixins' for Indian tacos.

Lisa, sitting where my mom once did, regales her guests with tales of growing up as one of Granny T's five daughters. How their hands would smell for days after digging up wild onions in the spring. Or the time she and her sister Jena were tasked with killing a chicken for that night's dinner, and the thing got up and ran headless around the yard, spurting blood everywhere.

Somewhere along the way, I relax and enjoy myself along with everyone else. Lisa's storytelling has taken the pressure off this homecoming. The food is a great distraction too. I can't remember the last time I ate frybread, and *goddamn,* I've missed it. Bruce and the Irish boys like it, too, devouring every last bite.

When we've eaten our fill, our bellies aching with laughter, Lisa stands and announces, "I hope you boys have saved room for dessert. I've made something special for tonight. I'm told it was Jake's favorite."

All eyes turn to me as Lisa disappears into the kitchen, only to return a moment later carrying a hot pot of grape dumplings, no doubt Granny Sixkiller's famous recipe. I'm nearly brought to tears at the scent and struggle to swallow my last bite of frybread around the lump in my throat.

Lisa ladles the piping hot dumplings into small bowls and passes them around. When little Kiah hands me my portion, he asks, "What's it like to sleep on a bus, Jake?" Of all the "your cousin is a rock star" stories they've heard tonight, the detail which most fascinates the boys is the bus.

"Uh..." I blink at his wide-eyed expectation, with absolutely no clue how to answer his question.

Fortunately, I don't have to. With a lilting tone in his voice, Aidan tells a story about the time I fell out of my bunk and rolled all the way up the aisle to land in the front passenger seat beside Bruce. The story is only about 5 percent true; it was Sean who fell out of his bunk, and he didn't roll anywhere, he just laid there complaining of a pain in his arse. But the truth of the story hardly matters when Aidan is telling it, his eyes as wide as his smile, his arms flopping around dramatically. Then Glenn takes over, spinning a yarn about the time the back wheel came off the bus, and we all had to chase it down the road.

I am in awe. The guys are covering for me. In some sort of silent solidarity, they've recognized I'm in no condition to talk, so they've huddled defensively around me. It's touching.

Cousins Kiah and Tommy are absolutely enchanted by their stories, and the boys' laughter, blended with the smells and flavors of the food, melt the years away. I close my eyes, and instead of sitting at this table at the ripe age of thirty-two—surrounded by an estranged family I haven't known for nearly two decades, and a band I've only known for two weeks—I'm a kid again.

I'm finally big enough my feet touch the floor in the tall ladderback chair. Sitting next to me, Tommy's legs still dangle, and he's excitedly kicking his feet for some reason. With one leg aimed toward my chair and one aimed at Dad's, he's driving us both nuts with the rhythmic slap of his little socked feet against the legs of our seats. I grumble and whine, irritated. Mom tries to hide a grin as Dad puts on a stern expression and clasps his big palm over Tommy's shoulder. Granny pauses from her work of dishing out food to see what Dad will say to Tommy to make him stop.

"Now, Tommy, little boys with ants in their pants don't get dessert."

"Why?" Tommy asks, his brow furrowing with horror at the prospect of being denied the sweet treat.

Dad has to force himself not to smile as he calmly explains, "It's the grapes. They make the ants go crazy. Trust me, son, you don't want crazy ants in your pants."

At this, Tommy explodes with excitement. His legs kick even harder at the chairs as he wiggles and shimmies in his seat. He scratches at his whole body like it itches, all the while, squealing, "Crazy ants, crazy ants, crazy ants."

I can't help it; I laugh. As irritated as I am with the little brat, his crazy ants dance is pretty danged funny. Mom and Granny laugh too, and finally Dad joins in as well. Tommy scratches at the imaginary ants as they march all the way up to his shoulders and then down his arm. When they reach the tips of his fingers, he reaches over and touches me. I scream with laughter, then begin to wiggle and shake like they're on me now too.

I reach over and touch Mom's shoulder; she squeals and begins to wiggle as well. Always the copycat, Tommy takes his cue from me and touches Dad. We all pause for a minute, really impressed with Dad's crazy ants dance, which is far more elaborate than any of ours. When Dad reaches for Granny, she bats at his hand with a serving spoon, like his touch is deadly—

"Excuse me," I say as I rocket to my feet and exit the room. I need a moment to myself. I hurry to the bathroom and splash water on my face. I grab for one of the hand towels in the old familiar place, but instead of Grandma's little pink towels, which matched the antislip butterfly decals in the tub, they're beige now. The butterfly decals are gone too.

Everything I knew of this place is gone, and yet here I am, a stranger to the people who live here now. I even feel like a stranger to myself, with memories so real I can practically touch them but so far removed, it's like I've stolen them from someone else's life.

At some point long ago, I divorced myself from the person I was in this place. I put all of who I was—my past, my family, my heritage—in a box and locked it away. And now, as these memories surface and bombard me, I don't recognize them. Or rather, I don't recognize my place among them. It's me who doesn't belong. The memories, like the ghosts, have been here all along. I'm the interloper.

I look at my reflection in the mirror, and all I see is my father. I close my eyes and open them again, and still the reflection shows my dad, not me. I reach toward the glass to touch the likeness of a face that isn't mine—

"You all right in there?" Uncle Eli's voice shakes me back to reality.

I blink and blink again. I take a deep breath in and out. "Yeah. I'm fine."

I listen for the sound of his heavy steps marching a path of retreat away from me. But instead, only a bated silence hovers as he waits for me to come out of the bathroom. It's a standoff. I surrender and open the door.

Eli is there, leaning against the wall, his arms crossed over his big chest. He stares at the floor, just beyond the tips of his cowboy boots. I appreciate the courtesy of avoided eye contact.

"Listen," he stammers, then clears his throat, still staring at the floor. "I know this is a lot for you, but...I was hoping we'd get a chance to talk. Is that—"

"Yeah. Whatever. Sure." I aimed to express a tone of numb indifference, but the shakiness in my words betrays me.

Eli leads me down the hall. I don't look into any of the doors. I don't want to see the bedroom where Tommy and I once slept. I don't want to remember the way Granny's bedroom was painted her favorite shade of green and decorated with white lace. Eli goes to the big room at the end of the hall, where Mom and Dad once slept, and presumably where Eli and Lisa sleep now.

How can Eli sleep in his dead brother's room, his dead mother's home? I flinch and shake the cruel thoughts from my head. Eli pauses at the door and looks back at me, then frowns. "Jesus, Jake, I'm sorry. If this is too much for you?"

"I'm fine."

"No, we can take this outside, if that'd be better—"

"I'm fine," I say again, then push past him into the bedroom. This room, like all the others, is unrecognizable. The walls are a deep burgundy, and the bed is one of those big sleigh types, with more pillows than anyone could possibly need. It looks nothing like the peach and ivory bedroom my dad worked hard to buy for my mom when I was twelve. Back then, the bed was only a queen-sized mattress with squeaky springs. Now, the thing is as big as a studio apartment. I take the liberty of sitting on the side that had been my dad's, and there is no squeak, no sound at all.

Across the room, Eli takes a spot near the closet, the old louvered closet doors replaced by mirrored sliders now. I have to look away— not liking the sight of my reflection, so much like Dad's, in this room, on this bed.

"What would you like to discuss, Uncle?" I'm pleased by the sound of my voice, solid and sure; like a man, not a boy.

Eli slides away from the wall and comes to sit on the bed beside me, staring at the floor between his boots as he finally speaks. "Listen, Jake, I know you're angry, and you have every right to be. I didn't do right by you, and I'm sorry about that."

"Sorry about what? That you left?" I glare at him. "Not even a week after we put them in the ground, you fucking left."

Eli clinches his jaw. "I know, and it was wrong, but—"

"But what, man? In life there are the people who leave, and there are the ones who stay. And it's the ones who stay that matter."

"I regret leaving. I do. But..." Eli pauses and swallows hard. At least I'm not the only one close to tears here. "I had to go. I would have been no good to you if I'd stayed. I was a drunk, Jake." He rubs at a frayed spot on his jeans. "I was broken. I'd just lost my brother—"

"So did I!" I yell so loudly, the conversation in the other room stops. I take a deep breath before continuing, more quietly this time. "In one night, I lost my entire family. Then a few days later, my uncle fucks off to California and never looks back. You didn't even come back for Granny's funeral—"

"I know."

"Your own mother—"

"I know."

"I said goodbye to her, alone, and you know what? I was too little to be a pallbearer. Greg's dad had to help me."

Eli shakes his head as he whispers, "Jesus."

"It should have been you—"

"I know, God, I know—"

"You should have been there for me. Or, at the very least, you should have there for *her*. But you weren't."

Eli's breath hisses out of him like a deflating balloon. "I know."

"Look, Eli, I'm glad you got your shit together. Lisa and the boys are great, and I'm happy for you. But you and me, we're not okay, and we never will be."

Eli clenches his jaw, like he's holding back the words he wants to say. When he speaks, his voice is little more than a whisper. "Did you really want me to stick around? Would you have preferred to live with your drunk uncle instead of out west in that big white-boy house on the other side of the boundary? You know as well as I do, if I'd been here, the tribe wouldn't have let you go."

It's true. As angry as I've always been at Eli for leaving, it was his absence that made moving in with Greg's family possible. If I'd had any family in Cherokee—aside from Granny Sixkiller in the nursing home— the tribe's social workers would have pushed for me to stay with family and within the community. Generally, I agree this is a good policy. But in my case, I desperately wanted to leave, and Eli's departure was the only thing that made my exit possible.

"*Utana Yona*, losing your family...I know how much that hurt you, and if I'd been any kind of a man, I'd have stuck around to help you deal with it, but..."

But what?

"But I lost my brother that night, too, my twin. There wasn't a single day of my life that he wasn't there, and then...he was gone, and all I had were bottles and pills to fill the void he left. I should have been a better man, for you and for Mom, but I wasn't strong, not then. I joined the navy as a way to find my strength, to make something of myself. It took a lot of work, but... I've been sober for seventeen years now."

"Good for you."

Eli exhales a long, slow breath. "I carry a lot of guilt, Jake, a lot of regret. How I did you wrong tops that list, but that night fucked me up too. I still...some nights I can't sleep...thinking back to that moment when we found you and Tommy on the floor..."

Eli's voice catches, and I go rigid at the memory of what Eli is describing—his arms wrapped around my chest as he tells me to be calm, as if the idea of remaining calm while my brother died right before my eyes was remotely possible.

He continues, "I know what it is to lose a brother. I didn't know that was your goodbye. I didn't know I was taking away your goodbye. I thought the doctors could help him. I didn't know..."

The watery, shaky sound in his voice guts me. This man has been as haunted by that night as I have.

Something inside me breaks. The anger drains out of me like a leak from a dam. In its place is emptiness, a hollow sadness.

"I failed you, Jake, and I will never be able to apologize enough. But I want to try and make things right with you. I want to be in your life in any way you'll let me. I want to show you the love and family I didn't show you when I should have."

I don't trust my voice, so I say nothing.

"I've wanted to reach out to you for a long while but didn't have a way to contact you. When Kiah was born, you were the first person I wanted to talk to. I thought of your dad on the day you were born. Lord, I've never seen him look more proud or more terrified. He held you like you were made of glass, like he thought he might break you." Eli smiles a little at the memory. "I never understood that, not until I was holding my own son. The joy of that first moment is...it's incredible, but then there's this terror, this fear that I might fail him, that I won't be the man he needs me to be. God, the weight of that. I thought of you and how I failed you, and I just wanted to hear your voice, you know? I wanted to know you'd grown up okay, despite me and despite...everything. I think maybe having kids of my own made me realize just how badly I failed my brother's son, and I want to make it right, if that's even possible."

I don't know what to say. It's too much to process. I feel a bone-deep exhaustion as the weight of all I've experienced today presses down on me.

Clearly sensing I've had enough of the heart-to-heart talk, Eli sets his hands on his thighs and exhales a deep breath. But apparently, we're not quite finished with the family share time. "Listen, I...uh...I have some things for you."

Eli lumbers to his feet, crosses to the closet, and rummages around the top shelf until he finds an old cardboard box and pulls it down. On the side, my name is scrawled in Eli's handwriting. He sets it on the bed between us. I think he's waiting for me to start digging through it, but I don't want to touch it. I stare at the thing like whatever's inside might bite.

After a moment, Eli opens the top flaps and starts to pull items out. "Mostly it's a lot of photos I thought you might want. I'll let you go through those later. But I wanted to show you a couple things in here I thought you ought to have."

I blink several times like I might cry as Eli pulls out an old finger-woven belt made of blue and white yarn.

"This was your dad's stomp sash."

I recognize it immediately but hesitate to touch the threadbare garment, like it will disintegrate in my hands.

"You may not remember this, but when you were little your dad would carry you on his hip as he'd sing and dance, trying to teach you the songs."

I do remember. I remember everything about those magical nights that stretched long past my usual bedtime. I remember Dad looping the sash across his chest, the ends tied at his waist. Mom would strap her turtle rattles onto her legs under her long skirt, and they'd smile at each other, young and in love, as they'd walk toward the fire, ready to join the dance.

I can still hear the rich, resonant sound of the men's voices as they sang the songs up into the night sky, and the hypnotic rhythm of the tortoiseshell rattles the women used to keep the beat with their steps. I can still smell the fire. I remember being mesmerized by its glow and flicker as I caught glimpses of it between the men's legs and the women's skirts. The flames of that central fire like a living thing, twisting and twirling up to the heavens, moving with the dancers as if one of them, then raining down a shower of tiny embers that glowed like fireflies.

"Kiah would want you to have it," Uncle Eli says and hands the belt to me.

I touch it like it's sacred, a relic, carefully running the material between my fingers. Dumbly, I say, "There aren't any Stomp grounds in Austin."

"Well, maybe you could go up to Oklahoma or come back here for a visit."

I nod absently.

Eli draws my attention back to the present when he reaches back into the box and pulls out a jewelry box to hand over to me. I hold my breath as I flip it open, and inside are two gold bands. Dad's is slightly wider, while Mom's is slim and adorned with a small diamond.

I can't contain myself any longer. Tears fill my eyes and spill over, and I cuss myself for showing so much emotion. But when I glance over at Eli, he's wiping tears away too. It's the most emotion I've ever seen him display. Eli was always the tough guy. Dad was the lover, and Eli was the fighter. The Eli I knew then is so different from the man here with me now.

"You know," Eli clears his throat. "Your dad was in love with your mom for as long as I can remember. Even when we were kids, he was always mooning over her. If you dig a little deeper"—he points at the box between us—"there are a couple of sappy love songs he wrote about her when we were...twelve, I think, or thirteen."

Part of me wants to dig out the lyrics and read them, but I'm not sure how much more of this walk down memory lane I can handle tonight. So instead, I gently close the jewelry box lid and set it back in the cardboard box. When I do, I spot something shiny glinting in the light. I reach in and carefully pull out a folded piece of red felt with several merit badges sewn on. Tommy's Cherokee Scouts medallion— a small brass disk adorned with a bright red arrowhead—catches my eye and stops the breath in my lungs.

"He was so proud of that thing." Eli grins out of the corner of his mouth.

"I remember. He wore that sash around everywhere, strutting like he was an army general."

The tears come too fast to stop. I hunch my shoulders in as I stare down at Tommy's little merit sash. At this moment, I feel his absence more acutely than I have in years, decades.

"I'm sorry," Eli says as he lays his palm on my shoulder. He clears his throat before continuing, "I know this is a lot."

"Yeah." I wipe my eyes. *It's a lot.* When I woke up in Atlanta this morning, I had no idea what today had in store for me, but I certainly wasn't anticipating the day I've had.

After a moment, I compose myself, then shrug off the heavy memories. I carefully lay Tommy's merit badge sash back inside the box, then close the flaps, neatly packing all those emotions back inside...for now. With a stoic nod and a gusty exhale, I stand and tuck the box under my arm. Eli stands too, and together we walk back out to the dining room.

There, Lisa holds court. Her boys have fallen asleep, their heads resting atop their arms, folded on the table. The three Irishmen and the war vet, though, are all laughing at something she's said.

It's Glenn who asks, "How do you know it will be another boy?"

Lisa, her back to us as we remain in the doorway, laughs animatedly. "Oh honey, the Sixkillers are always boys. Your friend Jake was one of two boys, Eli and Jake's dad were twin boys, Eli and Kiah's dad was one of four boys, and their granddaddy was one of..." Lisa glances at us over her shoulder, beseeching Eli for assistance as she tells her story.

"Six sons," Eli offers.

"Six. Yikes." Lisa laughs again, and I enjoy the sound of it. Lisa looks happy, really happy, and Eli too. When she gently presses her palm to her abdomen, I start to put together the pieces of the story we've walked in on. I look to Eli for confirmation.

He says quietly, so only I can hear, "We're going to call him Jacob."

In that moment, whatever remaining hostility I have toward my uncle melts away. I recognize in him the same thousand-yard stare and battle-hardened heart as my own. But I can also see the good man he's become. The man I'd needed then is here now, and this time, he's not letting go. In that moment, I do what I've been doing a lot today: I forgive him.

Aidan suggests we need to hit the road. It's long past nightfall and time to head to Charlotte for tomorrow night's show. Lisa insists on wrapping up some leftovers for us, and no one complains. Loaded up with food, Eli drives us back to the casino, where our bus is still parked in the lot. When my mates have all carried their spoils onto the bus, Eli and I take a moment to say our farewells. I press a torn piece of paper into his hand with my phone number and email address. Hell, I even give him the details of the Nebulous Myspace page.

He smiles wide, then rummages through the van to find a pen and a fast-food receipt. On the back, he writes down his number and pushes it into my palm. "Call me anytime. And our door is always open to you. Hell, the house is as much yours as it is mine."

We nod and he comes in for a hug. This time, it's a real hug. When we step away, both clearing our throats and wiping our eyes, I collect my box of memories and back away toward the bus door, grinning slightly when I say, "*Stiyu, Edutsi.*" *Be strong, Uncle.*

He nods and says, "*Dodadagohvi, Gvdutsi gvtlogi.*" *Until we meet again, Nephew.*

We don't have a word for "goodbye" in our language, and a goodbye would be too final anyway. I feel deep in my soul we will meet again, and that thought fills me with warmth.

• • •

After helping Bruce navigate to the interstate toward Charlotte, I retire to my bunk. It's quiet, just the hum of the wheels on the road to lull us to sleep. But I'm not tired. I reach into the box of memories and pull out the jewelry box with the two wedding rings. I brush my thumb across the shiny gold metal, then slide them on. Dad's ring fits me. Mom's fits my pinky finger. But it doesn't feel right. No one should wear these but them.

I don't want to tuck them back into the box though, and in a moment of genius, an idea grabs me. I pull my duffel bag from the foot of my bunk and dig for my necklaces; I'm pretty sure I packed either the bullet or the razorblade. In a side pouch, I find one and pull it out.

Fumbling with the clasp, I dump the razor blade pendant back into the duffle and carefully fish Mom's and Dad's rings onto the strand. I like the tinkling sound they make as they tumble together down the chain. Then I dig through the big box again and come up with Tommy's merit badge sash. I unfasten the small safety pin that attaches his shiny brass Cherokee Scout medal and string it onto the necklace as well.

I slip the chain over my head, letting it fall against my chest. It looks a bit funny, the gold bands on the silver chain—I'll need to buy a gold chain when I get home—but it feels right having these precious keepsakes of my family so close to my heart. It's a strange sensation, actually, and—

The curtain to my bunk sweeps open, and I yelp with surprise as Sean pokes his head into my space.

"Dude, knock first whydon'tcha? I could have been naked."

"As if we haven't all seen your knob by now. Learn the proper way to wrap a towel, *dude*."

I scowl. "What do you want?"

Sean clears his throat. "I just want to thank you for today. I don't know your whole life story, and I'm not asking for it, but I know enough to know today was no' easy for ye, and I appreciate you letting us come along. We've been on the road for almost a quarter of a year. I'm real fecking homesick. So the food, the conversation, it was quite nice. Thank you."

From the bunk above me, Glenn leans down to pop his face into view, upside down. "Aye, what he said. T'anks."

Aidan pushes his curtain aside from across the aisle and agrees.

"Yeah, sure, no problem," I try to shrug it off, but the truth is I owe them too. I owe them for all the times they filled the void with conversation while I fell apart inside. "Thank you guys too."

"For what?"

"For...everything."

"Aye," Sean winks, "Yer welcome *for everything*." He chuckles as he wanders off to the back of the bus.

I close my curtain and curl onto my side. But I'm still wide awake. I contemplate calling Nicole. It's late, but—

My phone chimes to signal the arrival of a text. I scramble to see it's from Nicole. It's like she can read my mind. I flip my phone open and the breath whooshes out of my lungs as I read her message. Just three words. Three little syllables: **I miss you.**

That's all it says, and it's just enough to crack my face wide open with a smile.

I dial her number as I rocket out of bed and make a dash for the privacy of the bathroom.

It's occupied. *Fuck.*

Just as I realize I have no safe haven, Nicole answers. "How's life on the road?"

I look around the back-lounge area, seeking out the farthest corner from prying ears. "Good, it's good."

"What'd you do with your day off?"

"I went home, actually," I whisper as I sit on the back couch and turn my face toward the window, cupping my hand over my mouth and the receiver. The guys love to rib me about my budding affection for "the lady in red," so I try not to give them more ammunition.

"Why are you whispering?" She laughs and it sounds like music.

"Because," I whisper, "I'm on the bus, and these fuckers are nosy as hell."

"Damn, so I guess that means no phone sex tonight?" she asks, sounding downright disappointed.

"You're killing me," I groan.

"How was home?"

The abrupt subject change catches me by surprise, but I steady my thoughts. "It was...strange. I saw my uncle again for the first time in almost twenty years, and he's...he's a better man than I remember. So..."

"It's nice when people surprise you in a good way, especially family," she says with a wistful tone, and it makes me wonder...

"What's the story with your family? You mentioned they never paid much attention..."

Nicole takes a deep breath in and lets it out in a huff. "Some people just shouldn't have kids, you know? Not because they're bad people, but because they just don't want them. I was a mistake, and I think they expected me to be more grateful they didn't abort me or send me off for adoption."

I feel a bit heartbroken for her. I was a mistake, too, but I never felt unwanted, not for one single day.

"My dad's a photographer, a good one, award winning and all that. But, naturally, that meant he traveled a lot. Even now, when he's supposedly 'retired,' he's always somewhere else. My mom is a therapist who spent a lot of time psychoanalyzing me but didn't spend much time, you know, mothering me."

Damn, that sounds lonely. "How did they react when they learned about"—I stop myself from saying "your rape and the pregnancy" out loud, not wanting to be overheard, and just go with—"everything that happened?"

Nicole knows what I'm referring to. "They don't know. I never told them." She takes a deep breath, then continues. "My dad was in Germany at the time. He was there to photograph the fall of the Berlin Wall, you know, really important shit. And with Mom, I learned early on I couldn't actually talk to her as a daughter would talk to a mother. She was always a doctor, and I was always a patient. And I didn't want to talk to a doctor about it, so I never said anything."

"I'm sorry, Nicole. That sounds lonely."

"I mean..." She clears her throat. "It could have been far worse. I always had a roof over my head, they bought me a car for my sixteenth birthday, and they fully paid for my college tuition. They never molested me or beat me. All told, I was a lot better off than a lot of kids."

"It's not a competition."

"You're right; it's not," she agrees, her voice soft and sweet, "but I've met a lot of kids through the after-school program at the library who remind me that, even as bad as I thought I had it, there's so much worse out there."

That's true for me too. I was orphaned, but I never spent a day in the foster care system. As bad as I had it, it could have been far, far worse.

"I really miss you, Nicole." The words just tumble out of my mouth on a long breath.

"Hey, Nicole," Sean hollers as he comes out of the toilet and makes his way back to his bunk.

I give him the two-finger victory salute, which is apparently considered insulting where he comes from. Nicole laughs, and sighs when she says, "I miss you too, Jake."

I grin and get a little sappy when I ask, "You know what I can't wait to do when I get back?"

"What?" she asks in a naughty tone, clearly expecting some dirty talk.

But I aim to surprise. "I can't wait to make you sigh."

"Not what I was expecting." *Success.*

"There's this spot right at the base of your left ear; every time I kiss you there, you sigh. And, right now, there's nothing I want more than to hear the sound of your sigh."

Silence.

Usually, her silences make me nervous, but something has changed today. I'm not sure if it is a change in her or a change in me, but it's a relief not to panic when she pauses. As if to validate my sense of calm, Nicole lets out a soft sigh, and whispers, "Just one more week."

I sigh and whisper back. "Just one more week, *Quana.*"

"*Quana?*" Nicole repeats.

"It means peach in Cherokee."

"Are you fluent in Cherokee?"

"I used to be. And I think I will be again."

10—Saturday August 6, 2005

In the week since my trip back home, I am recharged, my energy on and off stage amped up to eleven. The catharsis of that emotional day lightened life's burdens enough to put a spring in my step and more power in my playing.

But it's not just me. Since sharing that experience with the guys, we've grown closer, tighter; we're all feeling that magical charge of electricity on stage. I half expected we'd be road weary and worn out by now, but it's the opposite. As we've played our way up the east coast—Charlotte, Richmond, Baltimore, Philly, Boston, and tonight we've come back down to New York City to wrap up—we've become stronger and better with each performance, our starts and stops so synced, the cues are practically telepathic.

Going out on a high note, tonight is my last show with the band. Tomorrow, I return to my old life of playing at three-hundred capacity venues to recognizable crowds while the guys fly back to Dublin to meet Claire, Ian's newborn baby girl, and continue to ride their shooting star of success. A part of me mourns the end of this epic odyssey, but then I remember the wondrous woman who awaits my return home. I grow antsy with anticipation and desperation to see her, to touch her.

The cab rolls to a stop in front of Greg's Time Square hotel, and I pay the man before climbing out and stretching to my full height, staring up at the glass and steel tower before me. I shiver at the sight, terrified of what I might be walking into.

Greg hasn't returned a single phone call since he left for New York almost three weeks ago. Yesterday, I finally relented and called Kate, Greg's assistant/ex-girlfriend, and was surprised to learn Greg is not in Manhattan on business. In fact, he requested all his vacation time in one lump sum to nurse his injured wife back to health after her car accident.

That lie sets my nerves on edge. Kate is clearly concerned too. She offered to help me find him. Posing as his assistant— technically, not a lie—she called every five-star hotel in Manhattan until she found where he was holed up. And now here I stand.

Unease twists my stomach into knots as the elevator takes me to one of the top floors. I find the room number Kate gave me near the end of the hall, a Do Not Disturb sign dangling from the door handle. I disturb, knocking incessantly for what feels like hours until Greg finally swings the door open and greets me with an angry snarl. He looks me up and down, then mumbles something under his breath as he allows me entrance into the suite.

My relief at finding my friend still alive is short-lived. He looks terrible. He's mostly naked, wearing only a pair of black boxer briefs that look like they were yanked on one-handed. And, when he turns to lead me into the room, I see a set of angry, red scratches that run the length of his back and disappear beneath the waistband of his underwear. I'm starting to understand why it took Greg so long to answer the damn door.

The hotel room is as disheveled as the man. The floor and flat surfaces are littered with room service trays topped with dirty dishes, cutlery and partially consumed meals as well as an impressive collection of empty liquor bottles.

I sense movement from the corner and glance over at a brunette sprawled across a chaise lounge near the balcony doors. She looks a little too much like Ari, and she's doing a piss-poor job of covering her nudity. She has a freshly fucked air, and the reddened hand marks on her breasts tell me more than I ever wanted to know about Greg's sexual predilections.

I turn away, and Greg flops down on the couch. He picks up a credit card that he uses to cut lines of cocaine onto the glass-top coffee table, then leans forward to snort a line up one side of his nose and another up the other. Still sniffing and pinching his nose, he offers me the snuff straw he's been using. I try to say, "no, thank you," but all that comes out is a judgmental grunt. Sure, in college, we both did plenty of partying, but that was over a decade ago, and Greg's usage was always recreational—nothing resembling the wasteland I've walked into here.

The woman by the window makes a big display of getting on her feet. She yawns loudly to capture my attention, then stretches her arms over her head to capture my gaze. When she has both, she stands and saunters across the room. She sits on Greg's lap, and he grabs a couple fistfuls of her hips as she leans forward and snorts the last two lines of coke. When she stands, stark-raving naked, sniffing her nose, she eyes me. She's telegraphing her message loud and clear: threesomes welcome.

I roll my eyes, and Greg frowns at her, mumbling, "Put on some clothes."

With a bored sigh, the woman saunters off to some other room in the suite, leaving Greg and me alone.

"Who the hell is that?" The first words I've spoken to Greg in three weeks, not counting the voicemails.

Greg shrugs. "Some girl."

"Yeah, I could see that."

"Met her at a bar. We worked out a deal—blow for blow." He lets out a hollow laugh, then adds, "Get it?"

"Jesus, dude, could you be more cliché?"

Greg narrows his eyes at me, then turns his attention back to his drugs. He shakes more powder onto the table and organizes it into neat little rows. "Why are you here?"

"That's all you got for me? I haven't seen or heard from you since I drove you to the fucking airport...in fucking Texas...three fucking weeks ago, and all you got is, 'Why are you here?' "

"What'd you expect, a Macy's parade? It's a legit question. Why are you here?"

"Have you not listened to any of the voicemails I've left for you?"

Greg shrugs.

"Have I done something to piss you off, or have you been body snatched by a complete prick?"

Greg snorts more cocaine.

Body snatched by a complete prick, clearly. I sit in the chair opposite him, and try to connect with his bloodshot eyes to see what's going on in his head.

Greg tries to ignore me but grows increasingly agitated with each passing moment, his gaze bouncing between me and his drugs, his body moving in twitchy little tics. When he's had enough, he sneers and angrily spits as he says, "What? Fuck, man, what do you want?"

"Well, I wanted to spend time with my best friend, but he's not here."

I'd had such plans for tonight. I wanted to connect with Greg, bring him backstage for the show, and tell him about my life since we last talked—the tour, the trip home, Nicole. I'd wanted to share this, the last night of the greatest tour of my life, with my best friend. Sitting here now, facing off with the coked-out douchebag who's body snatched him, my shoulders slump with exhaustion.

"Talked to Kate this morning."

Greg flinches at the sound of her name but says nothing.

"She was surprised when I told her I thought you'd come here for work. Seeing as how you asked for all vacation time to care for Ari."

Greg shrugs.

"What is wrong with you? Why did you lie to me?" I ask. The fucker glances at me, then shrugs again, and the gesture has me red with rage. "Shrug one more time, and I will break your goddamn nose. I swear to fucking Christ, Greg."

Greg scowls.

At least it's not a shrug. I take a deep breath to calm my anger. "Come on, man, talk to me."

"About what?"

"About why you haven't returned any of my calls or texts for weeks. About why you've holed yourself up in this room with a mountain of blow when your life is back in Austin."

"My life?" Greg scoffs bitterly. "There's nothing for me in Austin."

"Seriously?" I recognize he's going through a rough patch with the separation and all, but... "What am I, chopped liver?"

Greg looks me dead in the eyes and smirks. The fuckwit *smirks*.

"So, your plan is to, what, stay in this room until you've burned through all your money, then let housekeeping discover your bloated corpse on the floor?"

Greg ignores me as he works out his nervous energy, shaping his coke into lines. Then he snorts one into each nostril and bounces to his feet, pacing around the room.

My paper-thin patience shreds to nothing. I rocket to my feet, and as Greg goes to walk past me on his third lap around the room, I grab him by the neck and straight-arm him backward until he hits the wall.

"The fuck is your problem, man?" Greg complains, trying to pry my fingers off himself.

"Excellent question." I get up in his face, angrier than I've ever been with the guy. "What the fuck is *your* problem?"

"Fuck off," he growls at me, his teeth flashing, spittle flying off his words.

The girl who could be Ari emerges from some other room and makes a beeline for the drugs. With one hand still closed around Greg's throat, I snap my fingers to get her attention and shout, "Hey, Tits McGee, get the fuck out of here."

She scoffs, twists her lips into a scowl, and pushes her hip out in a defiant attitude. "But I—"

"Get. The Fuck. Out. Now." I put a little growl in my voice when I add, "Please."

She pauses, staring at me and my hand wrapped around Greg's throat. She's trying to determine how fuck-with-able I am. I give her my most un-fuck-with-able scowl. With a roll of her eyes, she leaves.

When the door slams shut behind Greg's guest, I let go of him and shove. He tumbles to the side, landing halfway on an ottoman and halfway on the floor. While he squirms awkwardly like an upside-down turtle, I jog across the room, grab his bag of blow, and beat feet toward a doorway that leads to a disheveled bedroom. I keep running until I reach the attached bathroom. There I dump the full contents of his stash into the toilet.

That puts the fight back in Greg. In an instant, he's on his feet and chasing me, only to reach me a split second too late. We watch together as the cocaine cascades into the bowl, saturates with water, turns into a mushy paste, and sinks to the bottom.

"You fucking shit!" he explodes with anger, and before I see it coming, he throws a right hook that hits me square in the chin.

The force of the punch knocks me backward, and I hit the wall, seeing stars as my head rings like a bell. I try to shake it off, blink it away, but before I can fully recover, he hits me again. A left jab gets me in the eye. A right uppercut to my ribs knocks the wind from my lungs. I grapple with him, avoiding more blows as I bend over, gasping for air.

He calms a bit, and now it's my turn to rage, Hulk-smash style. I hit him three times in quick succession—chin, eye, and ribs. *Eye for a fucking eye, you ass.*

Greg hits the wall, winded and cupping a hand over his eye. I do too. I take a deep breath to calm down, then offer up some empathy. "Look, man, I get it. Divorce is rough. And losing a woman like Ari…shit, yeah, I get why you're so miserable. But you've got to get your shit together."

"Are you really going to bring up Ari here? Now?"

"She's what this is all about, isn't she?"

"It's always the same with you? Ari, Ari, Ari!" Greg sneers at me.

He doesn't even look human. He's some monstrous version of himself, a Greg-shaped figure formed out of pure vitriol, corrosive and caustic and burning through everything he touches.

"You think I don't know, man?" he snarls.

"Don't know what?"

"That you fucked her."

"*What?*"

"Oh, come on. I'm not stupid."

"Clearly you *are*." I point at the toilet full of his ruined drugs. "You've done so much of that shit it's fried your brain."

He mumbles like a madman, "I told her you were off limits. I told her I wouldn't be able to handle it, but I should've known I couldn't trust you. Always been sniffing around, always inserting yourself into every fucking thing. You were a third wheel in our entire marriage. You're why she left me."

I can't imagine a more devastating accusation than the one he's just leveled at me. When I speak, my voice is surprisingly steady, considering my anger. "I've never fucked Ari, Greg, that's your department. Or it was until you neglected your wife and fucked your assistant, and Ari decided to leave you. That's on you, not me. Don't blame *me* for *your* marriage problems, brother."

"You're not my brother." Greg says it like it's nothing, like he hasn't just delivered a gut punch that hurts worse than any of his actual hits.

I force myself to shake it off. *The guy's coked out of his mind. He's not himself.* I tell myself I won't take it personally as I scowl at the muttering madman in the corner. I can't even look at him anymore, so I leave the bathroom.

In the adjoining bedroom, I find Greg's luggage and start tossing his clothes and shoes into the bag. Greg follows, still muttering like a loon, and each time I grab an item of clothing, he tries to wrestle it away from me. When I've packed his bag, I head for the living area.

Greg grabs my arm to stop me, demanding, "What the hell are you doing with my stuff?"

I yank my arm away and loot the living room, collecting his wallet and room key from the credenza. "Good luck buying more drugs with no wallet, pants, or shoes, asshole."

"Who do you think you are?" Greg charges at me, looking for another fight, but stumbles and stubs his toe on a room service platter on the floor. He falls to his knees but scrambles back up to stop me at the door.

He goes to hit me again, and I dodge, but his fist comes down at my shoulder. Too late, I see the metallic glint of something in his hand. Greg's punch lands awkwardly, and the fork he's got clutched in his fist stabs me at the base of my neck.

Pain shoots through me, excruciating and heartbreaking. I drop Greg's luggage to grab at the fork. I yank it out and stare in abject horror at the polished silver, my blood coating its narrow tines.

"Shit, Jake, I'm sorry."

I've been stabbed. I've been stabbed by my best friend. I've been stabbed by the man I've considered a brother since we were boys. "You stabbed me."

"I...I didn't mean to. I didn't realize I was holding it."

"You stabbed me." I'm stuck, like a skipping record. I throw the fork across the room and cup my hand over the wound, the blood seeps out but doesn't gush. Greg didn't hit anything vital, and yet he's killed something I needed to live.

I look at him. He's as pale as a ghost, and there's a sobriety in his eyes that wasn't there a moment ago. I try to find my friend there, but all I see is a stranger, the asshole who's just *stabbed* me.

"Jake..."

I shoot him a warning look and grab his luggage to leave. Over my bloody shoulder, I issue curt instructions. "I'll return in the morning. Nine o'clock sharp. Be ready."

Greg is smart enough not to try to stop me again. He stands in the doorway of his room, shouting down the hotel hall. "I'm sorry, brother. I'm so sorry."

The elevator doors open, and I step inside. As the doors slide shut, I look up. Greg watches me, a hollow desperation in his expression. He's waiting for me to say something, so I say the only thing that comes to mind. "My brother is dead."

• • •

"Jaysus, the fuck happened to you?" Aidan asks, staring at my battered face and bloody shirt.

"Long story." I stow Greg's shit beside my guitar case. In the bathroom, I pull off my shirt and clean the wound on my shoulder. It's hardly anything to look at: just four little pricks at the base of my neck, the bites of a vampire. The wound probably won't even leave a scar. Yet, I feel ravaged.

Forcing my thoughts away from Greg, I put all my energy into my preshow ritual, needing that routine to center my mind. The comb is in my back pocket, where I always keep it. I set it on the sink rim and yank my hair out of the braids I made this morning. Running the comb through the waves to detangle, I close my eyes. It feels soothing, like a kind touch, the sort of touch I desperately need. *God, I wish I could hug Nicole right now.* I scrape the teeth along the center to form a perfect part. Then, one at a time, I deftly plait each side into a long, tight braid, using leather straps to wrap the tips.

Finished, I stare at myself in the mirror. The long ropes of hair lay neatly over my chest and discreetly disguise the place where my best friend stabbed me. The bruises on my face, however, aren't as easy to conceal. They fuck up my symmetry, which pisses me off. But there's nothing I can do about it now: it's showtime.

I follow the guys out onto the stage for the last time, and that dreary thought brings my mood down even more. As much as I long for home, I don't want this to be over yet. The show is massive, the crowd is going wild, but my heart just isn't in it. My fingers move from rote. My singing is nothing more than habit, honed by weeks of practice. With one eye already swollen shut, I close the other and just work to get through the set.

When the show is over, my job here is done. I feel bereft. On a couch in the green room, sandwiched between Aidan and Glenn, with Sean balancing on one of the arms, I press a cold can of soda to my swollen eye. Beside me, Aidan does all the talking while some cute little music writer with magnificent legs interviews us.

"What's next for Mammoth?" she asks, her bright blue eyes focused on Aidan as she nibbles on the end of her pen.

Aidan turns on the charm when he answers her, and I get the distinct impression he has plans for her later. I watch the exchange with an odd flutter of envy, longing for such simplicity of human interaction. Love 'em and leave 'em has always been my favorite form of contact. Relationships are just too damn hard, and they hurt too damn much. I touch my puffy eye as a reminder of just how much loving someone can hurt.

"Jake." Aidan turns to me as the reporter leaves us, and the rest of the band moves a bit closer too. "We'd like to talk to you about something."

I glance around at the guys' somber faces and pop the top on the can of soda I'd been using to ice my eye. "Listen, I'm sorry about the bruises. I know I must have looked like shit onstage—"

"You must be joking." Glenn shakes his head. "Your face is so feckin' *metal* right now. And when the cut on your neck started bleeding during 'Inside,' I think the whole place had a spontaneous orgasm. Had me laughin' me cacks off."

"What?" I reach up to my neck wound; it has indeed started bleeding again, and it's leaked blood all over my bare chest, staining the chain that holds my parents' rings and Tommy's medal. "Shit."

"You're a metal God, ye gobshite. Stop being so bloody miserable about it," Sean says.

I'm about to say something smartass in reply, but Aidan interrupts. "We want you to join the band."

Stunned, I blink. "What?"

"We want you to join the band," Aidan repeats.

"But what about Ian?"

"Ian's wanted out for a while. He wants to be a family man with Siobhan and the baby." Aidan shrugs. "The road isn't for everyone. Look, the thing is, when we asked you to join us for the tour, it was also an audition of sorts. We're sorry for not telling ya. It's just, we knew we wanted ya, but we needed to be certain. And, well, job's yers if ya like."

Holy fucking shit!

Holy fucking shit! Holy fucking shit! Holy fucking shit!

"But..." Why am I arguing? Just say *yes*, you moron. "I'm not really doom metal. I'm more...gloom, you know?"

Aidan shrugs. "We've never felt that 'doom' classifies us. We're looking to explore new sounds, and we like what you've been writing on the bus. Plus, your vocals are brilliant, and you're one of the most talented guitar players we've ever played with." Aidan says that last part like they're just words, like they don't constitute the most incredible compliment I've ever received.

I choke up a bit when Sean and Glenn both nod in animated agreement. I'm just...so...damned...surprised. I hold my soda up to my bruised eye again, needing something to do with my hands as I process all of this.

"Take your time in thinking it over. We'll no' make an announcement until—"

"Yes." I blurt the word out like it's burning the inside of my mouth. Then, just to make sure we're clear, I affirm, "Fuckin-A, yes!"

And just like that, I'm a member of Mammoth.

In the blink of an eye, my life has changed dramatically—again. Only this time, the change is for the better. Sitting here—half-naked, bruised and battered and coated in blood—I've been reborn into something new, something bigger. From caterpillar to butterfly, from poor little Indian kid to rock star: it's a motherfucking metamorphosis.

I wish my family could see me now. I smile along with my new bandmates, but my smile is sad, bittersweet, and a bit weary. All my life, the good stuff never happened for me, so I'm suspicious. I mean, why would a universe that killed my entire family in one night grant me this boon? *Where's the catch?*

And then I figure it out, the catch. The weight of my mammoth future with Mammoth hits me all at once as I consider the implications to every other part of my life. What will this mean for my future in Austin, my other band, my relationship with my friends, even if our path is already unclear? What about my future with *her*—my green-eyed goddess, my lady in red, my sweet peach? Do I even have a future with her? I'd hoped for the time to find out.

"Wait," I grimace as I turn to Aidan and ask, "does this mean I have to move to Ireland?"

11—Sunday August 7, 2005

I don't bother to knock, just use the keycard to let myself in. Greg is out on the balcony in a bathrobe, smoking a cigarette as he stares at Times Square. He looks surprised to see me, and that pisses me off. I told him I'd be here, and I'm a man of my word.

"Here's your shit." I set his bag down. "You have ten minutes to get dressed and meet me in the lobby. If you're not there, I leave without you."

I turn to go and hear him scramble behind me, calling out, "Jake."

"Ten minutes."

Greg comes out of the elevator five minutes later. He looks terrible; we both do. We have a matching set of black eyes. His jaw is swollen and purple, and there's a cut on his chin. My cut is on my lip. It hurts to smile, not that I want to.

Thankfully, Greg keeps quiet for the cab ride to the airport. I have nothing to say to him and don't want to hear from him either. My sole goal here is to get Greg back home to Austin, where he has a fighting chance in this battle with his demons.

At the airport, we check in and head toward security. Greg follows me, shadowing my every move like an annoying little brother. That thought—that instant association between Greg and Tommy—pisses me off.

When we're past the X-rays and metal detectors, I lead the way to our gate. Greg, on my tail, grumpily asks, "So, how long are you going to ignore me?"

I shrug.

Greg huffs, "Jake, come on, man. I'm sorry. Okay? I'm sorry. Can we talk about this?"

"Are you kidding me right now?" I stop and turn on him so fast he nearly walks into me. All around us, irritated travelers divert their flow of foot traffic. We're a sandbar in the middle of a raging river of hostility.

"You stabbed me, Greg." I yank at the collar of my shirt to reveal the gauzy bandage I put on this morning. It hurts like a bitch, a literal pain-in-the-neck reminder that one of the best nights of my life was also one of the worst.

Greg opens his mouth to talk, but I'm not finished.

"Stop trying to make this okay. It's not okay. I know you were high. I know you're going through some shit. And I know you have a hundred other excuses if those don't work. But right now, I don't give a fuck why you did it. When I look at you right now, I don't see my lifelong friend, I see the motherfucker who stabbed me in the fucking neck with a fucking fork. So shut the fuck up."

I go to walk away, but turn back and add, "Has it occurred to you to ask why I'm in New York? Is your head stuck so far up your own ass you think I came here just for you?"

Greg blinks.

"Last night, was supposed to be one of the best nights of my life. It *was* one of the best nights of my life. I would have given anything to have had my brother there, but he's dead. So I turned to you, the next best thing, and you fucking stabbed me, you dick, and worse than that was every fucking thing you said to me. So we're not okay, Greg."

With that, I turn and join the flow of human traffic through the airport terminal. I don't know if Greg follows me or not. I don't care. I'm tired and cranky. I need a nap, a fuck, and a hug—not necessarily in that order.

At the gate, I try to catch that nap, and when they call for boarding, I'm relieved the seat I booked for Greg is on a different row. Right now, I need the distance.

I don't see him again until we land in Austin a few hours later. He catches up with me as we're clearing the terminal, keeping pace as he asks in a somber tone, "What happened last night? Why was it the best night of your life?"

Three weeks. Three fucking weeks I'd been calling him and telling him about my escapades. I'd called him every other day, my messages growing increasingly alarmed with his extended silence. And for three weeks, he ignored me. I glance at him and shake my head. "Check your voicemail. It's all there."

• • •

I've missed the first whistle—had to stop by my apartment to shower and change before coming to the skate rink—but I'm here now. And despite my exhaustion, I'm sparking like a live wire, excited to finally see Nicole.

But I'm nervous too. I'm not sure how this reunion is going to go. On the flight home, I did the math. Nicole and I have been dating—or whatever this is we're doing—for less than a month. And in that time, we've been in each other's physical presence for fewer than twenty-four hours, all told. And much of that time we've spent fighting, fucking, or fighting *and* fucking. When we're together, we're as combustible as dynamite.

Which is hot, sure, but during all those long-distance calls, we connected in a different way. We shared a tranquil peace I hadn't known I'd been missing. What if that peace isn't possible when we're together? What if we can only feel close to each other when we're separated? When I see her again, will I meet the sweet, funny, gentle Nicole I've come to know these past couple weeks? Or will I be greeted by the cold, hard, aloof Nicole I first knew?

At the entrance, I tell a woman with blue hair and full-sleeve tattoos my name and suggest Arson Nic might have left a ticket for me.

"Yep. There's a seat reserved for you right up front, hot stuff. Just look for the Texecutioner's Chair; it's to the right of that."

Damn. More than just her comp ticket, this time Nicole has reserved a seat for me. I smile when I remember the fireworks from the last time I sat to the right of the Texecutioner's Chair. I nod and head into the big room.

If I thought it was packed before, I was mistaken. It's beyond fucking Thunderdome in here tonight. People are everywhere: cramming into the aisles, standing on tables, and balancing on railings and any other surface they can find in order to see the bout. The sound inside the place is almost as loud as one of my shows.

At the outer edge of the rink, I hear my name hollered louder than all the other noise in the place. I perk up, my gaze scanning the crowd. When I spot her, I stop dead in my tracks, She's the most gorgeous woman I've ever seen. In that hot little schoolgirl outfit, her cheeks rouged, her lips painted candy apple red, her hair gelled back into a severe look—she has my mouth watering.

This woman is one hundred percent grade A man-eater, and I can't wait to be devoured. Whatever worries I had about which version of Nicole I'd find here in the flesh melt away with the sight of her. Sure, I really like Nicole's softer side, but any pretense that I don't also treasure her hard edges is absolute bullshit. Looking at Nicole now, I crave everything about her. I want it all: the hard and the soft, the challenge and the reward. I've never felt so motivated to know another person and to let her know me. I've never been so compelled to earn someone's trust, to prove myself worthy of the privilege of knowing the parts of her she keeps so carefully concealed.

I'm not sure if it's the sight of her or the stunning revelations running through my head that knock me out, but I just stand there like an idiot who's forgotten even the most basic motor functions.

I watch, helpless, as Nicole barrels toward me on those lethal skates of hers. Wisely, the crowd between us parts to let her through, and in an instant, she's in my arms. I stumble to keep us upright as she wraps her legs around my waist. Then she kisses me, and I'm stumbling again.

She tastes better than I remember: tart as strawberries, sweet as ice cream, and fresh as mint. God, I'm starved for her. The kiss hurts as much as it titillates, the cut on my lip sending sharp pains through me. I don't care. I'll take any amount of pain, so long as Nicole is there to kiss it and make it better.

When we come up for air, I whistle through my teeth. "Goddamn, *Quana*, if this is the homecoming I get, I should leave town more often."

She giggles—she fucking giggles—and it's adorable. "You're not allowed to leave for a while. I'm horny and need tending to."

"Noted," I say with a waggle of my brow, then smile so wide the cut on my lip reopens and I taste blood.

"What happened to your face?" Nicole asks, gently stroking my temple, careful not to touch my black eye. "Who hurt you?"

She's so sweet. Here in the flesh, wrapped in my arms, she's being so damn sweet. Any notion that ours is a romance best-suited for long distances gets tossed aside as I hug her tight and whisper, "Don't know what you're talking about. I feel no pain."

Nicole tilts her head and quirks her brow, but she lets the subject rest. With a wiggle and a hop, she unwraps her legs from my waist and lands on her skates with a clatter. I'm reluctant to let her go, but when she hooks her fingers through the front belt loops of my jeans, any protest dies on my tongue.

Using me as her mooring, she starts to skate toward and away, back and forth, close and far, with subtle little sways of her hips. The sensual rhythm hypnotizes me.

Goddamn, it's good to be home.

Home.

What a strange concept *home* is. There's no place like it. It's where the heart is. And, all this time, I'd thought my *home* was that place from my past. I'd thought homesickness was the thing you felt for a place you could never go back to again. But that's different; that's grief and nostalgia. Standing here now, feeling Nicole's little tugs on my jeans each time she pulls herself nearer to me, I know: this is my home, and I've missed it intensely. I've finally found the place where my heart is, and I don't ever want to leave. There's nowhere else I'd rather be, and no one I'd rather be with—

"Holy shit. Dude, it's Jake Sixkiller." The voice is male, and unfamiliar. I look away from Nicole to a pair of metalheads sporting Slayer and Testament T-shirts. They look at me like I'm Santa Claus on Christmas morning.

"No way," the other one says, his voice airy with awe.

The guys both start to speak at the same time.

"Dude, it's really you, and you really do have a black eye," Slayer-tee says.

"Told you it wasn't fake, asshole," Testament-tee quips to his friend.

"Fuck, man, that video of your solo during '*Inside*'...with all that blood...fuckin' brutal," one of them says.

"So fucking brutal," the other agrees, flashing a set of devil horns as punctuation.

"Video?" I ask, dumbly.

"Yeah, on YouTube."

"What's YouTube?" I ask, lost by the conversation.

The guys ignore my question, moving on to a new topic. "Dude, can we, like, get our picture with you?"

I blink, absolutely dumbfounded.

"Here." Nicole gestures for Slayer-tee to hand her his camera. She rolls a few feet away, then turns and readies the shot while I'm flanked by Beavis and Butthead.

I don't smile, still too confused by the encounter to react with anything but a scowl. But my scowl will look a lot more "brutal" in the photo than a smile, so I don't go changing. Nicole snaps the shot, and I'm temporarily blinded by the flash. When I regain my sight, one of the guys has pushed a pen and a copy of the derby bout program into my hands.

The fuck is this shit? I stare at his pen like it's from Mars—a fascinating specimen not of this world—until Nicole nudges me with an elbow to the gut. I snap out of my stupor and sign my name a little too neat and legible, then return the guy's pen and brochure.

The other one asks, "Dude, are the rumors true?"

"Rumors?" I ask, still frowning.

"That you've officially joined Mammoth. Cuz that'd be so fuckin' brutal."

I glance at Nicole, who's back at my side, her finger looped through my belt loop. She frowns at the hefty revelation. Now she's waiting for my answer too.

"Well..." I hedge. "I haven't signed the contract from the label yet, but...yes?" *Wow, I sound so awkward.* But I'm still not used to this new reality where the answer to the question "Are you in Mammoth?" is *yes*.

The metalheads jabber a few expletives, flash me more devil horns, then wander away.

Once they've vanished back into the crowd, I look down at Nicole's pretty face turned up toward me, her gaze curious but cautious. "Any news you want to tell me, rock star?"

"So much news to tell you." I cinch my arm around her waist and pull her against me. "But that can wait until after your bout and after all the sex we're going to have tonight."

She smiles, but it's guarded.

"What's on your mind, *Quana*?"

She furrows her brow, thinking for a moment, then quietly asks, "Does this mean you'll be moving to Ireland?"

I raise a brow, trying to play it cool even as I'm howling with excitement at the pouty tone of her voice. "Does this mean you'd like me to stick around?"

She smirks with stubborn defiance and gives me a nonchalant shrug. She can't fool me, though, and the thought that she wants me to stay close warms my heart.

All my adult life, I've never had a problem with leaving on tour. I've always loved touring. It was an adventure, an escape. But that was before. Now things are different. Now I have a pretty compelling reason to stay.

I touch her cheek. My fingertips, calloused from years of guitar playing, are as course as sandpaper, too rough against her soft skin. I lighten my touch. I don't want to hurt her. I want to be gentle, tender in the ways I touch her and in all the ways I treat her. It'll probably drive her nuts. Nicole is not a handle-with-care sort of woman, but every instinct in me is screaming to be careful with her.

Just as I lean in for another kiss, the ref blows a whistle, signaling the end of the first quarter. The sound acts as a trigger, flipping a switch in Nicole that transforms her from Dr. Jekyll to Ms. Hyde—or rather, from Nicole to Arson Nic. Suddenly all business, Nicole flattens her palm against my chest, holding me and my kiss at bay. She straightens her spine, perks her head up to glance toward the track, then clasps my hand in hers and tugs, telling me over her shoulder, "Come on, I'll show you to your seat."

I have to jog to keep up with her skates as she leads me to the chair with my name on it, written in purple marker on a sheet of paper taped to the back. Nicole pushes me into the seat. I half expect her to just roll away, her focus narrowed on the upcoming competition, but she surprises me when she bends at the waist and plants a soft kiss on my lips. Then she skates away, leaving me wanting more.

"Jake-i-poo!" Sheryl squeals as she climbs over the announcer's booth and crawls across the Texecutioner's Chair, all in an effort to reach me without setting foot on the track—which would be a penalty for her team as they line up. When she reaches me, she chokes me with a hug, plops her little ass right in my lap, and fires off a volley of questions: "How was the tour? Is it true you joined Mammoth officially? Did you know Ari boned Aidan at SXSW last year? I mean, I boned Glenn just the once, but Ari and Aidan disappeared for, like, days. I can't believe she never told you. What happened to your face?"

"Tour was great. Yes, I'm officially in Mammoth. That's way too much information about Aidan and Ari and you and Glenn, let's never discuss any of that again, and no comment."

Sheryl giggles. She's always liked that I can keep up with her machine gun-style interactions; not many people can.

"So, what are you doing on my lap, sweetheart?"

"I'm trying to make your girlfriend jealous. She skates faster when she's mad. She doesn't look very mad, though. Usually her nostrils flair like an angry bull. Oh, I have an idea. Let's make out."

She's kidding...I think; I hope. And I hope Nicole knows there is nothing happening between me and the sexy little thing in my lap. If I were to list Nicole's few flaws, her jealousy would top that list. I venture a glance at Nicole. She's balanced on a toe stop, slipping on the red fabric helmet-coverlet adorned with a gold star to signify she's the team's jammer for this round. When she glances at us, I gesture to Sheryl and shrug, indicating my helplessness. Nicole gives me a wink just as the first whistle sounds. Then with the second whistle, she shoots forward like a bullet. Sheryl claps excitedly, congratulates me on a job well done, then quietly crawls off my lap to sit in the Texecutioner's Chair.

Sheryl's departure leaves me free to focus entirely on Nicole. She's as gorgeous as I remember, but something has changed in her between when I left and now. Her face is softer, the hard lines of her usually stern expression relaxed. I'd like to think it comes from happiness, and I'd like to think I had a little something to do with it. When she looks up at the pack of skaters in front of her, there is a broad smile on her face, and it's real, not the fake spokesmodel kind. It's beautiful. She's always beautiful, but when she smiles, she glows.

I'm in awe, the sight of her glee permeating every part of my being, like the oxygen feeding my cells. *Goddamn, I really like this woman. No, it's more than just like; I adore her.* I admire her spirit, treasure her mind, respect her independence, and worship her body. I cherish every smile and laugh. I savor every moment I get to spend with her, and I want more.

Nicole rockets past my seat, making it around the track at a clip and through the pack of other skaters almost untouched. When she's looped around again and is on the heels of the pack once more, she crouches low and moves with the deadly stealth of a leopard. In and out and in and out, she weaves her way through the pack until she's out front again. Once she's cleared the other skaters, she smacks her hands on her hips to signal the end of the jam, then skates in a lazy circle around the track to catch her breath. Bent at the waist, hands on her knees, ass hanging out in the breeze in a pair of bloomers that read "bite me" in red sequins—she winks at me and spanks her own ass as she passes by.

Annnnd, I'm a goner. I'm completely head-over-heels in love with this woman.

It's a relief, to finally admit it. I lean forward, my elbows on my knees, balancing on the edge of my seat as I settle in to watch the woman I love kick total ass. The rest of the rounds are divided evenly between Nicole and Sheryl skating as jammers for their team. When Nicole isn't skating, she sits on her team bench, stretching her calves and hamstrings and guzzling water as she agrees with whatever the team coach is saying to her. When she's skating, she's winning. She's on fire tonight, and I'm not the only person who notices. Skaters from the two teams who competed in the first quarter slide down onto the floor near my feet and fill up the penalty chair just to watch her, in awe of her stunning skill and grace on the track.

In this round, Nicole is once again off the line first and overtaking the pack before her opponent can catch up. At the back of the pack, one of her teammates turns around, and Nicole grabs her arms as the other woman spins and whips her forward, a move that slingshots Nicole even faster toward the blockers. She's almost clear. Just one defender stands between her and open track, but the blocker is a fighter and putting all her might into stopping Nicole.

The announcer's voice sounds shrill as he excitedly narrates the play-by-play. "*Large Marge tries to take down Arson Nic with a hip check, but Arson Nic pays her back with interest.*"

Nicole's payback is a shoulder block to Large Marge that packs enough punch to capsize a ship. She hits the blocker with all her momentum, and the hit sends the woman spinning toward the crowd at turn three.

It looks like a clean fall until the last instant, when the blocker's leg twists to the side and catches Nicole's right skate. Nicole's leg goes out from under her, and she hits the deck, hard. Watching her fall is like witnessing a train wreck—a horror more enormous than my mind can comprehend, with a devastating outcome that I can do nothing to stop.

The sound of Nicole hitting the ground echoes through the enormous space like a cannon shot. It's followed by a collective, audible gasp from the crowd. And then, everything stops. The jam forgotten, some of the skaters break protocol to circle back to their fallen comrade while others respectfully take a knee beside their bench. Overhead, the music—which has rumbled in the background all bout—is cut off, leaving all twelve hundred of us in a terrible silence.

I wait with bated breath for some sign that she's okay, but that sign doesn't come. Instead, Nicole groans in pain as she tries to move. Fear grips me like a vise around my chest as Nicole's coach and teammates surround her, their faces ashen and lined with worry.

One of the skaters rushes off the track toward the front of the building, the crowd murmuring with concern and curiosity in her wake. The cowboy-pimp announcer clicks his microphone on and in a gentle voice says, "Ladies and gentlemen, we have a skater injured on the track. Please remain in your seats and clear the aisles for EMS to tend to her."

EMS?

Just then, Nicole twists from her fetal ball and moans in agony. My panic hits a new level. The déjà-vu factor is working me toward hysteria. My mind volleys between the here and now and my memories of another place and time, when another person I love writhed and suffered on the floor, surrounded by people who couldn't do enough to help.

It's intolerable, this waiting and worrying and watching from a distance. *I can't do this again. I can't do* nothing *again. I need to help. I need to be with her, comfort her.* I rocket to my feet, on the move. Desperate to be at her side, I storm across the track toward the melee surrounding Nicole.

The announcer comes over the loudspeaker, chiding me to stop, and others are yelling too. I'm deaf to it. I'm deaf to everyone but her. All the way across the track, despite the murmur of the capacity crowd and the constant chatter of the pimp cowboy over the loudspeaker, I hear Nicole cussing and moaning in pain.

Before I'm even halfway to my goal, two giant tattooed guys in red security T-shirts stop me. One places his palm flat against my chest and in a booming voice says, "Sir, please return to your seat."

The words register as random sounds in my head, nothing decipherable or important. And in the gap between the security guards' heads, I see the muscles of Nicole's neck pull taut, strained with agony as she tries not to cry out from the pain.

I push the security guys aside and move between them. Surprised that I'm defying their order, they don't immediately move to stop me. But I don't get far before they're onto me again.

It's like that night, all over again, with Uncle Eli's arms wrapped around me in a suffocating hold, keeping me away from Tommy. *Not again. Not this time.* No one will keep me away from Nicole. But the two grapple to hold me back, and a thick arm loops around my neck, squeezing my windpipe. I struggle to breathe as I fight to break free—

"Stop it!" Sheryl hollers from somewhere near me. "Mike, John! He's her boyfriend. Let him go to her. Please. She's asking for him."

She's asking for me. My heart pounds at the sound of those words, pumping adrenaline through my veins to make me godly in strength. I'm ready to tear Mike and John to pieces, but they quickly step away from me, their hands in the air like it's a stickup, finally letting me pass.

I sprint the rest of the way to Nicole. The skaters who encircle her make room for me as I fall to my knees at her side. I grab one of her hands and gently squeeze. She looks at me with sad eyes and a tense expression, her brow damp with sweat, her skin white as snow. She's in intense pain but trying not to show it. *So brave, so fucking strong.*

"Where are you hurt?" I ask.

"Knee." She pants as she speaks, gritting her teeth when she finishes with a mournful "I felt something snap."

I look down. Her leg doesn't look broken, but it doesn't look right, either. Before I can say anything further, two paramedics crouch down on the other side of her and start to assess her injuries. Nicole squeezes my hand as they poke and prod her leg. They speak to each other in some sort of strange medical language, then, as they work her into a neck brace and onto a backboard, they explain they're taking her to the hospital.

Nicole remains strong and stoic, a total fucking warrior, trying so hard to hide her pain and weakness. I run my fingers through her hair and lean in close to whisper in her ear, "Let them know you're okay. Everyone here is worried about you."

She turns to look at me, and I can tell what I've said surprises her. She's never considered people might actually care about her. The paramedics lift the backboard, and I stand, too, not releasing her hand.

She silently stares at me as they strap the board to a nearby gurney. When they start to wheel her toward the exit, Nicole lifts her free hand and waves a set of devil horns in the air.

The place erupts with cheers, almost as loud as the crowd at my New York show last night. Nicole looks shocked, and a single tear traces down her temple to wet the shell of her ear.

The paramedics move quickly, and the crowd parts as we head toward the front door and then out to the waiting ambulance. I keep Nicole's hand in mine all the way there. I couldn't let go even if I wanted to. Nicole has an iron grip on me, squeezing so hard all the sensation has left my fingers.

One of the paramedics explains I will need to follow them in my truck to the hospital downtown. Nicole protests, so I assure her, "I'll be right behind you, *Quana.*"

She squeezes my hand tighter, like she never wants to let me go. It's a powerful feeling, to be needed and wanted by her. I don't want to let her go either, not ever.

"Nicole, listen." I speak with an urgency that draws her attention. Her eyes focus on me, and I say the words I so desperately need her to hear right now. "I love you."

She blinks, then furrows her brow, confused. Her voice registers about two octaves higher than I've ever heard it when she says, "*What?*"

The paramedics, seemingly oblivious to what's happening between Nicole and me, start to lift her into the back of the vehicle. I'm forced to release her hand. I feel the absence acutely, sharp pricks of pain as the blood and sensation rush back into my fingers.

"I love you." I say it again, shouting it this time, in case the issue was that she couldn't properly hear me the first time. With the rumble of the ambulance engine and the clatter of her gurney wheels rolling into the back of the van, I'm not sure if she can hear me the second time either. So I say it again, even louder. "I love you, Nicole. And I'll be right behind you. Okay? You're not alone. I love you, *Quana.*"

In that last glimpse of her before the doors close, Nicole looks utterly bewildered, and were the situation different, it would be cute as hell. As it is, I'm frustrated by the forced separation.

As the paramedic hustles around to the front door he turns and gives me a thumbs up, then hollers, "Smooth, dude."

Yeah, real fucking smooth. First time I tell a woman I love her, and it's while she's being wheeled into the back of an ambulance.

I stand there, at a loss for what to do next. Adrenaline pumps through me and sends my mind into panic mode as I watch the vehicle pull away from the building and disappear around the corner, lights and sirens blaring.

I turn around and see I'm not alone. Sheryl and about two-thirds of the flat track derby league stand behind me. They all look at me now: some with pity, some with curiosity, some amused by my declarations of love. I pause for a second, staring dumbfounded at my audience, then I run.

I run faster than I've ever run before. I run like my heart is in the ambulance that just drove away, and if I don't catch up with it, I'll die.

I find my truck where I left it, hop inside, and crank the engine. It comes alive with a growl, and I haul ass down the road toward the hospital. The drive is excruciatingly long, and without a spinning light bar and siren to explain my urgency, none of the cars in my way sense my need for speed. When I finally arrive, I ditch the truck in the lot and sprint for the emergency room doors. They open with a gasp of stale air, but I hardly notice as I jog to the nurse's station.

Breathless, I huff, "Nicole Rollins, please, where can I find her?"

The woman frowns at me. She looks familiar, and it takes me a moment to remember her—the nurse with the messy ponytail who'd lit my cigarette right before I called Nicole. How long ago was that, a few weeks? It feels like I've lived a lifetime since then.

She doesn't respond right away, so I repeat, "Nicole Rollins. Please"—messy ponytail's nametag reads *Amy*—"Amy, I need to find her. She was just brought in by ambulance."

"But," Amy points at my chest, "do you need to get that looked at?"

I glance down at my shirt; it's covered with blood.

What the...? Oh, for fuck's sake!

I reach up and touch the wound at my neck. The bandage is ripped off, and the cut has reopened. That security guy's choke hold must have torn at the scabs.

Awesome. First time I tell a woman I love her, and it's while she's being wheeled into the back of an ambulance AND I'm covered in blood.

"I'm fine. Nicole Rollins. Where is she, please?" I say the please with my teeth clenched tight, beyond frustrated at this point.

Amy frowns at me a moment longer before glancing down at her computer. She types something and glances back up at me. "The doctor is with her right now."

"Can I go to her?"

"No. You'll have to wait. Are you sure you don't need a doc—"

I grumble and turn away from her, walking over to the far corner of the waiting room to pace, but my energy soon flags. I slump against the wall, then slide down into a chair. It's a few minutes before I recognize it's the same chair I parked my ass only a few weeks ago, worried about another woman in my life.

Déjà-fucking-vu!

I can't help but consider how much my life has changed since I sat here last. From a directionless, affectionless, mess of a man, to a warrior in love and a budding rock star to boot. I could laugh at the absurdity of it all, but I'm too anxious to laugh right now. Instead, I tap my fingers on my knees and my feet on the floor, working through some rhythm that's been bouncing around in my head. Music: the only thing that's ever effectively calmed my nerves.

I don't know how long I sit there, stewing and writing a new song, miserable and shaking with the need to be with Nicole. *All I want is to hold her hand and kiss her cheek and tell her that if she'll have me, she's got me—*

"Jake Sixkiller?" I look up as Amy stomps across the waiting room toward me, her messy ponytail swishing from side to side with each step.

"Yes, ma'am," I say and stand up nervously as she stops in front of me.

"Come with me, please."

"Is everything okay?" I ask as I follow her toward a wide hallway.

"She's upset you're not with her. She's threatening to sue the hospital."

I chuckle. "It's good to see her charm hasn't suffered from the injury."

Amy rolls her eyes, then leads me up a flight of stairs to a separate wing of rooms. About halfway up the hall, she stops and points at an open door. Inside, Nicole is stretched out on a hospital bed with her leg immobilized. She looks tired and irritable and cute as hell with her makeup and hair mussed up. She doesn't appear to be in any pain now, courtesy of whatever drug they're pumping through that IV hooked into her left hand.

Nicole glances up at me, and her eyes sparkle. My heart races at the sight. It takes only two steps for me to reach her bedside. I clasp her right hand in mine.

"I hear you're planning to sue the pants off this place."

"Well, it worked, didn't it?"

Touched that she's so hell-bent on having me at her side, I slide down into a chair and pull it as close to the bed as I can. I take her hand again, bringing her knuckles to my lips for a gentle kiss.

"You're covered in blood. Why are you covered in blood?" She frowns at me.

"Minor disagreement with your security staff. Nothing to worry yourself over." I focus the attention back on her. "What about you? Do they know what's wrong?"

"Torn ACL. They're saying I'll need surgery and physical therapy. I'm waiting for another consult or something. They're trying to schedule my surgery for tomorrow, and they want me to stay overnight."

When she speaks, her words sound matter-of-fact, void of emotion, but her eyes give her away. She pauses and clears her throat, but her voice shakes when she adds, "They won't tell me how soon I can skate again."

"It's gonna be okay." I squeeze her hand. "Athletes come back from this all the time. You're strong, Nicole. You'll be back on that track in no time."

"I'm not that strong."

With exaggerated exasperation, I throw my hands up in the air and huff, "Enough with the false modesty. You're the strongest person I know, *much* stronger than me."

At that, she laughs. "Well, duh."

"You know what you are? You're a diamond."

"Compressed coal?"

"Yes, you're definitely compressed coal, but you're also really hard and really beautiful and strong enough to cut through steel."

Her eyes glisten like she might cry, and I'm mesmerized by the way the institutional fluorescent lighting makes them shimmer and sparkle like emeralds.

She watches me carefully, assessing. I let her. I don't flinch from her stare, even when holding her suspicious gaze takes every ounce of strength I have. After a long moment, she opens her mouth like she's going to speak, but nothing comes out. I wait. She goes to speak again, and with a quiet voice she whispers, "Jake, did you mean what you said?"

I have a pretty good idea what she's talking about, and yes, I meant all three words. "I only ever say what I mean."

"So you think I'm a colossal cunt?"

I squeeze her hand in mine. "I never said that, I said 'prove you're not the colossal cunt everyone *else* thinks you are.' And you did, again and again. All I had to do was get to know you to see the truth."

Defiant, she asks, "You think you know me?"

"Yeah, I think I know you."

Her chin juts out, challenging when she asks, "You think you love me?"

Without hesitation, I answer, "I love you."

She scans my face, as if she's looking for something that will reveal me as a liar, some hint I can't be trusted. I let her look; she won't find anything here but the truth.

"You make it sound so easy. But they're just words."

I understand her suspicion. Words are hard to trust. They can be used to make such pretty little lies. "Give me time. Let me prove it to you with more than words."

She raises a brow. "You're not going to start singing 80s hair metal ballads, are you?"

"Oh baby, if singing is the key to your heart, then I'm a lock. I'll have you know, I'm an excellent singer."

Her smile beams brighter than the sun. I lean in and gently kiss her. She sighs, as if my kiss has the power to relieve her of all her troubles. It's a heady feeling.

"Sorry to interrupt..."

Nicole and I bounce apart like we've been caught behind Granny T's garden shed. A young doctor stands near the door in her white lab coat, glancing down at a clipboard in her hands.

"I'm Doctor Wallace. I was called in to take a look at that leg." Dr. Wallace pushes her glasses up her nose. "So, Nic—oooooh my goodness, sir, are you okay?"

I keep forgetting I'm battered and bruised and covered in blood. "No worries. I'm fine." I point at Nicole. "She's the one you want."

Doctor Wallace looks between us like we're a bit crazy but crosses the room to take a look at Nicole's leg. After a few moments of poking and prodding and a couple notes written onto the file in her hands, Doctor Wallace pushes her glasses up her nose again.

"The good news is—"

Nicole blurts out the one question that's weighing on her. "Will I skate again?"

Doctor Wallace gives her a patient smile. "Let's take this one step at a time. I've scheduled your surgery for tomorrow afternoon. From the look of things, it will be pretty standard, and I don't see any reason why your recovery time won't be average. But let's get you walking first before we talk about skating. Okay?"

Nicole frowns.

The doctor continues, "Get some rest tonight, and tomorrow we'll get you started on the road to recovery."

"So I can go home now." Not a question.

"I'm sorry, but no. You'll need to stay overnight."

Nicole's expression hardens, and she opens her mouth like she's about to unleash a tirade on the good doctor. I squeeze her hand and lean in to whisper in her ear. "*Quana*, if you want to heal quickly, you need to do what the doctor says. I'll stay here with you tonight, okay?"

Nicole stares at me for a moment, then nods.

"Great." Dr. Wallace has lost none of her pep, even under Nicole's withering glare. "Then I'll see you tomorrow, and we'll get you fixed right up." She turns to leave, then catches herself and turns back. "By the way, there are some people down in the lobby wanting to see you. You can have guests for a brief visit, but they can't stay long." She turns to walk away, hollering over her shoulder, "I'll send them up."

"Who is coming up here to see me?" Nicole asks.

"People who care about you."

She looks confused.

"Why is it so hard for you to believe people care about you?"

She opens her mouth to answer, but she's interrupted by a ruckus in the hall. It sounds like an invasion—the echoing slaps of quick footsteps hitting the linoleum floor and several voices talking at once. Someone attempts to shush the noisemakers, but to no avail, and the rollicking rumble just grows louder as it draws near.

Nicole and I both stare at the hallway through the open door just in time to see a wave of people—possibly Nicole's entire team and a few skaters from the other teams as well—press into her room.

The room, which wasn't very large to begin with, seems to shrink to the size of a sardine can as more and more people pack inside. Some of the skaters have changed into their after-party attire of sexy little black dresses or comfy sweats, but most are still wearing their track gear, in such a rush to get to Nicole's bedside they didn't even take the time to change clothes. They encircle her bed, asking their questions all at once.

"Are you okay?"

"What is it? ACL? I'll bet it's your ACL, isn't it?"

"Do they have you on the good drugs?"

"Nic, if you die in surgery, can I have your skates?"

"Who's the tall, dark, and bloody arm candy, Arsy?"

"When can you skate again?"

Nicole is too overwhelmed to answer, shifting her gaze around the room, her eyes glistening with unshed tears.

I'm a bit overwhelmed with emotion myself. I squeeze Nicole's hand and whisper, "See, *Quana*? People care about you."

A shrill whistle cuts through the chatter, and there's motion near the door as the crowd shifts to make room for Sheryl. The ghost of a jammer manages to make her way to the foot of Nicole's bed without any interference. Once there, she lifts a giant trophy emblazoned with a big roller skate over her head.

"We won, bitch!" Sheryl shouts, then launches into a rousing rendition of Queen's "We Are the Champions." The entire room breaks into song, and after a few bars, I join them, belting out my best impersonation of Freddy Mercury. We're loud. We've probably woken this entire wing of the hospital, but no one stops us as we sing the whole damn thing.

When we finish, Sheryl whistles another ear-piercing call to order. Silence reigns, and Sheryl turns to one of the other skaters, who hands her another trophy. This one is smaller, and instead of a giant roller skate on the top, a woman on wheels crouches as if about to move.

"Also, after a quick deliberation postgame and a unanimous vote," Sheryl amps up her voice like she's the pimp cowboy announcer when she bellows, "Nicole Rollins, a.k.a. Arson Nic, a.k.a. Hell on Wheels, a.k.a. Wild Bitch of the West—we award thee MVP!"

With that, the trophy is held aloft and passed around the room so each skater can kiss it like it's a sacred relic. I watch the ritual with rapt fascination. Finally, the trophy reaches the last skater, Doctor Mid-Nite—the skater Nicole hit at the last bout. She gives it a smooch, then holds the trophy for Nicole to take.

Nicole pulls her hand out of mine so she can clutch the trophy with both fists. For a moment, she holds it at arm's length like it's a squirming baby and she doesn't know what to do with it. Then she pulls it in and smacks a big kiss right on the statuette's face. The room erupts in cheers.

I'm stunned, amazed. I haven't seen a community like this since I was a kid. It's incredible, this family Nicole helped create without even realizing what she's done.

When they've settled down, the skaters take turns coming to Nicole's bedside to hug her, wish her well, and offer their support.

Then they leave, and it's just Sheryl left. The petite jammer comes over and hops onto Nicole's bed. She crosses her legs, looking demure and strangely professional, even in her tiny plaid skirt and fishnet hose. "Hit me with the truth, babe. How bad is it?"

Nicole reports the details of her prognosis. Sheryl listens closely, then gives Nicole's fingers a little pat. "Okay, so listen up. Once you get out of surgery and it's time for physical therapy and all that rehabilitation shit, you call me. I'll drive you. I'll be your PT buddy. Whatever you need, you just ask, and it's yours. Gotta get you well and back on the track, cuz we can't win without you, Arsy Nic."

Nicole hides her emotions behind a mask of impassivity, but I know Sheryl's words have touched her.

Sheryl turns to me and points at my shirt. "Did Mike and John do that to you? Cuz if so, I'm going to give them a piece of my mind in the form of my boot up their ass. Or... I guess it'd be my boots up their asses, which sounds challenging when you think about it—"

"No," I interrupt her derailing train of thought. "They were just doing their jobs. This is from a prior injury. I should get cleaned up."

I pull my stained shirt over my head as I cross to the little bathroom attached to Nicole's room. Sheryl giggles like a schoolgirl and whispers something to make Nicole laugh. I leave them to it as I approach the mirror in the en suite and finally see what everyone has been commenting about.

I'm a mess. The shirt is ruined, so I chuck it into the trashcan beside the toilet. There are streaks of blood across my neck and down my chest. I rinse them off, tug my hair out of messy braids, and comb the waves and tangles into submission, then splash some water on my face before I head back out to Nicole.

"Sheryl gone?"

Nicole glances up at me, wearing a serene smile as she cradles the MVP statuette in her lap.

"That was pretty cool how everyone came here and sang."

She looks back down at the trophy, running her fingers reverently over the skater figurine, then shrugs when she says, "Yeah, it was all right. But God, I'm tired. I thought they'd never leave."

I see right through her words. She's touched, deeply, but just as I needed to take baby steps on my road home, Nicole needs to take some baby steps on her road to being loved.

I move toward the door, set my hand on the knob and give her a grimace as I announce, "Okay, well I'll get out of your hair too. Let you get some rest."

"But..." Nicole glances up at me, her eyes beseeching, "I thought you were staying. You said you would—"

I grin at her. I can't help it. The tone of her voice, that look in her eyes; it's a heady feeling to be wanted by her.

She frowns. "You're fucking with me, aren't you?"

"I'm totally fucking with you. Of course I'm staying."

"Asshole," she grumbles, but she shifts in her bed to make room for me.

I shut off the lights, cross the room, and set the trophies in a prominent spot on her bedside table. Then I climb into the small hospital bed beside her. It takes a few awkward shifts, me arranging my long arms and legs around Nicole like we're playing a game of Twister. But finally, we find a good position, me on my side with Nicole's head on my shoulder, my other arm draped across her belly.

Nicole whispers, "This is not how I expected tonight to go."

"Me neither. I thought there'd be more foreplay before you got me into bed."

Nicole giggles and I love the sound of it. "Thank you," she whispers.

"For what?"

"For staying."

"Always." I kiss the top of her head as she nestles a little closer in my arms and falls asleep.

12–Monday August 8, 2005

Thank you.

For what?

For staying.

Always.

I rest my head on the pillow beside Nicole's, watching her sleep, and all I can think about is how badly I want to be the guy who stays for her, always. But how will that work with a busy recording and touring schedule? How can I be the guy who stays, even as I plan to leave?

The Mammoth contract, a mammoth pile of paper, sits on my kitchen counter, read but still unsigned. It's everything I've ever wanted in my life. It's the brass ring. Or at least, I thought it was. But lying here with Nicole, faced with the prospect of leaving her, disappointing her, it surprises me just how little the band actually matters to me. I've already got the brass ring here in my grasp, so what am I still reaching for?

"Is she sleeping?"

I look over to the familiar face that peeks in at us through a gap in the door. It's Doctor Mid-Nite, only she looks different today. Instead of her usual puff of hair, she's wearing a colorful scarf knotted over her head. And instead of her skate garb, she's dressed in a long, white lab coat and teal scrubs that compliment her ebony skin. Hold up, is Doctor Mid-Nite an actual doctor?

"I'll come back," she whispers again.

But Nicole stirs and blinks her eyes open. She glances around the unfamiliar room, then looks at me and slowly smiles. "You stayed."

"Of course I stayed."

Her smile grows wide. "Of course you stayed."

"Hey," Doctor Mid-Nite's voice wavers hesitantly. "As much as I hate to interrupt, Nic, we need to talk."

Nicole looks to our guest at the door. "Ty?"

"Hey, Nic." She steps into the room, then looks to me. "We haven't formally met. I'm Dr. Tynisha Johnson."

"Jake Sixkiller."

After introductions, she looks back to Nicole. "So, listen, I'm here in a professional capacity."

Nicole's expression instantly changes from one of sleepy curiosity to tense surprise. She pushes up a little higher on the bed, her jaw hanging open, and my own nerves start to snap to attention.

Tynisha clears her throat, then turns her gaze back to me. "Jake, I need to discuss a personal medical matter with Nicole, would you mind—"

"He stays," Nicole asserts and grabs my hand, squeezing it.

"Okay." Tynisha comes farther into the room. She glances at a file in her hands, then back at Nicole. Finally, she clears her throat and says, "As you know, upon admission, you provided a urine sample. This is standard protocol to ensure your safety when administering medication or performing surgical procedures. In your case, Nic, everything was normal. However, your sample revealed elevated levels of the hormone hCG, the human chorionic gonadotropin hormone."

What does that mean? What is hCG?

Nicole squeezes my hand, suggesting she knows, but she says nothing, just stares at Tynisha. Time stretches like putty in my head, forming minutes, hours, whole days of worry and confusion like some surreal nightmare. *Shit, maybe I fell asleep, and this is just a dream—*

"You mean..." Nicole says.

Tynisha nods, then clears my confusion right up when she says, "You're pregnant."

I blink once...twice...twenty to thirty thousand times. I try to process the information, but nothing registers. The entire English language fails to register. In my head, I hear the song I've been writing and start to drum the fingers of my free hand to the rhythm of the tune, while in some other part of my brain, I hear bits and pieces of the ensuing conversation.

Nicole: "...I had an ectopic pregnancy nine years ago..."

Tynisha: "...OB can perform a transvaginal ultrasound..."

Nicole: "...soon, before the surgery..."

Tynisha: "...I'll coordinate with obstetrics."

The song I've been working on starts to fade away, replaced by a high-pitched squeal. Am *I developing tinnitus? I really need to start wearing ear plugs when I play, and—*

"Jake?"

I blink like I'm waking from a deep sleep. Tynisha has left the room. It's just Nicole and me now, and she's frowning at me.

Yeah? I think but don't say. I don't trust my voice right now.

"You haven't said a word."

I open my mouth, but nothing comes out. I'm at a loss for words. I search my mind, but it's too cluttered with half thoughts to make any sense of things.

Pregnant...preeeeegnant...pregunta...no, that means "question" in Spanish. What was the question? Holy fuck. I got Nicole pregnant. But she can't get pregnant, right? Holy shit. I'm gonna be a dad!

How exactly am I supposed to put the mess of my thoughts into coherent sentences with subjects and verbs that agree and objects and prepositional phrases and all that other shit? When I finally muster my voice and open my mouth, the only thing I manage to do is admit a sad truth. "I don't know what to say."

Nicole frowns, and I know I've gotten it wrong. There was something specific she needed to hear from me, and I missed the mark. She shifts away, and I feel cold in all the places where we no longer connect.

Desperate to stop her retreat, I open my mouth to speak, but all I get out is an awkward squawk when the door opens again. In walks Tynisha, and with her is a woman with silver hair and a warm smile.

Tynisha makes introductions, and Dr. Laura Douglas talks to Nicole and me. Dr. Douglas's voice is soothing, so calm as she explains about a procedure she would like to perform in order to determine the viability of this pregnancy. It's when she says that word "viability" that the reality of this situation sinks like a stone to the bottom of my stomach. *What if something's wrong? What if Nicole's health is at risk? What if the baby's health is at risk?*

I don't know what they say after that, my ears are ringing again. But finally they leave, and I'm alone with Nicole again. I think this will be my chance to talk to her about everything, but she's in her own space now. Staring at her hands, she ignores me like I'm not in the room, like my bicep isn't stretched out beneath her head like a pillow. How did I fuck up so royally to end up outside her walls again?

"Nicole—"

Before I can express my thoughts, a nurse steps through the door, pushing a wheelchair. "Good news! An exam room is open."

I've missed my window. The time for talk is over; now it's time for action. Which works for me. Right now, it's a lot easier to get my body working than my brain. I scramble off Nicole's bed, taking care not to jostle her as I do, then help the nurse transfer Nicole to the chair.

Soon, we're on the move. I don't pay attention to where we're going. My attention is focused solely on Nicole, her expression stony and blank. I can't bear how isolated she looks right now—just inches away from me, yet completely alone.

The nurse takes a left into a room. Dr. Douglas is already there, arranging a set of medical instruments on a tray. I watch the nurse maneuver the chair within the cramped exam room, then follow everyone inside and shut the door behind us.

It's a distinctly feminine space, with walls painted mauve and decorated with inspiring landscape vistas of waterfalls and starry nights, interspersed with illustrations of the female anatomy and a poster of a woman with a bruised face advertising a toll-free help line for abuse victims.

I feel conspicuously male, and I'm acutely aware of all the black and blue on my own face. I glance down at myself, still shirtless, and my discomfort ratchets up a notch. I cross my arms over my bare chest and dip my chin low, trying to take up less space, to disappear like an ostrich with my head in the sand.

No such luck. The room is barely large enough to fit us all, and when I move to stand against the wall, my back hits a bracket filled with pamphlets in English and Spanish about unplanned pregnancy, STDs, and breast self-exam guides.

"Janis, he's looking a little lightheaded, Can you grab him a seat?" the doctor's gentle voice cuts through the thick fog in my head, and I snap my gaze to the end of the exam table, where she's peering at me over the sheet she's draped across Nicole's legs. The nurse appears at my side with a stool, directing me to sit. I blink at her in thanks.

"Jake, you can go," Nicole says.

Confused, I ask, "Where do you want me to go?"

Nicole rolls her eyes, then says, "No, I mean, you can leave. You don't have to stay."

I frown, still confused. *Doesn't she know I'm the guy who stays?*

"Listen, Jake," Nicole props herself up on an elbow so she can properly scowl at me. "I don't expect anything from you, okay? I know you said all those nice things to me last night, but I'll understand if you..."

I shake my head, still not following. "If I what?"

She hedges and glances at the other women in the room, but finally says, "I know you didn't sign up for this. You have a huge opportunity happening with Mammoth, and I won't hold you back. This baby...if this happens...I want this baby, but I'll understand if you don't, and I won't—"

"Are you fucking crazy?"

Nicole blinks, then blinks again.

Suddenly, my head is clear, my thoughts sharp as knives cutting through the muck in my mind. I rocket to my feet, take two strides across the room to reach Nicole's bedside, grasp her hand in mine, and speak with resolve when I inform her, "I'm not going anywhere, *Quana.*"

"But—"

"You call me an asshole because I say what I mean, but then you don't believe the things I say."

Now it's Nicole who looks confused.

"All those things I said last night, I fucking *meant* them. I'm not going anywhere. I admit, I'm a little overwhelmed, but I'm staying, okay? I'm staying."

Nicole looks surprised. She scrutinizes me for a good long moment before she stammers to ask, "You are?"

"I am."

"Do you want this...?"

This *baby*. She doesn't have to say the word for me to understand her meaning. I take a shaky breath as the truth hits me square in the chest: "Yeah, I do."

"You do?"

This time, when I whisper the words again, I'm absolutely certain. "I do."

There's a noise from the foot of the exam table, and I'm reminded that we're not alone in the room. Dr. Douglas asks, "Are you ready?"

Are we ready? What a loaded question. These next few minutes could be the most exciting or the most devastating moments of my life with Nicole. If something is wrong, if the pregnancy isn't "viable" and has to be terminated, will this be the end of us? Will I lose Nicole before I've even had the chance to win her? And what about this baby? Somewhere deep in my heart, I think I've always wanted a family. Now, the thought of sharing that with Nicole has me electrified. My heart races in my chest. My mind spins with excitement at the thought of watching Nicole's belly swell as she carries our child, then spirals into panic at the thought that we could lose this kid. We're standing at a crossroads, and are we ready to move forward, no matter the outcome?

"Jake, you look like you're going to faint again," Nicole says with a gasp.

Who, me? I'm fine, I try to convince myself as I sway a little on unsteady legs. The nurse hustles over with that stool again, and I sit.

Nicole squeezes my hand tight. "Breathe," she says to me. Then to the doctor: "We're ready."

Taking my cue, I do as I'm told and breathe deep. Taking her cue, Dr. Douglas disappears behind the makeshift curtain, calmly saying, "Expect to feel a little pressure as I insert the transducer." She holds up a device that looks like a magic wand and is covered by a condom. *Ironic.* "Just breathe deep in through your nose and out through your mouth. I'll be as quick as I can."

Nicole winces and follows the doctor's directions, with deep inhales and exhales through gritted teeth. At the first sight of Nicole's discomfort, my pathetic weakness washes away, and I find my strength. I need to be strong for her. It's her turn to be the weak one for a change.

I squeeze her fingers with one hand and use my other hand to brush a few strands of hair behind her ear. I haven't felt terror like this since that moment I took my brother's hand, and together, we walked into Mom's hospital room to find her broken body being kept alive by machines. I'd lost everything in those next few moments, my entire family.

Please, God, if you exist, don't take this away from me too. And please don't hurt Nicole any more than she's already been hurt. Don't dangle this miracle in front of us if you're only going to take it away.

Nicole's eyes tear, and I know she's thinking the same thing I am, all those thoughts of loss circling in her mind. I wish I had the right words to soothe her, but I'm shit out of luck with words today. So instead of talking, I do the one thing that comes naturally to me—I sing. I cup her cheek in my palm and brush her tears away as I sing the first song I ever learned, the Cherokee version of "Amazing Grace."

As I sing, I'm flooded with memories of my mom singing it to me at night when I was a boy, scared of shadows. Now, like then, the song chases away my fears. My heart fills with warmth and comfort as I stare into Nicole's eyes.

When I'm done, Nicole tearfully whispers, "I love you, Jake."

Her words wash over me like the waves of the ocean; they shine a light through years of darkness and crack my chest wide open to make room for my once-atrophied heart to beat again. *Holy shit!* This incredible force of nature loves *me.*

"Yeah?" I dumbly ask.

"Yeah."

"Good." I grin like an idiot. "That's good news."

The only thing that could make this moment any better—

"I have some more good news for you two," Dr. Douglas announces. "The embryo appears to be well attached within the uterus."

Nicole lets out a gasp and then a sob as relief washes over her. I cry with her, holding her fingers to my lips as I try to control my trembling hands.

"Holy shit" is all I can manage to say. "Holy shit."

Dr. Douglas smiles at us, and I imagine this is one of her favorite parts of the job. She poises her pen over the chart in her hands, ready to take notes. "Do you know when the date of conception might have been?"

I remember this well, so I remind Nicole. "The first time was when the condom broke the night you nearly broke Dr. Johnson's nose."

Dr. Douglas blinks at me. Nicole clarifies, "Tynisha and I are in roller derby together. And the date was July 17."

"Then we went without a condom the night before I left for tour, which was Thursday July 21...and again that next morning...twice," I add helpfully.

"Jake!" Nicole laughs. "I think she gets the picture."

I glance up at the doctor, who is trying to suppress a smile. "We'll just say about three weeks." She writes a note in her chart. "Given that timeline, everything looks normal. You do have quite a bit of scar tissue, Nicole, but we can work with that. We'll just need to keep a close eye on things." They talk a bit more about a health regimen and insurance before Dr. Douglas shakes our hands and leaves.

I'm working with the nurse to get Nicole back into the wheelchair when Tynisha pops her head in the door. "Girl, you are full of surprises, aren't you? I did not see this one coming."

"Came as a surprise to me too." Nicole grins bashfully.

That makes two of us. I wink at her.

"Y'all are real cute." Tynisha rolls her eyes. "Now stop flirting and get her in the wheelchair."

I do as I'm told and push Nicole back to her room to get her into bed. When Tynisha goes to leave, Nicole grabs her hand. "Ty, thank you. I'm sorry I'm always such a bitch. You're so great, and I just...thank you."

"Goodness, pregnancy has turned you downright sweet." Tynisha gives me a thumb's up. "Job well done, Jake."

I grin like an idiot. Tynisha tucks a blanket under Nicole's chin. "Now get some rest, Little Miss MVP. You're gonna need it. And as soon as you're healthy, and this little bun is out of the oven, I expect to see you back on the track. You won't be the first skater mom out there." With that, Tynisha kisses Nicole's cheek and gives my shoulder a squeeze then leaves the room.

Nicole murmurs, "Skater mom." It's like she's trying to get used to the sound of the word "mom."

Mom. Dad. Such small words, such big meaning.

"Holy shit," I say with pure reverence in my tone. I repeat the phrase again, because out of all the phrases in the English and Cherokee languages, it's the only one that comes to mind.

My knees give out as the weight of my new reality settles on my shoulders. I collapse into the chair at Nicole's bedside with a huff, overwhelmed and in awe.

Holy shit, we're going to have a baby. We're going to be parents. I'm going to be a dad. How the fuck did this become my reality? From a directionless, affectionless, mess of a man—to a warrior in love, budding rock star, and future *dad* in zero to sixty.

Suddenly, I'm swamped with terror. *What if I'm terrible at being a dad?* I have no clue what it takes to be a father, let alone a *good* father. And what's more, how will I be a good father if I'm out touring or off in Ireland recording an album? Ian left Mammoth because he wanted a family. Is that the choice I'm faced with now? After hearing about Nicole's absentee father, the reality of tour life has taken on a whole new weight.

Fuck. This is a lot to deal with. How will we do this? How will we raise a happy, healthy, well-adjusted kid when neither of us have the first clue what we're doing?

At my side, Nicole takes a shaky breath and lets it out with a slow whistle, like the sound of a bomb about to hit the ground and explode. The sound makes me laugh. She smirks at me and it's adorable.

Jesus, this is so surreal. Less than a month ago, if you'd told me I'd find myself here, I'd have laughed my ass off. Surely Nicole would have done the same. But so much has changed since that first night with her. I've changed. Now, looking at this fierce, wondrous woman beside me—I'm out of my head with joy at the thought of being the father of her child. And her being the mother of mine.

I lean forward and rest my cheek on the pillow beside her as I move my hand to her abdomen and gently caress her belly. Her muscles flex beneath my touch, and she presses her hand over mine, lacing our fingers together. I look into her eyes, and she's watching me too, worry lines wrinkling her brow.

"What's the matter, *Quana*?"

"I'm scared," she whispers, as if there is anyone but me within earshot.

"Of what?"

"Everything."

"Me too." I kiss her, and it's a good one, the kind of kiss that addles the mind and curls the toes. The kind of kiss I've been aching to give her since I left on tour. When I pull away, she looks practically cross-eyed.

"As much as I hate to interrupt you guys..." Dr. Wallace stands just inside the door, pushing her glasses up her nose. "Nicole, we need to prep you for surgery."

I move to stand beside Nicole's bed as Doc Wallace comes farther into the room with a couple assistants. This time, they don't move her to a wheelchair; they move the whole bed, and before I know it, they're taking her away from me. The doctor kindly explains I will have to wait here, but I step around her, jogging to catch up to Nicole. Now that my mind and mouth are in sync again, I have so much to say to her.

"Nicole, I love you. I'll be right here waiting when you get out of surgery. Okay? I'll always be here, I mean that."

Nicole looks nervous, but nods stoically. I steal a quick kiss before they start to push her bed forward again. Then I watch them take her away, and all the air rushes out of my lungs, hollowing me out.

. . .

I'm no good at waiting. I turn to make another loop of the hallway that stretches in front of Nicole's empty room and nearly jump out of my skin when Amy, the nurse with the messy ponytail, blocks my path.

"It's Jake, right?"

"Yeah."

"Want to join me for a cigarette?"

"I don't smoke."

"But..." She frowns, confused, then shrugs. "Well, then, how about we go downstairs and get you a shirt to wear and a cup of coffee or some food from the cafeteria?"

I shake my head, not willing to move from this hallway. I told Nicole this is where I'd be, so this is where I will stay. But Amy isn't taking no for an answer as she turns me toward the elevator and gives me a gentle push. "Listen, Jake, you're distracting the staff with all this pacing. Plus, technically, there's a no shoes, no shirt policy, so..."

I glance down at myself. *Fuck, I need a shirt.* Before I can agree with her plan, she's maneuvered me into the elevator, and we're traveling down to the first floor. In the gift shop, I buy a neon tie-dyed "Keep Austin Weird" tee and tug it over my head. Next, we proceed to the cafeteria, and Amy piles items onto a tray she's set in my hands: two cups of coffee, a Cobb salad, a couple breakfast tacos, and a banana.

At a table near the window, Amy puts cream and sugar into both cups of coffee. She pushes one at me as she drinks the other. I stare down at the milky brown liquid, still spinning from her stirring.

"Eat something," she directs. "Stress is no substitute for nutrition."

"Huh?"

"Eat the banana, Jake."

Hesitating only a moment, I do as instructed. I eat the banana. And then I eat the tacos and the salad. I'm famished, only now remembering the last meal I ate was a bagel in New York City over twenty-four hours ago. Was that just yesterday?

"Amy," I say when she finishes her coffee and stands to leave. "Thank you."

With a smile, she returns to her shift, and I'm alone again. I look out the window, surprised it's cloudy, a murky gray day. I blink and squint at what I can see and what I can't see, all the things that lie ahead and just out of sight.

I'm overcome with fear of the boundlessness of it all—my future in music, my future with Nicole, my future as a father. It's vast, as wide and deep as an ocean. Will I sink or swim?

Vaguely, I recall feeling this way once before, on the day I buried my grandmother. That day—more so than the day I buried my mother, father, and brother—was the day I stared into the void of my future, unsure of what I would find there. On that day, I remember the one comfort I had was my best friend sitting at my side. When they'd lowered my grandmother's coffin into the ground, Greg had put his hand on my shoulder and—

I startle at the sensation of a hand on my shoulder. It's like I'm feeling the ghost of that memory. Except...

I look to my side; Greg stands there, his hand on my shoulder, a look of concern on his battered face. How did Greg turn up right when I need him the most? *I could cry.* The comfortable familiarity of his presence overwhelms me with love, and any residual anger I have over our fight in New York washes away. I rocket to my feet and pull Greg into a tight embrace, nearly sobbing with relief.

Greg hugs me back, holding on a little longer than usual. When we come apart, he stares at me for a moment before asking if I'm all right. I consider his question, then burst into laughter.

Am I all right? That's got to be the most absurd question anyone has ever asked me. I laugh until tears are rolling down my cheeks. Greg's wide-eyed confusion only makes me laugh harder. Finally, when the lunatic laughter subsides, I dry my eyes and answer, "Yeah, I'm all right. I'm good, great actually. And I'm glad you're here. Why are you here?"

"Sheryl called. Said Nicole got hurt at the bout last night. Said you were shouting 'I love you' at the back of her ambulance as it drove away, and that you're, and I quote, 'a total basket case who could use a friend.'"

I smile. "Thanks for coming."

Greg frowns. "It wasn't even a question. Of course I came."

Of course he came.

"Jake." Greg clears his throat. "I'm sorry about...everything. I listened to all your voicemails, and...that's awesome, man. It really is, and I wish... I wish..."

"I know."

Greg clears his throat and asks, "So, you're in love with her, huh?"

"Yeah."

"I'm happy for you."

I open my mouth, ready to tell him the other big news—he doesn't even know the half of it—but I hesitate. It's not right. I can't tell him, not without Nicole. It's not my story alone to tell. I close my mouth again; news of the baby will have to wait.

Greg watches my face as I'm sure a whole array of new and strange expressions cycle through, corresponding to this whole array of new and strange emotions. He doesn't ask for an explanation, just smiles at me—maybe sensing that something good stirs in the air, and I'll tell him when I'm ready.

I change the subject. "You hungry? If so, grab something, and let's take it upstairs. I want to be up there when they bring Nicole out of surgery."

Greg isn't interested in food, so we take the elevator back up to Nicole's floor and make our way toward her room. Ari and Alex are at the nurse's station, asking the staff questions. Ari is still in her cast, and it's been decorated since last I saw her. There's a colorful patchwork of messages and sparkling rhinestones. Her crutches have been bedazzled too.

The sight of her healing injury reminds me of the accident, the event which set all this into motion. Suddenly, I'm overwhelmed with how random it all is. God, the Creator, the Universe, luck: whatever it is, this is the second time a car accident has changed the course of my life.

I shake those heavy thoughts aside and holler, "When you gonna be in two shoes again, Two Shoes?"

Ari jerks around, brandishing a big smile, but her expression slips at the sight of me. "You look like shit."

"Thanks." I pinch at my new tee. "It's the shirt. These colors do nothing for my complexion."

Ignoring my attempt at humor, Ari crosses the distance between us and pokes at the bruise around my eye. "What the hell happened to your face?"

"Ouch," I hiss. "This is how you welcome me back to town, with a poke in the eye?"

Now Ari frowns at the bruises on Greg's face. "You too? What happened?"

I'm prepared to shrug off her concern and make a joke, but Greg steps up to the plate and knocks it out of the park. "Jake found me on a cocaine bender in New York and flushed my drugs, so I attacked him and stabbed him in the neck with a fork."

"*WHAT?*" Ari's expression is priceless.

"It's true; he forked me." I can't help but laugh; it's all too absurd. Greg chuckles too.

Ari stares at us like we've lost our minds. "Why were you fighting?"

Oh no, we're not going to rehash that conversation. I wave her question away like it's nothing. "Just family stuff. Right, brother?"

Greg lifts his chin higher. "Right, brother."

Ari stares suspiciously but finally just rolls her eyes as she comes in for a hug. "Whatever. I'm just glad you're home, big guy. I missed you."

I wrap my arms around her and kiss the top of her head. "Missed you, too, little sis."

Ari hugs Greg next. It's awkward but sweet nevertheless.

"How's Nic? What happened?" Alex asks.

"Torn ACL. She and a blocker tangled skates." Alex grimaces, and I add, "She's in surgery now. Everyone seems pretty optimistic about the prognosis."

Sheryl surprises me from behind with a squeeze around the waist. "What are you wearing, rock star? Does this thing glow in the dark?"

I smirk. "Whatever. I'm still hot."

"Yeah, in the ball-shriveling, radioactive kind of way."

I'm about to make some quip about her Sher Noble moniker when I see Dr. Wallace round the corner. A few staffers follow behind, pushing Nicole's bed.

Dr. Wallace comes to me with an update. Nicole has already woken up from anesthesia, but she's groggy and tired and might sleep for a while longer. I nod vacantly as she explains the procedure and prognosis—it went well, and she expects a full recovery—and when she shakes my hand and leaves, I head straight for Nicole.

Everyone follows me. I stop them. "You all need to wait out here. Nicole won't want to wake up in a room full of people."

Everyone frowns but Alex, who beams a big smile at me and answers for all. "Of course we'll wait out here."

Finally, I'm alone with Nicole again. I settle into the chair beside her bed, take her hand in mine, and watch her rest. It's peaceful and perfect and I enjoy the quiet. I sit up a little when I feel the first movement of her fingers. Then her eyes flutter open. It takes her a moment to adjust, then she smiles, and it's like a sunrise.

"Hey gorgeous," I whisper.

Glassy eyed, she whispers too. "Was it real, or did I dream it?"

"Dream what, *Quana*?" Worry lines start to form on her face, explaining what "it" is. "Our baby? It's real."

She lets out a shaky breath. "I was afraid I'd imagined him."

"Him?"

"Tommy."

The breath catches in my lungs. "Tommy?"

Nicole clumsily moves her free hand to her belly, resting it there. "Thomas Jacob Sixkiller."

Speechless. Stunned. It takes me a moment to find the words to ask, "You named our baby?"

"I think he named himself."

She named our baby. She named our baby after my brother. Does she have any idea what this means to me? Probably not; she's still stoned from the anesthesia. I can hear it in the slow drawl of her words. But, stoned or not, I'm on cloud fucking nine. I lay my head beside hers on the pillow as I place my hand beside hers on her belly, where she nurtures our son.

Son. But of course he's a son. "*Sixkillers are always boys,*" Lisa had said, and she's not wrong. A son named Tommy. *Fuck.* The thought brings me to tears. I try to sop them up with the shoulder of my shirt.

Suddenly, the door swings open, and Sheryl pokes her head inside. Nicole and I both yank our hands away from her belly, caught red-handed.

"See?" Sheryl hollers over her shoulder, "Told y'all they were just making out in here. Totally caught Mr. Frisky Fingers working his way down to Fun City. Get a room, you two."

"We have a room," Nicole grumbles, and she sounds so much more sober than she did just a moment ago. Her walls are back up, and this time, I'm on the inside.

She catches me by surprise when she grabs the collar of my shirt and drags me closer to whisper, "I don't want to tell them yet."

"Tell them what?" I whisper back.

"About Tommy," she says. "I'm not ready to tell anyone about him."

The idea of keeping such a monumental piece of news a secret is completely foreign to me. Since I was fourteen, I've shared everything with Greg, and in more recent years I've shared everything with Ari too. They're my family.

But Nicole doesn't have that. While I'm the technical orphan, she's the one with no family. She's never shared parts of herself because she's never had anyone to share them with...until me.

That revelation—like so many others in the past few hours—knocks me on my ass. I resolve, then and there, that I will share my family with her. I will help her see how much she can be—and already is—loved. But for now, I agree.

Turning to Sheryl, I raise my hands and wiggle my fingers like jazz hands, happy to play the role of Mr. Frisky Fingers. "Guilty as charged."

With that, Sheryl stomps into the room, chattering a mile a minute as everyone else follows behind her, and it's so many more people than

I was expecting. At some point, while I waited for Nicole to wake, a lot of her derby mates arrived. I gladly take a back seat while they file through the room to wish her well.

Ari deftly swings her way over to my side of Nicole's bed and whispers when she kisses my cheek. "It looks good on you."

"The shirt?"

"No. Burn that thing." She grins. "I'm talking about your smile, dummy. I've never seen you in love before; it's a good look for you."

I just smile wider.

Around the room, the mood is light as people tell their favorite "remember when" stories. Almost all the stories feature something weird, brutal, or badass that Nicole did. They tell the stories with such adulation, it's clear to me now no one ever really thought Nicole was a "crazy bitch" or a "colossal cunt," as I'd so delicately put it. She's a prickly one, certainly, but she's extremely lovable, and I'm not the only one in this room who loves her.

After a few moments, Nicole's head wobbles a bit and her eyelids droop. Concerned, I glance at the monitoring equipment behind her bed, but there are no bells and whistles of alarm, no warning sirens. Her eyelids flutter like butterfly wings and close, and I watch her drift back to sleep.

The rest of the room is too caught up in their storytelling to notice, so I interrupt with a deep whisper and a wave of my arm. "Hey, uh, she's sleeping."

Everyone stares for a moment, stunned by the sight of Nicole looking so peaceful, then they quietly shuffle out, blowing kisses our way. Finally, the door shushes shut, and it's just the two of us again. I like these quiet moments, little respites from the world, when it's just Nicole and me together. I settle a little deeper into my bedside chair and stretch my legs out in front of me, settling in for another night of watching Nicole sleep.

"Are they gone?"

I yelp and my feet fall off the edge of the bed. Blinking, I look over at Nicole peeking at me with one eye open. "Were you faking?" I laugh at her. "Bad girl."

She waggles her brows and wiggles over to make room for me in her bed. "Want to sleep together?"

"The answer to that question will always be yes," I say as I crawl into that tiny bed with the woman I love, the mother of my unborn child. She snuggles close and lets out a little sigh, and it fills me up, heart and soul.

13—Tuesday August 9, 2005

"Who's ready to get out of here?"

I startle awake at the noisy clatter as a hospital worker pushes a wheelchair into the room.

"Me!" Nicole answers with glee as she squirms like she's going to climb right out of bed.

I blink, trying to catch up. "Is it tomorrow already?"

"Yes, Jake, welcome to the future." She grins. "Now, come on, get your ass up and help me bust out of this place."

Suddenly wide awake, I hustle to help, aiding Nicole as she climbs from the bed to the wheelchair, and then out we go, with me following behind the woman pushing Nicole's chair, lugging her clothes, crutches, and derby trophies. Outside, I try to remember where I parked my truck, and once found, I steer it over to the patient loading zone.

When she's fastened in and ready to leave, I freeze, just staring out the windshield.

"What are you waiting for?" Nicole pipes up from beside me.

I laugh when I admit, "I have absolutely no idea where you live."

Nicole's house is cute; yellow with black trim, a little bumblebee bungalow. I stare in awe for a moment, but Nicole snaps me out of my reverie when she moves like she's going to walk inside. I quickly veto that idea, hustling around the hood of my truck to pick her up and carry her to the door.

Fumbling a bit with her key, Nicole manages to open the way in, and I'm greeted by a gust of cool air from inside. It smells like her, and I take a deep breath. Then I take my first step into her home. I try not to make a big deal out of it as I cross the threshold with her in my arms like she's my bride, but the significance is not lost on me.

From somewhere within the house comes a jangly scratching noise, and a black-and-white French Bulldog rounds the corner of a hallway, racing to greet us. *Nicole is a dog person? I wouldn't have guessed that.*

"Gomez!" Nicole coos and squeals at him, and it's adorable.

The chubby little rascal careens right into my boots. With an awkward scramble, he recovers and circles my legs excitedly wiggling his stubby little tail in a whole-body wag.

Nicole directs me to a plush purple couch, and I gently set her there. Gomez hops up to be with her, and while Nicole gets busy petting him, I look for ways to make her more comfortable. I grab a pillow from a nearby chair to fluff and set behind her head. I cover her with a throw blanket too.

Not sure what else to do, I ask, "Are you hungry? I can cook...sort of. Or are you thirsty? Maybe a glass of water? Or...do you want to take a shower? Can you take a shower with that bandage on? Though, really, you shouldn't be standing up in the shower right now. How about a bath? Do you want me to run you a bath—"

"Jake, calm down." Nicole clasps my hand in hers.

Feeling too tall, I crouch down beside the couch. "What are you talking about? I'm perfectly calm."

"You're acting like my crazy Aunt Agnes. Next you'll lick your thumb and wipe smudges of imaginary dirt off my face."

I note the way I've tightly tucked the blanket under Nicole's chin and have to admit she has a point.

"Jake, you don't have to take care of me." She pets my hand as if to soften the blow of her words. "I can take care of myself."

"I know, but I *want* to take care of you."

Nicole grimaces at me.

"Shit. I'm crowding you." I flop down onto the floor and lean against the couch to look around her place. The walls are lime green and dotted with large pieces of abstract art. She has several shelves stuffed with books and a massive collection of vinyl records. I climb to my feet and cross the room to inspect her albums. Only a moment into my perusal, I love the woman even more than I did before. "You've got some great stuff."

"I used to DJ; now I just collect them," she says with a yawn.

I turn to her bookshelves to peruse the titles. Most of them, I've read.

"I like your place," I say as I stand in the center of her space and marvel at the nuances of the woman I've fallen for. Her world is full of color and art and beauty, and oddly enough, that surprises me.

What the hell is wrong with me? I've fallen in love with a woman I barely know. I don't even know her middle name, yet I'm shouting the L-word at the back of her ambulance like I'm Romeo fucking Montague. I don't know the way she likes her coffee. I don't know if she's a pancakes or waffles kind of person. Does she eat meat? Does she believe in God? Do I believe in God?

"What's your middle name?" I ask.

"Well, that's random. Marie. What's yours?"

"Mitchell. How do you drink your coffee?"

"I don't drink coffee."

"Really?" Good to know. "Do you eat meat?"

"Yes, but I hate chicken," she answers, then asks, "Jake, did Greg bruise more than your eye? You're acting a bit...concussed."

I blink at her. "How did you know it was Greg?"

"I have eyes and intuition."

Wow. Okay. Changing the subject back, I take a seat in the chair across from her and lean forward, elbows on my knees. "Where do we go from here?"

"What do you mean?"

"I mean...Just a few weeks ago, we were practically strangers. Then we were fuck buddies. And now..."

She nods, understanding my point.

"Look, bottom line is this: I want to be in your life. I want to be a part of this...this..." I can't find the right words. The words sound too strange to come out of my mouth, but it needs saying, so I steady my nerves and spit it out. "I want to be a father to this baby. And I want to be...whatever it is you'll let me be to you. But you're going to have to help me navigate that. I'm going to need you to tell me what it is you want me to be to you."

Nicole lets me talk, not in a hurry to jump in with her two cents. So I keep going. "I'm not going to force my way into your life, and it's obvious you don't need me. But what I need to know is this: Do you *want* me?"

Nicole takes a deep breath then lets it out. With a groan she rolls onto her back, staring at the ceiling instead of me. "Jake, can we not do this right now? I'm tired, which is odd considering all I've done for the last day is sleep, and I think I'm a little bit stoned from the painkillers. And I'm still just so, I don't know, overwhelmed, I guess, about our baby"—I like her pronoun selection, *our* baby—"and up until yesterday, I didn't even know there was a baby. It's completely crazy that there is this tiny little dot of a person inside me who's half me and half you, and that's just, I mean, wow, you know? And now here you are in my house, being so sweet you make my teeth hurt. And it's all too perfect and too good, and I'm getting too attached, and I'm freaking out. And I think I need a nap."

I have to bite my lips together to keep from smiling. Every word that's just come out of her mouth is like music to my ears, but yeah, she sounds a little stoned. This is not the time for a heart-to-heart about our future.

"Besides, it's tomorrow already. Don't you have something else to do besides hover over me?"

"Well—"

"Okay, you go do that, and I'll nap." With a yawn, Nicole turns over to face the back of the couch. Gomez rearranges himself around her feet.

"Okay. Do you want me to come over later?" I ask.

Silence. I wait for a moment, then quietly call her name. Nothing. "You awake?" *Nope.*

I cross to the couch and stare at Nicole for a moment. She's sound asleep. I don't think I'll ever tire of the sight of her peaceful, resting face.

I glance around the room—looking for paper and pen to leave a note—and there at the entrance to a hallway sits a black cat. The creature reminds me of its owner—a dark, aloof beauty with big green eyes.

"Well hello there. What's your name?"

The cat meows softly and saunters toward me. When it's close enough to touch, I crouch and offer my hand for inspection. After a sniff of my fingers, the animal rubs against me and meows. The tag reads Morticia. I smile wide. Gomez and Morticia Addams: the woman is a dark romantic and I love that about her.

Morticia purrs as I pet her, then leaps onto the couch and curls up with Nicole and Gomez. I watch them together, Nicole's family, and I want in. I want to be a part of this scene of domestic bliss. All my adult life, I've been looking for where I fit in, and finally I think maybe I've found it—right there in that cuddle puddle on the couch.

But I haven't been invited.

On a desk near Nicole's bookshelf, I spot a pen and paper and write a note to Nicole:

"When you wake, if you need anything or want anything, call me, text me. Anytime. All the time.

Love, J"

I have to force myself to leave. I take my time about it, too, making multiple trips in and out as I carry Nicole's things in from the truck. I set her trophies on a prominent shelf near the door and rest her crutches within reach of her spot on the couch. Finally, I take one last look at the sleeping beauty, and go home.

• • •

Home.

That's the wrong word to describe my apartment. Nothing about this space feels like home to me now. The bare walls close in on me. The stale air, still tinged with the sour smell of cigarettes, weighs heavy in my lungs, choking me. The secondhand furniture that was never really mine looks uninviting, uncomfortable.

I don't fit here anymore. It reminds me of those years as a gangly kid, growing faster than my clothes could keep up. Time after time, I'd outgrow my shoes, seemingly overnight. But I'd have to wait until the end of the month when Dad got paid before Mom could buy me a new pair. For days, weeks sometimes, I'd walk to school in shoes that didn't fit, my toes and heels stretching the seams until they'd burst, and Dad would have to duct tape them back together. My Humpty Dumpty shoes, Mom called them. I went through several pairs of Humpty Dumpty shoes before my feet finally settled on a size thirteen. It was Margie Hendricks who'd bought me the pair of enormous Chuck Taylors that finally lasted for a few years.

Now, looking around at my Humpty Dumpty apartment, where I've gathered the broken pieces of my Humpty Dumpty life, I can see I don't fit here anymore. Something's changed in me. I'm a bigger person now. I've outgrown this place and the life I led before, and I don't want to tape it back together and pretend it still fits.

Claustrophobia starts to close in on me. I head for the kitchen and pour myself a glass of water, guzzling it and pouring myself another. I glance at the Mammoth contract on the counter.

Now that's different, isn't it? That's not one of the trappings of my old Humpty Dumpty life. There's a future there, possibly *my* future.

But how does it fit with my other possible future? Can I have both—the family and the career?

Groaning, I grab my guitar and leave. Heading for my home away from home, I make a grocery store pit stop to pick up cleaning supplies. It takes me almost an hour to clean the band room, but when I'm done, the place actually looks kind of nice and smells slightly less awful.

I settle into my usual metal folding chair, prop my feet on my amp, and play. I work on the song that's been rattling around in my head. I'm humming along, considering what lyrics to pair with the tune, when Ryan walks in.

"Good God almighty, the rock star returneth." Ryan gives me a high five. "How was the tour?"

"Epic."

"Cool." Ryan frowns. "The fuck are you wearing, dude?"

I glance down to see I'm still in the tourist T-shirt. I shrug.

"What's that smell?" Ryan asks as he turns in a circle, taking in the new and improved space.

Before I can answer, Dillon ambles into the room and slams the door shut behind him, complaining, "It smells like my mom's house in here." At me, he bellows, "What are you doin' here? I figured you'd be halfway to Dublin by now."

"Why does everyone think I'm moving to Ireland?"

"You joined an Irish band, fuckface."

"If I join, then it's an *international* band." *If*. I said *if*, not when. I try to joke it off. "And it's good to see you, too, assholes."

"Yeah, yeah, you were missed. Stop fishing for compliments." Dillon sits down behind his drum kit and with a solemn expression asks, "You quittin' us?"

"Why would I quit?"

"Mammoth, dumbass."

"It's possible to be in more than one band at a time, dumbass." They both just stare blankly at me, so I reiterate. "No, I'm not fucking quitting."

Dillon glances at Ryan. "Guess we should cancel that *Chronicle* ad looking for a new singer."

"Don't be too hasty," Ryan jokes.

"This is my band, douchebags. I'm not quitting the band I started, so fuck off with all that noise," I say with half a smile.

Dillon shrugs as he grabs his drumsticks and starts to tap them on the edge of his tom. "It's for the best. We weren't likely to find a new singer before our show on Friday anyway."

"We have a show on Friday?" I ask.

"Yeah, man, where've you been?" Ryan quirks a brow at me. "Oh right, on an *epic* tour with rock gods."

I laugh. *God, I love these assholes.*

"Less talk. More play," Dillon says, channeling his inner Animal. He taps his foot pedal and the sound of the double kick booms through the room. It's our cue to start as Dillon leads us into our first song.

Practice goes well, despite our three-week hiatus. I could play these songs in my sleep; we all could. Once we've covered our usual set list, I start to play the new song I've been working on.

Ryan and Dillon listen to it once, then on a second pass, they join in and work with me to write it out, playing with the different parts until it forms a good tune. We go through it several times, changing things here and there to make it flow better. When we finally have something workable, we play it one last time, and I record it so I can listen to it later as I write lyrics. But already, the song is mostly written in my head.

"I'll send you guys a copy tonight. Learn it. I want to play it on Friday."

Dillon and Ryan raise their brows but agree. It's on.

14–Wednesday August 10, 2005

She didn't call.

I try not to overthink it. I try not to dwell. I consider all the perfectly reasonable reasons why she didn't call. But it gnaws at me. It makes me cranky.

It doesn't help I'm tired. All night, I lay awake in my Humpty Dumpty apartment, staring at the ceiling, working out lyrics in my head, fantasizing about a clearer path for my future, and begging my phone to ring. But she didn't call—

My phone rings.

I scramble to answer it. "Did you finally start to miss me?"

"Jake?" Not Nicole. *Shit.* It's Caroline Evans, calling to confirm her son's guitar lesson. *Awesome.*

"Mrs. Evans, I'm sorry. I thought you were someone else. Would you still like me to come at ten?"

She clears her throat. "Uh...yes."

"Okay. Great. I'll be there soon," I say before I end the call, then cuss up a storm as I stomp into the shower.

Twenty minutes later, I'm driving out to West Lake Hills, listening to the new song and playing with some lyrics that came to me last night as I pined for Nicole...who still hasn't called.

As I pull up to the Evans house, I force thoughts of Nicole away from my mind. I wave to the yard guys like I always do and make my way to the door, but Mrs. Evans opens it before I get the chance to knock. She has her hip cocked to one side, giving me a good show, but she looks irritated.

"Hello Mrs. Evans. Good to see you again."

Skipping the niceties, she asks, "What's happened to your eye? Were you in a fight?" Adding with a scoff, "Guess that's to be expected when you tour with a heavy metal band."

"This had nothing to do with the tour. Just a misunderstanding."

She frowns at me.

I change the subject. "How's Jimmy? Has he been practicing?"

"Of course. He practices daily," she asserts. "But it's just not the same without you here. You were gone for quite a while; too long."

I swallow the words I want to say, and instead say, "Well, then I better not keep him waiting any longer."

When she finally grants me entrance, she doesn't leave me much room. I shimmy through the gap so that no part of me touches any part of her.

Jimmy is in the den, that giant Les Paul on his lap, almost as big as he is. He strums a couple jangly notes and stretches his little fingers to form the chords I've taught him. When he spots me, he shouts my name with a squeaky voice and kicks his legs with excitement.

"Hey, my man, your mom says you've been practicing pretty hard while I was away."

"I have," he announces with pride.

"Well, come on then, show me what you got." I sit beside him and pull my own guitar from its case.

Jimmy's face lights up. I can see where his grown-up teeth are starting to push through his gums to replace the baby teeth he lost a few weeks ago.

I imagine a future where it's my own son losing the last of his baby teeth. Where I'm the one tiptoeing around at night, sneaking tooth fairy cash under his pillow. I imagine the joy and pride of teaching these same guitar lessons to my boy. Or maybe he'll prefer athletics, like his mom.

I shake the pleasant but distracting thoughts from my head and turn my focus back to Jimmy. We work through a couple scales before we dive into the songs he's been learning for the past month.

When the lesson is over, it comes to the part of these trips that I dread the most. Working with Jimmy, that's easy. Dealing with Jimmy's mom, that's when I really *earn* my money.

"Jake, honey, may I have a word?"

"Yes ma'am."

"Oh, please, not *'ma'am.'* It makes me feel so old."

I say nothing as I follow her toward the front of the house. But instead of the front door, which would have been my path of choice, she veers off down a long hallway to a home office. It's all dark wood and heavy furniture. It doesn't suit this bright butterfly of a woman at all. I imagine this was once Mr. Evans' home office...until he lost the house in the divorce.

Mrs. Evans waits for me to enter, then closes the door behind us, blocking my escape. I watch with wary eyes as she circles around me and leans against the desk, then shimmies her ass up onto it, crossing her legs.

I keep my eyes high, really high. I stare at a portrait of a pretty young woman in a pageant gown and crown. It's Mrs. Evans but fifteen years younger.

"Jake," She says my name with a combination of affection and frustration, like I'm a little boy needing admonishment, a bend over her knee for a spanking. "We need to discuss your schedule."

"How do you mean?"

"Well, the school year is starting soon, and Jimmy has expressed interest in performing guitar at the quarterly talent performances. So, I'd like to set up a more rigorous schedule moving forward." Rigorous? What an odd choice of words. "I was thinking three lessons a week in the evenings after school."

"Well," I almost call her *ma'am* again and have to stop myself or risk another verbal spanking. "I have some personal matters that take priority right now, so I'm not sure—"

"Oh?" She quirks a brow and crosses her arms over her chest so her breasts push up a little higher in her tight dress. I dutifully avoid staring at them. "What sort of *matters*?"

"*Personal* matters." My answer is curt, borderline rude, but I'll be damned if I'll tell Caroline Evans anything about my life. "In another week I'll have a better grasp of my schedule, and we can coordinate adding a few more lessons, but I doubt I'll be able to accommodate three evenings a week."

"Well, what do you think you *can* accommodate?" There's a strange bite to her question, her tone almost mocking.

I repeat my prior answer. "If you can give me a few days, I'll know more, and we can coordinate then."

Mrs. Evans stares at me long and hard. "Very well. Call me once you have your *personal* matters sorted. But Jake, I'll need your full commitment to this new schedule. I can't have you canceling lessons just so you can run off on tour. Jimmy was inconsolable when you left, and I won't allow it to happen again."

I'm stunned. "Inconsolable?"

"You have to understand; Jimmy depends on you. He's been dished a lot of disappointment from the men in his life. I hoped you were different. But when you vanished with little notice, it broke his heart." She huffs with indignation. "And now you turn up looking like you've been in a bar fight and acting like you can just waltz in and out of his life on a whim. Frankly, I'm disappointed in you."

I'm stunned. Where is this coming from? She's painted me as the deadbeat dad of someone else's kid. Maybe some of the frustration she's directing at me is transference, misplaced anger meant for Jimmy's actual father. Or maybe I'm just an easy target. But whatever the reason she's laying this shit on me doesn't matter. What matters is she's wrong about me. I may be guilty of a lot of shitty things in my life, but this is not one of them. I'm not this kid's father. I'm his guitar teacher. I'm an employee and nothing more. And after this conversation, I'm not even that. I grit my teeth but manage to sound restrained when I say, "Mrs. Evans—"

"Caroline, please," she interrupts, exasperated.

"Mrs. Evans," I say again, a bit louder this time, brooking no argument. "I'm afraid I cannot commit to the schedule and expectations you've set forth. But I will gladly recommend a few people who can take on Jimmy's lessons."

Caroline Evans' cast-iron grin falters. Her brow furrows, and she lets out a surprised gasp. "You're quitting?"

"I wish I didn't have to. Jimmy is a great kid, and I've enjoyed working with him. However, I'm not the right person to meet your *rigorous* expectations."

"But—"

"With your permission, I'd like to speak with Jimmy. I feel I need to apologize to him for my absence before. I was unaware it had affected him so deeply. I'd also like to explain to him why I have to resign now."

She looks gobsmacked. I've surprised her, and I get the impression that doesn't happen often. But there's no pleasure in it. I hate to leave Jimmy like this. After what feels like hours, I ask, "Ma'am, may I speak to your son or would you prefer I leave?"

"Just leave." She waves a hand at me, dismissing me. "I'll explain it to him." In an exasperated tone, she adds, "He'll be so disappointed."

I don't take the bait, just clutch my guitar case in a white-knuckle grip as I exit the room.

Behind me, she hollers, "Don't you want your check?"

I don't bother answering. *She can keep her fucking money.*

I storm out to my truck in a huff. But in the back of my head, I know Caroline Evans isn't entirely the problem here. Reluctantly, I have to admit she's hit a nerve. My mind drifts back to the decision weighing on me, the decision I didn't know I had to make until a little tiny person and his mom popped up on my radar.

How can I pursue my dream and join Mammoth, knowing all that entails, if it could compromise my ability to be a good dad? If I sign that contract, will I be signing away my chance at a family? If I'm touring all the time, won't that make me just as bad as Nicole's father, perpetually absent? But if I don't sign it, if I let the dream go, will I turn into my dad—a sad shadow of myself, drowning my sorrows in alcohol?

Am I doomed to commit the sins of our fathers, regardless of which choice I make?

My phone rings in my pocket. I half expect it to be Caroline Evans, calling me from the inside of her house to give me a piece of her mind. To my surprise and delight, it's Nicole. It's like a sign from God. All she has to say is "Hi," and my anger melts away.

"Hey, sleeping beauty. How you feelin'?"

"Very rested. I don't think I've slept that well in decades."

"Good. Rest is good." Suddenly, instead of feeling drained and cranky, I am refreshed just by the sound of her voice. With the phone pinched between my shoulder and ear, I crank the engine and ramble out of the winding, hilly roads of West Lake Hills.

"How are you doing, Jake? You sound funny."

"Funny?"

"Off."

"Eh." I let the shrug linger in my voice as I answer, "I just quit my job."

"What?" She gasps, then says the thing that is my undoing. "But honey, babies cost money. How are you going to buy diapers for little Tommy without a job?"

Speech. Less. Absolutely speechless. Those words. The new reality that those words represent mean *everything*. "No worries, *Quana*, I've got twelve more."

"Twelve? What exactly is it that you do?"

"I teach guitar to rich kids."

"Really?"

"Really."

"You're a teacher?" She says it with such awe.

"Kind of. I guess." I merge onto the highway and push the pedal to the floor. "I like to think of myself as a rock star who teaches on the side."

"Do you ever teach for free?"

"I did today. Why do you ask?"

"Well, at the library we're organizing a fall after-school program for at-risk kids. Everyone at the library is signing up to volunteer a night. I'm going to host a reading night every Thursday. There are a few kids in the group who love music. I think they'd enjoy learning guitar from a bona fide rock star."

"I'm in. Sign me up."

"Really?"

"Pick a night, and I'll make it my priority. Though it should be Wednesday nights."

"You're serious? You'll do it?"

"Of course I'll do it. You know, I was an at-risk kid once, and music saved me. I can't think of a better use of my time."

She lets out the sweetest sigh and says, "I was so wrong about you."

"What does that mean?"

"You're not an asshole. Not even close. You're actually kind of awesome."

"*Kind of?*"

"I could consider raising your status to *totally awesome* if you were to bring me a pizza."

There it is, the invitation I've been hoping for. I nearly rear-end the car in front of me. I can't get there fast enough. "What do you want on it?"

"Pepperoni, mushrooms, and black olives."

"Black olives? You have terrible taste in pizza."

"Hush, you! Bring me food."

"Yes, ma'am."

• • •

My theory was correct; the cuddle puddle on Nicole's couch is exactly where I want to be. It's a comfortable couch, way more comfortable than mine. I like the color and texture too: purple crushed velvet, the sort of fabric I'd expect to see in a castle in Europe, royal and regal and bold.

And best of all, it's Nicole's creation. I asked, and she explained about how the couch was itchy and the color of an avocado when she'd bought it secondhand, so she reupholstered it. I'm equal parts amused and turned-on as I imagine her wrestling with fabric and unruly tufts of cushion stuffing, trying to staple and glue and sew it all together.

I like that Nicole made this couch her own. I think about my secondhand couch with someone else's cat scratches on the arms, and I'm a little embarrassed I never thought to *make* it mine. Just sat there like an idiot on my Humpty Dumpty couch for years, waiting...for what?

This.

I stretch forward—trying not to jostle Nicole's legs, which lie across my lap—and grab another slice of pizza. I hand that one to her, then grab one for myself.

Gomez presses his smushed face against my knee, urging me to drop the slice. I resist his powers of persuasion and take a big bite of my pep, shroom, and olive slice. Irritated by the commotion I've made, Morticia relocates to the chair across from us, and licks her belly.

Since I arrived, pizza and root beer in hand, it's been like this. Quiet. Peaceful. Nice. *Top Gun* plays on the television. I've seen it before, about a million times, but Nicole never has, and I enjoy watching her see it for the first time. She snorts a little when she laughs at the overly macho quips and dumb dialogue. It's adorable. I wait, knowing another one-liner is coming up—

Yep, there it is, that giggle-snort. I smile to myself and shove the last of the slice into my mouth. When I've wiped my hands clean, I clasp them on Nicole's feet and start to rub. She moans with pleasure. I rub harder. She's got on Star Wars socks. They're blue and dotted with little green Yodas.

"Cute," I point out.

She wiggles her toes in response, her mouth still full of pizza. I settle back into my seat, prop my feet on the coffee table, and revel in the sounds she makes as I rub the arches of her feet.

I wake up and the movie is over, replaced by some cop drama. Nicole has fallen asleep, too, still stretched across my lap, her feet still clutched in my hands. I watch her sleep for a moment, but she looks uncomfortable. Her head has fallen to the side of her pillow, and the angle looks awkward. I don't want to disturb her but don't want her to get a crick in her neck either.

"Nicole," I whisper.

She gently stirs and blinks open her eyes, then smiles as she stretches and yawns.

"Want me to carry you to your bed?"

She smacks her lips a couple times, still mostly asleep, and nods.

I work my way out from under her feet and lift her off the couch. She cuddles close to my chest, looking adorable in her comfy pajamas, her hair rumpled and spiked with bedhead.

Moving deeper into Nicole's space feels intimate, almost erotic. Walking down her central hallway, peeking into each doorway I pass, is like peeling off layers of clothing to glimpse the woman beneath. Her bedroom is in the very back. It's painted a moody midnight blue, but the bed shines with satiny silver sheets. It fits her perfectly.

I carry her to the bed and gently lay her down. She sighs with relief when I pull the covers up and tuck them under her chin.

Should I stay, or should I go? Nicole quickly settles that debate when she reaches for me and sleepily squeezes my hand in hers.

"Jake," She whispers groggily, "sleep with me."

You'll get no argument from me, Quana. I strip and slide under the covers with her. When I reach to turn the bedside light off, my necklace jangles and the sound stirs Nicole. She clasps the keepsakes in her palm and runs her thumb around the circumference of Mom's ring.

"What's this?" she asks in a tired whisper.

"These are my parents' wedding rings and my brother's medallion from Cherokee Scouts." I settle onto an elbow at her side, and the keepsakes make a soft tinkling sound.

Nicole says nothing as she carefully caresses each of the objects with such sweet reverence, it nearly brings tears to my eyes.

Feeling oddly self-conscious in the silence, I explain further. "My uncle gave them to me. I could have kept them in the box, but I don't know, I just like having them...near." I smirk, feeling like an overly sentimental sop. I shrug. "I should get a better chain for them, though, if I'm going to keep wearing them. This thing's a piece of crap."

Nicole glances up at me with a sweet expression, and she points toward the wall. "See that dark wooden box on my dresser? Bring it to me."

I chuckle. "Yes, ma'am."

"Pretty please," she adds, with extra sugar in her tone.

I slide out of her bed, grab the box, and bring it back to her.

Nicole sits up and pops the lid, revealing a veritable treasure chest. "You wear jewelry?"

"Rarely," she says as she digs through the jewelry box full of shiny baubles. After a moment, she comes up with a gold necklace adorned by an opal-winged bird pendant.

"It's pretty."

"My dad gave it to me as a gift for my sixteenth birthday, which he missed because he was in Croatia." With a quick snap of her fingers, she springs the clasp and dumps the pendant unceremoniously back into the box. She holds out the chain toward me. "Here."

I blink, confused. "Huh?"

"You said you needed a new chain." She holds the chain a bit higher toward me, offering it to me. "It's gold, so it matches, and it's thick and manly, like you."

She's giving me her chain? She wants me to wear my parents' wedding rings and my brother's medallion on a chain that belongs to her? *Does she have any idea how meaningful this is to me?* I hesitate, not sure how to accept such a gift.

When I do nothing, Nicole asks, "May I?" She reaches for the chain around my neck.

I lower my head so she can pull it off and watch in awe as she delicately strings the rings onto her gold strand. When she gets to Tommy's medallion, she frowns at the small safety pin I've used as a connector.

"Can you go to the garage and grab the needle-nose pliers from my tool chest by the washing machine?"

I blink at her, then follow the instructions. She has an impressive tool collection, but I save that revelation for another day as I hurry back to the bedroom, handing over the tool she needs.

Nicole collects the opal bird from the box and uses the pliers to pry open the jump ring at its top. With a couple adept manipulations, she manages to replace the safety pin on Tommy's medal with this gold loop, then bites her bottom lip as she pinches the sides of it back together. After carefully inspecting her work, she fishes the gold chain through the new link.

Without a word, she leans forward and brushes some of my hair out of the way so she can clasp the new chain around my neck. Practically breathless now, I look down at the rings and medal and her thick-gauge gold chain that rests against my bare chest.

It's perfect. Nicole smiles like she feels it too, the rightness of it all. I'm overwhelmed with emotion and the desperate need to kiss her. I cup the back of her head and pull her to me. Brushing her lips with mine, I whisper, "*Gvgeyui.*"

She whispers back, "What does that mean?"

"I love you."

"Because I gave you a chain?"

I pull away just enough to meet her gaze and say, "Because you've given me everything."

That earns me a kiss, so achingly soft and sweet. Then she yawns.

I shift the jewelry box to her nightstand and click off the light, then lay back in Nicole's bed, pulling her down with me. She curls against my body, her head resting upon my chest, her palm pressed flat over my heart. I sigh with contentment. *My God, this is what peace feels like. This is bliss.*

A brief commotion follows as Morticia jumps up onto the bed and settles like a mound of coal at Nicole's feet. Gomez, too, joins us, using a set of steps Nicole has installed to help him reach the top of the bed. He circles a few times before finally settling with a huff and a snort against my foot, his chin resting on my ankle.

At my side, Nicole nestles a bit closer and on a sigh, whispers, "I love you too, Jake."

Correction: this is bliss.

15—Friday August 12, 2005

I don't want to leave. I'd much rather spend another day lounging around the house with Nicole, but I have two guitar lessons scheduled and a Nebulous show tonight.

These past days have been pure domestic bliss. Between my occasional guitar lessons and band practice sessions, I've spent all my time at Nicole's house. We've talked and laughed and cuddled and napped. I've helped her with her bandages and her physical therapy exercises. I've cooked and helped her keep the house clean while she's been ambulation challenged. Not to mention we've been fucking like rabbits, almost nonstop. We've found every position that works with her injury, and we've been giving them all a lot of practice.

Even more than all the great sex and the excitement of the fire and ice between us, I really enjoy these quiet times. I like hanging out with her. Being here, doing nothing, I've come to know her on a different level, and she's come to know me in all the mundane and boring ways, and it's been fantastic.

She rubs the stitches on her knee.

"Stop picking at it, *Quana*."

She frowns at me. "It's going to leave a scar."

It's the same thing she says to me each time we change her bandages. I give her my standard reply: "It'll be a beautiful scar, just like all your scars. Beautiful, just like you."

Her lips twitch like she's hiding a grin, but she doesn't say anything; she never does.

When I'm ready to leave, I lean in for a kiss, and she delivers with such sweet affection that I want to say screw it, tear off all our clothes, and take her back to bed. Instead, I collect my guitar from its new home by the front door and wink at her as I leave. "I'll be back after the lessons to pick you up for the show, okay?"

Somehow, I focus and get through Tim Collins's lesson, followed by Marcy Springer's hour. As soon as her mom hands me the wad of cash, I'm out the door, in my truck, and hauling ass back to Nicole.

Maybe she'll be naked and waiting for me, game to fit in a quickie before the show. But when I arrive, Sheryl's ugly green car is parked in my spot on the driveway.

Inside, the living room is empty, a Sonic Youth album playing on the turntable. I set my guitar by the door as I holler, "Nicole?"

"Don't come back here." The reply comes from a trio of female voices. Then Ari pokes her head out of the bedroom doorway. "You can't come back here."

Did hell freeze over? "What are you doing here, Two Shoes, and why can't I go back there?"

Ari smirks at me. "Because it's bad luck for the dude to see the chick before the gig. Duh."

"What?" I frown, confused.

"Don't you have load in and sound check? Why are you here?"

"I'm here to pick up Nicole and take her to the show." I take a step forward.

Ari steps forward as well, challenging me. Then Sheryl appears at her side. They block the doorway with their arms crossed over their chests like a pair of bouncers.

"She has a ride to the show," says Sheryl.

"Huh?"

"Look, rock star, this is Nicole's first time leaving the house since her release from the hospital. She wants to get dolled up. We're helping. Now, go on, get."

I go to leave, but apparently not fast enough. Ari waves a hand at me and says, "Shoo, fly, shoo."

From inside the bedroom, Nicole laughs. "Did you just shoo him? I think I could grow to like you, Goody Two Shoes."

At that, I smile. But both bouncers start shooing me out the door, so I take my leave, grabbing my guitar on the way out as I holler, "Okay, well, I'll put y'all on the guest list. Alex and Greg too."

After picking up my amp, I head to the venue, fill the guest list with my people, then load in. I meet Ryan and Dillon onstage for sound check, and then the wait begins. At the bar, I settle onto a stool beside Ryan.

"Here ya go, man," Ryan says as he tries to hand me a beer.

I stare at the thing for a minute, then shake my head. "Thanks, but I'm not drinking anymore."

"You're not?" Ryan furrows his brow, confused. "Why?"

I hadn't given it much thought, but since my trip back home, I haven't wanted to drink. Then, on that magnificent Monday morning, hearing Doctor Mid-Nite say those magical words, "You're pregnant," cemented my resolve. If I'm going to be a dad, then I'm going to be a sober dad. I count the number of days since I last had a drink; I'm twelve days sober as of today. "I'm just not."

Ryan shrugs, too, then guzzles one beer as he nurses the other. Behind him, the door guy opens things up and starts letting people in. Soon, the bar is packed, an invading horde of leather- and latex-clad fans fighting for a space near the stage.

"Jesus." I turn to Tom as he slides a glass of water my way without being asked. "Big crowd."

"Expecting it to sell out tonight," he answers as he wipes the bar down with a rag.

"Why?"

Tom and Ryan exchange an amused look, and Ryan punches me in the shoulder. "Enough with the false modesty, rock star."

Oh. Right. That. I look out over the crowd. I hadn't expected this crush of people. How is Nicole going to handle this with her injury? I glance around, looking for a spot where she can sit unmolested—

"Jake?"

I swivel my head around as Rebecca slides onto the stool beside me. It takes me a moment to remember my manners. "Hey, Rebecca."

"How've you been?"

Awesome, it's small talk. "I'm good. You?"

"Good. So, is it true you're in Mammoth now?"

I scratch my neck for something to do. Rebecca takes my hesitation as confirmation, and her expression turns smug and self-satisfied. *Oh, this is about fucking a "rock star."* As my ex, her stock just rose.

I roll my eyes and turn away, scanning the room again.

"Listen, Jake." Rebecca scoots her stool a little closer to mine. "About that night when we were last together. I hate the way things ended."

You mean the last time you slapped me?

"Could we maybe get together to talk?" She stretches out the word *talk*, and it's not hard to read between the lines. I cringe.

Ari and Sheryl have just come through the door, Nicole between them. She looks incredible in a shimmery green dress that matches her eyes and sparkles in the light like a goddamn emerald. Her hair, often gelled back for a severe look, is styled soft and curly. And all I want to do for the rest of the night is run my fingers through it, feel it tickle my cheek, my neck, my thighs...

I rise to my feet, about to head over to her, when Rebecca grabs my hand and tugs my attention back to her. She jumps to her feet and presses herself to me. "Please, Jake, just give us another—"

I'm not listening, distracted by thoughts of Nicole. I look back toward the door. Nicole sees me, and she sees Rebecca. I watch the smile slip from her lips as she says something to Ari. Then she turns and leaves, her dramatic exit hobbled a bit by the crutches.

"*Fuck,*" I rasp.

"You read my mind," Rebecca purrs and starts to rub her hands down my chest.

Wait. What? "No. Rebecca, stop." I peel her hands off me, holding her at bay by the wrists. "That's not going to happen. We're done."

"But—"

"Jake." Ari has made her way through the crowd, looking worried as she approaches me.

"Where is she?" I ask Ari.

"Sitting outside in the smoking area. She said her leg was bugging her and all of the seats in here are"—Ari eyes Rebecca with animosity, then finishes with a single telling word—"taken."

I leave them both and go to Nicole. Pressing through the crowd is like running the gauntlet, a barrage of people wanting to hug me and shoot the shit. I kindly ignore them all.

Finally, I reach the door and push outside. Nicole sits next to Greg, who's smoking like a chimney. That can't be good for the baby, but I have other concerns at the moment.

"Nicole, that was not what you think."

Nicole pushes to her feet and balances on her crutches. She wobbles a little, and I reach out to help her balance, but she pushes my hand away and snaps at me. "I've got it. I don't need your help, Jake."

And there it is. She's shut me out again. I huff and she scowls and we both glance around at the crowd of people stuffed into the small smoker's patio, all blowing toxic fumes into the air. "Please come back inside. We can talk about this in there."

With a smirk, she makes her way back into the club and I follow, feeling like a dog on a leash about to get whacked with a rolled-up newspaper. Inside, we find a dark corner near the bar, and Nicole turns on me. "I can't believe you didn't tell me that the alley blowjob bitch was your ex-girlfriend. Yeah, I know. Ari let it slip."

Really? That's why she's pissed at me? "Does it matter?"

"Of course it matters."

"Why?"

I don't think this is the direction she expected the conversation to go. She frowns at me and tries to cross her arms over her stomach, but her crutches get in the way, so she gives up.

"If it matters so much, then yes, Rebecca is my ex. I dated her for a few months, and that was eight months ago."

Nicole frowns at me. "Obviously, that's not the whole story if she's still sucking your dick every time I turn my back."

I'm stunned. "Seriously? You think I'm cheating on you?"

"I saw you with my own eyes just now. And I saw her on her knees in the alley right outside that door, Jake," Nicole huffs. "Do you deny it?"

"Are you fucking kidding me?" *Okay, now I'm pissed.* "That wasn't cheating! If you're going to keep throwing that night in my face, then get your facts straight, Nicole. Fact one: On the night in question, you'd just gutted me, or did you forget that part? You made it very clear that I was nothing to you but a prop for your petty revenge scheme. So, yeah, I fell back on a familiar habit. Fucking sue me! Fact two: I didn't even finish with her that night. After you left, I broke up with Rebecca again, and then I went home and fucked the shit out of you. Or don't you remember that part?"

Nicole's scowl takes on a stubborn bent, like she's trying to maintain her righteous indignation even as the foundation for her anger starts to crumble.

"Listen. I feel like total shit about that night. I was an ass. But not because of how I treated *you*. I feel bad for how I treated *her*. I was a dick for using her like I did, and I regret that."

That surprises her.

"Nicole, I've had exactly two 'relationships' in my entire life, and that's *including* this thing I've got going on with you. Rebecca was the first woman I ever attempted monogamy with. It lasted barely three months, and I was miserable the whole time. She and I were not a good match, so I ended it. But after we broke up, she was always...there, you know? And it was easy. She made it easy to just keep fucking her, so I did. God, that sounds shitty, but it's the truth."

The scowl on Nicole's face is gone, replaced by what looks like shock. But she's listening, so I keep talking. I reach for her hand and she doesn't jerk away from my touch. A good sign.

"Fact is, I'm not very good at this relationship shit. I've got no practice at it. And until now, that didn't matter to me. But, with you...I'm trying really hard not to fuck this up with you."

Her expression softens with each word I say, and when I finish, she's almost smiling.

"I need your help, though. I need your trust. This jealousy shit has got to go. If you can't trust me, then I don't know how this is going to work." Her smile fades, but I can't stop now. *This needs saying, so I'm going to say it. Come hell or high water.* "Look around." I swing my arm out to encompass the whole venue. "I'll bet I've fucked at least a dozen of the women here. I've fucked a lot of women, Nicole. I'm not ashamed of that. I won't apologize for it."

Nicole huffs at me, and looks like she wants to interrupt, but I'm not finished.

"But do you know how many of those women I've fallen in love with? One." I hold up one finger, the middle one, then I poke her in the shoulder with it. The awkward gesture has the effect I hoped for; she kind of laughs at me.

I dip my chin low so my eyes are level with hers. I meet her gaze, unblinking and unflinching, when I say, "Nicole, I have fallen stupidly, helplessly in love with you. What I feel when I'm with you, it's like nothing I've ever known, and I don't want to lose it. I don't want to lose you. I need you to trust that. I need you to trust me. Can you?"

Nicole considers for a moment, and I like that she's actually giving it thought. Finally, she nods. I exhale the breath I've been holding and burst into song, warbling about the challenges of loving a music man.

She furrows her brow. "Did you just sing Journey at me?"

"Of course I did."

Nicole giggles. "You're such a dork."

"It's part of my charm. I'm a charming dork."

Nicole rolls her eyes.

"Admit it," I say as I pull her in for a kiss.

She melts against me, finally relenting with a sigh. "Yeah, yeah, fine, you're fairly charming...for a dork."

"By the way, you look amazing."

She sighs, and I love the sound of it.

"Hey, you guys." Ari steps up to us. "I talked to Tom, and he said you can sit on a stool beside the soundboard, Nicole. It'll be out of the way but give you a good view of the stage."

I shift my gaze from my best girl to my girlfriend and watch with pure, greedy satisfaction as Nicole smiles at Ari and thanks her. I pull Ari into a hug and kiss the top of her head as I whisper, "Thanks for being you, little sis."

When Sheryl and Alex join us, I give Nicole a quick kiss before Ari and Sheryl help her to her VIP seat beside the soundboard. I head in the opposite direction, toward the stage, focusing on the show now. Ryan and Dillon and I stand near the stage, in support of the opening band, and Alex joins us.

When Ari comes to stand between Alex and me her expression is serious and she leans in close to say, "Jake, Nicole is completely head over heels in love with you. You know that, right?"

I blink. Not sure I've let myself believe it just yet.

"Don't screw this up, big guy."

"I'm doing my best."

"Well that's good. Your best is pretty damn good."

"How do you know she loves me? Did she say something?"

Ari bursts into laughter. "Listen to you. You're like a twelve-year-old girl. No, she didn't come right out and say it, but whenever she talks about you, she gets this glint in her eyes. Looks a lot like the glint you've got in your eyes right now. It's beautiful to see."

From her other side, Alex hugs his arm around Ari's waist and plants a lingering kiss on her temple like it's second nature, like he doesn't even realize he's touching her...and he's always touching her. *Relationship goals.*

Over Ari's shoulder, I see Greg working his way through the crowd to reach us. He smells like an ashtray and looks—to use one of Granny Sixkiller's favorite expressions—rode hard and hung up wet. He's carrying a stool, which he sets down between me and Ari and then steps aside to reveal that Nicole is behind him, with Sheryl as her escort.

Nicole situates herself on the stool, then answers my unasked question. "Greg thought I'd be lonely back there by myself, so he stole the chair out from under me."

Greg, Sheryl, Alex, and Ari circle around Nicole on all sides, sentinels making sure that no one hurts her bum leg.

My God, I really love these people.

When the first band finishes their set, it's my cue—showtime. I give Nicole a toe-curler of a kiss, then head for the stage.

From up top, Dillon and Ryan stare down at Nicole. "What's the story, dude?"

"Fell in love."

"And it's mutual?" Ryan asks.

"Hell yeah, it's mutual, asshole," I grouse as I tug my shirt off and tuck it into my back pocket. The cool metal of Nicole's chain and my keepsakes hit my bare chest and come to rest right over my heart. I smooth my hands over my hair to tame any flyaways and flop my braids forward so they fall down the front of my chest. When everything is in order, I loop my guitar strap over my neck and pluck the strings to check that I'm still in tune.

When I'm ready, I turn back to the other guys, who are still staring at Nicole in awe. Dillon grumbles, "Lucky bastard."

"Hell yeah, I'm a lucky bastard." I wink at him, and he flips me the bird. He kicks his foot pedal, and we launch into our set. It feels nice to be back. After the tour, I wasn't sure how I'd adjust to returning to the smaller venue, smaller crowd, and smaller stage. But it's good, familiar.

I've played this venue dozens of times. I've seen most of the faces in this room at other shows. This is my crowd, my home, and there at the edge of the stage is my family. The love and positive energy I feel from them—*for* them—is nearly overwhelming.

We save the new song for last. I turn to Ryan and Dillon and check that they're tuned. When we're ready, I turn back to the crowd, and into the microphone, I say, "This next one will be our last song for the night."

That garners a collective grumble from the audience.

"But it's a new one, never before performed."

That gets a loud cheer.

"As many of you know, I've had a hell of a lot going on in my life lately. A lot of changes."

More cheers. They think I'm talking about Mammoth. And, in part, I am, but there's so much more, and most of the people in this room don't know the half of it. In fact, there's only one other person here who knows it all. I latch my gaze to hers and give her a wink. She grins wide, our shared secret a bond between us.

"To be honest with you, I've always been a little afraid of change because shit always seems to change for the worse."

Mass agreement.

"Though sometimes—not often, but sometimes—the changes turn out to be really fucking beautiful."

Roaring applause.

"And it's one of these beautiful changes that inspired me to write this song." I look down at my guitar, setting my fingers for the first chord. Then I look back out at the crowd and quietly add, "It's called 'Beautiful Scars.' Hope you like it."

I hit the first chord, even as the crowd's applause threatens to drown it out. I lock gazes with Nicole again, whose eyes go wide with realization: this is her song.

With another wink at her and another chord struck, I turn to sync with Dillon and Ryan, and we start the song. It's a slow, moody tune that works from a quiet start to an emotional climax. For the early build, the crowd sways along with the melody of my guitar. I sway, too, entranced, until it's time for the lyrics. No one's heard them yet, not even Dillon or Ryan, and it's with a strange sense of intimacy that I sing this song just to Nicole, but with the whole world listening.

Your cut is sharp
Straight to the heart
Say it won't hurt
Leave a beautiful scar

But that can't be all
It's not enough
I want the pain
I need it rough

Lash me, hurt me
Make me bleed

Then kiss it right
I beg, I plead

Take it all
It's yours to keep
My heart, my soul
My body in deep

Your beautiful scars are mine now
And mine yours

Jagged lines form a map
You're teaching me to read
The scars are a path
It's the road home I need

Your beautiful scars are mine now
And mine yours
I'm yours

I scream the last lyrics, while I hit the notes of the guitar riff with so much force that I break my G-string. Behind me, Ryan chugs to the end of his bass riff, and Dillon pounds a repetitive beat on his kick and cymbals; then we hit a full stop. And there's just absolute, pure silence.

The whole room is so quiet you could hear a pin drop...for about two seconds. Then the crowd goes batshit crazy. But it's the tears in Nicole's eyes and the smile on her lips that lift my spirit to the sky.

I sling off my guitar, go to the edge of the stage and hop down into the crowd, destination *her*. When I reach Nicole, she's wiping at her eyes and grinning sheepishly at me as I pull her into a hug.

"You wrote me a song?"

"Yeah."

"You wrote me a song." She says it with such awe.

I pull away so I can look her in the eye, then dumbly repeat, "Yeah."

"Jake..." And then she starts to bawl. She goes from normal to sobbing in the snap of a finger.

I'm at a complete loss and a bit terrified. What the hell do I do? I've had to console Ari when she goes full basket case before, and it was always a bit of inappropriate humor that brought her out of her funk. But Nicole is different, and I have no clue what to do in this situation.

"*Quana*, baby, why are you crying?"

"You wrote me a song...about my scars..."

Oh. Shit. She hates the song. "Your *beautiful* scars," I dumbly defend.

"Jake...no one's ever made me feel like you do. I'm just so...happy...and that scares me," she says between watery sobs.

Relief washes over me, and I rub my hands up and down her back as I whisper. "Me too, *Quana*, me too."

"Oh shit, I'm crying...in a bar. I'm crying in a bar. Is this a hormone thing; do you think? Because...fuck, when did I turn into the chick that ugly cries in a bar? I must look a fright." She pulls away from me and wipes the tears from her face. Her eyes are puffy and bloodshot. She's cried off most of her makeup, which now forms dark smudges across the backs of her hands, and mascara streaks down her blotchy red cheeks.

"You've never looked more beautiful to me."

She fails to suppress her grin. "You're a liar but a sweet one."

I drape an arm around her shoulder and jostle her a bit, like I'm trying to shake dry her tears. "Come on, let's go home and fuck."

She laughs through the tears. *Heh, I guess inappropriate humor works with Nicole too. Noted.*

16—Monday August 15, 2005

Clay Croft struggles through his scales, and I try to focus on correcting him, but my mind is elsewhere. My mind is with Nicole, the little man inside her, and our 2 p.m. appointment with Dr. Douglas.

It's been a week since the last ultrasound gave us good news. All week, we've shared this strange little secret between us. But we haven't talked about it. Not once. He's the elephant in the womb. *Heh.* I almost chuckle at my own lame joke but force myself to focus my attention back on Clay.

It's just...there are so many unanswered questions that come with this kiddo. Do I take the gig with Mammoth? Or do I get a regular job? Guitar lessons won't pay for college, and there's no health insurance. Will we move in together? Does she even want me to live with her? Should I ask her to marry me? Does she even want to marry me? Which of Nicole's two extra bedrooms would make the best nursery? Probably the one closest to her bedroom, so she can hear him cry in the night. Or will it be so *we* can hear him cry in the night?

We haven't addressed any of these questions. Haven't even asked them. Instead, we've focused on other things, the mundane everyday things. All while we inch toward that thing we're not discussing.

Each night—after we've watched movies, talked and laughed, had dinner, and fooled around for a while—she asks me to stay, and each night I do. Each day, I drive out west to teach lessons, then swing by my apartment to pick up more essentials to bring back to her place so we can go another round.

It started with my toothbrush, but it's snowballed. Last night, I washed the clothes I've brought over, and it was a full load of laundry. While I folded my shirts, she quietly made room for them in one of her drawers.

And yet neither of us has said a word about any of this. It's just sort of happening. We're merging our lives in small baby-steps but on an accelerated schedule that feels too fast and yet not fast enough.

I suspect, though, that all this unspoken progress between us is going to come to a head at approximately 2 p.m. today. That's when we'll learn if our baby is still a healthy and happy little bun in the oven...or not.

"Jake?"

"Huh?" I look back at Clay, who's got his fingers stretched along the neck of his guitar. My attention has drifted...again. *Shit*. "That's great, Clay. Now try this." I show him the next chord we're going to learn and let him study my hand as he tries to copy it.

With my other hand, I check the time on my phone. Almost finished here; then I'll drive to Nicole's to pick her up, then drive to the doctor's office for the appointment. My stomach aches with anxiety. I can't remember ever being this nervous about anything. The waiting is only making it worse. The minutes seem to stretch to hours and days, until finally, months later, I finish my session with Clay and his dad pays me as I head out the door.

Halfway to the truck, the sun beating down on my head, my phone vibrates in my back pocket. I yank it out to check caller ID.

Shit. It's Aidan.

"Hey man, how is it to finally be back home?" I ask, forcing a jovial tone into my voice.

"The Guinness is better here, so it's great," Aidan jokes. "And you? How's life with your lady in red?"

How would I even begin to answer that question. "Good. Life's good."

"Good." Aidan agrees. I let myself into the truck and crank the AC as I wait for him to explain the purpose of his call, though I already know. "So, I wanted to check in. Have you had a chance to read over the contract?"

"I have, yes." I've read it cover-to-cover...three times.

"Do you have any questions or concerns? The label says they haven't received it back yet."

Here we go. With a deep breath, I try to explain. "Aidan, I need to be totally honest. My situation has...changed. I have personal obligations which could interfere with my music plans."

"Personal obligations?"

"I can't say more than that. I'm sorry. I promised. But let's just say I find myself in a similar position to Ian, having to choose."

Silence. Then a deep inhale and exhale. "I see."

"I'll know more soon. I won't keep you hanging for long, but I need to talk to Nicole about all of this. It's not just my decision to make anymore, but there hasn't been a right time."

"Jake, we're in no hurry. I only called to check in, not to rush you. We're all a bit road weary, not ready to travel or record anytime soon. If you need time, then take it. And if you sign, understand that we can work around your schedule and your home life as much as possible. You can remain in Austin most of the year. We could use a webcam for practice and writing."

"A what?"

"A webcam. I've been using one to chat with Ronnie. Saves a bundle on long distance, plus I get to see her."

"Ronnie?"

"You remember the music writer from New York? Veronica."

"Ah, the one with the legs."

"She does have legs, yes." Aidan chuckles, but then he's all business when he continues. "Listen, Jake, bottom line is we want ye in the band, and I think it's what you want too."

"I do, it's just—"

"I understand. Life gets complicated." Aidan adds, "But Jake, when Ian left, it wasn't just because of his family. He never wanted to play music. We came up together in primary school and played together for years, but it was never important to him. When he left, I wasn't surprised. I would be surprised if you made that same decision. Music is different for people like us. It's like air or water; it's vital. Wouldn't you agree?"

I've never heard it put like that, but he's absolutely right. Whenever I've been at my lowest, it was music that saved me, kept me on my feet, made me happy. I take a deep breath and let it out. "Yeah. Yeah."

"Okay. Well, call me if you want to discuss anything," Aidan finishes.

I agree that I will, then sit stunned, listening to dead air on the phone as I stare out the windshield at the Austin skyline on the horizon.

•   •   •

Traffic is light, and twenty minutes later, I pull into Nicole's driveway and take a moment to get myself together. I'm not sure if my jitters are due to fear of the pending appointment or the weight of the decision I need to make, but I feel twitchy.

I carry my guitar to the door and let myself inside with the key Nicole gave me because, and I quote, "It's more convenient than always having to let you in and out like a persnickety cat." Speak of the devil, Morticia is there at the door to greet me. She purrs as I set my guitar on the floor and give her a good scratch behind the ears. Nicole is not in the living room, so I call out to her.

"Back here," She hollers in response.

I make my way to the end of the hall and peek into her bedroom. Nicole stands naked in front of the mirror, her palm flat on her belly, gently rubbing. She catches my eye in the reflection and admits, "I'm scared."

I cross the room to her and wrap my arms around her waist, covering her belly with my own hands, hugging them both. "What are you scared of, *Quana*?"

"What if he's not in there? I mean, if he's there, shouldn't I feel him? But I don't feel any different. I'm not even sick in the mornings. Aren't I supposed to be sick in the mornings? What if he fell out...or what if he never existed? Maybe it was just a dream, and now I have to wake up."

I tighten my embrace as I ask, "How could it be a dream if we're both in it?"

"Maybe I dreamed you too," she whispers as she stares at me through the mirror.

"Does this feel like a dream?" I ask as I kiss her neck.

"Yes." She moans as my fingers move down and come to rest at the apex of her thighs, cupping her sex in my palm. I start to massage her, and she groans, "Oh, yes. No. Wait. We can't."

"What's this word '*can't*'?"

"We're not supposed to have sex before the procedure."

"Says who?" I ask as I run my tongue over the spot just below her left ear that always elicits a sigh.

She does not disappoint, sighing when she says, "The experts."

"See, this is definitely real life. If it were a dream, I'd be buried balls-deep inside you right now."

Nicole rests her head back on my shoulder, and the weight of her in my arms feels so right.

I glance at the clock and see that we still have a few minutes before we need to leave. I ask, "Question: Do the experts say anything about oral sex? Because I skipped lunch today, and I'm starving."

I come around to I stand before her, then sink to my knees. The subject kneeling for his queen, I silently beseech her, begging for a taste.

She stares down at me for a moment, then shifts her bum leg a few inches to the side, making room for me. I latch onto her and feast. She tastes so good. Her legs shake, and I use my shoulder and hands to steady her as I devour every drop she gives me, savoring the flavor and sounds of her ecstasy.

When I'm finished, Nicole moans, "I'm definitely dreaming."

"Nope." I smack her ass. "This is the real deal, toots. Now get your sweet ass dressed. We have an appointment to keep."

"Toots, really?" She raises a brow at me.

"Would you ever have dreamed that you'd be in love with a man who calls you 'toots'?"

"Good point." She smiles and limps to the closet. A few minutes later, she's dressed and ready.

At the doctor's office, we're ushered into an exam room. There, a nurse takes Nicole's vitals and asks a few questions, then has her change into a cotton frock, white with little blue flowers all over it, and I help her onto the elevated exam table.

It's not long before the doctor enters the room. She perches on a stool in front of the exam table and asks, "How are you feeling, Nicole? That leg is looking much better."

Nicole glances at her healing knee and shrugs. "My knee's fine, but I'm not puking."

Dr. Douglas furrows her brow in confusion.

Nicole clarifies, "I'm not having morning sickness. I'm worried. What if he fell out?"

The doctor gives her a supportive smile. "Have you experienced any bleeding?"

Nicole shakes her head.

"A miscarriage is typically accompanied by bleeding or spotting." With a kind, patient tone, she goes on to explain, "Not all pregnancies exhibit the same. While it's true that most women do experience varying degrees of nausea during their first trimester, that's not always the case. If you're one of the few who doesn't, I'd say count yourself lucky."

Hope shining in Nicole's eyes. "So, then, maybe he's okay."

The doctor frowns, but quickly masks it. "It's still too early to know the sex. This baby might not be a boy."

"It's a boy," Nicole and I say in unison, with full confidence.

Dr. Douglas shakes her head. She continues to ask us questions and answer ours, then she waves the ultrasound wand, and has Nicole assume the position on the exam table. I hold Nicole's hand and the doctor turns the monitor so that we can all see the images on the screen. She points out the scar tissue in Nicole's uterus, but reassures us that it isn't cause to be overly concerned, just something to keep in mind as the pregnancy advances. At the word "scar," Nicole glances at me, and I squeeze her hand, giving her a little wink.

Finally, Dr. Douglas stops moving the wand around and directs our attention to a black spot in the middle of the monitor. It's just a small circle, but she points at it and says, "This is the gestational sac. Consider it a sort of cocoon for your baby."

"He's in there?" Nicole asks with a gasp and lets out a little sob.

I stop breathing, just completely stop breathing. Then I let out a sob too. Now I'm the one crying like a damn baby, and Nicole is squeezing my hand. *This is real. This is my life now.* It's a life I never imagined for myself, and it's so much better than my wildest dreams.

"It's not a dream," Nicole says to me, a tear sliding down her cheek.

I raise her hand to my lips, kissing her fingers as I say, "It's a dream come true."

Dr. Douglas busies herself packing up the equipment and gives us a few minutes alone in the room. But before she leaves, she hands Nicole a little photo of the tiny black dot where our son grows. We stare at the thing for who knows how long, our heads touching, both sniffing back tears and letting out awkward little laughs from time to time.

When we compose ourselves and get Nicole back into her clothes, we set up a series of appointments, and it's an hour of running to grocery and drug stores before we have everything we think we'll need to grow a healthy baby...for the next week at least.

When we finally make it back to Nicole's house, we're so beat we collapse into her bed. I kiss the top of her head as I joke, "The kid is just a tiny little dot, and already this parenthood shit is exhausting."

· · ·

When I wake, the bed is empty, with the blanket pulled up over me and tucked neatly beneath my chin. Nicole's been practicing her mothering skills on me again. And speaking of Nicole...

I sit up and scan the room, but she's not here, and the door is closed. Odd, we always keep that door open when we sleep so the animals can come and go. *We*, we're becoming a "we" now, and man do I love the sound of that.

I hear a voice, then another, and one of those voices sounds suspiciously like Alex. *What the hell is Alex doing at Nicole's house?* And did she just laugh at something he said? *Curiouser and curiouser.*

I tug on a pair of jeans and go investigate. As I make my way up the central hall, the voices grow louder, and there are more of them.

When I reach the kitchen, I'm surprised to find that, indeed, Alex is here, leaning against the fridge and sipping on a Lone Star tallboy. Beside him, Ari slices a tomato as she retells the story of her run-in with the Honda. Her audience: Nicole, who sits on the counter by the sink; Greg and Sheryl, who sit in the vinyl diner booth along the back wall; Tynisha, who pulls something out of the oven; and another roller girl—Rachel, I think—who's beside Ari, slicing carrots.

What is happening here?

I stare at the vast amount of food covering most surfaces of the room, perplexed.

"Hey, you're finally awake," Nicole says with a smile in her tone.

"Did I sleep all the way to Thanksgiving? What's with all the food?" I cross the room to Nicole and give her a kiss.

"Want a beer?" Alex asks as he moves to open the fridge.

"Nah, but I'll take a soda."

Alex hands me a can, and I guzzle the thing in a couple gulps, needing the caffeine and sugar to get my brain back online.

"How can you drink that and have abs like that?" It's Rachel who asks the question, pointing her chopping knife at me in an assessing sweep.

I let out a loud belch as I answer, "Good genes."

Nicole lets out a loud guffaw. "Good genes, plus a three-mile run, followed by about two hundred crunches and pushups every morning."

"Two hundred and fifty," I correct her and lean in for another kiss.

Nicole playfully socks me in the gut, then shimmies off the counter to leave the kitchen. She returns seconds later with my Testament T-shirt in hand, tossing it at me as she chides, "Cover up, sexy boy. You're distracting the cooks."

"Which circles us back to my prior question. What's with all the food?" I tug on the shirt and look around at the spread with a growling stomach.

"It's a potluck," Ari announces.

"It is?" *I'm so confused.*

"Yep." Nicole digs silverware out of a drawer. Alex pulls a stack of plates down from an upper cabinet. And Ari starts taking drink orders.

"Jake?" Ari hollers, and I look over to see her holding up a Lone Star tallboy.

"Water for me."

Nicole hands me a plate and pushes me toward the start of the food line. There's a lasagna casserole, a bucket of fried chicken, a salad that Ari and Rachel dump their chopped veggies into, some au gratin potatoes, and a pecan pie for dessert. My stomach growls louder than before, and I help myself to the feast as the others follow.

When my plate is full, I help Nicole carry hers out to the dining table that takes up a corner of the living room. It's usually covered with books and paperwork, but it's been cleared for the occasion. There aren't enough chairs to seat us all. My solution is to set Nicole's plate beside mine at the head of the table and pull her onto my lap.

When we're all seated, there's a pause as we look around at each other, and then all eyes train on Nicole. It's her house, her grace. But it's not a grace she says. It's something so much better.

"You're probably all wondering why I invited you here." She pauses, takes a deep breath and looks at me. "Jake and I are both orphans, in a way. He is, literally. For me, it's more figurative, and...for most of my life, I just assumed that I didn't get to have a family. But one of the things I've learned in the last week is that I actually kind of do, we do"—she glances at me—"and it's you guys. Rach, Sher, Ty: you've been with me from the beginning, and I don't tell you enough how much your friendships mean to me." All three women beam, seemingly surprised by her words. Then she turns to the opposite side of the table. "Greg and Ari, you are Jake's whole world. I see how much he loves you, and I see how much you love him. It's inspiring. And Alex, it looks like we're stuck with each other, and that's actually pretty cool."

Everyone at the table smiles, a party of Mad Hatters. Nicole wraps up her remarks. "Anyway, I thought this potluck could become the first of many, a family tradition. Thank you for rallying with such little notice. It means a lot."

That gets a smattering of applause and a "fuck yeah" here and there. I look around the table, grinning like an idiot at these people, my family, our family. When everyone just sits there a moment, Nicole hollers, "Well, dig in before it gets cold."

So we do. As we eat, I listen to the sweet symphony of conversation and laughter. The roller girls try to recruit Ari. Greg and I crack up at the idea, and Alex looks terrified at the prospect of his cute little klutz on skates. We talk about everything and nothing, and it's wonderful. It's perfect, almost too perfect. *Maybe I'm still napping, and this is a dream.*

"How was the tour, Jake?" Ari asks, and I realize that there's been so much going on since my return that I haven't had a chance to talk to Ari—or anyone—about much of anything, let alone tell them my tour stories.

"It was amazing. The guys are great—fun to play with, professional, and *really* talented. They initially hired me to fill in for Ian, whose wife just had a baby." I squeeze Nicole just a little tighter. "But what I didn't know until the end of the road was that they were considering me as a permanent replacement. In New York, they offered me a place in the band."

"Holy shit." A few people gasp, and eyebrows rise. Obviously, the rumors haven't circulated as far and wide as I'd thought.

"Does that mean you're moving to Dublin?" Sheryl asks.

"Nope. I was just on the phone with Aidan this morning, and if I sign the contract, we'll work it out. But I'll live here."

Nicole frowns at me. "What do you mean, *if*?"

Shit. I stare at her and blink. This is not the time to talk about this. I pull her against me and kiss her temple, then whisper in her ear, "Let's talk about it later."

"Yeah, but...I mean, it's Dublin." Sheryl wiggles like she's got crazy ants in her pants, and suddenly I realize why I've always liked her so much: her infectious enthusiasm reminds me of Tommy. "I'd kill for the chance to live there. Literally, I would cut a bitch to live there."

I squeeze my arm around Nicole's waist again when I answer her, "Yeah, well, I've got some pretty good reasons to stick around here."

Nicole smiles, and at the same time, we go in for a kiss and smack foreheads, then crack up laughing at ourselves.

"Who are you right now?" Rachel says to Nicole, a look of astonishment on her face. "Because this"—she gestures at Nicole with a wide sweep of her fork, a clump of au gratin potatoes staked to the end—"is not the Nicole I've come to know and barely tolerate."

"I know, right?" Sheryl chirps cheerily. "It's like she had a lobotomy, and they poked the bitchy part of her brain with a stick and popped it like a balloon."

"Hey, fuck you very much," Nicole huffs. "My bitchiness did not pop like a balloon. My bitchiness is fully intact, and I should kick your ass for suggesting otherwise."

"You can try, Gimpy McLimpsalot." Sheryl sticks out her tongue to egg Nicole on. "I'm untouchable."

"I used to think that too." Nicole grumbles. "But look at me now: crippled, in love, and pregnant."

You could hear a pin drop as every face at the table registers shock. But not me, I'm grinning from ear to fucking ear.

"Whoops," Nicole says when she realizes what she's just revealed.

"Well, thank God it's finally out." Tynisha is the first to speak, pure relief in her tone. "I wasn't sure how I was going to keep that secret for much longer."

"You knew?" Sheryl gasps.

"Honey, I knew before they did."

"So...wait." Ari shakes her head, confused. "You two are..."

"Gonna have a baby," I say with a smile so big it hurts my face.

"Oh my God," Ari says in awe, then gasps, "Oh my fucking God!"

"I thought you couldn't," Alex quietly says.

"I guess I was wrong." Nicole takes a deep breath and shrugs when she adds, "So far, so good." Despite her attempt at nonchalance, I hear the shake in her voice.

Tynisha notices too. "Nic, you're in good hands. Laura is going to take real good care of you and that baby."

"You're serious? You're having a baby?" Sheryl is up and out of her chair faster than a Tasmanian devil on a rampage. She circles the table and yanks Nicole out of my lap, wrapping her in one of her trademark hugs. "This is so *cool*. I can't wait to buy tiny little punk rock onesies. Oh! And itty-bitty Doc Martens. Dude, I'm going to be such a cool aunt. I'm going to spoil this kid rotten."

Nicole smiles, and I do too. It's nice to have the news out there, a relief somehow, like now that it's official, it's somehow more real. I look over at my crew. Greg looks stunned, and a couple shades paler than normal. He rises to his feet and wraps me in a hug. "Good for you, brother. I'm happy for you."

When it's Ari's turn, she's fighting back tears as she hugs me, then asks, "How far along is the pregnancy?"

"About a month."

"You ass!" She smacks me in the chest. "You've known for a month and didn't tell me?"

"We've only known for a week."

She smacks me again. "You ass! You've known for a week and didn't tell me?"

I pull her into another hug. "I love you too, little sis."

"Jake." She looks at me, wearing her serious expression now, and levels me with her next words. "You're going to be an amazing dad. This kid is so lucky...and they're going to be so pretty."

"Yeah? You think?" I ask about the first part of her statement.

She elaborates on the latter part. "Well, you're both totally hot, so..."

I shrug and go with it. "Can't argue with science."

"Seriously, I'm so happy for you."

I kiss her forehead, then turn to her man. He gives me a firm handshake and pulls me into a hug, saying, "I've never seen Nic this happy. It's pretty great. I'm happy for you guys."

"Thanks, man. That means a lot."

When we've survived the gauntlet of affection, Nicole and I come back to each other. I wrap her in my arms and kiss the top of her head as I whisper, "I love you."

Nicole lets out a quiet sob, and I hug her tighter as she whispers back, "I love you too."

· · ·

I stand in the doorway of the kitchen and watch it all unfold. At the sink, Ari rinses dishes that she hands to Greg to put in the dishwasher.

Alex is fixing an electrical problem with the under-cabinet lights while Nicole asks him questions about an issue with the faulty doorbell. Ty and Rachel scoop leftovers into plastic containers, and Sheryl hip-checks me as she passes me, carrying a load of plates.

This is my family. *Family.* I try the word out in my head and like the sound of it. I've said it a million times in a million contexts, but right now it rings more true and more meaningful than it has in a very long time. This is my *family.*

I nearly choke up with tears again, so I turn away and walk to the end of the hall and into the bedroom. Morticia is curled into a ball under the bedcover. I take a seat beside her, and stare at the wall, breathing deeply in and out. The cat pokes her head out and meows at me, then leaps into my lap and curls into a ball again, purring as I pet her.

With my other hand, I grab my phone and scroll through my contacts. When I reach the one I'm thinking about, my thumb hovers over the call button for a moment before I press it.

It rings a couple of times. Then I hear, "Y'ello," from a distant, familiar voice, the twangy accent instantly recognizable even after all these years.

"Eli." I speak with warrior strength in my tone, trying to hide the shakiness.

"Jake?"

I nod, then remember he can't see me and confirm verbally.

"Well, good goddamn, this is a nice surprise. I never thought you'd call me, but I sure am glad you did. How ya doin', *Utana Yona*?"

"I'm gonna be a dad." I blurt out the words like they're burning the roof of my mouth. It's strange how much I want to talk to Eli about this. Before my trip back home, I hadn't even thought about this man in over a decade. But everything is different now, and I desperately want to share this part of my life with the one person who, more than anyone else in the world, will know just how much this means to me.

"Oh." I've surprised him.

"I'm in love with an amazing woman and...well...I knocked her up."

"This is good news, then?"

"Yeah, it's really good news."

"*Osda.*" *Good.* Eli sounds a little uncomfortable, not sure how to navigate this heart-to-heart with his estranged nephew.

It's a bit strange for me too. Still, I admit, "I'm scared." It's odd to say it out loud, to Eli of all people, but then I admit to much more. "I'm scared of letting myself be happy. I'm afraid I'll lose them, you know, and I don't think I can survive that again."

Eli pauses for a long moment before he clears his throat and says in a gentle voice, "Well, son, some things in life are worth the risk of losing them. That fear you're feelin', that's how you know what a good thing you got. And that shit is scary, I know. I've been there. But don't you let it get in the way. I damn near lost Lisa before I even had her because of my own chickenshit fear. Fortunately for me, she's a stubborn woman, and for some reason, she likes havin' me around." Eli chuckles, and so do I. "Take it from me. Make yourself easy for her to love and get real comfortable with that fear, because it never goes away. But, son, let me tell you, it's worth it. That moment when you finally get to look your son in the eyes and kiss his momma, you'll know—you'll suffer anything for them."

I wipe at my eyes, trying hard not to cry as I imagine the day when I can look Tommy in the eyes. Will they be dark like mine or bold and bright green like his mom's?

I joke, "Ah, man, she's already got me sufferin'. There are times when all she has to do is look at me and it hurts. It's like sharp little pricks in my chest."

"Ah," Eli commiserates. "That's just her clawin' her way deeper into your heart, son."

"Yeah. Sounds like something she'd do."

We sit on the phone in silence for a few moments. But that's okay. For now, neither of us has anything more to say. It's a start, though.

"I best get off the phone. We got guests. I was just callin' to give you the news." It's funny; the longer I talk to Eli, the more my old Appalachian Cherokee accent comes out.

"Well I'm real glad you did. And you can call anytime, Jake. Don't need to have a reason, neither."

"Will do." I hang up and stare at the wall, taking another deep breath in and out. Behind me, the bedroom door clicks closed. I snap my head around to find Nicole standing there, watching me from across the room.

"How much of that did you hear?" I ask her.

She crosses to me and shoos the cat out of my lap, then sits down, her legs straddling me. She brushes a strand of my hair behind my ear, and the gesture is so achingly tender it makes my chest hurt. *There she goes again, clawing her way deeper into my heart.*

She wraps her arms around my neck and says, "I came in on the part about how you're scared of losing me." She glances down at her abdomen and looks back at me. "Scared of losing us."

Deep inhale in. Deep exhale out. I nod.

"I've been giving this some thought, and I've decided that you're not going to lose us," she says in a lilting voice that sounds like music to my ears.

Confused, I furrow my brow. "I'm not?"

"You're not." She gives her head a solid shake and rests her warm palm against my cheek. "All my life, good things never happened to me. I didn't believe in miracles or happily-ever-afters because I thought I would never experience either. But then you came along, and you gave me a miracle. So now I pretty much expect you to give me a happily ever after too."

"I can do that." I say it with absolute, unflinching confidence. I've never known anything with more certainty. I can and will be the man Nicole needs. It's not even a question.

"Good. Now that that's settled, what's the story with 'if'? I thought you were a member of Mammoth."

I shrug. "The gig's mine if I want it."

"Which you do...want it."

"Yeah, but—"

"What *but*? This is your dream come true."

I squeeze her tighter against me. "You're my dream come true; I just didn't know it."

Nicole frowns at me.

I clear my throat to elaborate. "It's just not a good time to pursue my career in music when we're...you know, trying to start a family."

"Jake." Nicole's eyes search my face for a hint of what I'm feeling. "I don't expect you to give up music for this family. In fact, I don't want you to. I don't want to be the reason you give up your dreams. I mean, shit, I'm not giving up derby to be a mom, and I don't see why you should give up music to be a dad. This is everything you've worked for, handed to you on a silver platter. If you truly don't want it, then turn it down. But if this is about me—"

"But..." Now it's me searching her face for the answers. "If I take this, I'll be on the road touring, recording...I could be gone for months. Won't that make me just like your dad? I don't want to be the kind of dad who's known more for his absence than his presence."

Nicole's expression softens. "Jake, my dad was absent even when he was present. You are nothing like my father. I see it in your eyes— you love this baby, and you will be a good dad to him, even if you have to travel from time to time. When I said some people shouldn't be parents, what I meant is that parents should *want* their kids, that they should *want* to come home to their kids. But that doesn't mean that they can never leave. We'll be here when you go on the road, and we'll be here when you come home. Okay?"

"Okay."

"So, sign the damn contract."

"Yes, ma'am."

Nicole gives me a full-wattage smile, and like the flash of a camera, it freezes this moment in my mind, a moment I will never forget. The look on her face, the weight of her in my lap, the sound of laughter coming from the other room: every detail is drawn with indelible ink in my mind, marking one of the best moments of my life.

I stare at her, the woman I love and the mother of my unborn son, and howl with glee. In a flash, I twist around until I've pinned Nicole under me on the bed, then savor the sound of her gasp and sigh as I start to kiss her, all of her, every inch I can reach, mumbling against her skin as I ask, "So, what's this happily-ever-after position look like?"

Nicole bites her bottom lip. "I wouldn't know. This will be my first time trying it."

"Mine too," I mumble as I kiss my way down her body. "Might have to try it a few times to get it right." I waggle my brows at her as I smooth my hands under the hem of her shirt, ready to pull it over her head, when we're interrupted by a bang on the door.

"Are y'all fucking in there?" Sheryl hollers through the wood.

"Yes. Go away," Nicole shouts in response.

"Well, hustle, loverboy, cuz it's Karaoke on Crutches time, bitches!"

Nicole whispers, "What's Karaoke on Crutches?"

"A new tradition. You'll love it."

She blinks at me, then raises a dubious brow. "I hate karaoke."

"Not the way I do it. I'll melt your panties while I blow your mind. Prepare to be amazed."

"Oh good lord." She rolls her eyes and giggles with that little snort-laugh I've come to love so much.

Out in the hallway, Sheryl huffs and bangs on the door again. "Get a move on, you two. We don't have all day!"

We respond together, shouting in unison, "We're coming."

Sheryl shouts back, "Ew, gross. TMI!"

At that, Nicole bursts into laughter, and my God, it's *everything*.

All my life, I've been a wanderer, always seeking, though I never knew what it was I sought. And then, I found it, I found her, I found my family, I found myself. I took the road home and it brought me here. And as I look at this woman in my arms, I know that we *are* the miracle, and we will have our happily ever after.

ᏣᎳᎩ ᎦᏬᏂᎯᏍᏗ
Cherokee Language

The Cherokee origin story of the strawberry is a love story. Maybe that's why, as a "Berry," I love writing love stories. This particular love story is very close to my heart because it's afforded me the opportunity to write my very own Cherokee love story. And, with a little help from my friends, I was able to include some Cherokee phrases too.

Below is the Cherokee syllabary for the words and phrases used in this book.

Cherokee Syllabary	Cherokee Phonetic	English Translation
ᏣᎳᎩ	Tsalagi	Cherokee
ᎦᎵ	Wado	Thank you
ᎣᏍᏓ	Osda	Good
ᎤᏍᏗ ᏲᎾ	Usdi Yona	Little Bear
ᎤᏔᎾ ᏲᎾ	Utana Yona	Big Bear
ᎣᏏᏲ, ᎡᎵᏏ	Osiyo, Elisi	Hello, Grandmother
ᏍᏗᏳ, ᎡᏚᏥ	Stiyu, Edutsi	Be strong, Uncle
ᏅᎵᏓᏙᎲᏗ, ᎬᏚᏥ ᎬᏠᎩ	Dodadagohvi, Gvdutsi gvtlogi	Until we meet again, Nephew
ᎬᎨᏳᎢ	Gvgeyui	I love you
ᏆᎾ	Quana	Peach

| JGᎯ | Kuwahi | Cherokee name for Clingmans Dome |

It you're interested in learning more about the Cherokee language, visit the language section of the Cherokee Nation site at language.cherokee.org.

Acknowledgments

To the readers, thank you! I hope you enjoyed Jake's story. There's still more to come. Next up is Greg.

A heartfelt thank you to everyone who helped make this book the best it could be. Christina Consolino, you were exceptionally generous with your time and editing expertise to get this beast ready for print. Thank you! Lisa Rutherford, Roy Boney and Jeff Edwards, thank you for fact checking my Cherokee cultural details and fine-tuning my novice Cherokee language skills. Meghan Scott, without your help those hospital scenes would have been an absurd mix of HIPAA violations and wrong diagnoses. Terry "Muffin Tumble" Cordova, Amy "Electra Blu" Sherman, and Virginia "Cheap Trixie" Evans Aloy: your roller derby feedback was exactly what I needed to get it right.

To my amazing family, thank you for always supporting me, and encouraging my creative endeavors. You constantly inspire me with your art and creativity. I love you all. And my husband, who went so far as to build the greatest writer's loft the world has ever known: you're the best, and I sure do love you.

All my love to my extended family of friends. I could not ask for a better support network. Y'all are always there to listen, love, hug, and laugh. You breathe life into me, when I'm running low. Even during this pandemic your Zoom Happy Hours, masked yard chats, and

Quarantine Care Packages have saved me from Depression's cold grip so many times. I am one lucky lady to have you all in my life.

And, finally, to my Cherokee kith and kin, as well as the Austin music and roller derby communities: you're the inspiration. That's right, I just sang Chicago at you.

About the Author

Christina Berry is the author of the *Lost in Austin* series. A citizen of the Cherokee Nation, Christina owns, operates, and writes all the content for the website All Things Cherokee (allthingscherokee.com). Originally from Oklahoma, she lives in Austin, Texas with her husband and two robot cats. Keep up with her latest at christinaberry.com.

Note from the Author

Word-of-mouth is crucial for any author to succeed. If you enjoyed *The Road Home*, please leave a review online—anywhere you are able. Even if it's just a sentence or two. It would make all the difference and would be very much appreciated.

Thanks!
Christina Berry

Thank you so much for reading one of **Christina Berry's** novels.
If you enjoyed the experience, please check out our
recommended title for your next great read!

Up for Air by Christina Berry

"Every turn of the page is like sipping a smart and sexy
cocktail I wish was bottomless." –Allison Dickson, **author of**
The Other Mrs. Miller (review for *Lost in Austin, Book One*)

View other Black Rose Writing titles at
www.blackrosewriting.com/books and use promo code
PRINT to receive a **20% discount** when purchasing.